FLEET *of* WORLDS

Larry Niven

AND

Edward M. Lerner

A TOM DOHERTY ASSOCIATES BOOK • NEW YORK

This is a work of fiction. All the characters, organizations, and events portrayed in this novel are either products of the authors' imagination or are used fictitiously.

FLEET OF WORLDS

Copyright © 2007 by Larry Niven and Edward M. Lerner

All rights reserved.

A Tor Book
Published by Tom Doherty Associates, LLC
175 Fifth Avenue
New York, NY 10010

www.tor-forge.com

Tor® is a registered trademark of Tom Doherty Associates, LLC.

ISBN-13: 978-0-7653-5783-0
ISBN-10: 0-7653-5783-6

First Edition: October 2007
First Mass Market Edition: September 2008

Printed in the United States of America

0 9 8 7 6 5 4 3 2 1

DRAMATIS PERSONAE

HUMANS / CREW OF *LONG PASS*

Diego MacMillan   *Navigator*
Jaime MacMillan   *Doctor*
Sayeed Malloum   *Engineer*
Barbara Nguyen   *Captain*

SOL-SYSTEM HUMANS

Sigmund Ausfaller   *Amalgamated Regional Militia (ARM) investigator*
Sangeeta Kudrin   *Senior executive at the United Nations*
Julian Forward   *Physicist (native of Jinx, in the Sirius system)*
Miguel Sullivan   *Racketeer*
Ashley Klein   *Racketeer*

CONCORDANCE COLONISTS / CREW OF *EXPLORER*

Kirsten Quinn-Kovacs   *Navigator and a math whiz*
Omar Tanaka-Singh   *Captain*
Eric Huang-Mbeke   *Engineer*

CONCORDANCE COLONISTS / OFFICIALS OF THE ARCADIA SELF-GOVERNANCE COUNCIL

Sven Hebert-Draskovics   *Colonial archivist*
Sabrina Gomez-Vanderhoff   *Governor*
Aaron Tremonti-Lewis   *Minister, Public Safety*
Lacey Chung-Philips   *Minister, Economics*

CONCORDANCE CITIZENS

Nessus   *Political officer on* Explorer; *Experimentalist neophyte*

Nike   *Deputy Minister, Foreign Affairs; Experimentalist radical*

Eos   *Leader of out-of-power Experimentalist Party*

Hindmost / Sisyphus   *Leader of the government and the Conservative Party*

Baedeker   *Engineer at General Products Corporation*

Vesta   *Nike's senior aide*

FLEET OF WORLDS TIMELINE
(All dates in Earth-standard)

PROLOGUE   Earth date: 2197

Long Pass crossed the sky in a series of shallow curves, because Diego MacMillan willed it so.

Interstellar space is not uniform. The tenuous interstellar medium isn't just a few atoms of hydrogen per cubic inch, forever. There are pockets of greater density, some thick enough to form strings of stars, given time. Between the dense patches there is nothing. A Bussard ramjet like *Long Pass,* which eats interstellar hydrogen and accelerates by spitting out fused helium, must coast between the denser clouds.

This is worse than it sounds. At any reasonable fraction of light speed, interstellar muck comes on like cosmic rays. As much as propulsion, a Bussard ramjet's purpose is to guide that lethal muck away from the life support system.

Every simulation run in Sol system had reached the same inconclusive conclusion: Course tweaking to exploit density fluctuations in the interstellar medium was "likely to be" unproductive. Between Sol and the target star the muck was thick enough. Sure, a course tweak might funnel a bit more hydrogen into the ramscoop *here,* but was it enough to compensate later? A slight diversion at these velocities took a heavy toll in kinetic energy. And what would you find when you reached the end of a detour? Maybe that was where the law of averages caught up with you, and the near-vacuum of interstellar gas became vacuum indeed.

Of course, flatlanders had built the models. Diego MacMillan had nodded noncommittally at their advice. Technically he was also a flatlander—spacers pinned that label on every Earthborn—but he had traveled across the solar system. Once *Long Pass* launched, whether he undertook the experiment was beyond their control.

The question had never before come up on a manned mission. *Long Pass* was experimental, a crew-rated ramscoop.

In the abstract, Diego respected the mission planners' conservatism. The ship's failure could discredit the new technology for a long time.

Flatlanders! He and his wife were aboard. That was more than enough to keep him from taking foolish chances.

So *Long Pass* had followed its wobbly curves for decades now. Maybe he'd saved a few months' travel. That was okay. Studying the variations, plotting alternate courses, assessing probabilities—they kept him busy. What had the experts imagined the ship's navigator would *do* for decades?

They could never have imagined what, in his obsessive peering ahead, he would find.

AND TO WHAT do we owe this honor?" Captain Nguyen asked.

Meaning that by the current schedule Diego would normally be asleep. It was all he could do not to blurt out the answer. *One step at a time,* he told himself. "All will be revealed," he intoned with his best mock pretension.

The ship's population numbered just above ten thousand. Most were embryos, sharing the freezers with forty-three hibernating adult passengers. The crew numbered only four, between them covering three daily shifts. Together, they filled the ship's tiny dayroom.

He had arrived early to configure the claustrophobia-denying decor. Undulating, verdant forest, the Andean foothills of his youth, receded into the digital wallpaper. Fluffy clouds scudded across the brilliant blue sky glowing overhead—he had no use for the cave-parks his Belter crewmates thought normal. Leaves rustled and insects droned softly in surround sound. Most of one wall presented a well-remembered mountain lake on which a sleek, two-toned power boat cruised. Its hundred-horsepower inboard motor was throttled down to a barely audible purr.

Nothing, alas, could mask the ubiquitous odor of endlessly recycled air, nor could the rough-hewn planks projected from the dayroom table disguise the plasteel slickness beneath his fingers. He twiddled the cabin controls, tuning chirps and twitters down a notch, while his curious shipmates took coffee and snacks from the synthesizer.

Barbara Nguyen sat first. She had the tall, gangly frame of a Belter, and her head was shaved except for a cockatoo-like Belter crest of thick black hair. She was their captain and the most cautious among them; which was cause and which effect remained stubbornly unclear to Diego. Throughout their hitherto uneventful voyage, she had let decisions emerge by consensus. With luck, consensus-seeking had become a habit.

Sayeed Malloum, their engineer, was taller still but stocky for a Belter. Each of them handled the tedium in his own way. Sayeed's latest affectation, dating back several weeks, involved dyeing his crest and disposable jumpsuit in matching colors. Today's hue was chartreuse, shading to deep yellow.

Jaime MacMillan, ship's doctor and Diego's wife of fifty years, slid into the last chair. She was built to earthly scale, nearly matching his six feet, but otherwise illustrated the old adage about opposites attracting. She was lithe while he was pot-bellied, blonde where he was dark, and as fair as he was swarthy. Those were shipboard skin tones, of course. Flat-lander full-body dye jobs and elaborate skin patterns had been left on far-off Earth.

Jaime slipped a hand beneath the tabletop to give his knee a reassuring pat, although not even she knew what he was about to reveal. With a start, he noticed she had printed her jumpsuit in Clan MacMillan tartan: another silent vote of confidence. How anxious did he seem?

Barbara cleared her throat. "Spill it, Diego. Why did you call everyone together?"

Oh, how the details and analyses, all the terabytes of specifics in his personal journal, yearned to be free. This was not the time. "Have a look." Above the picnic-table illusion he projected a navigational holo. Amid the scattered pink, orange-white, and yellow-white specks of the nearest stars, a brilliant green asterisk blinked: You are here. As his friends nodded recognition, he superimposed, in tints of faint gray, a delicate 3-D structure. Would they see it? "Density variations in the interstellar gas and dust."

Sayeed frowned, likely anticipating another pitch for rerouting the ship on one more just-a-bit-off-our-planned-course wrinkle in the void.

"You've shared density plots before. It's never involved much fanfare." Barbara eyed him shrewdly. "And you've never before struggled so hard not to bounce in your chair."

Words alone would not suffice—not for this, not with Belters. That was not a criticism. Growing up inside little rocks, they lacked the background. Diego said, "Jeeves, give us Boat One."

"On full throttle, sir, as you had specified." The virtual speedboat slewed until its stern faced them and the shore. With a roar, the boat's bow rose. A great vee-shaped wake formed. Diego tracked the boat as it receded, the ripples of its wake dwindling as they spread.

Sayeed's gaze flicked between the simulated lake and the 3-D graphic that still hung above the table. "There's a shock wave in the interstellar gas. A . . . a *bow* wave."

Barbara narrowed her eyes in concentration. "I concede the resemblance, but we're comparing two simulations. Diego, are you certain about the underlying data?"

It would be *so* easy to dive into minutiae about years of observations patiently culled and collated, about converting those observations from the ship's accelerating frame of reference to a stationary frame, about estimating and correcting for the perturbations of stellar winds. He could have discussed at length vain efforts to match his readings to the sky survey with which they had departed Sol system. He yearned to explain the extrapolation of the full pattern from the mere fraction so far glimpsed, even after so many years and light-years of observations.

He must have had a fanatical glint in his eye, because Jaime shot him the warning look that reminded: There's a fine line between scary-smart and just scary. Diego kept his response to a confident nod.

Barbara said, "I'll want to go through it later, step by step. No offense, just captain's prerogative."

"What could have made this bow wave?" Sayeed asked.

That was the right question. Diego started another simulation. A more nearly uniform background wash, modeled from a century-old survey, replaced the translucent ripples in the stellar display. "This is what we expected to encounter. And . . . now."

A new speck, this one bright violet, materialized in the holo. Gathering speed, it recreated the 3-D shock wave.

Jaime stood, squeezing behind his chair to study the image from another perspective. She poked a finger into the image. "Then whatever caused the waves is here?"

"Obviously, the simulation runs faster than real-time. I've given you no way to gauge the compression factor. The object producing the wake is moving at one-tenth cee, and we're nearly a light-year apart. To look at it, we aim"— Diego tweaked a program parameter, and a backward-extrapolated trajectory materialized—"where it *was*."

He linked their main telescope to the display. A dark sphere shimmered, faintly aglow in a false-color substitution for IR. Mountain peaks and hints of continental outlines peered out from beneath an all-encompassing blanket of ices.

Sayeed leaned forward to read annotations floating above the globe. "An Earth-sized world. At one point, it *was* Earthlike, its oceans and atmosphere since frozen. It's a bit warmer than the interstellar background, which is why we can detect it, perhaps leakage from a radioactive core. And somehow, you say, it's racing by at one-tenth light speed. How can that be?"

Barbara shook her head, setting her crest to bobbing. "A fair question, but I have a more basic one. Diego, you might have *begun* by showing us what you'd found. Why didn't you?"

"Because this isn't about an out-of-place planet. I need you to accept the years of observation and the model that showed us where to look." Diego took a deep breath.

Would they believe? "They prove that that world has been accelerating steadily at 0.001 gee.

"*Someone* is moving it—someone who controls technology we can't even imagine."

"ARE YOU AWAKE?"

Diego was reasonably certain he'd been prodded in the ribs to assure a positive response. "Uh-huh," he answered groggily. "What's on your mind?"

Propped up on an elbow, long hair looking stirred from tossing and turning, Jaime stared at him. "Are we doing the right thing?"

For days, the four of them had gone around and around on this. Even Nguyen had come over. The big day was *tomorrow*.

But decisions feel different in the dark. "Jeeves, lights to quarter bright," he told the onboard computer. It had the good judgment to comply without speaking. "Hon, we've all agreed. We can't let Earth decide! They're almost fifteen light-years away. Whether they signal the aliens directly—which they wouldn't, since there's no guarantee the planet won't change course in the meanwhile—or they tell us to proceed, that'd be nearly a thirty-year delay. What does *that* do for us?" Despite himself, a yawn interrupted his response.

Then she surprised him. "That's not what I meant. Maybe we shouldn't contact them at all. What if they're . . . hostile?"

That brought him fully awake. Ascribing violent intent was a good way to get sent for medical help—but aboard this ship, *she* was the medical help. "Advanced civilizations are peaceful," he said cautiously.

"I know." She raked a hand, fingers splayed, through her mussed hair. "War was a societal psychosis. With the resources of a solar system at our disposal, and with Fertility Boards to keep population levels under control, there's been peace for more than a century. We left behind violence with the era of scarcity that the mentally ill used to excuse it." The words came out like the secular catechism that they were. "They"—no antecedent was needed—"move entire worlds. How could they possibly covet the resources humans administer?"

She was shivering! Sitting up, he put an arm around her. "Then why are you worried?"

She snuggled against him. "Because aliens must surely *be* alien. Can we presume to predict their social development?"

"Can we presume to decide for mankind *not* to try contacting them? We're almost a light-year apart. We're moving at thirty percent cee. The ice world is moving at ten percent cee, and accelerating. Contacting them by comm laser already requires extrapolation and faith. Deferring to Earth could mean losing the opportunity." He kissed the top of her head.

"We're not making this decision only for ourselves," she said softly.

He said, "There's a reason our computers, like every starship's computers, carry the UN's standard First Contact protocol. Sending us off with the protocol means the UN recognized we might have to—"

"I mean our children." She shifted into a sitting position, careful not to dislodge his arm. "Diego, they may be only frozen specks, two among thousands, but the decision we've made affects them."

The children they were permitted only by leaving Sol system behind. "I think companionship in the universe will be a wondrous gift for them."

For a long while, the omnipresent hum of fans was the only sound. Then she said, "I might be worried about nothing. There may be no answer to our signal. Some unknown natural phenomenon could explain that planet's movements." She squeezed his hand. "The first extraterrestrial intelligence or a brand-new cosmic force. Either way, you've made one heck of a discovery."

If its acceleration were constant, the ice world had taken

about a century to reach its current velocity. In that time, it would have crossed a bit over five light-years. A red-dwarf star lay more-or-less in its backtracked direction, at about that distance. One of its worlds, a gas giant alongside which Jupiter would seem puny, had a separation in its satellite system, a gap at odds with the accepted theory of planetary formation. "It could be a natural phenomenon," Diego agreed.

But he didn't believe that.

THE NORMAL COURSE of shipboard events was that there were none. One could get very bored, even at full cruising speed, between encounters with significantly sized dust motes. Every excuse for a celebration was quickly embraced.

Four birthdays and New Year's Day (despite Diego's railing at the pointlessness of commemorating a random spot on the orbit of an increasingly remote planet) left long stretches of mind-dulling routine.

The liquid in Diego's glass was undeniably of that morning's vintage. "Jeeves, did you *taste* this stuff?"

"Harmless," the Jeeves program said. "Mostly harmless."

"Good enough," and Diego raised his glass. Fine wine would significantly overtax the synthesizer's capabilities. Today the four of them celebrated something *real*. Ice World, months ago promoted to proper-noun status, should now have received the first-contact greeting lased more than a year earlier. Should . . . for such a simple word, it conveyed a satisfying and very newfound conclusiveness. They had signaled to where they projected the distant, speeding planet would be—if it continued without interruption on its steady course and acceleration.

It had.

A miniature Ice World, unanimous choice for the party's décor, glittered above the dayroom table. Months of continuous observation had yielded details far beyond the crude holo he had first shown his shipmates.

His shipmates. With a start, and to Jaime's knowing smile, he returned his attention to the party. "To new friends!" Glasses clinked, contents sloshing a little, and were enthusiastically emptied.

Sayeed shrugged. In the steadfastness of the Ice World's hurtling trajectory, which three of them saw as evidence of intelligent intervention, he saw a mindless, if unknown, natural force. On one point all agreed: At least one of them was spectacularly wrong. Long after the discovery of pulsars, astronomers still remembered the hasty misattribution of the celestial rhythms to aliens. None of *them* planned to be forever remembered for announcing imagined aliens— or for failing to recognize real ones.

"In another year-plus. Two if they ponder and muse for a while about how to respond." Barbara poured another round of the *vin* très *ordinaire*. "I wonder what, still assuming someone *is* there, they will have to say."

Any alcohol is potable by the third serving. The day was special; they imbibed enough of today's wine to render it superb. Eventually, they had Jeeves draw virtual straws. Jaime lost. She was taking a very strong stim when the rest of them headed to bed.

THE VOICE OF Jeeves brought Diego instantly awake. "All hands to the bridge!"

He burst through the cabin door shouting, "What happened?"

Barbara beat him onto the bridge, but only because her cabin was closer. He and Sayeed were left to loiter anxiously in the corridor. The bridge couldn't accommodate them all.

"Radar pulse hit us." Jaime's chair spun as she relinquished it to the captain. "There's nothing on our sensors."

"Jeeves, alarms off." The warbling screech mercifully faded. Barbara settled into her seat and triggered a ping. Above a monitoring console, a spherical volume grew and grew: the representation of the space probed by that pulse. "Nothing," she finally concluded. She downed the stim pills Jaime offered. "That's as it should be. We must have a flaky sensor."

Diego nodded jerkily. *They couldn't have reached us.*

A new alarm blared. Parallel rows of floor lights blinked, painfully bright, their sudden manic cycling drawing Diego's attention down the curved corridor. Emergency hatches slammed; the siren and the whooshing stopped. "Hull breach in storage bay D," Barbara said. "Check that out, Sayeed."

Diego's head pounded. He dry-swallowed the pills Jaime now offered him. The alarms resumed, joined by the windstorm of a second breach aft. Something was poking holes in their ship. What, if nothing were nearby, had breached the hull? They were moving at thirty percent of light speed. What could possibly overtake the ship from behind? *Light speed! They couldn't have reached us!*

"Jaime! Trade places."

They squeezed past each other and he dropped into the lone chair beside the captain. Radar, lidar, maser—the instruments reported nothing, regardless of the frequency they sent.

Oh.

"Barbara, let's just *look*. No active sensors, just Mark I eyeballs." She spared him a sideways glance—light-years from the nearest sun, what could he expect to see, and how? But she did as he proposed.

The exterior cameras spun with the hull. Computers compensated for the gravity-simulating rotation, projecting a stationary star field onto the bridge. The stars behind were reddened and dimmed; the stars ahead flared, visibly shifted toward blue. And to one side: a large, circular patch of pitch-blackness. Whatever blocked the starlight was huge, or close, or both. Its immobile appearance meant it was orbiting them, matching the ship's rotation.

"What the tanj *is* that?" Barbara focused their radar and lidar on the apparition. "Still no return signals. The echoes are being nulled somehow."

"They're—" Jaime bit it off, but Diego could finish it for

her. *They're poking holes in our ship!* Enemy aliens. She thought they were under attack.

"Sayeed, report." Diego's words echoed from speakers across the ship. There was no answer.

Another alarm. More wind rushing from the bridge. More emergency bulkheads slammed shut. "I'm on it." Jaime's voice quavered as she dashed off.

There was precious little privacy in the *Long Pass;* by mutual agreement, the corridor cameras had been powered down early in the mission. Muttering under his breath, Diego hunted for the command sequences to awaken them. The first reactivations came a tantalizing few moments late. Was that shadow disappearing around a corner Sayeed's? Jaime's?

One more ear-piercing alarm and again sudden wind tugged at his clothes. This alarm, too, faded as Barbara reset it. What was that scurrying sound?

"Pressure continues to drop throughout the ship. I'm closing all interior hatches," announced the main bridge computer.

"Thank you, Jeeves. Give us the corridor cameras."

At last they were all on. Diego cursed as one revealed Sayeed, crumpled and motionless, face down on the deck.

Black, many-limbed figures scuttled past the camera at a nearby corridor intersection, moving too fast for Diego to integrate what he was seeing into a meaningful picture. Aliens, or robots, or alien robots. . . .

Barbara had seen it, too. "We've been boarded."

The bridge hatch burst inward before he could respond. There was a brief glimpse of serpentine limbs, an impression of something pointing at him, and a nearly subsonic vibration.

Then there was only darkness.

EXILE   Earth date: 2650

Alone in his cabin, behind a triply locked hatch, within a vessel constructed from the most impenetrable material ever made, light-years removed from any conceivable hazard, Nessus cowered.

"Nessus" was a label of convenience. His actual name, Citizen speech requiring two throats for proper articulation, was unpronounceable by his crewmates on the opposite side of the sturdy hatch. He had once overheard an irreverent Colonist remark that his true name sounded like an industrial accident set to music.

Curled into a ball, heads tucked safely inside, Nessus saw and heard nothing. He unclenched only enough to breathe. The herd pheromones continuously circulating in the ship's air would eventually calm him. Meanwhile, surely, his anxiety was appropriate.

How could he *not* panic? He represented a trillion of his kind. Only the merest fraction of the Concordance could bear to take leave of the home world. Yet here, by his own initiative, he was—because the alternative, for all of the trillion, was even more unthinkable.

The panic attack ebbed, and a head emerged for a peek. Sensors hidden throughout the ship reported that conditions remained normal. His three Colonist crew were unaware of or properly respectful to his mood. Two were within their respective cabins, one softly snoring; the last stood watch on the bridge.

Had he truly thought: normal? Normality existed only on Hearth, in the time-tested rhythms of life, amid the teeming multitudes of his kind.

He rolled once more into a tight, quivering orb. Without radical changes and much luck, everything *normal* was doomed.

* * *

YOU NEVER SAW hyperspace; quite the opposite. The brain refused to acknowledge that a dimension so strange could exist. Objects all around a cabin window somehow came together, the mind denying the nothingness between. You covered the window, but a coat of paint or a scrap of fabric only taunted you that oblivion lurked behind. You had to get used to hyperspace, and some never did. Hyperspace had driven many people mad.

Kirsten Quinn-Kovacs, alone on the bridge, studiously ignored the covered view port. There was much else to do, and much more to occupy her thoughts. Everything was new and wondrous. Merely to be aboard was a tremendous honor.

At every moment, the strangeness of it all threatened to overwhelm her.

The bridge of *Explorer* was a chimera, a superposition of improbable parts. Chimera: The word itself was a fanciful novelty, describing a fantasy creature. Nessus had taught it to her, claiming to have learned it on an alien world far, far away.

What could be more improbable than that *she* was on her way to study an unexplored alien planet? Though there was little chance she would set foot on that new world, this trip was an amazing opportunity. Except as a passenger or on training flights, always within sight of the Fleet of Worlds, no Colonist had been on a space ship—until now.

She stretched and her crash couch stretched with her. Whoever had built it truly understood Colonist physiology. The flight and navigation controls within her reach were likewise comfortable and intuitive. The General Products company knew their stuff. It amazed her that *Explorer* was only a prototype.

The other seat on the bridge, a padded bench, was as clearly meant for Nessus. The console before Kirsten had its analog near that empty couch. She could, in a crisis, interpret those other instruments; she could barely operate those controls. Her hands did not begin to approach the dexterity or strength of a Citizen's lips and jaws.

Although half the bridge's seating accommodated Colonist physiology, the room itself was clearly designed to Citizen standards. There was not a sharp corner to be seen. Consoles, shelves, instrumentation, the latching mechanism on the hatch—everything looked melted and recongealed. Citizens perceived an unnecessary hazard in every crisp edge and pointed corner.

The nothingness that was hyperspace whispered to Kirsten, daring her to acknowledge its presence. She fixed her eyes instead on her console. The heart of the instrumentation was a large transparent sphere: the mass pointer. Each blue line radiating from its center represented a nearby star. The direction of the thread showed the direction to the star; the length of the thread represented the star's gravitational influence: mass over distance squared. The longest thread by far pointed straight at her: their destination.

Logic said that a glance every shift or two was more than sufficient—even at hyperdrive speed, they took three days to cross a light-year—but logic seemed a flimsy thing indeed while the nothingness stalked her mind. She shuddered. Ships in hyperspace that too closely approached the singularity around a stellar mass, vanished. The mathematics was ambiguous. None knew where the disappeared had gone, or whether they even still existed.

Monitoring seemed like a process that could be easily automated—simply drop out of hyperspace when a line got too close—but it was not possible. The mass detector was inherently psionic; it required a conscious mind in the loop.

Even splitting the responsibility three ways, the stress was intense. They dropped into normal space every few days, if only for a moment to remind themselves that stars were more than hungry singularities reaching out to devour them.

"Does a thirty-day journey still seem like a simple

thing?" The voice was a rich contralto that women envied and men found disturbingly alluring.

Kirsten looked up, the clatter of hooves on metal decking that should have alerted her to Nessus' approach only now making a conscious impression.

One head held high, the other low, he watched her from two directions at once. With the instinctive caution of Citizens, Nessus had paused half-inside, half-outside the hatchway, poised to dash in any direction.

Her whole life she had been beholden to Citizens. So it had been for generations. But while Kirsten knew about Citizens, and respected and revered them, she had *met* few of them. Her people, like sharp corners, were an avoidable risk.

Now, in the emptiness behind the void between the stars, Kirsten reawakened to how dissimilar Citizens and Colonists truly were.

Nessus stood on two forelegs set far apart and one complexly jointed hind leg. Two long and flexible necks emerged from between his muscular shoulders. Each flat, triangular head featured an ear, an eye, and a mouth whose tongue and knobbed lips also served as a hand. His leathery skin was a soft off-white, with few of the tan markings common among some Citizens. The unkempt brown mane between his necks covered and padded the bony hump that encased his brain.

He raised a neck. His heads swiveled toward each other, eye briefly peering into eye, in an ironic laugh. Her brave words at the start of the journey had not gone unnoticed. Despite her embarrassment, she was relieved that he had come out of his cabin. Relieved, but not surprised: The surprise would have been his continued absence as they neared their destination and its unknown perils.

Of course had Nessus not emerged in another shift or two to oversee the ship's arrival, she would have hit the panic button. The looped recording of a Citizen screaming in terror would bring him to the bridge, no matter what.

The room must have looked safe enough. Nessus entered

and straddled his thickly padded bench, arching one neck forward to more closely examine the mass pointer. "We will arrive soon," he said. The simple statement ended with a hint of rising inflection that was surely no accident.

He had run the experimental training program for Colonist scouts. Surely questioning his protégés was by now second nature to him. But what was the question? Whether preparations had been completed while he hid in his room? No, that topic would be reserved for the captain.

Twenty of the best and brightest had been winnowed from the Colonists' millions. Whatever their avocations or interests, until this time of crisis *every* Colonist contributed directly or indirectly to food production. The trillion Citizens on Hearth consumed vast amounts of food, and left scant open space on which to raise it. How she, Omar, and Eric performed on this mission would be taken as proof whether *any* child of farmers and conservationists could rise to the occasion.

Before departing the Fleet, the biggest risk the three of them had imagined was a lack of challenge. The unsuspecting aliens whose faint radio emissions had drawn Hearth's attention might prove too primitive. They might offer the crew no opportunity to show their talents.

How naïve those fears now seemed!

Risks motivated Citizens, risks and finding ways to avoid them. If Nessus were questioning her, most likely the unstated subject was risk. He wanted to know: Did she understand the dangers?

The only tasks in hyperspace were routine maintenance and monitoring the mass pointer. The one was tedious, and the other nerve-racking. In such a small crew, everyone took turns. They were about to emerge from hyperspace, though, and this time not only for a reassuring peek. When they did, the star that had been their target would instantly become the brightest object in their sky. In that instant, the crew's roles would cease to be interchangeable.

She would be a navigator once more, once more with stars to steer by.

"We'll assume orbit well outside the singularity," she answered, guessing at his implied question. "I can't imagine how they could detect, let alone waylay us—but if they do, we'll reengage hyperdrive and be gone."

Two bobbing heads, alternating high and low, left Kirsten convinced she had guessed correctly. She smiled too, in her own Colonist way.

EXPLORER BURST FROM hyperspace at furious speed.

The courage that enabled Nessus to be here meant that he was, by definition, insane. Kirsten had never met a sane Citizen, because they never left Hearth. Her hands never left the flight controls, but her eyes kept darting involuntarily to the right where Nessus rested upon his crash couch. He could take control of the ship from her at any time. The knowledge was simultaneously reassuring and demeaning.

The Fleet's velocity at *Explorer*'s departure was "only" 0.017 light speed. Setting out, that initial impetus had seemed a meaningless crawl in the context of the light-years they were about to cross. That same intrinsic velocity as they reentered normal space was an altogether different matter.

Under Nessus' watchful eyes, Kirsten shed excess speed using the ship's gravity drag. Three times she micro-jumped them back to hyperspace, looping them around their target for another braking pass. *Explorer*'s fusion drive would have accomplished the task much faster—but a miles-long column of fusing hydrogen, hotter than the surfaces of stars, would have shouted the news of their arrival to anyone watching.

"Well done," Nessus finally said.

"Thanks." Her mentor's words seemed both sincere and tentative. As Kirsten steered *Explorer* into orbit around the distant spark named G567-X2, she initiated a deep-radar scan. It was both doctrine and enigma. Neutrinos passed right through normal matter, so what were they looking for? "It is good practice," was the only explanation their trainer had offered. "Nessus will know what to do if there is a return signal."

As busy as she was, Kirsten could not help wondering what the aliens called this sun. Nessus would not care. Citizens exhibited curiosity only when their safety might be imperiled. At other times, they considered inquisitiveness to be at best a distraction.

Perhaps their curiosity made Colonists better explorers, and that was why they were here. Or perhaps Colonists were only expendable. Her parents and brothers thought the latter. *And if no one were willing to scout ahead of the Fleet?* Her family had no answer to that.

With a sigh of relief, Kirsten raised her hands from the controls. "We're in orbit," she announced over the ship's intercom. To Nessus, she added, "We're safely outside the singularity, as promised."

With one head high and the other low, he studied her. "Good. Our work here begins."

· 2 ·

Of the solar system they had come so far to survey, only the star that they distantly circled was visible to the naked eye. Their instruments reported one gas giant and three rocky worlds, plus an unexceptional assortment of asteroids and remote snowballs.

Radio signals had brought *Explorer* here; radio signals emanated now from only one spot in the solar system: the third moon of the gas giant. On close examination—*close* denoting high magnification, not proximity—that moon was tidally locked to its primary, airless, and sheathed in ice. Great cracks crisscrossed the icy surface. Nessus remembered seeing another world quite like it once, a long time ago. It was called Europa.

"There is probably a world-spanning water ocean under

the ice," Omar said. He was pacing the narrow aisle of the relax room, which, after the machinery-packed engine room, was the largest chamber aboard the ship. Eric and Kirsten were tucked into small spaces on either side of the treadmill.

Nessus watched from the doorway as Omar led a review of their early findings. Most of what they discussed was confirmation rather than discovery. The Fleet's instruments were *very* sensitive. The crew's findings would be matched to what the Fleet already knew. Nessus hoped the three of them had not figured that out.

". . . So by process of elimination, whoever is generating the radio signals is beneath the ice," Omar concluded. He glanced from time to time at Nessus for approval.

Captain Omar Tanaka-Singh was tall, wiry, and slope-shouldered. An unruly mop of brown hair—Nessus had wondered: Was that a conscious imitation of my mane?—emphasized the pinched features of his face. Omar organized and administered shipboard activities; he did not define them. Nessus, in role if not in title, was the mission's Hindmost: he who leads from behind. The captain coordinated such tasks as Nessus delegated.

Before his selection for training as a scout, Omar had been an agricultural logistician. In that role he balanced projected demand with long-term weather forecasts with transportation availability with plant-pest mutation probabilities with, doubtless, many more fuzzily defined factors. The work demanded multidisciplinary analytical skills and a broad tolerance for ambiguity. And yet—while deciding what to plant and when to harvest it were important, things agricultural changed *slowly*. How would thought processes attuned to the growing season adjust to scouting of the unknown?

Some things were unknowable from a distance. Were that not the case, Nessus mused, there would be no need for scouts. "Omar, how do underwater beings make radio waves?"

"Eric, why don't you handle that?" Omar responded.

Eric Huang-Mbeke was their engineer. He was stocky and short, with ocher skin, thick lips, small teeth, and dark and intense eyes. His naturally black hair was dyed in long, colorful strands elaborately braided in imitation of Citizen style.

Explorer's ability to sense through the ice was limited, but that constraint wasn't the chief difficulty. Why would the aliens deploy radios at all? Sound was a more suitable mechanism for underwater communication. Radio waves attenuated quickly even in pure water. *Explorer* had observed enough water bursting through fresh surface cracks to measure the covered ocean's salinity, and it was high. Radio could not be a useful medium under the ice.

And even more puzzling: How could parts for a radio or its antenna be fabricated under water? While Eric hypothesized about forays above the ice, unknowingly echoing speculations of the experts on Hearth, Nessus found his attention wandering.

Did any Colonist truly understand how coiffures encoded social status among Citizens? Nessus doubted it. His mane was unadorned because he considered the custom an affectation.

Nessus could have worn an elaborate style if he so chose. Powers high in the Concordance government, within two levels of the Hindmost himself, had authorized this mission. Those who had appointed Nessus to lead it mostly disdained him for the very traits that made him qualified. Nessus returned their not-quite-hidden sneers by wearing his mane not only plain, but occasionally disheveled. His parents were Conservatives; he had ample experience coping with disapproval.

He hoped his conduct toward the Colonists was less judgmental than what he had so often received. Eric in particular deserved better: His devotion to the Concordance was beyond question. With each new generation, more Colonists took their comfortable existence for granted. Eric would never be one of them.

The irony was not lost on Nessus. For all that *he*

questioned authority, instinctive loyalty to the current, utterly conservative, political order was a primary selection criterion for this crew. He would have it no other way. His safety might someday depend on their reflexive deference.

"Nessus?" Eric prompted respectfully.

Nessus quickly ran through his mind the highlights of Eric's briefing and Kirsten's occasional insightful interjection. On the one head, they had raised no points new to the Fleet's analysts. On the other head, despite being pioneers on their first separation from their own kind, their findings so far seemed sound. He could not reasonably have expected anything more.

"You've made some interesting observations. How would you propose we proceed?"

"I would like to get closer," Eric said. "Perhaps we can locate their above-the-ocean bases."

"Absolutely not," Omar glanced at Nessus for support. "That's why we carry unmanned probes."

Explorer's distant orbit around G567-X2 was not, as Nessus was happy for his crew to believe, a precaution taken against the still-unseen aliens. Out here where hyperdrive could be used, the hyperwave radio hidden in his cabin could *also* be used.

If *Explorer* headed sunward, they would leave behind a hyperwave radio buoy, with which the ship could then link by conventional radio. The light-speed crawl to the relay, however, was the problem. It would delay his access to Hearth's experts. The illusion of infallibility would be lost without fast access to a world of experts.

As Omar turned anxiously to Nessus for support, Nessus wondered whether his staffing decisions might already have proven him fallible. Perhaps the captain was *too* much like a Citizen. In a crisis, would Omar become hysterical or withdraw? Of course, Omar's wariness was another tool Nessus could use to mold and guide the crew. Problem or not, Nessus took satisfaction from having had the insight. He was getting to truly understand them all: cautious Omar, loyal Eric, and quiet but clever Kirsten.

This must be what it's like to raise children. The comparison seemed appropriate: If Nessus expected ever to have his own children, he must demonstrate success with these Colonists. He had once overheard his parents discussing the need for extreme caution in having progeny: "The disadvantage of advanced medical technology—we have to live with our child for a *long* time." It did not matter that Nessus was eager to take that chance, for there was no prospective mate in his life.

Success could change that.

Flight from danger was instinctive for Citizens. He certainly had the same reflex; no doubt there would be times he would regret the decision he was about to announce. Fortunately for the trillion on Hearth, he, and a precious few like him, could overcome the impulse.

Perhaps it was the prospect of a mate when they succeeded. Whatever the cause, a manic mood seized him. It was familiar from his other travels and at the same time wondrously strange. They were inside a General Products hull, made from the most impenetrable material known to his or any other species. Without a black hole or large amounts of antimatter, there was nothing the ice-moon aliens could possibly do to harm them. He felt liberated, even giddy.

Nessus fixed Omar with a hard, two-headed stare. "Actually, Omar, I think the level of hazard is acceptable. Everything we have discussed here suggests the aliens use only quite primitive technology. I believe we'll be quite safe.

"Let's go get a closer look."

ERIC WAS LEAVING the tiny galley as Kirsten arrived. He loitered while she got a glass of juice from the synthesizer.

He had been wearing the bold colors of a man seeking a wife and children, ready to settle down. Fair enough. But aboard this ship were only Omar, who was already mated and had two daughters, and Eric, and Kirsten herself.

She had worn only gray—and a pale gray, at that, for

added emphasis—to make plain that she was not presently open to any relationship. She had done so since the final crew selection, before *Explorer* ever departed their world of NP4. If asked, she would have told a partial truth: that her sole focus was on the success of the mission.

Eric's colors were bolder today than ever, his jumpsuit an eye-poppingly vibrant green. She had never encouraged him. That intense color, that overt proclamation of his interest, was the equivalent of a leer. He watched her drink. "You're looking very relaxed," he told her.

His clothes did not match his words, and Kirsten decided to address only the latter. "Relaxed" certainly overstated things. She could admit, however, to being relieved. "I'm just happy to be here," she said.

To be anywhere, in fact, besides hyperspace—merely thinking of the nothingness made her twitchy. After finding their way across ten light-years, wasn't she entitled to feel a bit of accomplishment and relief?

Eric said, " 'Here' is going to be a disappointment. You *getting* us here, and presumably home again, may be the highlight of the whole trip."

Was he mocking her? She had rejected his advances in training, politely, she thought. No word had been spoken; only clothing styles and body language expressed her disinterest. His attitude ever since, whenever they were alone, was inappropriate. It might be suggestive, or sarcastic, or belittling, or something else entirely.

Nessus had assembled a *very* bright crew—considering them individually. Perhaps it was too much to expect him to anticipate how three isolated Colonists would interact. Or maybe—Omar having a long-term relationship contract back on the continent of Arcadia on NP4—maybe Nessus considered himself a matchmaker between her and Eric. *That* idea made her fume.

She hiked enough to be fit, she supposed, although the treadmill in the relax room was a poor substitute for cross-country treks. Maybe she cleaned up all right. Neither was justification for Eric's unwelcome persistence. Regardless, the easiest way to deal with him was usually to ignore the subtext.

She said, "What we're here to do is *important*."

"In a way," he answered. "In the way that practice is always important."

She knew she was staring. Words refused to come.

"No, really. The mission can't be anything else." Eric perched on a corner of the room's small table. "We were sent to assess this specific solar system, of all those along the Fleet's path. *No* artifacts are visible, not from the Fleet, not even here on the borders of the solar system. There are only alien radio signals, too faint and intermittent to interpret over just a few light-years."

"Right," she agreed, wondering where he was going.

"Trust your friendly neighborhood engineer on this: The aliens' equipment could not be any more primitive." She must not have looked trusting, because he continued. "The signals we came ten light-years to investigate were scarcely more than big sparks. They evidently encode some kind of on/off system for sending information.

"These guys on their ice world are hardly a threat to anyone. We learn, or fail to learn, anything interesting about them, and get our final grade. If we're lucky, we show ourselves worthy of exploring someplace that really might be a potential threat. Regardless, the Fleet flies past in seventy years, by then accelerated up to three-tenths light-speed. If realistically there were any danger here, would Nessus be willing, even eager, to go for a closer look?"

Was Eric right? Might this be simply one more exercise? In her disappointment, Kirsten almost overlooked a subtlety. "Were, you said. Their signals *were* little more than big sparks. Are they something different now?"

"Well, yes," he admitted. "The signals are better controlled now. They've substituted an absurdly convoluted transmission scheme. The broadcasts remain staticky. They use spectrum with horrible inefficiency. Even their most sophisticated format has a slow, jerky frame rate, low resolution, and it's all in two dimensions. The content is mapped into an analog representation, of all unlikely choices. Despite the many oddities, I have most of the details worked out."

Big sparks was a much shorter description. Was he implying progress? "You're describing video," she finally said.

"True, in the sense a sled is like *Explorer*. They're both for transportation." Eric slid off the table. "Look, Kirsten, I didn't mean to upset you. Forget I said anything. Be as relaxed or tense as you wish, and I won't comment further." With a patronizing smirk, he was out the door and into the corridor.

Hyperdrive had brought *Explorer* across ten light-years, so Eric's big sparks were first broadcast just ten years ago. Was sparks-to-video in ten years fast development? The Concordance's vastly superior technology was *old,* mature long before the first Colonists arrived at the Fleet of Worlds. Maybe she could extract something germane about technical history from *Explorer*'s data archives.

Eric could be obnoxious and offensive, but he was also damned smart and he paid attention to politics. What if he were right? What if this whole trip was an elaborate exercise? She presumed that by getting them here she personally had passed. It did not seem like enough. Surely an equally important part of the test was threat assessment. The *mission* would flunk if they too quickly dismissed the aliens as a prospective danger.

Think like a Citizen, she told herself. Any avoidable risk should be avoided. Nessus had an expression about leaving no stone unturned. She got a sandwich and more juice, wondering all the while why that odd saying nagged at her.

Three-tenths light speed. Stone. She nearly dropped her plate as the realization dawned. In the presence of quite modest technology, the Fleet's very speed was its worst vulnerability. Strew some pebbles in its path, and the Fleet's velocity transformed them into fearsome kinetic-energy weapons.

Was such a scenario remotely likely? Sparks-to-video in

ten years seemed rapid to her, but truthfully she could not say. She intended to find out. What about alien intentions? If the ice-world denizens could harm the Fleet, would they?

From the Concordance's perspective, the better question might be: Who could say they would not?

Space was a dangerous place, as her ancestors had found to their misfortune. A chill came over her—and a wave of gratitude for everything the Citizens had done for her people. Training exercise or not, *she* would take this threat assessment seriously.

Eric was quite mistaken. She was *hardly* relaxed.

· 3 ·

Perhaps mathematics was not such an impractical career choice after all.

The Colonists' world was Nature Preserve Four, NP4 for short, and theirs solely through the great magnanimity of the Concordance. At that they held only the continent of Arcadia. With few exceptions, and Kirsten was not one of them, the Colonist population enthusiastically embraced their assigned role as ecological stewards. Much of their world was dedicated to biodiversity sanctuaries; the rest of NP4, including most of Arcadia, was intensively farmed. The Colonists produced huge quantities of food, for the vast population on Hearth and the few millions of themselves.

Not everyone is meant to be a farmer or preservationist, and that, too, was part of the Citizens' vision. People were needed to maintain the irrigation systems, manufacture the tractors and combines, process and transport the harvests, educate the children, run the power generators, maintain the records, house and clothe everyone . . . it took a great many skills to maximize production in a sustainable way. Sustainability was the key—Citizens planned for the long haul.

For all the breadth of Arcadian society, though, it took

real creativity to justify a career in mathematics. Kirsten found enough unresolved problems in weather forecasting and seismic prediction to make it work. Interstellar navigation was not an application she would ever have imagined for herself, but she could not fault herself for overlooking it. Things change.

Until five years ago, none of a trillion Citizens anticipated that the galactic core had exploded.

With that revelation, nature preservation took on a much broader meaning. The radiation blast from that long-ago supernovae chain reaction would sterilize this part of the galaxy in another twenty thousand or so years. It was impossible to imagine the Citizen flight reflex operating on a larger scale: the migration of Hearth and its five nature-preserve companion worlds to safer surroundings. In so doing, the Concordance was once again rescuing her people.

Nessus did not admit to knowing the aliens who had reported the core explosion. Maybe there was even sense to his refusal to say much about his past travels. "All aliens are different," he liked to say. "The less I share, the less I'll warp your thinking about what we encounter on this flight."

Kirsten liked Nessus a lot, and not only for having selected her to train as a navigator. Few Citizens could do what he did. Yes, the Fleet of Worlds was running *from* danger, but without someone scouting ahead, who could know what dangers they might be speeding *into*?

Sighing, she switched off her sleeper field and settled lightly to her cabin's floor. The universe had a way of keeping her awake. She might as well get up and *do* something.

Nessus was probably unique. Padding down the corridor to the treadmill in the relax room, she surprised herself by thinking: There may not be another Colonist who can do what *I* can—

And I have the pictures to prove it.

WITH FIVE EQUAL-SIZED, tapered, tubular limbs spaced equidistantly around a flat core, the aliens seemed equally adapted to swimming the world-spanning sea and crawling along sea-bottom muck. Prehensile spines covered their leathery skins. Their five writhing extremities made them gross parodies of Citizen and Colonist alike. From time to time, some of them would entwine, or crawl over one another, or manipulate unrecognizable objects for unknowable purposes. Most of the activity took place inside ice or stone structures. Nothing in the images offered Nessus any sense of scale.

He was marking a flat projection when Kirsten entered the relax room, a towel over one shoulder. She was svelte and athletic, fair-skinned with high cheekbones and a delicate nose. Her auburn hair was pulled back in a short ponytail, with unruly bangs that somehow made her dark brown eyes that much more striking. From the way Omar and especially Eric looked at her, Nessus guessed she was a desirable mate by Colonist standards.

She hopped onto the treadmill. "Are you learning much from the recovered video?"

Nessus said, "Despite what I always say, a picture may not be worth a thousand words."

She laughed, and Nessus guessed her good humor had little to do with his turn of phrase. While Eric had been disparaging noisy, low-quality signals and a primitive broadcast format, she had mathematically deconstructed the modulation scheme. Crisp video had popped right up after she mathematically described how to filter out superimposed data flows. It appeared she had found an audio channel and annotations of some kind where their engineer had suspected only noise.

Presumably the experts on Hearth would come to the same conclusion, which was something he himself would never have accomplished. The only numbers Nessus found truly interesting were polls. Success in the Colonist scouting program could give him the start he had so long wanted in politics. A mental image of his disapproving parents, near-catatonic with fright these past five years since the first news of the core explosion, almost made *him* laugh.

None of these ruminations were suitable for the crew. "What do you think of our new acquaintances?"

"They're sure busy doing *something,* but I can't begin to guess what." Her arms pumped as the treadmill kicked up to a higher speed. "It should get easier when the translator software starts making sense of the audio channel."

Nessus put his heads to use tweaking the projector controls. He was stalling: His attention was not on the magnified area he slowly panned across, but on what not to say. Concordance technology must seem limitless to the Colonists. There was much to be said for keeping them in a state of awe.

This manic phase would not last forever. Soon enough, Nessus thought, I'll surrender to tucking my heads tightly between my forelegs. When that happens, I'll be just a bit safer if these three understand what *Explorer* is, and is not, capable of.

"We can't translate the broadcasts. The way it usually works"—and the thought brought him *very* close to retreating into a tightly coiled ball—"is in a faces-to-face encounter. We say something, and it's unintelligible. They say back something unintelligible. There is much pointing and miming. The translator has to build the context. At first, only scattered words make sense. In time, there will be phrases, even sentences, but with maddening gaps for unrecognized concepts. Full translation takes a while."

"That's . . . logical," she huffed. Her ponytail flipped from side to side as she now ran full-out. "So we need to land and meet them."

A mosaic filled his mind's eye, populated by swarming hordes, grasping tentacles, and sharp-edged daggers of stone and ice. He had met aliens before but not like this: A first contact could go wrong in *so* many ways. Up here, in the ship, they were safe from anything such primitives could do. Faces to face was a very different situation. "It would be prudent to gather more information first."

Sweat dripped down her face and neck, to be wicked away and evaporated by the nanofibers in her tunic. She ran in silence for a long time. "Here's a thought. Most likely, some of the audio corresponds to the video information. Suppose—" and she fell silent again. "Okay, try this. We use scene-analysis software to model what's going on, tagging with English text our hypotheses about each object and activity. Most images are ambiguous, so we start with probability-weighted decision trees. Then we correlate the tagged scenes with the concurrent audio information.

"Sure, some of the seeming audio may be an independent voice channel. It might be music, if they have such a concept. The thing is, over time, the only statistically significant audio data will be speech that's related to the concurrent video. Everything else will be washed out by the significance filters."

"You could do such an analysis?"

Retrieving her towel, Kirsten blotted her face and neck without breaking stride. "Sure. Not easily, exactly. It will take some programming, and probably some experimentation with the weightings of alternative interpretive models. . . ."

Her math ability constantly impressed Nessus, but her casually assumed prowess at programming made him tremble. No, be honest—this *kind* of programming scared him. It scared all Citizens. Nothing was more intrinsically related to intelligence than language. Programs that modeled intelligence could, it was feared, all too possibly become intelligent. Translators, in certain circumstances, were a necessary evil, but . . .

I'm more like most Citizens than I realize, Nessus thought. Still, he was one of the very few to have visited civilizations that dared to undertake AI research. None had run amok yet. And her approach, if it worked, might eliminate the need for a landing.

"That is an excellent idea," he began to say in support.

The rapt expression on Kirsten's face made it clear no encouragement was required.

"CUTE LITTLE FELLAS." The curl of Eric's upper lip revealed his words as sarcasm. "Still, it's interesting to watch what the starfish are up to." He had proposed the name, and was all the prouder of it because it amused Nessus.

At times, Kirsten found Eric's deference annoying. Have your *own* values, she wanted to shout. She kept her response to a noncommittal grunt and returned her attention to the video. Officially, her interest was in ways to improve the correlation and decoding models. Interpretation of the data was more Omar's department. In truth, she was hooked. The more she learned about the aliens, the more fascinated she became.

Holos surrounded the video, each offering another perspective of the main scene: partially translated conversations; interpretations of any alien artifacts in view; the location on the globe of the video source; a highly magnified view from synchronous orbit of the encampment and a few roving aliens, taken by one of *Explorer*'s recently deployed probes. Kirsten said, "They call themselves Gw'oth, Eric. It's Gw'o if you're talking about just one."

"Maybe that translates to *starfish*."

"Whatever it means, they're adventurers, space travelers in their own way." He was so enamored of Citizen culture—just look at the curls and intricacies of his hair!—that Kirsten doubted he would ever appreciate how incredible the Gw'oth were. She felt compelled to try. Maybe she could reach him on *his* terms.

"Someone I know once suspected this trip was a test. If so, part of our grade will certainly depend on how well we figure out these guys. Think about it, Eric. They evolved in the ocean. Living underwater means no fire and no use of metal. Their first venture above the ice, into the *vacuum* above the ice, was a heroic undertaking."

If their scene interpretations and partial translations were correct, those first forays had involved the most primitive of gear. The early protective suits looked like no more than translucent bags trailing tubes back to underwater pumps that were little more than flexible bags manipulated by Gw'oth remaining beneath the ice. Bags, suits, and hoses all seemed to be made from the tough skins of deep-sea animals. She pulled some old imagery from *Explorer*'s archive. "Just look at this."

Nessus joined them in the relax room. He had a way, Kirsten had noticed, of appearing whenever a conversation became interesting. "Don't mind me," he said. "I just came for a bite to eat."

"So the starfish," and Eric looked to Nessus for approval, "cut a hole in the ice with stone tools and climb up wearing leather bubbles—where someone is already on the ice to capture it all with a video camera? Was that chipped from stones, too? Kirsten, that makes no sense."

Citizens ate often, but they ate with one head and kept watch with the other. Nessus was observing them now while he ate. Trying not to think about him assessing them, Kirsten gestured at the video she had just pulled up. "I assume it's a reenactment. Maybe that's a Gw'o who likes the challenge. Maybe it's a history show, or education, or entertainment.

"You're right, Eric, about one thing. They could not have had video cameras, or any type of electronics, until after they went above the ice. Their only prior experience with gases would have been from undersea volcanic eruptions, or vacuum boiling of the water in a fresh ice fracture. Look at them now: We've got video of them wearing their pressure suits inside their above-ice buildings so that they can contain an atmosphere. Why? They need fire! Fire for what they still see as new industrial processes." She wished she could say more, but it was far beyond her knowledge to guess what alternate paths to technology had been involved.

Nessus set down his bowl, the gruel within it still

untouched. "Eric, what do you think? Is such a scenario plausible?"

Eric struck an increasingly familiar pose that made Kirsten strangely uncomfortable: worshipful presentation to their mentor. "It's possible, Nessus. A big ceiling lens in an airtight room could focus enough sunlight to gradually photo-dissociate water. That would give a hydrogen and oxygen atmosphere. Such a lens could be carved from ice or a crystal like quartz. They'd need something they could add to the oxy-hydrogen mix to make it less explosive. Biological processes like digestion or respiration probably produce other gases, like carbon dioxide, in small amounts. They might have found catalysts to produce or separate gases. Yes, it seems possible. But how could they figure this all out?"

Nessus gave an involuntary shiver, the kind Kirsten associated with a mood swing to depression and withdrawal. "I certainly hope we convince ourselves they somehow did. The alternative is that an advanced, spacefaring species has visited this solar system without our knowing anything about it."

He did not need to remind them that this solar system lay near the Fleet's planned path.

FROM FIRE TO fission in two generations.

From the depths of his tightly coiled body, Nessus took solace that it could have been worse. At least the analysts on Hearth thought the Gw'oth had developed their technology on their own. And at least their report had reached him through the still-secret comm link in his cabin. The Colonists had not seen him in panic.

Those advising the expedition from the safety of Hearth had assigned a multitude of computer and math experts to enhance Kirsten's models. How many experts? His inquiries never got an answer. It probably did not matter, and it even amused him to picture their unease. None of the experts had had her insight to augment the standard translator.

Regardless, between *his* expert and the many at home,

there was now an answer to Eric's question: How could they figure this all out?

With great force of will, Nessus unwrapped himself. Without a doubt, this mission had already established the value of Colonist scouts. It was hard to be happy about that when a threat to the Fleet was involved.

The disturbing analysis from Hearth lay unannounced in the ship's main receive buffer. With a coded message, he released it to the comm subsystem on the bridge. Omar, currently on the bridge, would "receive" it while Nessus innocently made his way to the galley.

"All hands to the relax room," Omar called out over the intercom. Omar read fast.

KIRSTEN STUMBLED DOWN the corridor, groggy from being awakened suddenly. She found the rest of the crew in the relax room before her, discussion already begun. A laugh caught in her throat, because Eric's usual construction of elaborate braids was a straggle matted on the left. How much time, she wondered, did he normally spend to maintain that coiffure?

". . . Scientists back at Hearth have decoded a portion of a big Gw'oth data archive. What we've seen by tapping their broadcasts is a small part of what's available. The good news is, there's no evidence of spacefaring visitors helping the Gw'oth." Omar gestured to a complex holo graphic whose meaning was far from obvious.

Yawning, Kirsten almost dropped the bulb of stim juice Eric lobbed her way. She needed the caffeine badly; it took her a moment to synchronize her thoughts with the conversation.

It had turned out digital data streams were sometimes modulated over the analog transmissions between the bases above the ice. Reverse-engineering the protocol and cracking its associated simple authentication model had revealed to her a new surprise: a Gw'oth digital communications network and associated archives. Likely there was no way beneath the ice to develop electronics or other sophisticated technologies, but devices built above the ice could operate below. The wired network deployed below the ice seemed far larger than what they could directly see. Its addressing scheme implied planning for a very large network.

How much, she wondered, that was hidden from sight will now be revealed?

That, Kirsten realized, was what this no-notice gathering was about. The experts on Hearth had analyzed the archive. She felt a twinge of jealousy. She could apply only the computing power of this single ship. They had a world's computers to sift and organize the data.

"The timeline surprised the analysts," Omar said. "The Gw'oth calendar is based on the solar orbit of the gas giant they circle. We can translate their dates precisely. They first ventured above the ice fifty-two of our years ago. Roughly two Gw'oth generations."

Our year. It was an arbitrary unit of measure, maintained for consistency with old Citizen records. The Citizens had long ago moved Hearth far from its sun, as that star prepared to swell into a red giant. "Year" had been arbitrary long before the Fleet began its latest journey.

Looking around the room, Kirsten could see that everyone was struggling to absorb the news. Not that long ago, the only bit of technical history she wanted to better understand was the likely progression between broadcasting techniques. More sophisticated transmission was such a small part of what was implied by Omar's timeline.

Someone had to comment first, so she did. "Fifty-two years seems incredibly fast progress." It *had* been done, so she had to believe it. How could they learn so much so quickly? They had to build the tools to build the tools to build the tools, through untold iterations. They had to produce an atmosphere in which to first create fire to first smelt ores with which to craft their first metal tools. She could just barely believe the full sequence was achievable starting with a detailed knowledge of the underlying sciences. Experts on Hearth said there were no outside parties imparting the knowledge. So how?

The hideously complex graphic floating in the aisle suddenly made sense. It represented the many parallel and entwining technological projects the Gw'oth had undertaken. "They knew from the moment they cracked through the ice what they wanted to do and how to accomplish it."

"That is what's now believed," Eric said. "What I don't get is *how*. How could they create the plan before they had the environment in which to do the experiments to develop the science to envision the plan?"

Kirsten had no answer, but neither did anyone else. She pointed into the holo. "Is that a *nuclear plant* at the end of this sequence?" No one corrected her. "How could we fail to notice nuclear power plants?"

"They're beneath the ice, on the ocean floor," Nessus said. "We had noticed the heat sources, of course. We assumed they were seabed volcanoes. Checking those locations with full instrumentation, deep-penetrating radar, and radiation sensors leaves no doubt what they truly are. From fire to fission in two generations."

Nessus' body quivered, as though he resisted fleeing to his room or rolling himself up. "And there is one more detail we collectively overlooked. Radio signals don't propagate past the horizon, unless by bouncing off of an ionosphere. The ice moon has no atmosphere, but we never stopped to ask ourselves how the starfish communicate between their distant bases."

"Long wires run under the ice?" Omar guessed.

Nessus reached a head into the graphic. "No, low-orbiting communication satellites. So far they use only primitive chemical rockets, but it's a start toward space travel."

Comm sats. No one could claim *those* were out of sight beneath the ice. At least, Kirsten thought, Eric had the decency to look embarrassed.

· 4 ·

The walls were rough-hewn stone, the lighting an eerie bioluminescent green, and the occupants five-pointed sea creatures. Purplish-green fronds grew from cracks in the floor and walls, swaying in unseen currents and eddies. For all the strangeness, the setting suggested an office.

"What are you working on?" Kirsten asked rhetorically. She was watching the Gw'oth through a camera conveniently placed by the aliens themselves. Were they recording an important meeting? Monitoring workers for purposes of security? She had no idea. The camera was video only. That was too bad, because their translator was getting better. It produced logical-seeming results from nearly half what it was given.

Beep. Her viewpoint switched to a storeroom somewhere beneath the ice. Their scanning program probed Gw'oth network addresses at random, but as far as she could ascertain, a network address conveyed nothing about a camera's physical location. Maybe it didn't matter. No one was in the room, and the translated labels on the boxes identified only various foods.

Beep. Beep. Beep. Two random attempts had gotten no response. Another room, this time with two writhing Gw'oth. Alien sex, she thought. She was still blushing when the vantage point shifted again.

A knock rattled her cabin door. "How is it going?" Omar asked.

"Fine." It was a rote answer. Eric was investigating the primitive Gw'oth satellites—in plain sight, now that he knew to look—and scanning the surface for launch sites. Omar was assisting Nessus with analysis of the archive translations streaming to them from Hearth. By process of elimination, that left her to sample the array of Gw'oth cameras. She only wished her assignment had produced something useful. "I've tagged several scenes for ongoing monitoring. How goes your analysis?"

"The little guys are making me feel really stupid. I'm just glad we have a big head start, and the Fleet will be past here soon."

The little guys: Omar's favorite nickname reflected a small bit of progress. A medical database had provided typical Gw'oth body dimensions in their own units of measure. A physics database had shown the correspondence between their traditional unit of length and hydrogen wavelengths. An average Gw'o was no longer than her arm; its torso at its thickest was the length of her hand. "Keep me posted, Omar. I'll let you know if anything interesting pops up here."

The next beep-beep drowned out Omar's parting words. Receding footsteps suggested he had not expected an answer.

Bigger surprises than the size of a Gw'o lay within the medical databases. Each of the five muscular tubes was nearly an independent creature in its own right. Gw'oth researchers believed a distant ancestor of theirs was some sort of primitive colony. Omar, the closest among the crew to a biologist, suspected they were correct. It would take genomic databases to prove or disprove the theory, and so far nothing of the sort had been found. Gw'oth science seemed not to have ventured far into genetics.

The next scene showed a single Gw'o operating an apparatus she did not recognize. Whatever it was, the creature used four extremities to control it. The lack of an annotation said the translator could not identify the equipment either. "Pause scan." She watched for a while without enlightenment. "Keep recording this channel. Queue a copy to Eric." After staring a little longer without result, she added, "Resume scan."

Beep. An empty corridor. Beep. A writhing mass of Gw'oth: an orgy. She averted her eyes until a tone signaled a scene change. Beep beep. A vast spread of sea-bottom plant life, perhaps a farm. Beep . . .

She stood and stretched. The little guys were keeping

their secrets, she thought, followed by: Why do I care that they're smaller than me? Several more uninteresting scenes beeped by before she decided. It's a *defense mechanism*. Omar is not the only one they make feel slow-witted.

"Pause." Maybe her reaction did bear thinking about. It wasn't just that the outpouring of Gw'oth creativity shocked Eric and Omar—and her. In truth, Colonists had little experience developing technology from scratch. Her people's science and engineering was doled out by their patrons. Whatever she had learned before, she had always been aware it was merely a subset of Citizen knowledge. No, what was truly eye-opening was that the Gw'oth rate of learning astonished *Nessus*.

It was not her first such rude awakening. . . .

WHEN KIRSTEN WAS twelve, her parents took her and her brothers hiking in a forested conservation zone. Dad practically had to drag her there, stepping disc by stepping disc. Voluntarily leaving the grid seemed ridiculous. To intentionally walk into the wilderness was the most peculiar thing she had ever contemplated.

Still whining petulantly, she popped into a small woodland clearing where Dad and Carl awaited her. She took a step forward, and her mother and her baby brother appeared on the disc she just vacated. Teleportation: *That* was how civilized beings traveled. A ten-digit code was emblazoned on a nearby sign; she committed the stepping-disc's address to memory. It seemed impossible that there would be *no* more stepping discs in their path. She had vague hopes of finding one, evading her parents, and teleporting back along a chain of stepping discs to home and friends and urban comforts.

Five globes—four blue and white, one bejeweled—hung overhead in a straight line: the rest of the Fleet. She had never set foot on any of them; she did not expect she ever would. Still, any of those worlds, even Hearth itself, was less alien than the myriads of trees all around her. Each of those worlds had stepping-disc grids, too.

She had known in the abstract that farms and ranches and seas lay outside the stepping-disc network. Never before had she *felt* it. Her parents worked in a tractor factory. The factory and their neighborhood were in the heart of the grid.

A hundred paces into the woods they lost sight of the forest-ranger station and its end-of-the-line stepping disc. Chirps and rustles in the undergrowth made her shrink close to Dad despite her displeasure at being here. She knew both he and Mom carried some sort of Citizen-sanctioned stunning device in case an animal got too close.

Dad led the way into the park, babbling about permutations and combinations of trees. She did not share his enthusiasm. She remembered a downhill section along a stream bed, and a packed-dirt path. Had it been trodden by animals? The thought made her cringe. Occasionally they climbed hills for their different-only-in-the-details views, between longer periods spent among the trees and undergrowth. Much of her time went to keeping track of little Philip.

Dad's commentary grew sparser and sparser. They came to a halt beside a pond she thought seemed familiar. He and Mom traded looks that said plainly: This is not what I expected. Mom checked her communicator, and shook her head. No reception.

"We're lost, aren't we?" Kirsten was scared and angry and ready to slug Philip, just because he was there. "Why would you bring us here? No stepping discs, no communications"—and a sudden thought hit her—"and no food."

"It was supposed to be a fun outing, Kirsten," Dad said. "I thought we were following a circuit that would lead us back to the entry disc, but obviously we missed a turn. This park *seemed* small enough that we couldn't go very far astray, and safe enough, because it's surrounded by farms.

"So yes, we're lost, but there's no need to worry. The

park staff will surely find us. They know we're in here. Or our friends will call them when we're late coming home."

The sky darkened with clouds, and the rain began. They huddled together for warmth under a rocky outcropping that kept off little of the rain. Philip hid his face in Mom's side, and even Carl was quiet. As the last of the orbital suns set for the night, the temperature plummeted. Her teeth chattered.

Were they animals, to die alone in the forest? It seemed insane.

Three yellow blotches in the dense cloud marked the visible worlds of the Fleet, a bit of normality in an existence suddenly become surreal. Through the clouds, she could not tell one world from another.

It was a useless skill, but she had deduced how to tell the time of day from the position of the worlds in the sky. It amused her, and provided a smart-aleck answer to Dad's questioning the value of studying math.

Wait! The line of the worlds had seemed different at the start of their trek. "Dad, you said the park is surrounded by farms." Farms meant warmth and food, and workers who could show them the nearest stepping discs.

"Yes. We could hike out of here if we could walk in a straight line." His shrug was barely recognizable in profile in the nighttime gloom. "Following stepping discs isn't the same, is it? I mean, a stepping disc or a sign for one is always in sight."

"That's the thing." She pointed skyward, suddenly excited. "We *can* walk in a straight line. It's even easy." She turned to face squarely the three glows overhead. "Just walk towards the Fleet."

They made their way slowly with only flashlights to guide the selection of a safe path. With Dad at her side, Kirsten led the way. Another world had set, leaving but two to guide them, when the edge of a cultivated field appeared through the trees. It was her first feat of navigation.

That near-disastrous outing was at once the start of her love of nature and the loss of innocence. Thinking her parents wrong and stupid about everything somehow had not yet translated into a visceral realization that parents did not know everything. But no one can know everything, not even parents. It was all right if she knew something they did not.

That wilderness adventure, her first act of navigation, was also the first step on the path that had brought Kirsten to the stars.

SO EVEN *CITIZENS* don't know everything, and Eric's question hung over the mission like a dark cloud. How *had* the Gw'oth planned their no-wasted-efforts, no-missteps, technological eruption before they mastered the environment in which to do the experiments to develop the science to envision the plan? If the four of them could not answer that, how could they begin to predict whether the Gw'oth represented a risk to the onrushing Fleet?

Running often helped Kirsten think, and the only place onboard to run was the treadmill. Her arms and legs pumped, and cityscape streamed past her in a wall projection, as she tried to reconcile the irreconcilable. She had a theory that only an applied mathematician could like. The Gw'oth could have *simulated* everything—science, engineering designs, and development projects—until they were ready to put their plans into effect. With sufficiently massive computing power, models and calculations could replace much messy experimentation. She had taken basic science classes on Arcadia. Simulation was a much more reliable guide to how the world worked than her typical lab technique.

But the Gw'oth wouldn't have computers until they developed above-the-ice industry. The riddle made her head hurt.

Dinner time came and went; she kept loping on the treadmill. She needed a clear head more than a synthed meal.

Not only would the Gw'oth need computers to do the simulations, but as far as their investigations had revealed, the aliens *still* did not have major computing capabilities.

They had huge data archives, and specialized devices to facilitate sorting and searching and networking that data—but computers? The scouts had not found any computing centers to speak of.

Her arms and legs burned and trembled; she ached from overexertion. Knowing she had overdone it, she slowed the treadmill to a cool-down gait.

Even Citizens don't know everything. How much less do *I* know?

· 5 ·

The four scouts watched a cluster of stone structures climb skyward from a mountain peak that poked through the ice. In the fast-forwarded playback, Gw'oth workers in pressure suits became nearly invisible blurs. Completed rooms and outbuildings were sprayed inside and out; whatever water did not immediately boil away froze into gas-tight seals. More and more test bores gaped nearby, giving the site the overall appearance of a mining camp. From the apex of the mountain rose a metal structure, too early in its construction to be conclusively identified. A steerable dish antenna on a tower pointed skyward; analysis showed it was tracking low-orbiting comm sats as they flew past.

This was a full hologram, the imagery taken by *Explorer*'s forward probes. *Explorer* itself shared an orbit with the ice moon. The gas giant they both circled blocked starship and moon from any direct view of each other. Chains of tiny stealthed buoys, each in a transparent and indestructible General Products #1 hull, relayed messages between *Explorer* and its observation satellites high above the ice moon. We're surely safe here, Kirsten thought. How much are we impeding our own investigation by hiding here?

They had gathered again in the relax room. Nessus gestured with one head at the holo. "Omar, what do we know about their building project?"

"Know? Not much," Omar said. "The project was well under way before we happened to notice it. It looks like the little guys are putting up a big antenna. I would guess they're going for a high-gain antenna to use with synchronously orbiting comm sats."

"We could land and *ask* them," Kirsten burst out. More and more, the Gw'oth impressed her. Observing them was fascinating, but she wanted to get to *know* them.

Nessus swiveled a head toward her. "Ask them what?"

Whatever, she wanted to shout. Her impatience and frustration surprised her. "What are they building? What is their approach to science? Can we trade information with them?"

The core question—will you become a threat?—could not be asked directly. Eric wanted to know how and from where they launched the satellites; she wanted to know why she had found data archives but still no major computing centers. Inquiries about either topic risked revealing their own spying to the Gw'oth. It's tricky, Kirsten thought. *Our investigations might make us seem a threat to them.*

"No landings yet," Nessus answered with a shudder. "We don't announce our presence, either. The Gw'oth probably do not even know that other intelligent species exist. Why reveal that fact, and perhaps in the process make them more likely to notice the Fleet?"

Eric was frowning at the fast-changing holo. "They might know sooner than we'd like, that they're not alone, I mean. That could be a radio telescope they're building."

"I'll continue to watch it," Omar promised. "We might also try an experiment to elicit more information."

Something about *experiment* sounded provocative to Kirsten. "What do you mean?"

"Incapacitate one of their satellites to see how they respond. It was Eric's suggestion, and rather good."

Kirsten struggled to find a suitable verb, finally settling on a word that described the behavior of predatory animals. "Attack them?"

Eric nodded. "We would use a laser-equipped probe, waiting until its line of sight to the Gw'oth satellite misses all other satellites and the ice moon itself. They won't see anything. There is no evidence they have lasers, so they won't have a clue what happened. A lost satellite will put a hole in their communications network, so they are likely to replace it as soon as they can."

"So yes, an attack," she replied.

Nessus plucked nervously at his unkempt mane. "We know they have *some* sort of spaceflight capability. We need somehow to extrapolate whether that capability can grow into a threat to the Fleet. Given their rapid progress in other fields, that risk could be substantial."

"I still feel we should start out by *asking*." Only as she realized she was shaking did Kirsten grasp how strongly she felt. "If radio contact with them does not work, I volunteer to go down myself."

Omar switched off the projection. "Kirsten, we are *far* from home. Your primary job is to get us back. After Nessus, you're the last of us I would put at risk."

She found herself thinking again of that long-ago hike in the woods. No one knows everything.

She just wished she knew whose ignorance—that of Nessus, or herself, or the still-mysterious Gw'oth—was the issue here.

FROM DEEP WITHIN a comforting nest of pillows in the sanctuary of his cabin, Nessus considered Kirsten's unusual request for a private audience. He had already reached his decision about the aliens. His full focus could now be on assessing the Colonists. "Please come by my cabin," he decided.

The knock on his cabin door was timid, but Kirsten had wasted no time getting to him. "We're making things worse, Nessus."

"What do you mean?" he asked.

"I believe our actions are stimulating the Gw'oth to develop in ways contrary to the Fleet's interests."

That was also his suspicion. "I don't see how that could be," he lied.

"You know we're deep inside their communication networks and data archives. There is no sign they know *Explorer* is here, but their R&D is being influenced by how we study them. We map their cities with deep-penetrating radar, and they detect radio-frequency anomalies. Their radio and radar research expands. We destroy one of their satellites, and they quickly develop a rapid-launch capability. The pattern goes on." Kirsten looked around the cabin for someplace to sit; finding none, she leaned against a wall. "The longer we test the Gw'oth for capabilities we consider undesirable, the more likely we make it that they will develop just those capabilities. Our very presence may give them the theoretical potential to endanger the Fleet as it passes."

She was methodical and insightful. If that intellect could be combined with Eric's devotion to the Concordance, how useful their children would be.

Thoughts of Colonists mating made his stomach roil. "Kirsten, do you *admire* these primitive aliens?"

"I do," she said. "That's all the more reason not to groom them into a threat meriting any action on our part. Respectfully, Nessus, I recommend that we leave this solar system now."

Kirsten was raising valid points. The Gw'oth were erecting large observatories above the ice. How could they not notice the Fleet when it approached? They already had primitive chemical rockets and fission. Would interplanetary capabilities follow? In the seventy years until the Fleet passed by, it was surely imaginable—which crossed his risk threshold—that the Gw'oth would have spacecraft exploring the fringes of their solar system. Should such probes be stealthed and maneuvered to lie undetectable in the Fleet's path . . .

Why do *anything* that might advance progress among the starfish?

The correct course of action was obvious. Nessus had decided several shifts earlier on his recommendation to those who lead from behind. The Fleet should adjust its course slightly. Over seventy years, even a minor course modification would steer the Fleet far from any possible Gw'oth danger. Slamming a comet into the ice moon was a last resort, and even if it came to extreme measures, he could imagine far more subtle actions.

"Nessus," she prompted him apprehensively.

Unfortunately for Kirsten and her crewmates, the investigation of G567-X2 was always his secondary objective. "I appreciate your input, but I believe we must continue assessing the Gw'oth."

She flinched at the gentle rebuke. "May I use your holo projector?"

"Of course." He wondered where this would lead.

Kirsten called up a file from the ship's archives. A bumpy sphere appeared: the hidden ocean floor of the ice moon. Scattered dots glowed, some blinking. "The red dots are major data archives. The blinking dots are archives associated with major Gw'oth development centers."

"They had to do their engineering somewhere. What is the significance of the locations?"

"Now look at this," she answered. Her face reddened as a second holo appeared.

It was a squirming mass of twisting, entangled aliens. His stomach churned as the view changed to another such scene, and another, and another. There were chains of convulsing aliens, pulsing arrays, and writhing piles. That the aliens performed these acts on camera revolted him.

Reproduction was a private matter. Among Citizens, sex meant reproduction. No Citizen was comfortable discussing sex with any other species. To sound sternly disapproving took no effort. "I have no interest in others' sex lives."

Her face reddened further, but she stood her ground. "I

know what this looks like. When such scenes appeared on our random video surveys, I turned away. Then an amazing thing happened. The longer we have been here, the more frequently such scenes appear in our intercepts.

"The outpouring of technological change, the above-ice journeys of exploration, perhaps suspicions of unseen observers—it must be very stressful for the Gw'oth. At first I thought, and please excuse me for this indelicacy, that they respond to stress with increased sexual activity."

She could not meet his eyes, and he guessed he knew why. Humans must also react that way to stress. Reluctantly, he gestured for her to continue.

"Then I noticed a perplexing correlation. This . . . activity corresponds with the growth of data in the archives. The activity is most prevalent where the archives are fastest growing. What could that mean? In desperation, I made myself watch these scenes." She froze an image. "Look closely," and she swallowed audibly, "and you'll notice that each Gw'o has, umm, linked tubes with four other Gw'oth."

Nessus forced himself to confirm her observation. As best he could ascertain, there were sixteen Gw'oth in the image, all linked as she described. "Why is that significant?"

Kirsten searched the cabin once more for a chair. Finding none, she settled onto a pile of cushions. "What I've not yet mentioned is near which data archive this scene happened. It's an archive specializing in rocketry development. *This* group interaction has been ongoing for days, starting and stopping, aligned with the apparent work schedule of the surrounding Gw'oth city. As this activity continues, there has been extensive growth in datasets related to rocket-nozzle design."

Rocket nozzles? Nessus struggled to imagine the need to design such things. It seemed as archaic as inventing a pillow or table. Such things had been standardized on the homeworld for many millennia. Yet his people, like the Gw'oth, had had to originate the technology sometime. He supposed the design process had had to consider variations in heat and pressure throughout the nozzle volume. Ah. "Three spatial dimensions and time. You're likening four-way linkages"—and despite himself, he could not keep disgust from his voice—"to a four-dimensional matrix calculation."

She leaned forward on her cushions, eyes bright. "Exactly. I found similar correlated expansions in other archives, where the number of inter-Gw'o links matches the apparent mathematical model. Lines of linked Gw'oth and simple, one-dimensional gas-diffusion models. Three-way connections and 3-D models of molecular bonds. I found more examples."

He was beginning to believe. "How is such a thing possible?"

"We already suspected from their medical records that the species evolved from a colony organism. The individual tubes are like hollow worms, with at least a vestigial version of every organ required for independent existence. Omar thinks the ancestral forms linked nervous systems and eventually evolved a large, shared central brain. It looks as though nervous systems can also connect at the *other* end, the freely moving end, of the tubes. If that's right, such connections would form multiperson minds."

Nessus' purpose was not served by admitting anything, but he was fascinated. "Biological computers. That would explain why you've found large archives, but no computing centers. It's an interesting hypothesis, although this may be only a coincidence." Could it be true? "But even if you are correct, why should I care?"

"Don't you *see*? We all wondered, and worried, about this sudden, unexplained outpouring of creativity. The Gw'oth must have been preparing for ages to break through the ice, waiting to act until they had a very detailed plan. Remember all the seabed ruins we've seen in deep-penetrating radar images and intercepted video—this is an old civilization. The eruption of capability only *seems* sudden."

He had never been more convinced of the value of the

Colonist scouting program. Would Citizen scouts have ever reached such a bizarre—but quite possibly correct—conclusion about the Gw'oth? He doubted it, even ignoring the difficulties in assembling an entire Citizen crew.

"Kirsten, say you are correct. Throughout their history, the Gw'oth have been limited to the energy of muscle power and tides and perhaps volcanic heat. Their collective memory was limited to what could be recorded on some underwater analogue of paper. They remained stuck beneath the ice.

"Now those constraints are all lifted. They have nuclear energy. Above the ice, they've had the means to create vast data archives. And they're on the verge of space travel, with all these other moons at hand. Perhaps all that remains unchanged is the will that sustained them until they could entirely plan their renewal. Consider how dangerous that focus might be coupled with their vastly expanding resources."

Her mouth gaped in shock. "Nessus," she finally managed. "They don't know we exist. They don't know the Fleet exists. They have done nothing to threaten anyone. And we all agree they're smart—if they do spot the Fleet, an undeniably more advanced civilization, why would they provoke us?"

"What are you suggesting, Kirsten?"

"What I proposed earlier. We should just leave."

A succession of insights was not Kirsten's only surprise. Obviously, she had developed an emotional bond with those *Explorer* had come to study. He sensed there was yet more she was thinking but not admitting to him.

How would her feelings for the Gw'oth affect her behavior? Might she oppose the application of defensive measures, should the Fleet's safety require such? He needed to know. "Your findings have brought me to a different conclusion. We must strive harder to understand certain implications."

His Colonists had compellingly proven their abilities to

be great scouts for the Fleet. Now, Nessus pondered a dilemma that had never before occurred to him.

It remained to be proven whether they would be loyal servants.

. 6 .

Starlight glistened off the icy, potato-shaped body on which Kirsten stood. With her visor photomultiplier turned up, it was as bright as a cloudy day on NP4. Boulders were scattered in the ice beneath her feet, and more rock protruded from the surface. Eric tramped nearby, crouching occasionally, inspecting the ancient and pockmarked surface of the proto-comet.

What made this region of the snowball safe for them to work on was what it lacked: gas pockets. Although they were much too distant from the sun for any significant heating, they had used deep-penetrating radar to find an intrinsically stable area for their landing.

This was her first time off *Explorer* since they had left the Fleet. *I'm on another world, if only a small one.* Not long ago, a mere chance of such an adventure would have elated her. Knowing the purpose of the excursion now sucked the joy from the experience.

Explorer floated at a safe distance. As Kirsten watched, a port opened, through which a small sphere emerged: a General Products #1 hull, not much larger than her helmet, hardware glittering within. Omar remote-piloted it toward them.

"Success," Eric called with satisfaction over the public channel. "Here's a suitable spot. I've got a clear view into the ice for as deep as my flashlight will shine."

She walked over carefully to see. The improvised crampons on her pressure-suit boots did more to hold her to the surface than the snowball's feeble gravity. She believed him, but wanted to speak alone. Private channel two, she gestured. "This is wrong," she began without preamble.

He dialed his flashlight-laser to its highest intensity setting and aimed it downward. Steam instantly boiled from the surface, luridly illuminated by the laser beam. "What do you mean? If we're careful, which I am being, this is perfectly safe."

"Not unsafe, wrong." How long did she have before Nessus became curious or suspicious? "We're endangering another intelligent species, Eric. We shouldn't be doing this."

He released the laser's ON button for a moment, allowing the steam to dissipate so he could have a look. "A nice shaft," he said to himself, before he resumed drilling. "No one is hurting them, Kirsten. We're testing them. The question is: Will they see and respond to a comet-collision threat? It's our best bet at predicting how soon they'll be able to detect the approaching Fleet, and whether they can launch anything that might endanger it. After we watch for a while, see whether they react or not, we'll divert the comet."

"Will we really?"

The laser beam wobbled as he jerked in surprise.

"Careful with that! I'm serious, Eric. This test is happening because the Gw'oth *might* be a threat to the Fleet. We know nothing about what they're like or how they think. Admit it: We're endangering the Gw'oth. And why? It's purely because they've acquired some basic technology. Ask yourself what Nessus will do if our monitoring shows they have detected a collision risk and made plans to divert our comet."

He switched off the laser. When the steam dissipated, he grunted approval at the hole gaping near them. "Kirsten, I have to talk to Omar now. I'm going public." He tapped buttons on his sleeve. "Omar, give me control of the probe."

The sphere approached slowly. "Reactionless drive. *There* is a technology I bet our little buddies don't have," Eric said. The tiny ship settled into the hole he had excavated, smacking the bottom with a thump they could just sense through their boots. "Piloting something that is practically indestructible makes the job a lot easier."

With his flashlight-laser dialed to a broader beam, Eric began fanning the surface around the hole. Less steam erupted than before, and the tube collapsed inward on itself. He slowly fanned the area until all that remained of the shaft was a shallow depression. Kirsten waved her flashlight laser about, too, but her beam was set so wide it contributed only harmless light.

Eric gestured for a return to the private channel. "You know this test isn't a danger to the aliens. At worst, they'll think it is. The thruster we just planted will slowly change the proto-comet's orbit, to make it a near-miss threat. If the Gw'oth don't see it, or if they are unable to respond, the thruster will be used later to nudge it off an intersecting course."

She knew the plan, too. It would seem from a distance as though the typical random eruption of gases from the comet had changed its orbit to something safe. "Or our embedded probe could re-aim the comet for an impact on a later orbit. Or the probe could rip through the comet on full thrusters, and shatter it into several large pieces to make it all the harder to divert."

"I guess you two wanted to be alone," Omar kidded on the public channel. "Fine, take a little while. I assume you know Nessus thinks every unnecessary minute you spend out there is a sign of insanity."

"Kirsten, what is this really about?" Eric asked.

"We have just built the means by which the Gw'oth civilization could be destroyed. Maybe the entire species. A comet striking their world would kill millions. To create such a device just in case . . . are we any better than those who attacked our ancestors?" She stared down at her boots. "Is the Concordance?"

He grabbed an arm and jerked her around to face him. "How *dare* you make such accusations against Citizens! Someone, and we'll never know who, attacked the starship transporting our ancestors. It was a Citizen vessel that found the hulk, dying and adrift. You *know* how fearful Citizens are, and yet they boarded the derelict, they rescued the frozen embryo banks, and they salvaged whatever few artifacts they could carry in a vessel no larger than *Explorer*.

"Kirsten, they might have left the hulk lost in space, and our ancestors with it. Instead, they saved us. They created a whole language and culture for us. They gave us our whole world. So don't expect *me* to think ill of them or their motives."

Every word he spoke was true, and yet . . . together, under Nessus' tutelage, they had created this frightful device. How could any sense be made of that?

Eric was staring at her. She had to respond to his outburst *somehow*. "I don't know what to say. Maybe this is just too far from home for me."

"I'm going back on public in a moment," Eric said. "But yes, we are a long, *long* way from home."

Meaning he accepted her rationale? Meaning he took her almost-apology as a long-awaited acquiescence to his advances? In either case, she breathed a sigh of relief. It seemed that her unworthy misgivings would, at least for the moment, remain between them.

· 7 ·

Kirsten did not know whether they had passed or failed.

All she knew—all Nessus had told the three of them— was that he had decided to return to the Fleet. Any danger from the Gw'oth was far into the future. The Concordance government could choose a course of action, which might be simply to change the Fleet's path slightly.

And the Gw'oth? Nessus assured them the comet experiment had been canceled. The altered snowball would stay far from G567-X2. She could neither confirm nor refute, much as she yearned to, that the danger to the ice moon had passed.

Nor could she cajole Nessus for reassurance. Once they had exited the singularity and reentered hyperspace for the flight home, he had locked himself in his cabin, and answered no inquiries. His manic phase had given way to its opposite.

On the other head, Nessus' withdrawal during the long journey home gave her unsupervised time to think.

GW'OTH VENTURES ABOVE the ice fascinated Kirsten. How brave they were to explore such a hostile domain with only the most primitive of technologies to sustain them! Their quest for knowledge, the expansion of their capabilities, and the vigor of their efforts were inspiring—

And they awakened in her a new attitude toward her own kind.

Colonists did not have pride. Why would they, without successes to call their own? NP4 had been tamed before they first set foot on it. Their technology had been handed to them, and even that technology, everyone knew, was far beneath what the Citizens controlled. Their benefactors considered them unworthy, or unprepared, or in some other as-yet undefined sense not ready, to share in all that the Concordance had researched and invented.

Knowing in the abstract of whole worlds with indigenous civilizations was one thing. Observing the strivings of the Gw'oth was so much more. The experience made the lost home of her kind *real* to her. Somewhere out there was a world, a place as real and unique as the ice moon of the Gw'oth.

In her mind was a pale blue spheroid that resembled NP4, but with all outlines blurred. Her ancestors must have tamed that world, and developed their own technology, and ventured unaided into interstellar space. If she could respect the Gw'oth for their accomplishments, how could she not admire her own ancestors?

What were they like? How did they organize themselves? To what goals did they strive? What language did they speak? Surely it was more logical and structured than this English the Citizens had invented for them.

Her newfound interest made all the more troubling how little could be found in *Explorer*'s library about the Colonists' long-ago rescue.

THREE ON THE bridge was a tight fit. Omar and Eric sat side by side, hips touching, sharing Nessus' padded bench. Omar had brought in a tray with three hot bulbs of stim juice. "Thanks for coming," Kirsten began.

"What's up?" Omar waved at the controls in front of him. She took the gesture to mean: Do we need Nessus here?

That Nessus continued to hide in his cabin served her purpose. Her ability to formulate such rebellious thoughts remained new enough to surprise her.

She had decreed a sanity break in normal space. Diamondlike points of light shone through the bridge's presently uncovered view ports. The distant Fleet remained invisible to the naked eye. "It's really *empty* out here, isn't it?"

"That's not exactly big news," Omar said.

"No, but it's hard to truly grasp *how* empty until you're living with it." She let them consider that for a moment. "Imagine how unlikely it was that a Citizen ship should encounter our ancestors adrift." How very unlikely, given that hyperdrive-equipped ships dropped back into normal space only occasionally. How especially unlikely, if adrift meant, as was always part of the story, that their saviors noticed a ship whose fusion drive was inoperative. *Explorer*'s sensors could not spot such a derelict unless it was nearly on top of them.

Eric glanced in the direction of Nessus' cabin. "We were lucky, I suppose. We should be thankful."

Had that passing look denoted fear? Skepticism?

Warning? She would know soon enough. If she were correct, this would be the hardest on him. "You both know I've been researching primitive technology. I thought it could be instructive to contrast the Gw'oth experience with what Citizens have seen in their travels."

She called up a holo to summarize her findings—or rather her paucity of findings. She opened a second display. "Here's how I queried the library. Am I doing anything wrong?"

Omar studied the images. "Your queries look fine to me."

"Nessus *told* us he didn't want our investigations influenced by knowledge of other aliens," Eric said. "I'm not surprised he removed such material from our library. He was obviously right—*some* of us couldn't be trusted not to look."

Kirsten ignored the criticism. "Next, I wondered if the history of the Citizens themselves might have relevant material." Two more holos she opened implied another excision from the library.

"Kirsten, *why* are we here?" Omar asked. "It wasn't to sympathize with what Nessus chose to exclude from the library."

Her eyes twitched involuntarily toward Nessus' cabin. Had her precautions been successful? "Bear with me." She offered another query. It was the opposite of what she had queried for before: everything *un*related to pre-spaceflight technology history.

A warning message chastised her for her overbroad search. The only hint the library provided as a measure of the relevant results was two very large numbers. One number was merely the count of related files. The second number, an even more prodigious value, showed the extent of the data in those related files. "Consider this, gentlemen. I ran complementary queries. The first asked for everything related to early technology history. The second asked for everything *not*. The combined results should encompass the capacity of the library. They don't."

"Obviously," Eric sniffed, "Nessus anticipated your prying. The unaccounted-for storage must be files he reserved for himself."

"Obviously. As a confirmation, consider *these* queries." Her next requests sought what was, and what was not, in the library regarding hyperdrive technology. It was no secret Citizens reserved hyperdrive theory for themselves. To no one's surprise, Kirsten's paired searches revealed another large inaccessible region. "Are we agreed? This is a valid way to measure the extent of hidden data on a given topic?"

Saying nothing at all this time, Omar looked pointedly at Nessus' controls.

Perhaps there was more to their captain than Kirsten had suspected. She ignored the apparent warning. "It works with searches using date parameters, too. Would anyone be surprised to know there's an off-limits region that continues to grow even as we travel home?"

Omar stood, clumsily dismounting from the padded bench. A shoe-tip caught, and he fell across Nessus' control console. "Crap!" He got back to his feet, juice all over his shirt, his beverage bulb squashed flat. "That's hot." The liquid beaded quickly, unable to adhere to the nano-cloth, and trickled to the deck.

More stim juice dripped down the controls. Omar removed his shirt and with it blotted ineffectively at the console. Reflexively, Kirsten looked away—it was unseemly for her to see Omar's bared chest. But she looked back at what his hands were doing.

That was no random spot on the console! Growth in the archives even while they remained in hyperspace suggested Nessus did not limit his eavesdropping to the Gw'oth. Kirsten had found a sensor hidden on the bridge—exactly where the spill had occurred and the location Omar's wadded shirt now covered and muffled. He, too, had located the concealed camera.

"We can get away with this only once." Omar was suddenly more direct than Kirsten had ever seen him. "Nessus may be suspicious regardless. Whatever you have to say better be important. And Eric—do *not* ask."

Eric looked ready to explode, but he stayed quiet.

"There was an unfortunate spill before I called you both here," Kirsten said. "Hopefully it worked." Nessus would never believe two innocent accidents could occur so close together. "I'll tell you what's so important.

"We've all been raised on the heroic tale of the rescue of our ancestors. How dangerous the tumbling derelict was, its hull agape, the victim of unknown and unknowable assailants. How back-projection along its apparent path suggested no plausible candidate sun for hundreds of light-years. Perhaps it had been adrift for a *long* time, or its crew had changed course in a desperate run from peril. Either way, there was no clue to its point of origin. After the embryo banks were rescued, the wreck was abandoned in deep space, its fate unknown. All in all, what we've been taught is how very little the Concordance knows of our past. Now watch."

Her final two queries revealed yet another inaccessible region within the library. Its topic was "pre-NP4 history of Colonists" and its extent was vast.

NESSUS HAD BEGUN to dare to hope that this mission would be deemed a success. The Colonists had functioned well as a team, operated the ship effectively, and learned a great deal about the Gw'oth.

As importantly, they had proven loyal. Kirsten's assertiveness, as respectfully expressed as it had been, had briefly worried him. He need not have been concerned. When the time came, she had helped implant the comet with a thruster-equipped probe. Obedience to Citizens was an ingrained part of Colonist society.

The Fleet would have more scouts and better preparation for its dash from the galaxy . . . and those happy, risk-reducing results were because of *him*. When he returned in triumph, in this, the Fleet's time of need, all things would be possible for him.

So many had doubted him. It had gladdened him to imagine what consternation his unorthodox success would evoke in his heads-under-their-bellies parents. He had day-dreamed of recognitions and honor from his new friends, the Experimentalists. The achievements of this mission could result, quite possibly, in that most precious of rewards: a mate. And not just *any* mate—

When he returned in triumph, even subtle, graceful Nike would surely be approachable.

Yes, he had begun to dare to hope . . . until the private recall message had arrived. Its few brief words left him cowering in his cabin, all thoughts of personal advantage forgotten. Nothing seemed to matter. He ate from the small synthesizer in his room. He could not be bothered to replace the sensor that had shorted out on the bridge. The Colonists would get him back to Hearth whether he paid attention or not.

The unexpected message read in its entirety: "Return immediately to the Fleet. Wild humans are close to finding us."

"I CAN'T EXPLAIN what's going on," Kirsten said, "beyond that the Concordance knows far more about our past than they have shared. I intend to discover the truth. To begin with, I'm going to find our ancestors' ship."

"That's impossible." Eric sat slumped on Nessus' bench, his belief system shattered. He looked deflated. "It was abandoned hundreds of years ago. How can we possibly know where to begin?"

How can *we* possibly know? He believed her! Kirsten set aside all her doubts and uncertainties. "Whatever clues there are will be found where we are now going.

"Whatever secrets the Concordance has, they hold on the Fleet of Worlds."

QUEST   Earth date: 2650

. 8 .

Nike's office was a stepping disc away from his apartment. Barring emergency, he never commuted that way. Teleportation offered efficiency, but neither comfort nor information.

He teleported now to his arcology lobby, walking briskly off a stepping disc there and pressing through the gentle force field that divided the climate-controlled atrium from the exterior walkways. Buildings extended up and down the mall as far as the eye could see. The least of the arcologies towered to a thousand times his height.

Herd scent embraced him like a warm bath. With a sociable nudge, Nike plunged into the unending stream of pedestrians. Chance bumping and brushing of flanks was as reassuring as it was unavoidable.

Heads craning as he walked, Nike surveyed utility belts and decorative sashes, the ribbons and jewels adorning manes, and ornamental brooches. As always, he spotted the greens of those declaring their Conservative loyalties and the orange shades that identified Experimentalists.

Declarations of allegiance to hobbies, professional affiliations, and social clubs greatly outnumbered any factional color. The spectrum of adornment only highlighted a reality Nike had sadly accepted: Passions had cooled in the years since the discovery of the explosion in the galactic core.

And why not? The sky glow of continent-spanning cities masked the shifting of constellations. Only sophisticated instruments could discern the operation of the reactionless drive that continued to accelerate the Fleet of Worlds. Departure from the galaxy would change nothing for the vast majority of Citizens, or their children, or their children's children, for countless generations—for those who still measured the passage of time in generations. Births were as rare as deaths among the Citizens.

Thus the extraordinary had become mundane had become all but forgotten. Escape from the galaxy had been entrusted to Conservatives too unimaginative to have initiated it. This was how the Concordance dealt with every emergency. With a tremble of frustration, Nike straightened the large orange brooch pinned to his utility belt.

Conversations ebbed and flowed all around him. They dealt with family and friends, art and theatre, shopping and government. The little political discussion he heard involved nuances and trivia, nothing that might favor reconsideration of those most suited to lead from behind.

Of course, few shared his knowledge. With that recollection, Nike declared this unscientific poll sufficient for the day. Nearing a public stepping disc embedded in the walkway, he dipped a head into a pocket. With nimble lip nodes he retrieved an address from his personal transport controller; his tongueprint authorized access to a secured file. The disc flicked him instantly to a restricted location: the employee vestibule of the foreign affairs ministry.

"Sir," whistled the guards who encircled the entry area. Taking turns, they briefly lowered their heads in respect. The motion began with the guards standing nearest to Nike and traveled around the group, so that at all times most sentries remained attentive to the discs.

Pulling his head from his pocket, Nike assumed the wide-legged, no-need-to-run stance of confident leadership. "My greetings," he chanted formally. He gestured, and two guards sidled away to clear his path. He walked briskly to a second group of restricted discs, discs that provided access to workspaces within the ministry. Another tongue-locked address delivered him to the maximally secured complex of offices that was Clandestine Directorate.

Functionaries emerging from their warren of work nooks repeated the gesticulations of esteem. "Deputy Minister. Sir. Your Excellency." Nike most savored grudging bows from the Conservatives in this herd. With the Conservatives in power, of course the Minister was a Conservative. *All* ministers in the present government were Conservatives.

Whatever the political balance, however, most positions of responsibility in *this* ministry remained with the Experimentalists. Despite generations of acculturation, few Conservatives could bear to deal directly with Colonists. There were never enough, and anyway, managing the Colonists was the simplest part of the ministry's mission. Only the truly exceptional could cope with wild aliens, and none but Experimentalists had the flexibility of mind to work with the exceptional. The Clandestine Directorate was and would remain an enclave of Experimentalists.

Too many in Nike's party bemoaned the short memories of the masses. He did not. To deny the wisdom of the majority was the very definition of insanity. Those who now led the Experimentalists from behind had resigned themselves to another epoch of powerless opposition.

Which was why, thought Nike, when we Experimentalists next return to power, the party will not be led by any of them.

Nike straightened again into the stance of supreme confidence. Heads held high, he strode toward his private office. Its personal door bespoke his high status. Just before shutting it, he announced to all, "I am not to be disturbed."

". . . DISAPPEARANCE OF GENERAL Products representatives continues to stoke interest in Puppeteer affairs. United Nations authorities continue their full search for your home system. They rationalize the hunt by claiming that in GP's absence some contractual commitments might go unfulfilled or warranty obligations become unenforceable. I have yet to gain access to the investigators' files, but it is thought a wide-ranging analysis of astronomical anomalies might—"

Nike paused the hyperwave message. The human in the recording stood unmoving. A thousand details, from her bold skin-dye pattern to the cut of her clothing, made clear that she was not one of the Colonists.

Her use of the term "Puppeteer" told Nike the same. When representatives of the Concordance had eventually revealed themselves to the indigenous civilization within the tiny bubble of stars so presumptuously deemed Known Space, the human explorer Pierson had likened Citizen anatomy to a three-legged centaur with two sock-puppet heads. The name Puppeteer had stuck.

The wild human's mouth had been open at the moment the image was frozen. Just now, that gaping orifice made the torrent of bad news seem unending. At least having a personal office meant Nike might compose himself a bit in private.

Perhaps the wild humans would have the last laugh. Following the success of the Colonist experiment, many Experimentalists had taken human names as an affectation. The appellation he had chosen was suddenly like ashes in his mouths: Nike, the deity of victory.

The question was: victory for whom? How might wild humans react if they were to discover the Fleet—and with it, the Concordance's human servants?

At least the wild humans continued to look, mistakenly, for a home world still anchored to a solar system. Not even the most trusted human agent had been told that six worlds had flown free of their sun.

Nike found himself pacing around the soft, padded work surface that occupied a significant fraction of his office. He needed to calm himself. With one mouth holding a comb, the second a mirror, he meticulously smoothed and layered and arranged his braids. As always, the grooming routine soothed him.

His intercom lowed. "Your Excellency." His assistant's voice was softly respectful over the intercom.

"Yes," Nike replied.

"It is nearly time for the rally. You asked to be reminded."

With a few deep breaths Nike banished a slight trembling from his limbs. What his distant agent reported made it vital that the Experimentalists reclaim power.

That, in turn, made his rally all the more crucial.

NESSUS TROTTED AS quickly as the teeming throngs permitted, hooves clicking on the hard surface of the wide boulevard. His destination remained unseen no matter how much he craned a head, but it never occurred to him to use the public stepping discs that might have sped him the final small fraction of his journey. "What a beautiful day," he hummed softly to himself. Despite the din of the crowd, several heads twisted his way in inquiry. He could not resist responding with a one-eyed blink. Why *not* smile? He was delighted to be off *Explorer*. To be home. He was *so* happy that his mane, although not stylishly coiffed, was uncharacteristically neat, combed and pulled back by two orange ribbons.

The walkway broadened as ne neared the park. Greeters spaced every few body lengths bobbed heads in welcome, bunches of bright ribbons for the party faithful clasped in their mouths. Nessus took two brilliant orange-and-gold streamers and merged into the waiting crowd. Many had draped their new ribbons about their necks. Nessus happily followed their example.

A Citizen to Nessus' left tapped his shoulder. "It's an excellent turnout."

"I completely agree." Nessus had spoken only English with the Colonists for *so* long. It still felt wonderful beyond words to warble and trill, to roll long arpeggios from his tongues, to harmoniously entwine elaborate speech with himself and others—to truly *talk*. The Gw'oth seemed only a distant memory. "It's for a great cause."

"Have you been to other Permanent Emergency rallies?" asked his new friend.

"Some." Not as many as I would like, Nessus thought. He made no mention of his long absence. Even the partial truth he was permitted to share, that he had been away on

NP4, would cause most people to back away. Association with the insane was but another risk the majority shunned.

Before thoughts of separateness could ruin his high spirits, Nessus immersed himself in the moment. The contrapuntal themes of thousands of voices, the milling herd, and the scent-rich air enveloped him. And soon enough, *Nike* would orate.

Speaker after speaker crooned about risks and perils, about the many dangers from which Experimentalists had saved the Concordance in times past. It was familiar and exciting at the same time. Nessus' heads, like those around him, bobbed agreement: up/down, down/up, up/down, down/up.

"Our flight from the galaxy is likely the first," warbled the current speaker. "It will surely not be the last. Race after race must follow us, all the more desperate for their unwise delays. Imagine their panic as the wall of radiation from the core explosion draws near. All the laggard races desperately seek energy and supplies where wiser races have already refueled and resupplied. Now picture some of these needy, desperate refugees encountering the Fleet of Worlds. They detect our prudently collected resources. Will the Concordance be safe then?"

"No!" The tens of thousands packed haunch to haunch in the small park roared as one. Around Nessus, hooves pawed at the ground in anxious contemplation of distantly glimpsed perils.

"Is the danger passed?"

"No! No!"

"Is our course of action so clearly a matter of routine that we should entrust the existence of the Concordance to Conservatives?"

"No! No!"

"When will it be safe?"

It began in a thousand jarring dissonances, and then converged into a chord of tremendous power. "After the emergency!"

After the *permanent* emergency, that was. It was a concept too new to judge, an upending of all norms, breathtaking in its audacity—and for that, frightening in its own way. Even most Experimentalists balked at the concept. For Nessus, scarcely split from his Conservative upbringing, it remained too great a leap. It did not matter. In his hearts, Nessus knew his interest in the Experimentalist Faction of the Permanent Emergency was not about policy.

A delicate figure materialized onto the park's central knoll, magnified many times in an overhead holo. His skin was a pale tan, without spots or other markings. Delicate filigree of orange and gold blended with the waves of his tawny mane, gleaming under the spotlights. Other than on the Hindmost himself, and perhaps on the would-be Hindmost who led the Experimentalists, Nessus had never seen such an elegant coiffure.

Nike stood, legs far apart, totally poised, in the stance of confident leadership.

Amid tens of thousands of ululating stalwarts, Nessus acknowledged a private truth. He would do *anything* to win the heads of, and the right to have children with, the beautiful and charismatic leader.

EVERY ARCOLOGY OFFERED many dining halls. The myriad conversations in each assembly freely started and ended, coalesced and diverged, waxed and waned to reflect the interests and experiences of thousands of diners. How could it be otherwise, with so many professions, hobbies, political opinions, and individual interests represented?

And yet, as Nessus exited a stepping disc into his usual dining hall, one topic clearly predominated: Nike's speech. The din was inordinate. How loud would it be, he wondered, without noise cancellation?

Row after row of triangular tables receded into the distance. Nessus paced deep into the vast room, searching for familiar faces. He nudged his way into the gap between two acquaintances, settling astraddle a long padded bench. Signaled by his weight on the bench, a shallow trough of

mush, a loaf of bread, and a bowl of chilled water materialized on the tabletop in front of him. The shipboard freedom to select his own diet was already a fading memory.

To each side of him, a head bobbed in welcome. Nessus
knew both Citizens from the dining hall, suggesting they
lived somewhere in the arcology. An orange ribbon on one
and orange utility-belt pockets on the other marked them
as fellow Experimentalists, just as an absence of gold suggested they were not of Nike's faction.

A lack of contact with humans, wild or domesticated,
was no obstacle among Experimentalists to the selection of
a human-style nickname. In his dining companions' case,
musical hobbies provided ample inspiration.

"Euterpe, Orpheus," Nessus acknowledged. He spoke
with one-head informality, his other already busy with his
food. He had skipped a meal in favor of an earlier start to
the rally, and now he was famished. "How goes the latest
composition?" Honestly, he did not care. It was a question likely to evoke two long answers during which he
could eat.

His plan failed.

"Good, good," answered Euterpe. Setting down his half-
eaten loaf, he double-warbled a short, mellifluous passage.
Partway through, Orpheus joined in. "That can wait. We were
talking"—Euterpe made a gesture with one sinuous neck
that encompassed the whole dining hall—"*everyone* is talking, about Nike's latest speech. Did you hear any of it?"

There was an undertune of skepticism to Euterpe's words.
Nessus answered cautiously. "Some."

"It's amazing. No, worse—it's unprecedented," Orpheus
said. His disdain did not hide in mere undertunes.

Nessus tapped a keypad on the table to recycle the rest
of his synthesized grain mush, his appetite lost. The half-
filled trough vanished. He said, "The chain reaction of
supernovae at the galaxy's core is unprecedented. The
wave front of radiation that will sterilize everything in its
path is unprecedented. Is it so surprising that our course of
action must also be unprecedented?"

"Not the course of action." Orpheus paused during a long sip of water, his opinion evidently too important to convey with a single throat. "Most people, well, most Experimentalists, would agree with you. Whatever our response is or becomes must surely be without precedent. But once we have followed that course of action for a time—Nessus, does it not become precedent? *Has* it not become precedent?"

From beyond Orpheus, a homey smell made itself known: manure. The soft plop had barely penetrated Nessus' consciousness. The dropping was already whisked away.

Tables covered with stepping discs to deliver sustenance. Aisles paved with stepping discs, imprinted with filters that passed excrement, and excrement only, directly back into the synthesizers. Grazing and fertilizing—the herd had done both together since before it became aware of its own actions. Technology merely made the process more efficient.

No other known intelligent species was herbivorous and only herbivores eliminated where they ate. Part of Nessus' preparation for visits to other intelligent species had been bowel training. Once again, he felt out of place.

"Nessus," fluted Euterpe impatiently. "Do you not see Orpheus' point?"

Sadly, Nessus did, or rather the deeper reality that lurked beneath his herdmate's observation. Success created familiarity, and familiarity bred complacency—even among Experimentalists. His travels had revealed but the tiniest fraction of the galaxy, but that limited exposure often amazed him. The Gw'oth were merely the latest wonder. What other surprises, what unimaginable perils, yet lay in the path of the Fleet?

In the unprecedented flight from the core explosion, complacency could kill them all.

Once more, companionship shifted without warning into an unbearable reminder of how maladjusted, how unlike his own kind, he had become. Excusing himself, Nessus took the closest stepping disc that would return him to the doorless, windowless little cube that was his home.

Nike, he realized, was correct. Escape from the core explosion was a permanent emergency, or so close to permanent that the difference could not matter for many generations.

For all Nessus' dread on behalf of the Concordance, his heads now tucked snugly between his forelegs, he could not help but notice the irony. The very fear that threatened to immobilize him also provided his best hope of finally meeting the object of his affections.

· 9 ·

Waves crashed against the rocky cliffs that rimmed the Great North Bay. Salt spray leapt high into the air. Between crests, phosphorescent foam undulated and sudsed amid the scree. Atop the craggy heights at the head of the bay, it was just possible to sense the wall of water onrushing from its mouth. A gorgeous blue-and-brown-and-white world, the source of the oncoming tidal surge, hung overhead, dominating a clear night sky aglitter with stars. NP3's single string of orbiting suns was doubly bright for their reflections from its equatorial ocean.

"Wow." Omar's mouth opened and closed experimentally a few times, but he failed to find any word more suitable. "Wow," he repeated.

Five companion worlds meant ten tides every day, and nowhere on NP4 did the tides surge as high as in this remote fjord. Kirsten had been awestruck on her first visit. She had not budged from the spot for days. Remembering, she grinned. "Then it's all right that I rousted you guys a little early from your sleeping bags?"

"It would have been wrong to come this far and *not* see this." Eric paused for effect. "Now about coming out here at all . . ."

"You have *got* to be kidding, Eric," Omar said. "We all

grew up in cities. The woods we hiked in through and this rugged coast are as exotic as anything we found on the Ice Moon, but *this* we get to experience in person. How can you not appreciate such a spectacular view?"

Eric wiped salt spray from his forehead with the back of a hand. "You're right. I am kidding. Good idea, Kirsten, to drag us out here—even if it is the farthest corner of Arcadia."

The night was chilly. She raised the heater setting on her coveralls before answering. "We don't really see much of even our own world, do we?" She let them think about that as, with a roar, another great wave smashed into the cliffs. "Truthfully, only our own continent."

"Arcadia is more than ample. If this were our world entirely—" Eric began.

Omar cut him off. "We know, Eric. One isolated continent given over to the species preserved on our ancestors' ship. The remainder of NP4 dedicated to growing crops for the Citizens. Kirsten, I can't help but think there is more to this outing than the view. What, exactly, is out here?"

More to the point, she thought, was what was *not* out here: any Citizen presence. The closest stepping disc was half a day's hike distant through thick forest. Not even Nessus would care to approach this precipice and its spray-slick rocks. "Privacy is out here. Privacy to discuss my doubts."

Omar leaned against a nearby boulder. "Meaning the pre-Arcadia history files you found hidden aboard *Explorer?*"

"I was taken aback by that, too." NP3 light gave Eric's face a blue tinge. "I've had time since to think it through. Maybe I overreacted."

Implying that *she* had overreacted. "We've been lied to. I don't like that."

"I acknowledge information was withheld from us," Eric said. "At a minimum we were lied to about that information's existence. But have Citizens lied about anything substantive? We have no reason to believe so."

Kirsten felt her eyes widen in disbelief. "Why keep our history secret from us?"

"To protect us," Eric said. "Maybe our ancestors did something shameful, and they want to spare us the knowledge."

Something shameful? Her mind spun. "Or maybe the Citizens did something shameful to our ancestors, and want to keep *that* secret from us!"

Omar broke a lengthening, awkward silence. "Either way, the Concordance knows things about our past that we don't. It's a big file. They're hiding a lot." He stood and walked nearer to the precipice to stare at the surging tide. "We're not the first Colonists to see such discrepancies."

She remembered that Omar, too, had known about the sensor hidden on *Explorer*'s bridge. "Omar, who are you really?"

"You mean other than your captain: above all reproach, beyond any question, and more than a little obsequious?" Omar smiled, and Kirsten could not help but think how different this self-confident, self-deprecating man was from the Omar who always deferred to Nessus. "I'm someone who was asked in confidence by someone in the Arcadia Self-Governance Council to keep my eyes open.

"I'm glad that you arranged this secluded outing. It's time we started working together."

THERE WAS A bit of conventional wisdom in which Kirsten had never placed any stock, that any Colonist was only a few degrees of separation removed from any other. As she kept her eye on her cousin's next-door neighbor's visiting friend's mate—who just happened to be the chief archivist for Arcadia—she thought she might have reason to reassess.

The apparent chance meeting was Omar's doing, or at least he had brought the opportunity to her attention. Her questions about how he had identified the opportunity elicited only a knowing smile. Leveraging her celebrity sta-

tus as an *Explorer* crew member to obtain an appointment
with Sven would have been easy. The trick was to talk with
the archivist without leaving an audit trail. Were Citizens
monitoring the network activities of *Explorer*'s crew, or of
Sven Hebert-Draskovics, the archivist, or of Omar's undisclosed contacts in the Self-Governance Council? The
microphone hidden on *Explorer*'s bridge made such unannounced supervision all too plausible.

This community party provided a perfect venue for an
innocent encounter. People filled the streets, food and
drink in hand, chatting and milling about. Kirsten eventually wandered to where Sven stood in conversation with
someone she did not recognize. With casual nods and comments on the day's fine weather, she worked her way into
the conversation. In time, Sven's friend went looking for a
fresh beverage.

"What do you do?" she asked after a while.

"Nothing interesting, I'm afraid," he answered. "I keep
dusty old records."

"Dusty?"

Sven laughed. "Pardon my whimsy. Of course, most records are computerized. That was a metaphor, to denote
age."

"You lost me," Kirsten said.

"That's one of my skills." He glanced about for someplace to exchange his empty beer bulb for a full one. "I
deal with obscurity for a living. I'm the Colony archivist."

"I didn't know we had an archivist," she lied. "Dusty old
records, you say. You must know all about the founding of
the colony, with all that information at your disposal."

"I generally deal with more modern times. Production
data, census compilations, weather statistics, that sort of
thing. Still, I may know more than most about the early
days." He looked a bit wistful. "That may be less than you
would expect."

"Hold on." Kirsten grabbed the sleeve of the man walking by with a tray of sliced cheese. Feigning disinterest in
what Sven had just said, she took her time pondering her

selection. Did her lost ancestors have words for devious and unsanctioned data collection? Certainly the vocabulary developed for the Colonists did not. "Sorry. You were saying something about 'less than I'd think.'"

"Few records and artifacts survive from those early times."

Despite herself, Kirsten blinked in surprise. "I didn't think information was ever lost. Citizens have backups and backups of backups."

"Of course," Sven agreed. "That is, Citizen computers are massively redundant and frequently backed up. The Citizens who established Arcadia colony chose not to interface the recovered computers to their own networks. They were concerned a connection would be unsafe. Events proved them correct."

Youngsters dashed past, flapping their arms and whooping, their antics random as far as Kirsten could judge. She let the noisemakers recede before cautiously following up. "Recovered computers? Oh, you mean salvaged from our ancestors' drifting starship. Did they matter?"

"Nothing mattered more." Sven ran a hand, fingers splayed, through his thinning black hair. He wore a marriage ring and a progeny band with three small rubies. "Maintenance of the embryo banks, real-time control of the artificial placentas, nutritional requirements of the newborns—it *all* depended upon our ancestors' computers. And it's all lost."

"Lost? How?"

"A fire. It's believed a piece of the recovered equipment must have started it."

Of course Citizen equipment could never fail dangerously. But still . . . "Sven, I'm confused. That equipment maintained the embryo banks safely from the attack until a Citizen ship arrived. Then it withstood experimentation while Citizens learned how to operate it. It ran long enough thereafter to gestate at least one generation, or none of us would be here. And *then* one day it burst into flame?"

"Unfortunate, I know." He coughed. "There's no helping it, though."

Her ancestors' computers were insufficiently trusted to be connected to the Citizen network. The same computers were entrusted with the primary Citizen records of the founding of the colony! At least one of those statements *must* be incorrect. Perhaps both were.

What would the archivist have to say about the extensive, if inaccessible, pre-NP4 history files she had unveiled aboard *Explorer*? "So our past is lost. As you say, there's no helping it." Smiling to show she was joking, Kirsten added, "We won't know until we inspect the derelict. I don't suppose you have any records where it went."

"Now there's a crazy idea," Sven laughed. "Imagine, finding that ancient ship, lost in space, after all this time."

Doubtless, it was a crazy idea. Like Nessus, Kirsten was not about to let a little matter of insanity stand in her way.

• 10 •

The summons was both exhilarating and unnerving. Approaching the appointed time, Nessus tongued the message's stepping-disc coordinates.

His tiny sleeping quarters vanished; he reappeared inside an even smaller, clear-walled chamber that looked into an unoccupied waiting room. A blue beam scanned him, presumably checking for dangerous implements even as it took his retinal prints. His gentle rap on the foyer wall confirmed his suspicion: This was no ordinary entrance. He was enclosed in the near-impregnable material used in spaceship hulls. Ceiling-mounted high-intensity lights shone brightly on him. Their intensity could surely be raised to lethal levels—and visible light was one of the few things that could penetrate General Products hull material.

Nessus was suddenly outside the security chamber, delivered by the stepping disc on the isolation booth's floor. "Welcome to the Ministry of Foreign Affairs," a recording fluted and trilled. "Please wait here."

He settled onto a pile of plush cushions. Nessus took no offense at being made to wait; the security precautions had unnerved him. He appreciated having time to regain his composure. Of course, much more than security was on his mind.

Had he ever *not* been infatuated with Nike? For as long as Nessus could remember, the charismatic politician had been a darling of the media. Nike had such vibrancy and wit, such presence and poise—and such beauty—that he was constantly in the news. Nike's exotic political positions had only increased Nessus' fascination.

Parental disapproval had only encouraged Nessus' youthful obsession. He recorded Nike's every major public appearance, viewing them again and again. Many political events were open to the public; Nessus had attended at least sixty. Intellectually, he knew Nike's positions had changed repeatedly over the years. In his hearts, those shifts made no difference.

To his supporters, Nike was creative, flexible, and original. To his detractors, Nike was ambitious and bold. Ultimately, which description best fit did not matter. Nessus abandoned his family's generations-long tradition of Conservative allegiance. His family abandoned *him*.

While most of Nessus' peers wasted their time in idle socializing and frivolous hobbies, Nessus had volunteered for every experimental project that might attract Nike's attention. None did, so Nessus proposed his own, even more innovative programs. His Colonist explorer initiative had supposedly risen to Nike's personal attention.

Today, he would finally meet Nike!

"Follow me." A tall, green-eyed aide, a green brooch pinned to his utility belt, had appeared across the room. His posture hinted at disdain for this scruffy visitor. "The Deputy Minister will see you now." Then he was gone.

Nessus trotted, hearts pounding, to the temporarily active stepping disc. He emerged outside an open office door. Merely the wide padded work surface visible through the doorway was larger than his living unit. Lush meadow-plant covered the floor. The green-eyed aide ushered Nessus inside, bobbing farewell as, from the outside, he closed the door.

"Your Excellency." Nessus lowered both heads submissively.

"Be comfortable." Nike extended a neck gracefully, brushing heads with Nessus in greeting as though they were equals. "You may wonder why I asked you here."

Nessus settled awkwardly onto a guest bench. Artwork lined the large office. Much was holographic, of course, but crushed meadowplant showed that several of the large sculptures were carved from rock or cast in metal. Physical art, like the oversized office, bespoke vast power. It was surely meant to intimidate—and it succeeded.

He had imagined this day so many times, in so many ways, that he was at a loss now for what to say. It was all Nessus could do not to pick at his mane—or to cross his necks flirtatiously. "Yes, sir."

"Nike. And may I call you Nessus? Good. Those human-style designations are especially apt given our subject—

"—The recent *Explorer* mission."

Faces to faces, Nike's elegance and charisma were overwhelming. Nessus had missed something in his delighted shock. What about the mission? His report on the Gw'oth? The crew's capabilities? That was it. "Yes, Nike,"—how he reveled in speaking the name—"I consider the trip a success. A longer stay would have yielded more data, but not changed my positive assessment of the Colonists."

"Did you know I personally approved the experiment?" Nike watched Nessus closely. "I did. The Concordance is gifted with too few individuals able to search for danger in our path. Your imaginative solution to our problem is to be commended." Nike paused, for no apparent reason other than to let Nessus bask in the compliments. "I did not lightly call you back to the Fleet."

"I understand." The praise was exhilarating. "Then why, Nike?"

"We face more immediate dangers."

Nessus had not forgotten the hyperwave-radio recall message. "Have the wild humans discovered the Fleet?"

"Not yet. Our agents on Earth report that a serious search is under way."

"That has long been the case." Very few Citizens could confidently say that, but Nessus was one. In his early attempts to advance among the Experimentalists, he had served as a General Products Corporation representative in Human Space. Quite possibly, he had recruited the human agents of whom Nike spoke. "They have yet to succeed."

"They never before expended such resources in the effort," Nike persisted.

The earlier, unexpected flattery suddenly made sense. Nike's newfound interest in Nessus was not about the *Explorer* mission. This summons was about Nessus' earlier experiences. A hundred human-standard years earlier, a mere fifty human-standard years after Citizens had made themselves known to wild humans, Nessus had first entered Human Space.

Remembered fear and isolation flooded Nessus' mind. Only Nike's presence kept Nessus from rolling into a cowering, quivering ball. He told himself: Nike needs me.

Would returning really be *so* bad?

Every human world, even Earth itself, was an unpopulated wilderness. The poorest human tenements wasted volume profligately in hallways, stairwells and elevators, and individual food-preparation areas. And conditions in Human Space were primitive. When the Colonists' point of origin had finally been located, wild-human technology had advanced little beyond that of *Long Pass*. The Concordance, directly or otherwise, was the source of what few improvements had been made since. How much of that technology, Nessus wondered, would have been transferred to the humans absent experiments and experience with the unsuspecting, easily manipulated Colonists.

Primitive, but still dangerous.

Nessus had challenged *Explorer*'s crew with thoughts of pebbles turned into kinetic-energy weapons. Should humans find the Fleet, a stealthed ship jumped by hyperdrive into the Fleet's path could utterly destroy Hearth. And if the wild humans were to discover the Colonists and their history . . . would that not guarantee hostility?

Concentrate! After striving for so long to meet Nike, how could his thoughts have strayed?

He heard, ". . . Agent quite highly placed in the United Nations bureaucracy. This United Nations search for the Concordance is wider ranging than any before."

Knowledge would impress Nike. "Respectfully, that search cannot be sustained. The wild humans' primitive economy had become dependent on our General Products Corporation. Now that GPC has withdrawn, their economy has contracted. It will suffer for years."

The idea for GPC had originated in an historical entry in the *Long Pass* computers: the British East India Company. Concordance influence was more subtle, of course, than the crown-awarded monopoly over trade with the East Indies. GPC sold humans its indestructible hulls and accumulated vast sums of human money—funds whose main use was the purchase of behind-the-scenes influence. And much as India's sepoy armies battled Great Britain's enemies, the wild humans were readily manipulated into constraining other spacefaring species that might otherwise grow to trouble the Concordance.

Nessus had left behind highly placed agents, including a deputy undersecretary of the United Nations. Most had been recruited—compromised or bribed—very indirectly. They might still be reporting by hyperwave radio to the foreign-affairs ministry.

"Nike, wild humans sought the 'Puppeteer' home world the whole time I was in their region of space. The progress of some such efforts I tracked myself through the human news media. The UN also hunted us in secret. My agents reported on those efforts to me, often without knowing it. The longer those quests failed to find us, the deeper into space the humans looked." Each time Nessus appeared without protection under their yellow sun assured them that Puppeteers had evolved nearby a similar star. "While they keep looking at yellow suns, they'll never find us."

"And yet, despite their failures, they keep looking," Nike said. "Tell me about the ARM organization."

"The Amalgamated Regional Militia." It was an uncharacteristically modest name for an extremely powerful entity. "The ARM evolved as the law-enforcement branch of the United Nations. Its operatives are called ARMs, too."

"Are these ARMs capable?"

"Some." Once more, Nessus found himself struggling not to pick and tug at his mane. "ARMs are given psychoactive drugs to make them paranoid. When one such is smart, too—"

"I am told Sigmund Ausfaller is such a smart one," Nike said. "He is the organizer of the latest United Nations search for us. Our source says Ausfaller feels the haste in GPC's withdrawal from Known Space might have left traces, new clues. I fear his assessment could be correct."

Ausfaller! "He is among the humans' very brightest, a natural paranoid, and not easily distracted." Nor, despite several surreptitious attempts, had Nessus ever found a way to corrupt him. What might Ausfaller attempt if he were to find the NP4 colony? And yet . . .

Nessus had the start of an idea. It was not fully formed, nor necessarily practical. He would have to do a lot of thinking before he dared articulate it to Nike.

On the other head, it just might be brilliant.

WITH A FINE-TOOTHED comb in one mouth and tiny scissors in the other, the stylist made the final adjustments to Nike's mane. The dyes had already been touched up, the hair carefully teased and layered, and the braids reknotted and arranged. Hundreds of jewels had been woven into place. Nike craned his necks, admiring the effect from all angles. His elaborate coiffure required the twice daily ministrations of a master hair artist—and that was the point. Only one as successful and powerful as he could afford the expense.

Nike chanted his approval. The hair artist dumped his tools and unused ornaments into a sack and vanished from Nike's residence via stepping disc. The many instruments could be sorted and repacked elsewhere.

The figure in Nike's mirror was virile and commanding. Surely few in the audience of tonight's ballet would be more dashing. Completing a pirouette of inspection, he bobbed his heads high/low, low/high, in satisfaction both with what he saw and his upcoming appointment.

Nessus, despite his excellent record, had been distracted, sometimes all but tongue-tied, at their first meeting. Was he sexually infatuated? Another hero-worshiper? Either way, after the evening to which Nike had invited Nessus, the smitten scout would do whatever Nike asked.

Knowing just how spectacular he would look by farmworld light, Nike had directed Nessus to meet him on a shore promenade. They would go to the ballet soon enough.

Nike dipped a head into a pouch of his decorative sash—no utilitarian pocketed belt tonight!—and with a quick manipulation of his transport controller left the residence. He emerged to a place, rare in the world, devoid of lamps, chandeliers, and glow panels. Artificial light could only detract from the view.

Rising from the blackness of the sea was the planet NP1. Beneath its ring of equatorial-orbiting suns, that most ancient of Hearth's companions shone in full phase. Its seas sparkled in brilliant blues and greens; its icecaps were pure white. Countless reflections shimmered on the swells that rolled slowly up the shore. A crescent NP5 was setting on his other side. Its suns were polar-orbiting, to provide a more constant climate from pole to pole. The visible arc of that world revealed vast cyclonic storms. His still-to-be-conceived children would be old before those storms subsided and this most recent world to join the Fleet became fully tamed and productive. As for NP2, NP3, and NP4, Hearth's rotation had temporarily hidden them from view.

"It's breathtaking," Nessus said. The tremor in his voice suggested he had wished to say *you* are breathtaking. He stood nearby, one head resting on the stout railing that separated the promenade from the gently sloping beach. His mane was as plain as could be: unimaginatively cut, earnestly combed flat, and bound into large clumps by a few simple ribbons. Still, by comparison with the holos in his file, Nessus was being uncharacteristically formal. Nike appreciated the attempt.

"It is beautiful," Nike agreed. There was no need to mention the exclusivity of this location, for the restricted stepping-disc address, and the one-time-use access code, said it all. They were sharing one of the few, small parts of Hearth not covered in arcologies.

Also unspoken was the prospect that Nessus, by remaining in Nike's favor, might join the community of privilege. Nike felt a moment of shame. No promise would be uttered, but a thousand generations of social convention spoke as loudly as words. Peril to the Concordance *must* be averted. He would do what he must to see that Nessus returned to Human Space.

"This is not natural." Nessus looked himself in the eyes briefly. As Nike suffered another twinge of guilt, Nessus continued. "As beautiful as is this unending night, other worlds have suns to warm them."

Suns, not the waste heat of a trillion occupants. Alone among the worlds of the Fleet, Hearth had no suns. Nike extended a neck. He pointed a head, lips pursed and tongue extended, at NP1. "We can enjoy that perspective from here."

Nessus swung a head from side to side disapprovingly. "I know it will never happen, but I wish I could show you the beauty of a true sunrise. The sky shading from darkest, star-spangled black to pale blue. Clouds aglow in yellows, pinks, and reds." For a long time, they stood side by side, watching long waves rush far up the shore. "I will enjoy the sunrises on Earth."

The words meant success—and renewed pangs of shame. "It's getting late," Nike said. "We should be on our way."

· 11 ·

Kirsten led cautiously through thick underbrush, bending foliage from her path with a sturdy fallen branch she had retrieved from the forest floor. The dominant plants ranged from waist-tall to twice her height. Dense shrubs that she might almost call hedges predominated; they failed to qualify because of their plethora of colors. Fruits and flowers might fairly span the rainbow, she thought. Leaves should be green.

Like Omar and Kirsten, Eric wore muted colors today. It wasn't just for concealment. He had eased off on the styles and colors of a man seeking a mate. Perhaps his intentions had evolved during their time together aboard *Explorer*. Certainly his manners had.

"What's with that one?" Eric asked.

He was huffing from the unwonted exercise, and Kirsten suspected a stall. She hid a smile. "Which one?"

From the boulder where he had settled, Eric pointed. "That red thicket to my left, with dangling purple tendrils."

"I forget the name, but it's an insectivore. Citizens once planted them on the periphery of fields to protect crops." As though to demonstrate her point, several tendrils on the nearest red hedge lashed out, converging with a *snap*. A bit of diaphanous wing fluttered to the ground, the remains of a purple pollinator.

Omar grimaced at the display, and dropped his backpack.

The groundcover into which it settled with a soft whoosh was dusty yellow, mosslike in texture, with scattered spiky flowers. "And this little training exercise you talked Nessus into authorizing—you say it's safe?"

"Relax, guys," she told them. "We don't smell a bit appetizing to anything here."

Could anything here even smell them? Kirsten found the odors a bit overpowering. An artificial herd pheromone had permeated the air aboard *Explorer,* but that was a single scent. Countless pungent, spicy aromas surrounded them here. The next time, she'd bring nose filters.

Having twice navigated interstellar space, she had expected the jaunt across the ocean to the continent of Elysium would seem inconsequential. In practice, leaving Arcadia was visiting a whole new world, and the suborbital hop was the least of the experience. Amid all this strangeness, she had no impenetrable hull, nor even a sturdy spacesuit, to protect her. It was too easy to forget, especially when not a farmer, that most of NP4 was a *Citizens'* nature preserve.

Of course Citizens work here, she reminded herself. How dangerous could it be?

Omar and Eric were exchanging a look. "Now that you've brought up smell, did you know how badly it was going to stink?" Eric asked. "Did that detail make it into your research?"

The brief stop was encouraging her muscles to assert themselves: They were tired. Tough. There was a long way to go before anyone rested. Bending forward slightly at the waist, she shrugged her backpack into a more comfortable position. "I'd like to find someplace more suitable for camping before dark." They all knew she had a very specific spot in mind.

Grumbling, Omar retrieved his own backpack. "Someone explain again why we didn't step there directly and set up camp? First flying here and then all this walking . . . it seems so primitive."

"There's a limit to how much kinetic energy a stepping disc can absorb or impart." Despite having agreed to this adventure Eric looked embarrassed, as though admitting to a limitation in Citizen technology were somehow disloyal. "Simple example: We're on the equator. Half the world away on the equator is where we want to be. Both locations, being at the same latitude, rotate at the same speed—but their instantaneous velocities are in opposite directions. Do the math: We're dealing with big numbers.

"Across much of Arcadia, and surely all over Hearth, the huge number of stepping discs avoids the problem. If the velocity difference between two locations is too large for a single-disc jump, the system moves you through intermediate discs. It happens so quickly you never experience the intermediate points. We flew here because the ocean is too wide for a disc-to-disc jump. We're hiking now because this wilderness Kirsten is so keen to get us eaten alive in is sparse on discs."

Omar peered dubiously into purple underbrush where a scurrying *something* had set ground-hugging fronds rustling. "What's the limit?"

"Two hundred feet per second," Kirsten answered him. No one understood why Citizens had come up with English units of measure to accompany the English language they had invented. Maybe they only used them with humans. She had had to master standard Concordance units to fly *Explorer.*

"Let's get going." She lobbed a pebble beyond the rustling. Something resembling a cross between a Citizen and a koala, but smaller than her hand, burst from the bushes to rush past them. "If that creature isn't too *scary* for you."

That brought the laughter she had hoped for. They resumed their hike through the transplanted Hearthian woods.

Their path was mostly west. Until the final circle of suns set, the north-south line was unmistakable. She pushed briskly forward, leading them to the true objective of this outing.

KIRSTEN FELT HERSELF beginning to tire; her crewmates, who lacked her considerable hiking experience, were staggering. Around them, branches creaked and leaves rustled. Unseen animals chattered and scuttled in the brush and high in the trees. NP4's suns had long ago set for the day. The only illumination to augment their flashlights was Fleet light dimly filtered through the many-hued forest canopy.

Their goal was a safety shelter deep in the woods. She had wondered how visible the structure would be amid such a variety of foliage colors. Now her concern seemed foolish. The blinking lights that outlined the building would have been unmistakable even without their rapid but random color-hopping. This was a Citizen refuge—she should have known better than to worry.

The shelter sat in the center of a clearing, bathed in the light of worlds. Three were presently visible: a crescent NP2, a full NP1, and Hearth.

Sunless Hearth was a world like no other. Between oceans as dark as pitch, continents sparkled like a million jewels. Each of those lights was a city larger than any on Arcadia. No matter how often Kirsten saw it, the sight was humbling.

"Whenever you're done gawking," Omar panted. A smile took the sting from his rebuke. "Even a Citizen's padded couch will feel good about now."

"Or a padded floor," Eric agreed.

A fifteen-mile hike through the wilds entitled them to be weary. They had gone farther than was rational given their mid-afternoon arrival on Elysium. Had it been important to get specifically here, a stepping disc from the airport, or from a shelter closer to their departure, would have made much more sense—to a Citizen. Tomorrow, after a hike back out, none would ever suspect they had been here. Except—

"We'll be limping tomorrow," she said. "We'll take it easy. I know massage, I'll do you both." She waited for their nods.

Unlatching the door activated the inside lights. Kirsten led them inside. "All the comforts of home, my friends, and no records in the stepping-disc system." Were records kept of who went where when? She did not know, and asking might raise suspicions.

Wincing, Eric dropped his backpack. "I ache in places I didn't know had muscles. Maybe food will help."

"It never hurts," Omar said. He was sitting on the floor, boots off, massaging a foot. "Besides, whatever we eat will make someone's pack lighter."

"Good point." Eric started digging through his backpack. "Kirsten, any requests?"

"Whatever sounds good to you," she answered distractedly. Where was the comm terminal? No Citizen shelter could possibly be without one. "Remember to pack up the wrappers and any waste."

The terminal was behind her, immediately next to the door. With a second head, she would have found it sooner. "Here it is. I'm going to work."

The questions that obsessed her could be answered nowhere on Arcadia. She could not prove that assertion, but even if there *was* something there . . . how likely was she to uncover secrets that had eluded Sven, and all the archivists before him? No, it made more sense to search on the public Citizen data net.

That was her theory, anyway. This was her chance to test it.

With fingers interlaced, Kirsten cracked her knuckles. Eric's queasy expression made her chuckle. "I only have hands. This keyboard is meant for a Citizen's lip nodes."

"Then it *does* have keyboard input," Eric said.

"As backup to the voice-command mode, like aboard

Explorer." A pleasant aroma began to make itself known. Beef stew, she thought, from a self-heating pouch.

"Eat, Kirsten." Omar held out an open pouch. "Can you operate the terminal?"

Suddenly she was ravenous. She devoured a third of the contents before responding. "It's like Nessus' console on *Explorer.* Yes, I can use it." Barely. An experimental button push brought up the greeting screen she had expected. "Welcome to . . . Herd Net," she translated. Nessus had decided it was easier to teach his crew to read Citizen than to translate the shipboard library into English. "We'll know soon if I read well enough to make sense of the public databases."

Her first accesses were for the benefit of any logging software at the unseen public data center. They retrieved information any Citizen on Elysium might request. She navigated slowly through holos describing NP4 geography and climate, the flora and fauna of Elysium, and a brief history of the reshaping of the planet to resemble an archaic Hearth. As she read, she finished her stew and burrowed into her own backpack for a juice pouch.

Omar stood behind her, looking over her shoulder. "It's kind of interesting. Maybe we should save some of it. Agreed?"

"Uh-huh." She snapped a memory cube into the download slot. "If nothing else, copying this might make it less obvious which subjects really interest us." She returned to a previously viewed summary of NP4 history. Now she drilled down to Arcadia, the human settlement, rather than Elysium.

"Look at that." Eric crouched for a closer look. "I count far fewer links than before. Was Elysium settled before Arcadia?"

"Let's see." She tuned her requests to consider just the past two hundred years. "No, there's still more information about Elysium."

"Apparently Colonists aren't interesting." Omar sounded insulted. "Is anything new here about Arcadian history? It might be my language skills, or lack thereof, but I see nothing surprising."

Nothing caught Kirsten's eye either. "In the details, maybe. To be fair, there are words I don't know." She waited until Eric shrugged. "Regardless, I've downloaded all of it. Time for the big experiment."

She carefully entered a refined query: pre-Arcadian Colonist history.

After an agonizing few seconds, a list of topics materialized before them. Kirsten struggled with unfamiliar terms. Some struck her as English transliterated into Citizen characters. "Earth, humans, Long Pass, ramscoop, United Nations."

"Ramscoop sounds promising," Eric said. "Our ancestors' starship supposedly scooped interstellar hydrogen for its fuel. We're told they didn't have hyperdrive."

She selected *ramscoop*. Another multisecond delay got them only a "restricted" disclaimer. She tried Earth: restricted. Long Pass: restricted. Humans: restricted. She began timing the delays on her wrist clock implant. Her earlier, for-show searches had gotten near-instantaneous responses. "That's interesting. The time lag is consistent with a light-speed round trip to Hearth."

"Not an unexpected place for the Concordance to keep its secrets," Omar said. "Unfortunate, but not surprising. I guess it doesn't really matter, since the data are restricted."

Aboard *Explorer,* she had watched Nessus access restricted files. However clever they got, she saw no way to mimic a Citizen tongueprint. "No, I guess . . .

"Or maybe I *can* do something." The display was in its default mode, a format that efficiently allocated viewing volume to minimal file descriptors. With a few keystrokes, Kirsten changed visual layouts to a maintenance mode— and shivered. The inaccessible files were now time-stamped and sorted by their creation dates. "Whatever these are, they predate the founding of Arcadia colony."

Recent bravery was taking its toll.

Nessus cringed in his personal quarters, swinging between exhilaration and panic, too keyed up from his rendezvous with Nike to sleep. Their time together had been everything Nessus had dreamed. More. And yet . . . Nike was surely destined for great things. How dare a motley loner like him aspire to union with a likely future Hindmost?

Nessus plucked two-headedly at his mane, the few decorative touches he had so recently worn already picked apart. In all honesty, it had never been much of a decoration: a scattering of ribbons and a few lopsided braids. Nike's coiffure had been a work of art. What could Nike possibly think of him?

And so much for his principled rejection of mane adornment.

It had never before occurred to Nessus, but the quest to become Hindmost, to *seek* responsibility for the entire Concordance, demanded its own type of courage. The dangers to be faced were not physical, but the duty was surely unending. How could *he* possibly hope to conjoin with such a partner? And yet . . .

Their time together had been *fabulous*.

Fifty dancers, gliding and twirling in ever more intricate patterns, their hooves clicking ever faster in a frenetic crescendo. Afterward, a bejeweled gathering he could never have imagined, where he brushed flanks with some of the most powerful figures of the Concordance. Broad rows of grazing tables covered entirely with *grown* fare: grains and roots and freshly squeezed juices, without a speck of the synthesized food that sustained most Citizens.

All of it experienced with Nike.

Quivering muscles bespoke another swing back into

depression—and Nessus rebelled against his instincts. He stepped to a place that always calmed him.

The visitor gallery was always crowded at Harem House.

In Nessus's stage of life, Harem House was something of an abstraction. He could be on any of a thousand floors, in any of a hundred physical locations. Until he entered a registered union, until that pairing was awarded a license to mate, the stepping-disc system would continue to deliver him to a random viewing area. However often he returned, he was unlikely to observe the same Companion herd twice. Social convention held this was for his own good, lest he form an unseemly attachment to a specific female.

Where a Citizen arcology would enclose living units and offices close-packed like blocks, Nessus now saw an open, naturelike expanse. Meadowplant spread before him, interrupted occasionally by shrubs and stands of trees, by ponds and bubbling streams. Digital wallpaper extended the rolling heath to the distant virtual horizon, beneath a hologram blue-and-scudding-cloud sky. The mating fields were, of course, elsewhere and not viewable.

Nessus pressed through the milling throng toward the soundproof, one-way viewing wall. He tried to ignore the pitying looks from doting couples. The singles in the room were in the clear minority, and most were younger than he. Someday, Nessus thought, it could be Nike and me here, awaiting the birth of our child. It *will* be Nike and me.

The judgmental whispering stung. On past visits Nessus had occasionally lied that his partner had been detained, speaking a bit overloud to some sympathetic-looking pair of observers. His mood now was too complex for such pointless subterfuge.

"There is our Bride."

A new couple had edged up to the window to Nessus' left. The lovers stood side by side, their adjacent necks entwined. The one who had spoken was tall, with bright blue eyes and a lush, simply groomed red mane. His partner was nearly as tall, with a handsome tan-on-cream patterning that reminded

Nessus of a panda. Both wore brooches suggestive of an avocation in abstract art.

Using his free head and a straightened neck, one was pointing toward a cluster of three Companions. Their sides heaved slowly as they cropped the thick blue-green meadowplant.

"The middle one?" Nessus guessed. She was the thickest of the three, so most likely with child. There had been no introductions; Panda and Red were serviceable labels.

"That's her," Panda agreed. "She bears our child."

"Prosperity for you and your family," Nessus said. The traditional answer was the safest.

"She looks strong, don't you think?" Panda continued proudly.

"Very." Nessus said. In truth, Companions always seemed delicate to him. The tallest of them scarcely reached half the height of a Citizen. That was not the only difference, of course. The torsos of Companions, although brown-and-white patterned like those of Citizens, were entirely covered in fur.

Panda and Red prattled on about the intelligence of their Bride, oblivious to Nessus' torment. He wondered if he would lose all objectivity if—when—his own turn came. Size was only the most obvious difference between Citizens and Companions. Another differentiation was in the mane-covered cranial dome between the shoulders. In Companions, the hump was much flatter—because there was far less brain under the dome. Companions could not speak, nor were they capable of learning much, although the brightest among them, Nessus had heard, could understand a few words, and seemed to grow fond of their husbands.

That was far short of sentience.

There were times when Nessus thought the structured and unthinking life of the females was idyllic, and not only for the unimaginable luxuries of natural foods in this meadowlike setting. How liberating it must be *not* to strive, *not* to wonder for most of one's life whether he would ever be deemed worthy of siring children. But introspection was his doom; the diminutive and unthinking creatures before him faced their own. . . .

Panda and Red eventually departed. Nessus watched the Companions for a while longer, until being there without a mate became too awkward and painful.

All the while the possibility that had come to him in Nike's office continued to sharpen in Nessus' mind.

NIKE ROAMED DISTRACTEDLY about his office. Scouts are a precious commodity, he assured himself. They are exceedingly rare, no more than a very few identified each generation. Why, but for such scarcity, would he, a deputy minister, have studied the personnel records of all of them? Why else would he have deigned to *meet* one? Each scout was aberrant in his way, needful of coddling, jollying, and other distasteful encouragement. Their missions inherently relied upon self-direction, exercised in isolation, far from the Fleet.

Only a motivated volunteer could perform such duty.

How could it be otherwise? Safety in numbers had been wired into Citizen genes long before the first glimmer of intelligence. Beyond the herd waited predators patiently stalking, ready to pounce on anyone too young or too old, too infirm or too inattentive, to keep pace with the herd. Yet what if none were to scout ahead for new pastures? The whole herd might starve.

Hearth had long been purged of its native predators, but more sinister dangers lurked. Spacefaring alien races surrounded them. Hearth's once-yellow sun had swollen into a red giant, generations ago, initiating the planet's first epic voyage. The galactic core itself had erupted into a storm front of lethal radiation thousands of light-years thick. If none ventured ahead, who would warn the Fleet of new perils? Without scouts, how would the Concordance know where to flee from danger?

It was all a rationalization, of course. A secluded walk

on the shore, the ballet, the private party after . . . Nike knew he had crossed a line with Nessus. The wild-eyed, mangy-maned scout was all too obviously smitten with him. Without shame, Nike had exploited that infatuation.

There was ample shame now, however belatedly, and Nessus had requested urgently to see him again. Nike had agreed. Very soon he must ask Nessus to undertake another mission. For the safety of all, no other race must ever locate Hearth.

What Nessus must do in Human Space was horrible.

A buzzer interrupted Nike's dark thoughts. "Yes?"

"Deputy Minister, your visitor is here," an assistant said over the intercom.

"Show him in." Reflexively, Nike found some minor details of his coiffure to straighten. His assistant appeared at the door with the scout. "Please come in."

Nessus was bursting with scarcely restrained enthusiasm. Two uneven braids offered a token acknowledgment to social norms. Faint compression marks hinted where a few ribbons might once have been found. "I have an answer!"

That sounded unrelated to the feelings Nike feared he had so inappropriately encouraged. "How I envy you. What was the question?" he temporized.

Nessus shifted his weight excitedly between front feet. "An answer for the problem with the wild humans. I can save them. That is, I know how to preoccupy them."

Preoccupation sounded so inadequate. "Can you keep the ARM from finding us?"

"Yes, yes!" Nessus bobbed his heads in vigorous alternation. "I was at Harem House and—"

Had his encouragement already led Nessus so far astray? Nike's embarrassment deepened. Worse, the scout was not the only one influenced by their late private encounter. Nike found himself distracted by strange sympathies.

We Citizens, he thought, even the most ardent Experimentalists, are a conformist lot. What must it have been like to grow up tempted by curiosity, lured by risk? Somehow, Nessus had learned to wonder what lay beyond the next hill, and—more wondrous still—to go, necessarily alone, to look. His personnel file said Nessus was long estranged from his parents.

"—discrediting Earth's Fertility Board is the key."

An advanced civilization of only a few billions defied Nike's imagination. Regardless, the humans' United Nations had already instituted mandatory population controls. "You propose a scandal to divert the hunt for the Concordance."

Nessus fixed him with a two-headed stare. "Imagine if it were suspected Citizens were secretly buying Brides and the right to reproduce. How would our kind react?" Nike's horror must have been apparent, because Nessus added, "Exactly."

It made a certain depraved sense. Only the conviction that reproductive constraints were equitable made those restrictions bearable. Loss of faith in that fairness would incite strife even here on Hearth. How would wild humans react? With massive unrest, Nike supposed. With violence. It might very well preempt their security forces from speculative Puppeteer hunts. "Is it doable?"

"I believe so, given access to sufficient resources," Nessus said. "I envision our agents bribing some members of the Fertility Board, and compromising others by creating bank accounts in their names. The economies of the human worlds have yet to recover from the shock of General Products' disappearance. The more wealth people have lost, the quicker they will be to suspect conspiracy. Many will believe the rich are buying birthrights. A bit of innuendo here, some surreptitious funding to political opportunists there . . ."

It did not help communications that Nessus lapsed repeatedly into some wild-human language—Interworld, was it called?—for terms lacking in their common vocabulary. After several such digressions, Nike had an epiphany. For much of his life, Nessus had had only humans with whom to converse. Even when Nessus had finally returned to the Fleet, it had been mainly to the company of other humans: the Colonists.

Slowly, after many questions and lengthy discussion of wild-human traits, the proposed plan took shape in Nike's mind—if only in broad outline. "The retained earnings from the General Products Corporation are adequate to the task?"

"If the approach is valid, money will not be the limiting factor."

If? Nessus, who had entered Nike's office almost bursting with exuberant certitude, was beginning to slump. Nike saw he had pushed too hard. "I am very encouraged, but of course a great deal of detail must remain to be determined. I would like you to make this your top priority. Please get back to me soon with an update."

Amid the earlier torrent of explanations, Nessus had used a curious figure of speech. A surgical strike: It evidently related concurrently to primitive medicine, and warfare, and the application of force to points of maximum leverage. Nike had only partially grasped the metaphor, but that was sufficient. Nessus' gambit, if it could be made to work, would eliminate the need to lob stealthed relativistic objects at the human worlds. Gigadeaths, even among aliens, even in defense of the Concordance, should be a last resort.

And wild humans had proved helpful when deployed, however unwittingly, against the Fleet's other prospective opponents. Recalling the Kzinti, a fiercely aggressive species of carnivores who had repeatedly attacked—and been defeated by—the wild humans, Nike suppressed a shudder. If the Fleet were ever revealed, relativistic bombs might be directed at the Citizens' own inhabited worlds.

Terrible outcomes were easy to imagine: ARM hostilities upon the discovery of the NP4 colony. ARM survivors of a preemptive strike, even more enraged. And what if the Fleet were to be found by Kzinti no longer restrained by humans?

Kzinti made even *more* aggressive by the knowledge of the humans' fate. Any of those results was unthinkable.

Thinking the unthinkable was among Nike's chosen tasks. Nike steeled himself. Any hope for an acceptable outcome depended on the maverick who stood trembling before him.

The office door was still closed. With feelings of duty outweighing shame, Nike leaned forward to intimately stroke Nessus' scruffy mane. "Come back soon. I am depending on you."

SOMEONE FROM NIKE'S staff led Nessus to an isolation booth. Nessus knew his way out from his previous visit, but he was too wrung out from this encounter to object. His mane still tingled from Nike's gentle touch. Certain words had yet to be spoken, but some actions spoke for themselves.

The taciturn aide had not introduced himself. That was no surprise: Given the long chains of emerald-green beads woven into his braids, Nessus' escort was clearly a high-ranking Conservative. The bureaucrat was doubtless a factional watcher as well as an aide.

Nessus had worked himself into a manic state. How else could he have found the self-confidence to advise someone as hindward as Nike? But it was impossible to remain indefinitely self-agitated. Depression and panicked withdrawal could not be delayed for long.

Nessus stepped from the isolation booth to a nearby public nexus, and thence, in another step, to a favorite glen in a small park. Feathery purple hedges encircled him. Bright-winged germinators fluttered overhead. A few Citizens retreated from his wild-eyed stare.

His trembling worsened. He had promised much and implied yet more. His words had brought him, at the least, Nike's respect. He must return soon to Nike with a solution for every imaginable contingency.

For Nike, he would instill in his Colonist scouts the confidence they would need to explore ahead of the Fleet without him. For Nike, he would volunteer to remain in Human Space for however long the disruption and subversion of the wild humans required.

The task before Nessus would test and stress him like nothing he had ever attempted. His limbs trembled more and more; soon the fear of failure would exceed his ability to control. A final step deposited him into the cozy sanctuary of his sleeping quarters. Surrendering to the terror, he curled into a ball so tight he could scarcely breathe.

And yet, there was no doubt in Nessus' mind that he would undertake this mission. The safety of the Fleet was at stake.

To disappoint Nike—and so, to lose him—was unthinkable.

· 13 ·

Three arcs of little suns, one directly overhead, beat down on the vast expanse of concrete that was Arcadia Spaceport. Cargo floaters, huge when they silently emerged over or vanished from above the freight-sized discs, were dwarfed by the great spaceships that they serviced. The ceaseless procession of cargo floaters, impressive as it was, handled only the largest and most oddly shaped items. Teleportation discs built into the decks of cargo holds were used to onload and offload most interplanetary goods.

With a hand raised to shade her eyes, Kirsten stood watching a grain transporter settle to the pavement. Its cargo of biowaste tanks would be exchanged for grain containers. The spherical ship was easily a thousand feet in diameter. The nearby tapered cylinder that was *Explorer*, about three hundred feet in length, was a toy by comparison.

Kirsten stood to one side of a group of Colonists. Four

were family come to see her off; others were Omar's or
Eric's friends and relatives. By habit, Kirsten checked
people off by clothing and jewelry: these mated, these
mated and pregnant, there a young woman unmated and
interested—

She felt a tug on her sleeve. It was her niece, Rebecca,
wearing the muted hues of youth and unavailability. "What
is it, Honey?"

"Will you be safe, Aunt Kirsten?"

Nessus had yet to appear. Had a Citizen traveling companion been present, not even a six-year-old would have
asked. "I couldn't be safer." The serious face looking up at
her remained skeptical. "Ask your father."

Carl (pastels of a mated adult; a four-stone progeny
ring) gave Kirsten a brotherly hug. "Your aunt is right,
sweetie. She'll be back before you know it."

Carl had ad-libbed the last part. Kirsten wished he
hadn't. She didn't know how long they might be gone.
True, this trip was her idea, but the argument she had made
for it seemed weak even to her.

She was desperate to get to Hearth—and, once there, to
find or make an opportunity to surreptitiously access Herd
Net. No one was more surprised than she when the mission
planners actually agreed to meet with the crew to get some
Colonist-specific perspective.

Nessus' ready agreement, given with no questions
asked, still puzzled Kirsten. It wasn't the only matter troubling her. Where was Nessus now? Why he had chosen to
escort them? He might easily have arranged a ride for them
aboard one of the grain ships that ceaselessly shuttled
between NP4 and Hearth. It was rare, but not unheard of,
for Colonists to visit Hearth. Those who made the journey,
mostly associated with Arcadia's Self-Governance Council, rode cargo ships.

Nessus popped into view at a nearby stepping disc. He
cantered forward, scarcely trembling despite the Colonist
crowd, bobbing a head in general greeting. To Kirsten's
surprise he sidled up to the group. After meeting Omar's

and Eric's guests, Nessus made his way to Kirsten. She did
the introductions; he chatted with her parents and brother
as though they were old friends.

Nessus was in a manic phase, Kirsten realized. Had he
worked up his courage merely to meet the crew's family?
That seemed *so* unlikely. As she mulled that over, Nessus
arched a neck to stroke Rebecca's fine, blonde hair. "What
do you like, little one?" he asked.

Kirsten glimpsed an unexpected motion out of the corner of her eye. A loud "Baa," confirmed her suspicions:
Rebecca's pet lamb was bounding toward them. Schultz
trailed his leash, rushing to play with Rebecca and her
new friend. Hooves clattered on the rough surface. His
mouth hung open, tongue lolling to one side. How often
did animals bite their tongues before learning not to run
that way?

Nessus pivoted to flee, and Kirsten realized what *he* saw:
a large animal rushing toward him. Hearth was too crowded
to keep around even harmless animals. She stepped forward
and scooped up the lamb. He was nearly two feet tall now,
and mostly legs. "Good boy," she cooed. Schultz wriggled in
her arms, his tail wagging furiously. He licked her face.
"That's a good kid." She scratched him between the ears.
"Yes, you are. Yes, you are!"

Omar's wife, Evelyn (her tunic a rainbow of warm pastels: pointedly mated), whispered a bit overloud, "We've
got to find Kirsten a man." Kirsten pictured Eric grinning
at that comment and blushed.

"My apologies, Nessus," Carl said. "I'll take this little
guy away." There was a flurry of movement, part farewell
hug and part the transfer of the still wriggling lamb into his
arms. His parting words to Kirsten, called over his shoulder, were, "Stay out of trouble."

If you only knew, she thought.

Nessus had turned back to the Colonist gathering, but
his shaking had worsened. "I'll go ahead now. Join me
when you're ready." One head tracked the squirming lamb

until Nessus disappeared by stepping disc, presumably directly boarding *Explorer*.

Kirsten finished her goodbyes and followed. She found Nessus on the bridge, still quaking. "I'm sorry about Schultz. He was only being friendly. He wouldn't have hurt you."

"Do you like animals?" Nessus' voice was a monotone. He was still upset.

"I do." Clearly *he* did not. A change of subject seemed wise. "Nessus, I was surprised that you met us at the spaceport. I'm surprised you're on NP4 at all."

His heads swiveled so that he briefly looked himself in the eye. "I wanted Colonist company. I've been in Arcadia for several days."

Huh? Kirsten had not seen Nessus faces to face since the Ice Moon mission. No one had mentioned having seen him. Who had he been visiting on NP4? And why?

Omar and Eric appeared at the hatch to the bridge. "Is everything all right?" Omar asked.

"I am fine." Nessus' response sounded rote. "I was aboard earlier, before meeting your families. *Explorer* is ready for departure. Take your duty stations." One head watched the two men leave; the second accessed an exterior camera. "Good. Everyone is at a safe distance."

A flurry of radio communications cleared *Explorer* for departure. "I'm sorry," Nessus answered Kirsten's interrogatory look. "Your qualifications are not the issue. Only Citizens may guide large masses near the Fleet."

The apology sounded mechanical, like the answer to Omar. That was not like Nessus, she thought. First, he had been manic; now, he was operating on reflex. What made him so edgy? Perhaps their scheming had been detected. Perhaps *she* should be nervous. Kirsten shrugged inwardly. If that were the case, the Concordance authorities would do whatever they wanted to Eric, Omar, and her. Could their jeopardy explain Nessus' mood? Maybe the Colonists' snooping had gotten Nessus into trouble, too.

"Trust me," Nessus continued. "You will find this trip interesting regardless." NP4 receded beneath them. The cooling system briefly hissed at full power as *Explorer* sped between two of the orbiting suns.

"What will we be doing on Hearth?" she asked.

"Trust me," he repeated. A trace of his earlier manic mood had returned.

Above the atmosphere and beyond the suns, where the sky grew black and the stars came out in their myriads, the Fleet of Worlds shone in all its glory. Kirsten's breath caught in her throat. Neither abstract knowledge nor a few trips off-world prepared her for the sight.

She looked down on the plane of worlds, above which their flight plan had taken them.

Six like-sized planets defined the vertices of a hexagon. They orbited the empty point that was their common center of mass, at a radius approaching 900,000 miles. The five worlds lit by necklaces of artificial suns were pale blue-brown-and-white siblings: the nature preserves. The sixth orb, magnificently brilliant in its own light, was Hearth. Its continents glowed with the radiance of megalopolises. Its oceans were mostly black, scattered with gleaming island cities, the pale blue reflections of the companion worlds, and the greenish-blue sheen of plankton blooms.

A fiery red point caught Kirsten's eye. The star was only a fraction of a light-year distant. Once it had nurtured all life on Hearth. It had been a yellow dwarf then, of course. The Concordance had moved Hearth and its entourage—a mere two farm worlds, so long ago—before its sun bloated into its present, red-giant stage.

Hearth's shift into a distant orbit had alleviated another challenge: ever more heat. The planet held only half a trillion Citizens then, but their waste heat was destroying the environment. The world could support more Citizens without a nearby sun. In the panorama spread before her, that wisdom remained on display. One large artificial sun at the empty center of mass would have equally warmed Hearth and its farm worlds. The smaller suns that circled individual NP worlds imparted little energy to Hearth.

"It is an impressive sight," Nessus said.

Impressive was such understatement. Kirsten shivered and did not answer. Beings too risk-averse to leave their homeworld had instead cast off the final ties to their sun.

As NP4 shrank, a part of Kirsten yearned to abandon all scheming. The Concordance had incredible knowledge. They wielded scarcely conceivable power. Who was she to question their actions? What if secrets *did* lurk in her people's past? What could Colonists accomplish in the face of such might?

She thrust aside her doubts. The truth mattered. Colonists deserved to know their own past. Kirsten planned to uncover it.

FINAL APPROACH REQUIRED two mouths. That was a disappointment: Nessus would have liked to observe Kirsten's reaction. He would settle for watching the replay from the hidden bridge camera. That bit of repair had been within his capability.

"Crew, prepare for docking," Nessus called. He allowed himself a one-headed peek. Kirsten startled nicely.

"Dock where? There are no ships nearby. Once we're past the moon . . ." Her voice trailed off as she studied her instruments. "The surface is perfectly smooth. There's almost no gravitational reading. That's no natural moon."

"Correct." Nessus tweaked their course as a large hatch irised open. He activated the intercom. "We're about to board an orbital facility operated by General Products Corporation. They make spaceship hulls. They made this one."

He set down *Explorer* with a barely perceptible bump. "All hands, prepare to disembark."

He and Kirsten found Eric and Omar already in the relax room. Nessus pointed at the discs inset in the cabin's floor. His other head was already in a pocket, mouthing the transporter control. "Are we ready?"

Omar and Kirsten nodded. "Absolutely," Eric said.

With the flick of a tongue, Nessus rematerialized them inside a factory waiting room. Omar's eyes widened. Eric and Kirsten merely grinned knowingly. Eric grabbed at the first wall bracket he floated past. He said, "Orbital manufacturing said it all, Nessus. Microgravity. Why else make things out here?"

That was quick thinking. Nessus had an epiphany: He genuinely liked these Colonists. He could not say the same for all Colonists, of course, although increasingly they had his respect. The recognition made him feel guilty. Guiltier. Arcadia colony reflected long-ago Concordance meddling. The imminent Fertility Board manipulation would be his personal crime.

A second realization crowded upon the first. He had been wise to spend the past few days in cities across Arcadia. Colonists in their millions still made him want to run and hide. Living among them was the best available preparation for a return to Human Space. He did not intend to reveal himself to many, if any, wild humans, not even to his agents. Still, humans would be all around him.

The thought terrified him.

Eric found the display control that turned a wall transparent, revealing the vast enclosed central volume of the factory. Nessus saw six hulls in progress. Surely, this artificial world looked wondrous to them. Like the scenic flight plan he had chosen, this stopover was meant to instill awe. He needed their dutiful diligence when—soon—he could no longer accompany them.

The nearest construct was a #4 hull, what Colonists knew as a grain ship. Its position near the view port was no coincidence. That placement hid a production space that was almost empty. Nessus had seen the same volume almost filled with ships. The export market no longer existed, of course: The Fleet would soon leave behind the many races too foolish to immediately flee the explosion at the galactic core.

"Can we get a tour?" Eric asked. His eyes never left the factory region.

"Of course," Nessus promised. On cue, a General Products executive appeared. He wore his mane in tight, closely packed braids, the hair a striking yellow-brown that approached a Colonist's ash blond. His utility belt and few ornaments disclosed affiliation only to the company. "Here is your guide."

Nessus exchanged introductions and greetings with the newcomer, who did not speak English. "I brought a translator. I'll activate it now."

"Hello," the executive said. "My name is . . . and I will be showing you around the facility."

Citizen names seldom translated. How should the Colonists refer to their guide? A label popped into Nessus' mind, unsurprising given his recent re-immersion in wild-human cultures. The word amused him, and with so much at stake he needed amusement. "For today, we'll call you Baedeker."

"I shall be Baedeker then. I'll start with an overview of our operation. We're looking into the main production volume of . . ."

KIRSTEN GAZED INTO the enclosure that Nessus had so casually called a factory and she had mistaken for a small moon. Omar was subdued; she guessed he was as awed as she. Eric, though, seemed ready to burst with questions. Unless he overcame the habits of a lifetime and interrupted a Citizen, those questions would go unasked. One-headed speech evidently sufficed for the translator, and Baedeker never paused for a breath.

". . . Familiar with the Number 2 model, of course. We built your ship around such a hull. *Explorer* is unusual, though, in that it has a fusion drive. As part of this refit we'll replace the fusion drive with more and larger thrusters."

"Thrusters are more compact," Nessus said.

Why had Nessus made that comment? They knew all about thrusters. Only thrusters made sense near populated worlds, which was why *Explorer* already had some thrusters. He clearly knew about this refitting. Why hadn't he mentioned *that*? Swap-out of the ship's main normal-space drive struck Kirsten as a major change. Eric's furrowed brow showed he was equally surprised.

"Our most popular model is the Number 1 hull." Baedeker held his heads about a foot apart. "They're excellent for free-flying sensors, small satellites, and such."

The air was redolent with a spicy chemical smell, reminiscent of the pheromones with which Nessus flooded *Explorer* but somehow different. These scents were more varied, Kirsten decided, more like the forest smells she had encountered on Elysium. Perhaps this factory/moon recycled its atmosphere biologically. Certainly it was large enough.

"We have prototyped several of the changes you Colonists suggested." Baedeker suddenly vanished. He had not moved from the room's stepping disc since his first appearance, a position he had maintained despite the microgravity conditions by hooking hoof claws through some of the fabric loops that surrounded the disc. Doubtless he was prepared to flee the Colonists. Perhaps the three of them were Baedeker's first.

A nudge against the wall sent Kirsten floating over the disc. It remained active; she found herself drifting in a chamber twice as large as the room she had left. This space was crowded, mostly with new computer cabinets. She was happiest to see keyboards whose layouts looked better-suited to fingers than to lip nodes and tongues.

Omar appeared before she could identify the other equipment, and then Eric. Nessus arrived last.

"Also, notice the modified crash couch we have designed for the bridge," Baedeker said. His second head adjusted the seat as he spoke. "I understand that for your next mission you will all be flight-trained. This reconfigurable couch accommodates whoever is piloting." He circled around his visitors to occupy a place above the room's stepping disc. "Someone try it."

"I will." On his first try Omar bounced from the chair. "This would be much easier with gravity. Can we get some in this room?"

"No," Baedeker said. "Is that comfortable?"

"Why not," Eric burst out. He seemed surprised at his own interruption.

Baedeker looked unhappily at Nessus. "Our manufacturing processes are quite sensitive to gravity. How is the couch?"

"It's a good fit for me." A nudge against an arm rest sent Omar floating free. "Someone else try it. Eric?"

"I'm an engineer," Eric said. Kirsten understood that to mean it took more than an adjustable seat to impress him. "Room-scaled artificial gravity produces minimal fringing fields. Pardon my curiosity, Baedeker. What is so sensitive?"

Shut up, Eric! This trip might be their only chance to uncover their long-hidden history. Excessive curiosity now could lose them that opportunity. Kirsten had to change the subject. Using a bolted-down table for leverage, she pulled herself to the prototype couch. "My turn."

Eric frowned, but he took her hint. He managed to keep quiet through a presentation about new sensors. Then he asked, "When will we see hulls being made?"

"You have seen that," Nessus said.

"I mean in person, Nessus. Up close."

"It is not allowed." Baedeker answered. "That region is a controlled vacuum."

"I'll wear my pressure suit. It's aboard . . ."

Baedeker's heads wobbled from side to side on the hinges of their necks. Kirsten had seldom seen the gesture, but knew it denoted strong disagreement. Eric needed to drop this! "It is *not* allowed," Baedeker insisted. "The traces of gas and dust that cling to the outside of your suit would contaminate the process."

"I don't understand," Omar said. "Nessus, you told us

only large quantities of antimatter could harm *Explorer*'s hull. How can a bit of dust harm anything?"

"What I told you is correct," Nessus said. "I was speaking of completed hulls. During construction, hulls are fragile."

Eric would not let it go. "Extreme sensitivity to gravitational variations. Extreme sensitivity to trace contaminants. It sounds like a very-large-scale nanotech process."

Baedeker made a noise like a slow-motion boiler explosion. His howl did not translate. Nessus responded in kind, but louder and longer, until Baedeker lowered his heads submissively.

"General Products Corporation does not often disclose this information," Nessus said. "Given what you now know, it is best that you hear the rest. It would be unfortunate if you lost trust in your ship.

"*Explorer*'s hull is impervious to damage. If not, would I have ventured out in it? Still, there is a fact I had not shared. The hull takes its strength from its unique form: It is a single supermolecule grown atom by atom by nanotechnology. During construction, the incomplete hull *is* unstable. The slightest chemical contamination or unbalanced force can tear it to pieces. That's why there is no artificial gravity here, and why communication here uses optical fibers."

Kirsten gulped. As dependable as the rising of the suns, hundreds of grain ships visited NP4 daily. Each was like a soap bubble a thousand feet in diameter, grown atom by atom. How could such a thing be done? "Baedeker, are there only the four hull styles, each always the same size, because those are the superstrong molecular configurations?" In the back of her mind was the geometric oddity that there could be only five regular polyhedrons.

Eric disregarded both pairs of vigorously bobbing heads. "I don't think so, Kirsten. Hull shapes are standardized, but the details differ. Think about the number and placement of airlocks, the number and placement of openings for cable bundles, that sort of thing. And when I requested additional external hull sensors for *Explorer*, there were no restrictions on where to attach them or to route through the cable bundles. Since hull penetrations are that *un*constrained, I can't imagine how the molecular strength could stem from specific sizes or shapes."

Baedeker screamed again, louder and more discordantly than before. It only ended when he activated the stepping disc and vanished. Maybe he fled, Kirsten thought. Or maybe he was seeking higher authority.

"Too much logic?" Eric asked. The hurt look on his face added, "From a Colonist?"

"As I stated, this construction process is not widely shared," Nessus said. "You lack only one final detail. The supermolecule's imperviousness derives from interatomic bonds artificially strengthened using an embedded power plant. The stiffened bonds can absorb virtually any impact, and temperatures up to hundreds of thousands of degrees.

"Reinforcement of the bonds only becomes possible once the hull is effectively full-grown. Until then, as Baedeker explained, the construct is extremely fragile.

"Are you satisfied?"

Eric averted his eyes. Perhaps he had finally realized the extent of his assertiveness. "Yes, Nessus. I hope you will apologize for me to Baedeker. My professional interest does not excuse poor manners."

"Good," Nessus said. "Overhaul of *Explorer* will continue, but we have likely rendered ourselves unwelcome as guests. We will take the next available shuttle."

It wasn't until the shuttle was halfway to the surface, hull vibrating from the forces of reentry, that Kirsten took notice of a critical detail. Nessus and Baedeker alike had nodded at her analogy, moments later proven untenable, of four stable hull types. Up/down; down/up; up/down; down/up . . . like a Colonist's vigorous head nodding, it denoted firm agreement. Yet Nessus knew reinforced chemical bonds actually explained GP hull strength.

Nessus *lied* to us, Kirsten thought. What else has he lied to us about?

Explorer's crew exited the shuttle onto a vast expanse of concrete. Intellectually, Kirsten had known what to expect. Arcadia spaceport was merely one of several spaceports on one of five farm worlds. *This* was the main spaceport of Hearth itself.

Viscerally, she could not have been less prepared.

The unimaginable scale froze her in place. They had disembarked deep within an array of grain ships that extended in all directions. Cargo carriers, thousands of them, teemed everywhere. Strips of white lights embedded in the pavement provided ground-level illumination, while the clouds throbbed with the reflected blue running lights of arriving and departing vessels. In the distance, speckled blocks, prisms, and cylinders rose above the ships. To tower over the grain ships like that . . . those *were* towers. The smallest building must stand at least a mile tall. The tiny speckles were windows.

"I don't believe it," Omar said wonderingly. "I see it. I've read and been told about it. I still can't believe it."

"Believe it." Eric turned slowly, savoring every detail. "A trillion Citizens. One planet. Do the math."

Nessus watched them taking it all in. "Are you ready to proceed?"

They had exited the shuttle by stepping disc. They could have gone directly to wherever Nessus wanted them. Was his purpose a tourist excursion or understated intimidation? "Where to, Nessus?" she asked.

He pointed, neck and tongue extended, at the tallest tower in sight. "Soon enough, there. I arranged a meeting with a Concordance official to discuss scouting missions. Although almost anyplace is convenient to the spaceport by stepping disc, the deputy minister chose to place his department in sight of the spaceport."

"How long until then?" How long did she have to some-how gain access to Herd Net?

"I intended you to have an NP4 day here for sightsee-ing." Nessus picked at his mane. "That has changed. There were complaints about our visit to the General Products orbital facility. The deputy minister is rearranging his schedule to see us earlier. We have until we're summoned, no longer."

Was there an undercurrent to Nessus' reference to the deputy minister? A slight pause before the title? An espe-cially careful pronunciation? Were Nessus a man, Kirsten would have had no doubt.

A nearby grain ship lifted off. Eric craned his head to watch it recede, running lights pulsing, into the perpetual night of Hearth's sky.

"Come." Nessus vanished.

Swallowing hard, Kirsten stepped onto the disc he had just vacated—and into complete sensory overload.

Unimaginably large buildings loomed over her, their tops hidden in low cloud. She stood in a plaza, amid tens of thousands of Citizens jostling together like . . . what? They clumped like sheep, flank by flank without visible space, but entering and exiting the flock, veering and converging, with intent purpose. Herd pheromones saturated the air, so pungent that her eyes watered. And the din! It sounded like a thousand orchestras tuning up at once, while tens of thou-sands of hooves beat a counterpoint on the pavement.

Blunt teeth grasped Kirsten's arm and tugged. "You must vacate the disc." Nessus spoke from one mouth, for his other one still grasped her elbow. She stepped back and Eric appeared. His jaw dropped; she felt better seeing his reaction.

By the time Nessus jostled Eric aside and Omar appeared, another impression struck her. "Nessus, everyone is staring at us."

"Colonists on Hearth remain a rarity." Nessus began walking across the plaza. "Stay with me. You will not be bothered."

"We're in your mouths," Omar said shakily. "What can we see?"

The clear area around them moved with them, a bubble adrift in the sea of Citizens. Rare meant unknown meant, to Citizens, prospectively dangerous. What threat might the three of them possibly pose, she wondered.

"We are in a communal courtyard," Nessus answered Omar. "It is typical, although smaller than average. I did not want to overwhelm you."

"What are the surrounding buildings?" Eric asked.

"Three edges of the square are arcologies, modest by Hearth standards but you would consider each a large city." Nessus pointed at the fourth and nearest side, toward which they continued to walk. "This is a local entertainment and shopping complex."

Kirsten was about to ask a question when a distinctive warble intruded. "Excuse me," Nessus said. His head poked into a pocket of his utility belt. There were muffled orchestral sounds, and then his head reappeared. "That was the deputy minister's office. He will see us in a little less than an hour."

Kirsten's mind raced. A trip to Hearth had seemed their best hope to ferret out the facts about the Colonists' past. Among so many Citizens, with so little time, what chance was there to gain access to Herd Net? Would they have a moment without Nessus' supervision? It *had* to be now. After a high official had rearranged his schedule to get the three of them off-world sooner, she could not count on a repeat visit.

"Many artists exhibit in the main promenade." Nessus continued his recitation. "Classical holostatues remain the most common, but dynamic holoforms are increasingly popular. My favorite is—" He trilled something in both throats. "Sorry, his name has no meaningful translation."

He's manic again, Kirsten realized. The meeting is almost upon us, and Nessus is working himself up.

". . . A secondary entrance. The interior lobby has stepping discs, of course, for access to the stores and artistic venues. We can spare the time for a quick look."

As they reached an overhang, Kirsten encountered a slight pressure. A weak force field to keep out weather, she decided, pressing through into the lobby. Translucent holograms floated overhead, both abstract art and scrolling directories. Stylized fonts, rapid scrolling, and unfamiliar vocabulary rendered most labels unrecognizable. A few made sense: hair salons; stores selling jewelry, belts, music, and books; art galleries; concert stadiums. Aha! "Nessus."

He stopped. "What, Kirsten?"

"I'd like to get some souvenirs." She ignored Omar's baffled expression. "Maybe some picture books."

Nessus swiveled a head to scan the nearest directory. "Follow me." He vanished. This time Omar and Eric beat her to the disc Nessus had activated.

She emerged into a small, congested shop. Media players lined several shelves at the front of the store. Captions and illustrations floated over bins brimming with packaged media.

"Omar, would you mind picking out a reader for me?" She squeezed through the narrow aisles, Citizen customers staring at her, until she found a range of bins labeled "History." She plucked up a handful of coin-sized data disks under an assortment of titles. Most dealt with Hearth, but she included several about the NP worlds and Colonists. She added geography and art books from other racks.

Nessus was deep in conversation with another Citizen, a cascade of wild music, when Kirsten returned to the front of the store. She set her selections on the counter beside the media reader Omar had picked. As the clerk waved a scanner over everything, it occurred to her to wonder how to complete the purchase. Did stores on Hearth accept Colonist credits? "Nessus, may I pay you back?"

"Of course." He completed the transaction with a tongueprint on the scanner. "We must be going."

NIKE'S CAPACIOUS OFFICE had acquired a human-compatible sofa since Nessus' last visit. Tuxedo-style, Nessus thought. Its purpose might be simple hospitality. More likely, Nike hoped to render the Colonist visitors careless with a gesture.

Astraddle a proper seat, Nessus listened as Nike chatted with Eric, Omar, and Kirsten. Nike's mane was resplendent, richly woven with orange garnets. Nessus had to concentrate not to stare. When they had last met, the cascading of Nike's braids had merely indicated unmated status, without interest in being approached. The current interweaving declared prospective openness to a relationship. *This message is for* me, Nessus dared to hope.

Despite the casual conversation, Nike remained behind a massive, new desk. Nessus guessed that a stepping disc hid beneath Nike's own padded bench for an emergency exit. "Tell me about the aliens you studied," Nike said via translator.

"They call themselves Gw'oth. Physically, a Gw'o is small." Omar held his hands about an arm's length apart. "It's five-limbed, in a star shape. The sense organs and the brain are in the central area. The Gw'o appears well adapted to life under water."

"And under the ice." With typical delicacy, Nike showed he had seen their report.

"You'll be more interested in their capabilities and potential," Omar said, taking the hint. "Eric will cover that."

Eric straightened. "They are newly industrialized. They had to master life in a vacuum to gain access to . . ."

While Eric described Gw'oth technology and Nike probed Eric's depth of understanding, Nessus thought about the future. The crew *he* had selected and trained would warn the Fleet of any threats ahead. *He* would sidetrack the wild humans searching for the Concordance. *His* feats would earn Nike's undying respect and gratitude—and hopefully much more.

"My specialists say Gw'oth progress is exceptionally rapid," Nike said.

"I wondered about that," Kirsten replied. "We had no frame of reference."

Nessus' stomach spasmed at the implied criticism. His grand plans could unravel *so* easily. The complaints about the General Products visit already reflected badly on them. What if Nike insisted that he supervise the Colonists on their next flight? What if Nike canceled the Colonist scouting experiment altogether? Even the minor precaution of placing a substitute political officer aboard *Explorer* would be problematical. To prepare another Citizen to take his place on *Explorer* meant shared credit if all went well— and full blame if it did not.

"What impressed me most," Eric said, "is the Gw'oth rocketry program. We monitored several satellite launches. Every attempt succeeded. Each mission exceeded the last in sophistication and payload."

"The quality control, precision, and rate of learning impressed me," Omar added.

Good! The men appropriately respected the potential threat. This hastily rescheduled meeting would surely end soon. They would be safely out the door, his plans intact.

"On the other head, Nike, Gw'oth technology remains primitive," Kirsten interjected. "Their world is resource-limited. They are very unlikely to achieve deep-space capability before the Fleet passes them by forever."

It was all Nessus could do not to pluck and fuss at his mane. Generations of acculturation had yet to expunge from Colonists the casual human attitude toward risk. *Anything* dangerous was to be avoided. Likelihood did not matter. Humans curiously chose to ignore the unlikely. The marvel was that such self-destructive behavior had so far failed to cause their downfall.

"That is not a scout's decis—" Nike said.

"Excuse me, Nike." Kirsten leaned forward. "I believe you misunderstand my point."

On Elysium and again with a visit to the General Products manufacturing facility, Nessus had been sensitive to Kirsten's unfulfilled need to explore. Rather than satisfy her, he had emboldened her. Trembling with dismay and rage, he awaited disaster. No mere Colonist could interrupt a deputy minister.

"Explain." Nike's translated command was ominously curt and flat.

"I hadn't finished," Kirsten said. "Certainly we must avoid any danger to the Fleet. All we face now, however, is the potential for a threat. Should that threat materialize, Gw'oth technological limitations mean we can disable the aliens nondestructively."

Nike's necks tipped forward with interest. "How would that work?"

"Gw'oth networking is understandably primitive. It was neither necessary nor possible until they ventured above the ice, where they could no longer plug in as living computers. I can easily introduce a self-propagating, self-replicating program, let's call it a virus, to subvert their networks. The Gw'oth have no defenses against software attack. The virus would incapacitate everything their networks operate—including their launch- and spacecraft-control systems."

"Interesting." Nike ignored a discreet buzz that probably signaled another appointment. "But why respond that way?"

Nessus knew why. Kirsten disbelieved his assurances that he had deactivated the comet probe. She was correct, of course. Why not retain the option? Had he deactivated it, it was easy enough to build more.

"I'm considering the contingency in which we must preempt the Gw'oth from acting against the Fleet," Kirsten said. "If that happens, disabling their computers will limit Gw'oth casualties. The intervention would imperil anyone riding a computer-controlled conveyance at the wrong time, but most Gw'oth would survive."

"A surgical strike," Nike said.

The phrase obviously puzzled Kirsten; it spoke directly to Nessus. *He* had proposed a nonviolent stratagem against the humans. Now Kirsten proposed a ploy against the Gw'oth.

Nike's buzzer sounded again. "I have another meeting. Omar, Eric, and Kirsten, I found this discussion very helpful. Nessus informs me *Explorer* will soon depart on its next trip. I wish you an interesting mission."

Turning off the translator, Nike fluted four wonderfully complex double chords to just Nessus. "The human affinity to computing continues to appall me. Still, the opportunity to protect the Fleet without slaughter appeals to me, and these three seem capable and loyal. I accept your recommendation, Nessus. Next mission, they will fly alone."

· 15 ·

Nessus pored over the shuttle's maintenance log, seeking composure in the routine. The ground crew had made a few annotations, none involving more than a small tweak to the calibration of one or another component within a massively redundant subsystem. A hundred such minor glitches could go unaddressed without endangering the shuttle.

He was shaking! By force of will, Nessus calmed his trembling limbs. A quick scan revealed his crew talking among themselves; he doubted they had noticed his lapse. Only now, the meeting safely behind them, did Nessus admit to himself the gamble he had taken. Had the session produced a different outcome, he might easily have lost any chance with Nike.

Omar stowed his duffel bag. "Nessus, thank you for arranging this trip. We all appreciate it."

"You're welcome." Nessus whistled a few parameters to

the main bridge computer. It would record the data and uplink it to traffic control. "You three have done well."

"Thanks again," Omar said.

"Hearth is amazing." Eric checked instruments as he spoke. "Too bad *Explorer* can't accommodate four on the bridge like this shuttle."

Soon enough, *Explorer* would carry only three, although the refitting now nearing completion would retain a Citizen-friendly crash couch. Nessus decided the news could wait a little longer—until he achieved calm. "What struck you most about Hearth?"

"The crowds, even in what you called a small court-yard." Eric scratched his chin. "One thing puzzles me, though. Amid those throngs, I don't know if I saw any female Citizens."

Nessus froze. "You did not."

"Do they have their own communities?" Kirsten asked.

"Discussions of gender make Citizens uncomfortable," Nessus said.

"Everything seems fine." Eric looked up again from his own preflight checkout. "Nike is smaller than you and so elaborately coifed. I had wondered if Nike were female."

"Nike is also male."

"You would know, of course." Eric made a strangled sound, part laugh, part cough. "He kept looking at you."

Nessus had noticed that, too. Together with the mane signal . . .

"The few Citizens I've met are male," Kirsten said. "I would like to meet some Citizen females."

A lamb bleating and leaping playfully: Nessus remembered Kirsten hugging it and cooing at it. What would she think if she knew? What would any of them think? Their likely reaction was yet another worry pushing him toward withdrawal.

A traffic-control update let Nessus change the subject. "We're the third ship cleared for departure. Prepare for launch."

They took off soon after into the perpetually crowded

skies above Hearth. He kept the bridge conversation focused on air traffic control, then space traffic control. His inner doubts, however, refused to be channeled.

What would any Colonist think who knew about the Companions?

THE SMALL WORLD that was the General Products orbital facility receded in Kirsten's instruments. They had reclaimed *Explorer* quickly. Baedeker made no effort to hide his feelings. He was eager to be rid of them.

"I missed this ship," Kirsten said. "It's good to have her back."

"It's good that you like this ship," Nessus answered. He had slumped on his bench. "You'll be spending a lot of time on it."

He had been tense throughout this trip. Kirsten still had no idea why. "Shall I take over the controls? You seem . . . preoccupied."

"I appreciate the offer, but it remains impossible. Don't worry. I'll get you back to Arcadia." Nessus trembled, despite his assurances.

In hindsight, all her scheming for a visit to Hearth had been unnecessary. The trip's true purpose—for Nessus—was bringing them to meet Nike. Kirsten had yet to deduce his motives.

She probed. "Is Nike planning another scouting expedition?"

"Correct." Nessus straightened on his bench. It was a struggle. "We're on autopilot. Now that we're clear of the GP facility, I have news to share." He activated the intercom. "Omar, Eric, meet us in the relax room."

For a short while, at least, they *could* use the autopilot. Even without a natural sun, the worlds of the Fleet warped nearby space-time too much to use hyperdrive. Kirsten felt more and more worried about Nessus piloting in his present condition. She had to do something: Citizens distrusted computers too much to permit automated landings.

They reached the relax room before Omar and Eric. Nessus tugged at his mane, undoing its final remnants of order as he waited. At their entry, Nessus looked himself in the eyes while whistling an impressive fanfare. "The meeting with Nike went well. Lest you become anxious, I kept to myself what might result from that meeting.

"Nike had final authority to approve a recommendation of mine. You three will take *Explorer* on its next scouting mission. I must attend to other matters."

Eric blinked. "Just us three. There will be no Citizen aboard?"

"Correct," Nessus said.

"But *why*?" Eric squeaked.

Was she proud or worried? Maybe both. The bigger question for Kirsten was: How would this affect the quest for their past?

"It is inappropriate for me to discuss my own mission," Nessus answered Eric.

"When will we go? How soon will you go?" Eric asked.

"I expect to go in a few days." Nessus' tremors grew. "Scientists in Nike's ministry must select destinations before you leave. Perhaps ten more days."

How much longer could Nessus last before hiding in his cabin? "Nessus, respectfully, you are distraught. *Please* let me do the piloting."

"I will be fine," Nessus said. "I'm returning to the bridge."

"I'll join you in a minute." After Nessus left the relax room, Kirsten took a pen and notebook from a storage locker. Had General Products hidden new cameras? There was no time to look—and no guarantee they would find them. She had to risk getting caught.

Kirsten hunched over the notebook, the better to block the view of any new sensors. The posture did nothing for the legibility of her writing. She passed the notebook, closed, to Omar.

Omar opened the notebook a crack, read her note, and nodded. He passed the notebook to Eric, who also nodded.

"Now I'll join Nessus," Kirsten said. He seemed too close to a nervous breakdown to bother watching them remotely. But what if she were wrong? Her presence on the bridge could dissuade him from accessing any secret sensors.

She found him quivering in a corner of the bridge. Tufts of his mane protruded in every direction, all trace of order vanished. "Are you all right?"

He looked at her dully. "I will be. I'm resting before we land."

She waited as long as she dared before calling Eric. "We're landing soon. Is everything in order?" It was not a routine inquiry about shipboard systems. Per her scribbled note, the question meant, "Do the Citizen histories have any new information about our people?"

"Everything is normal," Eric answered. "Nothing new at all."

She had bought the histories on impulse. "Nothing new" meant the Concordance told Citizens the same fables as it told the Colonists. The past she sought was a Concordance secret.

Her last hope for recovering that lost past would be in *Explorer*'s own archives—if those records had not already been purged. But perhaps Nessus would not delete his private records until he was done with the ship.

She saw only one chance.

"You're in no shape to pilot. Respectfully, you know it." Nessus said nothing. "Nessus, to land the ship yourself is dangerous. You could kill us and countless people on the ground."

"I know." A neck, as though with a mind of its own, curved slowly toward the safe place between his front legs. "Kirsten, a Colonist pilot within the Fleet is forbidden."

"You'll have to change that rule before *Explorer*'s next mission. Why not bend it now?"

Silence. "Traffic control cannot know," Nessus finally responded.

"No one need know, Nessus, but you must decide now.

We reenter soon. There are only two *safe* options. One, I land the ship. Two, you give traffic control a reason for aborting into orbit around NP4."

He trembled in silence. Not even imminent danger was getting through to him. Could *anything* make him decide? Remembering the curious tone of voice whenever Nessus mentioned Nike, she took a chance. "Suppose we abort to orbit. *Explorer* is in perfect shape, just refitted. Will Nike still trust you for your own upcoming mission?"

The head about to hide between his forelegs whipped up to stare at Kirsten. "Would you keep this secret?"

"I promise," she said. "I assume I can communicate with traffic control solely by text messages and data transfers."

"Yes." He fell silent again until a fit passed. "I'll show you the message protocols."

She settled into her crash couch. "I'll need to be logged in as you."

"Right." He crept nearer. His voice trembling, occasionally verging on incoherence, he made his explanations.

When, the lesson completed, Nessus ran down the corridor to cower in his cabin, she fought to control two strong emotions. The first was pity for her stricken shipmate. Whatever his faults, Nessus had given the three of them unprecedented opportunities. The second was—

The urge to shout for joy.

EXPLORER SANK THROUGH NP4's outer atmosphere, hull thrumming. They would be on the ground soon, and Nessus would likely emerge from his cabin.

Kirsten stared at a secondary bridge display. The pre-NP4 Colonist history files were gone. She pictured Baedeker gloating as he purged information meant only for Nessus' eyes.

Neither anger nor despair was the answer. What should she try before Nessus reappeared and revoked her temporary privileges?

Backup files: nothing. Temp files: nothing. Associative

search: something! A few records remained in the library that pointed to the now-vanished information she sought. Paging through those records, her hopes sank again. Hints and allusions, nothing more.

She continued scanning, and a familiar word caught her eye: ramscoop. It was one of the restricted terms they had encountered in Elysium.

The ground rushed toward them. Reluctantly, Kirsten abandoned the search to concentrate on their final approach. She exchanged messages with traffic control, carefully following the protocols Nessus had taught her. Too soon, they set down at Arcadia Spaceport.

She skipped the customary announcement over the intercom, hoping Nessus might not immediately notice they had landed. Instead, she shot Omar a message. "Wait outside Nessus' cabin door. Stall him if he comes out."

A query on "ramscoop" found only the one cryptic reference she had found earlier. What were the other terms from Elysium? United Nations: nothing. Long Pass: nothing. Humans: several hits! Humans might be a plural; she queried again with "human" and got more hits.

A corridor camera showed Omar on station outside Nessus' cabin door. Kirsten skimmed the records that mentioned human or humans. Nothing she saw meant anything to her, and she dared not pause to analyze what she was reading. She copied her search results into new files with innocent-sounding names, and then globally replaced every occurrence of "human" in her copies with "squirrel."

The camera showed a cabin door opening. Nessus appeared, looking once more in control of himself. After a short conversation, he pressed past Omar. Omar followed, still talking.

Where but the bridge could Nessus be coming?

Logged in as Nessus, Kirsten had total access to the ship's computers. Using that authority, she created a pseudonymous account and delegated full privileges to it. As Nessus' unmistakable contralto echoed in the corridor, she purged all traces of her searching from the audit and security files.

Nessus entered the bridge. "Thank you for your help, Kirsten."

"I was happy to do it," she said.

Nessus settled onto his bench. "I'm taking back control." Kirsten's display flashed, and all Nessus' privileged-mode information vanished from it. "Thanks again."

The last file she had scanned mentioned a Human Studies Institute run by the foreign affairs ministry. Nike's ministry on Hearth.

"I was happy to do it," Kirsten repeated.

· 16 ·

Whom the gods would destroy, they first make mad.

Summoned by and left to wait for the Hindmost, Nike wondered how many Citizens, even among those who borrowed names from human mythology, had encountered Euripides. Probably none. The present crisis had renewed Nike's fascination with humans, enough that he again rued the hubris of his assumed name. He did not feel victorious these days.

Had meeting Nessus's crew been a mistake? They seemed so *normal*. The harsh choices to be made about humans felt that much harsher after speaking with the Colonists. Perhaps it was madness to make such decisions. Perhaps it was madness not to.

Dark thoughts only amplified Nike's isolation in the posh, eerily spacious antechamber. He needed distraction. What, he wondered, was a suitable human name for the most powerful of all Citizens? One by one, Nike considered and discarded every option among the main members of the pantheon.

Perhaps a legendary mortal: Sisyphus. The Hindmost was crafty, and yet spent much of his time on pointless and endless endeavors. Fiddling while Hearth burned, as it were.

The Hindmost, of course, disdained such whimsy as a human pseudonym.

In a flurry of activity, the Hindmost and a small retinue materialized around Nike. All were resplendent in shades of green, none more so than the Hindmost. Nike's host wore his mane intricately coifed with emeralds and jade. Despite his advanced years, the Hindmost's roan coat gleamed with good health. "Thank you for coming," the Hindmost said.

Nike dipped his heads minimally, balancing respect with more assurance than he felt. The Hindmost's aides looked on disapprovingly. "I am honored to be asked into your home."

The Hindmost brushed heads briefly with Nike, as though greeting an equal. "We live in interesting times."

"That is true," Nike answered cautiously.

With a graceful twist of a neck, the Hindmost dismissed his staff. They vanished quickly. "Come. Let us enjoy the fresh air."

Nike followed the Hindmost through a virtual wall and weather-resistant force field onto a long, marble-tiled balcony. The house hugged the side of a mountain. The view, of wooded slope and crashing surf and undulating sea, was spectacular. A diffuse glow along the horizon hinted at a distant coastline.

The Hindmost paused while brilliantly colored flutter-wings zigzagged past in formation. "I received your recommendation for a course change."

Nike took a deep breath. "The ministry proposes an alteration in the Fleet's path. It is a matter of prudence, given that the wild humans seek us. In less than a year, the proposed small course change will interpose a dust cloud between the Fleet and the humans' home solar system."

"The recommendation said as much. That maneuver seems to be of marginal utility. The Fleet will remain observable—if they deduce where to look—from other human-settled worlds. And they can seek us from any vantage by using hyperdrive ships."

It was all Nike could do not to blink in surprise. When was risk *reduction* not a sufficient argument? "Hindmost, it is the home-system humans, their United Nations, who are most curious, most insistent—"

"The recommendation will have my authorization," the Hindmost interrupted. "I bring up its limitations to show that the ministry's advice receives my personal attention." The interruption wasn't jarring. It harmonized perfectly with Nike's woodwind/violin voice.

Long, slow combers washed up the broad pebbled beach, the foaming crests glistening by planet- and starlight. Offshore phosphorescence marked a sea-polyp colony. Clouds far out to sea sparkled with lightning. Despite the churning of Nike's thoughts—what was this meeting *truly* about?— he could not help but admire the view.

"This is a restful spot," the Hindmost said. "A stepping disc away from anywhere and yet private and serene. Few places on Hearth can match it."

The sea breeze ruffled Nike's mane and raised a sigh in the woods that surrounded the mansion. He considered: Acceptance of the ministry's—Nike's own—recommendation. The gentle reminder who was in charge. The hint of potential rewards.

He was being tempted, as he had so recently tempted Nessus. The lure was of wealth and power, not mating, but this was seduction nonetheless. Work with me, the Hindmost implied, and the rewards will be great.

Nike had rationalized his manipulation of Nessus as vital to the safety of the Concordance. He would not sacrifice the Concordance for personal gain now. "Might we speak, Hindmost, about the coming consensualization?" The reassessment of the public mind and mood for which the Experimentalists were agitating.

The Hindmost swiveled his heads toward Nike. "Surely disturbing the public about a settled issue is unproductive."

"Respectfully, Hindmost, a revised policy is in everyone's interest."

"A policy of permanent emergency? I think not. And

what else does your party have to offer? We are already embarked on the escape from the galaxy favored by Experimentalists."

"Some Experimentalists." Nike paused as far-off lightning bolts lit the sea. "The reality of the matter is: We flee because flight is in our nature. The explosion of the galactic core is frightening, and so we sought to leave it behind. Yet in my opinion, flight from the galaxy is our worst possible course of action."

"You would have us *stay*?"

"We run from a long-ago chain reaction of supernovae explosions—from radiation. To escape that peril, we will move fast and far, so that the wave front, already thousands of light-years deep, will dissipate before it can overtake us.

"Because all sane beings shun the perils of hyperspace, we must accelerate to relativistic speeds in normal space. Therein, Hindmost, is the paradox: As the Fleet flees the radiation from the core explosion, it produces radiation just as deadly—and will encounter it far sooner—with our own ever-growing speed. Interstellar dust and gas will impact our worlds as cosmic rays."

"Our planetary force fields protect us from the radiation in our path," rebutted the Hindmost.

"Those same force fields would protect us from the core explosion's radiation, were we to stay and await it."

"Indeed." The Hindmost blinked amusement. "Public beliefs notwithstanding, *we* can agree radiation is not a threat."

Had the Hindmost come to his point? "Meaning the threat is something else. The counterproductive results to our past approach toward our neighbors?"

"Guiding alien affairs to our own advantage seemed wisest at the time," the Hindmost confirmed. "Of course, every intervention introduced its own complication. Too bad. Colonists tending our nature preserves seemed such a good idea."

An aide approached, clearing his throats. "Your pardon,

Hindmost. You asked to be reminded of your next appointment."

"Thank you." The Hindmost gestured dismissively.

Intervention was such a colorless word, Nike thought, and exploitation of the Colonists was but one instance. Now discovery of the NP4 colony by wild humans appeared to be the most imminent danger to the Concordance. "I see at last why Conservatives so quickly embraced flight from the core explosion. You seek to distance us from our neighbors, not the radiation."

"You are too judgmental." The Hindmost craned a neck downhill, sniffing the rich mélange of forest and sea scents. "Surely we agree that the safety of Citizens is ever paramount. That being so, wasn't a bit of social engineering preferable to genocide?"

Was concealed intercession in the wars between human and Kzinti mere social engineering? Was enslavement of the Colonists? How, Nike wondered, would Nessus react to the Hindmost's words? For all Nessus' quirks and idiosyncrasies, the scout was insightful—and increasingly an advocate for the Colonists. And yet . . .

How Nessus proposed to deflect the humans was more social engineering. What Kirsten proposed, if necessary, to hobble the Gw'oth was yet more social engineering.

In an epiphany, Nike grasped the Conservative vision. Where he would invoke permanent emergency to empower Experimentalists . . . the Hindmost sought permanent equilibrium in the emptiness between the galaxies. Hearth had already cast off its anchor to a sun; now, in the guise of institutionalizing Experimentalist policy, the Hindmost would have the Fleet cast off its anchor to even a galaxy.

There would be no more stars to misbehave. No more star clusters to erupt into a chain reaction of supernovae. No more alien races like those that had proven so difficult to control.

"Hindmost, let us not revisit past policy. For our own reasons, each party agreed that we must take flight. But to embrace the unknowable dangers between the galaxies—isn't this a risk?" Whom the gods would destroy . . .

"We can neither stay nor go," the Hindmost said. "Perhaps I have missed something."

The Hindmost had—but the course of action Nike might someday espouse remained unformed even in his own mind.

A proper discussion could not be managed before the Hindmost's imminent appointment. Nike settled upon a polite formality. "Surely the Hindmost would not miss anything."

The Hindmost motioned expansively at the private estate before them. "Consider what we have discussed." The advice served simultaneously as enticement, warning, and dismissal.

WHOM THE GODS would destroy, they first make mad.

Alone in his apartment, Nike resisted the urge to wrap his heads in a tightly rolled shelter of his own flesh. What madness it was to meddle in the destiny of other races!

Yet meddling was what the Concordance did. How misguided that policy must be, when to escape its consequences even the *Conservative* Hindmost embraced a headlong plunge into the intergalactic unknown.

The choices before Clandestine Directorate were limited and stark. Preemptive genocide. Or do nothing, and risk the discovery of the Fleet, of humans trapped on NP4, and with it the unknowable—and surely justified—reaction of Human Space. That way lay mutual assured genocide. Or interfere yet again, undertaking more *social engineering*.

Whom the gods would destroy, they first make mad.

Feeling an unaccustomed empathy with the scout he saw no choice but to dispatch, Nike recorded a brief message.

"Nessus: Proceed immediately with your proposed intervention against the ARM."

Kirsten leaned forward in her chair, listening attentively to final guidance for *Explorer*'s upcoming mission. At least she felt her bearing was attentive. A discreet nudge against her left shoe suggested Omar read her posture differently.

Her hands hurt. Glancing down, Kirsten saw they were tightly clenched. Nessus might have understood white knuckles, but he was gone, destination undisclosed, purpose undisclosed. That had left Nike to oversee scouting missions, and the deputy minister lacked Nessus' in-person experience with Colonists. Best to play safe, though. She willed her hands to relax.

". . . The great responsibility entrusted to you," Nike concluded. "Do you have any final questions?"

"We appreciate the honor, Nike. We aspire to merit your trust," Omar said. Eric nodded agreement. "We thank you and Nessus for the confidence you have placed in us."

Through her left shoe, Kirsten felt renewed pressure against her foot. "I have no questions, Nike," she managed, envying Omar's poise.

She held her tension in check long enough to escape Nike's office and the foreign-affairs ministry. Stepping discs delivered them to the spaceport at which their ship waited. Their home, NP4, was visible only as a narrow crescent. Whether its appearance in new phase was auspicious, she could not decide.

Either way, it was time.

In the shadows beneath the curved hull of *Explorer,* Omar took her hand. "You're sure about this?" he asked.

"I am." She was sure she wanted to attempt it—while she dared. "We can't know if we'll get another opportunity. With Nessus away, Nike apparently felt he needed to brief us. Once Nike feels more comfortable dealing with us, or after Nessus returns, or when Nike assigns another

Citizen to oversee us, there may be no more invitations back to Hearth." No other chance to uncover the facts of our past.

"Then I'm going, too," Eric blurted.

"Two of us going increases our risk of getting caught." She looked to Omar for support.

"Sorry, Kirsten. I agree with Eric," Omar said. "You can't know what you'll find."

Could they afford the time spent debating? "Fine, Eric, on one condition. You agree I'm in charge."

Eric nodded.

"Omar . . . if anyone gets suspicious, you don't know where we went. I just wanted to play tourist for a little longer while you finished shipboard preparations." Before he could comment, she stepped onto the nearest public disc and disappeared.

KIRSTEN EMERGED INTO a safety shelter indistinguishable from the one in Elysium. How long ago that seemed! She set the nano-cloth of her jumpsuit into a random conglomeration of red, purple, and yellow splotches. In theory, it would blend with Hearthian foliage.

Eric materialized behind her. His eyes widened at the unexpected change to her clothing, before, with a nod of understanding, he altered his own shirt and slacks to correspond.

"So far, so good," she said. "We have the place to ourselves."

He shrugged. "For the few moments we'll be here."

The exterior cameras showed nothing but empty woods, lit by the "daylight" glowing from the mile-high wall of a nearby arcology. She unlatched the door. "This is a *Citizen* park. There is nothing dangerous out there. You didn't need to come."

He edged past her through the doorway and into a small clearing. Bushes and trees, or at least their Hearth equivalents, soughed in the light breeze. "Maybe a third of the plants look familiar from our last hike. I don't suppose that matters."

"Probably not." Kirsten's attention was on the sky. By a succession of public stepping discs, and so, in theory, untraceable, they had jumped far around the globe. A full NP1 overhead instantly oriented her. "This way."

A few paces into the woods plunged them into shadowy gloom. Only Eric's fast grab saved her from a nasty fall as she caught a toe in an unseen root. He took a small flashlight from his pocket.

"Not even the Concordance can banish uneven ground," he said. "You could fall down a hill or into a gully—and then it's over."

He was right. "Thanks," she said, and meant it. They had miles to go, and they had to cross them quickly.

What would they find when they arrived? Perhaps the Human Studies Institute cited in files she had stolen from Nessus. Perhaps a home for wealthy Citizens. Perhaps nothing. The institute was "located" in the file only by its fifteen-digit stepping-disc address, highlighted in the manner that denoted an access-controlled location. Even if she had known Nessus' authentication code, the institute's entry was surely continuously monitored. The stepping discs into Nike's ministry were certainly well-secured from the uninvited.

It might never occur to a Citizen that someone would *walk* there.

Of course, walking there required knowledge of the institute's physical location. That critical detail appeared nowhere in Nessus' files. The institute went altogether unmentioned in Kirsten's souvenir books. That left only wishful thinking—and a hologram of the institute in Nessus' archive. The image showed an isolated hexagonal structure topped by a dome.

The murk grew ever deeper. Dim beams from their flashlights provided the only meaningful ground-level illumination. The overhead pattering that had begun early into their hike grew louder. Raindrops begin penetrating the canopy of leaves. Dense underbrush made the walking slow, and the uneven ground made it all too easy to veer off course.

Compass notwithstanding, were they even walking in the correct direction?

This expedition had seemed so much easier in the bright and warm comfort of her apartment. In the holo image, four NP worlds in various phases hung over the institute. The date stamp implicit in the image's file name indicated when the hologram was made. However computationally messy, it had been conceptually simple to derive the institute's physical location on Hearth. Those coordinates put it on the shore of a lake, deep inside one of Hearth's few large parks.

They talked of home and hobbies, of friends and family. Eric coughed. "How far do you think we've come?"

"Two miles, maybe a bit more."

"Less than half way. Kirsten, we're taking too long."

"I know." There was nothing they could do about it. At this point, they were committed. "I couldn't know how rough the terrain would be under the foliage, and I didn't think to plan for rain. The wet footing is slowing us down."

"I wasn't criticizing." His flashlight beam wobbled as, in a flurry of wet leaves, he slid down a slight incline. "What do you think we'll find?"

"I don't know." She batted aside a low-hanging branch. "I'm almost afraid to know."

"Humans," Eric answered. "Is that what we are?"

They crested a hill. Shadows hid the way down. "Maybe. Or maybe humans are another race the Citizens have encountered, who may know something about us. Or they're the species who attacked our ancestors' starship. I don't understand why they wouldn't just tell—"

Eric caught her arm as her feet slipped out from under her. A bit of wet clay? "Be careful," he wheezed.

Kirsten looked all around in growing panic. "I dropped my compass."

Crouching, Eric poked with his flashlight at the low groundcover amid which they stood. Fleshy, fan-shaped sheets filtered its light into dim pastels. "I don't see it." He chain-coughed as he stood.

"Are you all right?"

"Funny thing," he said. "Maybe not."

She stared at him. "What do you mean?"

"I had a condition when I was a kid. Asthma. Apparently, I still do." He sat on a boulder, breathing shallowly, as though he were sucking air through a sponge. "Humidity and chemical fumes can trigger it." A chuckle morphed into a hacking cough. "Stress aggravates it."

They were miles from anywhere, and the nearest structure was someplace they weren't supposed to know about. She patted a pocket, and was relieved to feel her communicator. "We can call for help."

"And wait for Citizens to extract us from the woods during a storm?" Another half-cough, half-laugh. He stood. "We might as well walk. At least that will avoid their questions."

Walk where? She had lost her compass. Thick cloud so suffused the NP glows that she could scarcely navigate by their light—and then, only in the occasional clearing from which the clouds were visible. The clouds hung only a few hundred feet over her, scarcely above the tree tops, blocking most of the now-distant arcology-wall light.

It suddenly struck Kirsten what an alien world Hearth truly was. It had no little satellite suns and no great fireball star. There would be no daylight to save them.

"I have an idea," Eric said. "The institute is on the lake, right?"

"Right."

"Maybe we can follow that creek"—he pointed toward a faint gurgle—"downstream to the lake, and then follow the shore."

"We don't know how much the creek wanders. The shore *does* wander. We'll have a much longer walk."

"You identified our destination mathematically." He coughed unproductively. "It's all right if we get there another way."

"Lead on." At the base of the hill she added, "I'm glad you came."

"I'm not." He coughed. "Well, that's not true. I had, however, envisioned our first date somewhat differently." Cough. "That's a joke."

"Why didn't I know about this asthma condition?" Kirsten asked. Suddenly her face grew hot. She was thankful for the dark that hid her blush. She had been thinking like a crewmate; Eric would almost certainly fail to take her question that way. You *never* talked about hereditary medical conditions, unless with a doctor, or family, or a prospective mate.

Eric asked, "Can you keep a secret?"

"If not, we're in a lot of trouble."

The shallowness of Eric's breathing rendered his laugh horrifying. "Respiratory problems aren't that uncommon where I come from."

"We come from the same place." And she had never heard of asthma.

Cough. Wheeze. "Here's the secret, Kirsten. I grew up on NP3, a world away from you. There's a small Colonist settlement there. Apparently growing Colonists from the embryo banks was trickier than the Concordance wants people to know, and problems can—do—recur generations later. Some problems take a *lot* of medical care." Wheeze. "I was a success story. I owe them."

"I had no idea." The depth of his loyalty to the Concordance, his deference to Nessus, his sometimes questionable social skills, began to make sense.

"How could you know?" Cough. He crouched to peer below some branches.

No wonder he felt so indebted to the Citizens. She was afraid to ask why he had not informed on Omar and her. Why he was here?

Her doubts must have been written on her face. "Because it's important to you." As though afraid of her reaction he continued without pause, "I think I see the lake."

Moments later, she glimpsed the lake, too. A few more

steps brought them out of the woods, to a narrow fringe of rocky shoreline. Around a curve of the lake, through the rain, she could just make out a hint of a domed structure.

The Human Studies Institute.

THE "TREES" BY the lake loosely resembled red saguaro cacti sprouting fleshy round leaves instead of spines. Despite the increasingly heavy rain, the NP light that diffused through the cloud cover and reflected off the water allowed Kirsten and Eric to move quickly through the woods near the shoreline. The institute itself provided no light.

They were nearly to the isolated structure when Kirsten's communicator trilled discreetly. "You need to get back," Omar said. "Spaceport authorities are getting impatient. I blamed our delayed departure on a small technical glitch. If I don't 'resolve' the problem soon, they'll send tech support to help me fix it."

They were *so* close. "I told you to blame the delay on me: gone shopping. Now you'll have to find a way to stall. We're almost at the institute."

"If this doesn't work, I'm not leaving you and Eric to take the blame," Omar answered. "I'll do what I can, Kirsten, but *hurry.*"

The building they had come so far to explore was scarcely taller than the surrounding trees. From where they stood, no doors or windows suggested themselves. She edged deeper into the woods to circle the building. "Follow me."

They stayed among the trees, straining to make out details of the building. "It's too dark," Eric said. "If there is a door, we might not see it." He crept up to the wall, hand over his mouth to muffle a cough. "Come on."

They reached the shore again, having closely examined four sides of the hexagon. The final sides, those nearest the lake, were sufficiently illuminated by sky glow not to need up-close scrutiny. They were unbroken.

"I can't believe it." Kirsten sat heavily on the ground,

her back against a tree. "To have come so far . . ." She meant not only this hike, but everything they had been through. It had been a long and arduous trail here from the ice moon.

"Hmm." Eric studied the inaccessible wall, head tipped thoughtfully. "Remember Nessus bringing us to a shopping complex?"

"I do. Why?"

"It used force fields for outside access, not doors." He walked along the building, trailing a hand against the wall. "Just a hunch." As he approached a corner, his hand sank into the wall. "Aha." He stuck his head through briefly, then gestured her over.

"What did you see?" she whispered.

"A viewing gallery, I think, overlooking a roomful of Citizens and terminals. The gallery itself is empty."

Muddy splotches marked their approach. The rocky ground didn't take full bootprints. She pointed at her boots, covered in muck. "We can hope the rain will wash away our tracks, but that won't help us indoors. Our boots have to stay outside."

With a shrug, Eric sat down through the false wall. His head, shoulders, arms, and feet remained outside. He slipped off his boots, setting them just outside the holo wall, and then leaned backward to roll the rest of the way inside. His disembodied voice called, "Come on."

Faster than she could mimic Eric's entry procedure, he was flat on the floor, peering through the railing at the activity below. His clothes had become a pale blue that closely matched the corridor wall. She reprogrammed her own clothes and joined him. Below them, ten Citizens were seated near terminals, three walked about, and seven more stood watch over an array of stepping discs.

Holograms floated among and over the institute staff. Even the nearest projections were maddeningly indistinct at this distance. Images of Colonists—or was humans the correct term?—their activities unrecognizable. Impressions of text, none readable. The holo of a Nature Preserve world, clouds masking its surface. Holos of General Products hulls. It was all tantalizing.

It told her nothing.

Kirsten crawled around the balcony area, hugging the exterior wall. She was sopping wet from the rain and left a damp trail. She hoped strong winds sometimes blew in rain, or that the water would evaporate before a Citizen appeared up here.

The unattended terminal she sought was at the railing, a third of the way around the gallery. For all Kirsten knew, it offered only administrative functions unrelated to the purposeful activity below. She scooted backward with its wireless keyboard in hand until the wall touched her back. If she managed to activate the terminal and set its display into flat mode, whatever she did should be invisible from the floor below.

Murmurs and music whispered, snatches of speech from terminals and conversations below. Acoustical vagaries, echoes from the dome overhead, and her limited fluency reduced it all nearly to babble. Nearly, but not quite: Scattered words and phrases were intelligible. "Human" and "wild humans" were distinct enough, and several mentions of known space, and something she must have misunderstood, about a suspicious arm.

She could not get past the welcome display. Administrative or not, the terminal expected biometric authentication. Beyond turning the terminal on, all Kirsten had managed to do was to dim the display, still in floating holographic mode, to pale translucence. Faint characters continued to invite an authorizing tongueprint.

She caught Eric's eye. He shrugged, as unsuccessful as she at spotting anything useful. His face was mottled, pinkish-purple and pale. His chest moved shallowly but rapidly. She thought she heard wheezing. Whatever asthma was, she had to get him to an autodoc.

The hike from the safety shelter and its stepping disc had taken hours. Could Eric make it back? He needed medical attention *now*. Without a stepping disc, that meant making their presence known. Surrendering.

The still-scrolling characters of the welcome prompt taunted her. She restored the terminal, as best she could remember it, to the brightness level where she had found it, and powered it down. It had all been for nothing.

As she slithered on her belly back toward Eric, her communicator trilled. Omar. "Not now," she whispered.

"Spaceport control has lost patience. In fifteen minutes, if *Explorer* is not ready to launch, they will send help. I'll have to tell spaceport control I've been covering for your absence."

On the level below, Citizen voices rose and fell, at once lyrical and discordant. Holograms floated about, appearing and vanishing to the unknowable purposes of the staff. Sentries still ringed the stepping discs. Even if they could be activated, they would only access another restricted area.

The only access she and Eric had found to the gallery was from outdoors. How did Citizens get to and from this level? They clearly never arrived at the institute by land, or there would have been guards outside. She began crawling the long way round to Eric. Halfway there she found a stepping disc in the floor. She waved for his attention. "Get our boots," she mouthed. "Wrap them in your shirt."

Most likely, the disc would only move them to the busy main area below the gallery. Maybe they could alter it . . .

Carefully, they pried up the disc. Eric, now shirtless, eyed the controls set in the edge. "It looks standard—with the minor problem that the customary maintenance keypad has been removed. Anything could be in the memory chip." His lips were blue and his breathing labored. "Maybe, if we remove the programming chip, it will reset to default settings." Cough. "Not that we know where its default setting would send us."

"There's no way to give it an address?"

"Only by communicator, and only then with an authentication code we can't give it."

They were out of options. "Eric, we have to turn ourselves in. You need medical help, and soon."

Cough. "I didn't know you cared."

"You came along to help me. That makes you my responsibility." And, if not in the way Eric would wish it, she found she *did* care. "Unless you have a better idea."

"You walk out. I tell them I came alone."

The offer made Kirsten feel even worse. "We're in this together."

The murmuring below continued to taunt her. Through the railing, holograms came and went: Colonists/humans. A grain ship. The nature-preserve world, now revealing enough continental outline through its clouds to suggest NP5. Still-indistinguishable hints of text.

Why a grain ship and NP5? The newest world in the Fleet was still being eco-formed. It had no grain to export. "Eric, that's NP5, isn't it?"

"I don't know." Cough. "Maybe. Judging by the amount of cloud cover. Geography isn't my strong point."

The Human Studies Institute had interest in NP5. That sufficed to pique *her* interest. Kirsten pointed at the disc. "Let's remove the memory chip. There's only one way to find out the disc's default address. Worst case, we'll surrender there."

"All right."

She pried out the part.

"Wait. Not like that." Cough. "Say we get away. The next time someone here uses this disc, they'll also be sent to the default location. Someone will check out the disc, and see that the chip is gone." Cough. "They'll see that someone has tampered with the disc." Wheezing, he took the chip from her, bent a pin and put the chip back into place. "Let them think the chip had a bent pin all along, and the bent pin just now came completely unplugged. Random floor vibrations, not intruders." Together they set the disc back into the floor.

He picked up an awkward parcel, their boots knotted inside his shirt, and stepped. He did not reappear on the level below. She stepped after—

To join him among a crowd of gaping Citizens. A holo-sign labeled the nearest structure as *Department of Public Safety*. The default disc address, of course.

"Let's go," she said. She took his arm and pulled/lifted him toward an array of public stepping discs.

After several random hops through public spaces, they popped aboard *Explorer*. Omar's eyes widened, and she could only imagine how bedraggled they must look.

"Two minutes to spare," Kirsten said. "I'll get Eric into the autodoc. *You* get us on our way."

· 18 ·

Nessus bowed to no sane sentient when it came to caution. Of course, he was *in*sane and sadly aware of it. He could not otherwise be so distant from Hearth and herd. He could not otherwise be hurtling through the nothingness of hyper-space. Alone with his insanity, grazing absentmindedly from a trencher of freshly synthesized mixed grains, he contem-plated another's insanity—and wondered if he had finally met his match.

For Sigmund Ausfaller was paranoid, and his delusions of persecution made him a formidable adversary. Nessus understood paranoia, although among Colonists it was treated. Among the wild humans, within the ARM, para-noia was nurtured—even induced.

To be paranoid was to inflate one's importance, to see oneself as worthy of persecution. Paranoids found things to worry about that no sane person could. Such a fear might sometimes prove not so irrational after all. Where Pup-peteers were concerned, Ausfaller's suspicions had become a self-fulfilling prophecy.

The meal was disagreeably dry. Nessus synthesized a flagon of carrot juice to accompany it. The beverage was totally without nutritional value for him but he liked it nonetheless. It was one of the few pleasures available to him aboard *Aegis*.

Another was the larger-than-life holo with which Nessus shared the bridge. He had taken the image at one of the earliest Experimentalist rallies he had ever attended. Perhaps Nike had meant the adoring expression for the entire crowd; Nessus chose to imagine it otherwise.

But first he had a mission to complete.

In his paranoia, Ausfaller hunted for Puppeteers years after all had departed. Nike had learned that fact from their most highly placed spy. Where, then, did the ARM seek? For what?

Reason as distrustfully as Ausfaller, Nessus told himself. Put yourself into his place.

General Products made its technology crucial to the economies of humans and their neighbors—and then disappeared, plunging those economies into chaos.

Perhaps it had been a mistake to humor the term "Puppeteer." To humans a Citizen's heads might look like a pair of sock puppets, but—imagine how a paranoid would interpret aliens embracing *that* label.

Put yourself in Ausfaller's place.

A world is too big to hide, hence it should long ago have been found. That worlds could be moved surely remained beyond the imagination of the wild humans, so failure to find the Puppeteers must only reinforce Ausfaller's theories of conspiracy.

A syllogism: All the UN's resources would have found the homeworld. The homeworld has not been found. Ergo: Some resources have been diverted, or some discoveries hidden.

Ausfaller deduced a Puppeteer secret agent in the ARM. QED.

Nessus shivered. The ARM had likely leaked news of his latest search, hoping to lure Puppeteers and their agents into exposing themselves. Any of Nessus' usual sources within the UN might now work with Ausfaller, or, unknowingly, be under his observation.

Nessus contemplated his dilemma, food and drink abandoned, picking anxiously at his mane. He needed a whole new approach to gleaning Ausfaller's strategy. He needed to recruit anonymously a whole new network. Could he act quickly enough to protect the Fleet?

All hope of return to Hearth and Nike receded into the very indefinite future.

SOL SYSTEM WAS home to scant billions, but those few knew no fear. They filled its skies with interplanetary yachts and liners, tugs and freighters, Belter patrol ships and UN frigates. To those argosies were added yet more, the many starships that plied the void to far-flung human colonies and the worlds of Kzinti and Kdatlyno.

Nessus intended that his presence go unnoticed by all those teeming craft. He approached Sol system tangentially, rather than head-on, and at a steep angle to the plane of the ecliptic. He dropped *Aegis* from hyperspace into the anonymous outer reaches of the Oort Cloud—

And, from habit, he reached toward his console to run a deep-radar scan.

He jerked the head back. *Aegis* had just exited hyperspace far from the singularity, the better to let dissipate unremarked the unavoidable ripples of his emergence. Why emit a discretionary neutrino pulse?

Did he think to find a stasis box *here*?

He looked himself in the eyes, appalled and amused at the near-lapse. It could be worse, he supposed. He could be mystified, too, as Kirsten had wondered at being trained to emit a deep-radar ping on approach to a new star system.

Nessus burst into song as, with full thrusters, he slowed the ship's headlong plunge. *Ride of the Valkyries* in full orchestration. The music seemed somehow apt. Doubly apt, really, in that his erstwhile crew had once thoroughly enjoyed a performance.

Trust Kirsten to notice phonetic similarities between

English and German. Coincidence, he had told her. What was one more deception?

Had she dutifully deep-scanned *Explorer*'s most recent destination, wondering what there was to be learned that way?

If she only knew.

Eons ago there had been a war of galactic extermination, of which naught remained but scattered artifacts preserved for eternity within stasis fields. Most objects recovered from stasis storage defied understanding. All embodied technologies of terrifying potency. The prevailing opinion was that these were weapons caches.

The one course of action more frightening than to locate and open a stasis box was to leave it for another race to find.

The stasis field was opaque to neutrino pulses. Only degenerate matter, like the collapsed central mass of a star, shared that property. A stasis field could not be missed—so it was foolish to look for a stasis box in such a heavily traveled region as Sol system.

As his singing swelled to a crescendo, enjoying his manic glee while it lasted, Nessus could not help wondering how Omar, Eric, and Kirsten were coming on *their* mission.

A WATER WORLD sparkled through *Explorer*'s view ports. Other than the peaks of a few volcanic cones, only an immense, equatorial landmass interrupted the otherwise planet-spanning ocean. The continent's coastal regions were bright with greenery, its high central plains brown and sere. Nike, in his only active participation, had responded to an early report by naming the planet Oceanus.

Life teemed in the seas and jungles below. If she let herself, Kirsten could stare for hours every shift. Despite countless differences, Oceanus reminded her of NP4. She missed home.

"It does look nice down there." Eric sat on the relax-room deck amid a scattering of parts, things to be configured into yet another remote-sensing satellite. He had regained his normal color since the nearly disastrous expedition to the Human Studies Institute, but not yet his stamina. "In a bugs-at-the-top-of-the-food-chain sort of way."

"Nothing here to match the Gw'oth," she said.

"Not even close." As a tiny component went flying from his grasp, he muttered about fingers being too stubby and inflexible.

Rather than her smaller fingers, all she offered him was a question. "Why bother with more sensors? Nothing below can possibly be a threat to the Fleet."

"You really *are* down," Eric said.

He'd been like that with her, solicitous, since the autodoc let him out. His taste in colors had become subdued, too. She said, "It was a fool's errand. I was the fool. The best that can be said for our outing is I didn't get you killed—not quite—and we weren't caught." She trembled. She had no idea what punishment might have been meted out. Somehow, the uncertainty only made it worse.

"Kirsten, I insisted on going. I kept my medical condition secret. It's not your fault." A cough ruined his protest.

"I don't understand why the autodoc can't *fix* that." At least, if he healed completely, she would have only the failure of their quest to depress her.

"The 'doc can only treat my symptoms. It can't keep my body from producing the proteins that predispose me to asthma attacks. Only time stops that process." He sipped something from a drink bulb. "And no, the 'doc can't switch off some magic gene. There's some complex dependency involved: environmental, or multigene, or environmental *and* multigene." Cough. "That's me. I'm special."

Eric went back to his tinkering and she to planetgazing. She had a great deal of thinking to do. Either activity served to spend the time until his health would accommodate a return to the Fleet without raising unwelcome questions.

UNSAVORY.

It was the adjective Nessus associated with underworld figures. It could hardly be otherwise. To be unsavory, or worse, was surely a precondition for acting against the common good of one's species. Unsavory, fairly or not, was how he labeled the man and woman in the holo before him.

No matter that they had come at his summons: his minions.

The wild humans spoke from a light-second away. If they were surprised to encounter a hyperwave radio relay rather than a ship at the designated coordinates, they did not comment. General Products produced a near-impregnable hull, but a sufficiently serious impact would still turn *him* to jelly. A sufficiently powerful laser would vaporize the hull coating and then destroy anything within, the hull itself being transparent to visible light. There could be antimatter. . . .

This line of thought would soon have him cowering against his own belly, which he could have done without traveling so many light-years. It did nothing to protect the Fleet or to impress Nike. Better to concentrate on his goals than on improbable hazards. "What results?"

"Fertility Board records are not easy to come by," Miguel Sullivan began. He was swarthy and round-faced, with close-set eyes, a smooth scalp, and a scruffy mustache. An Earther scrubbed of body paint for space. "That was no small matter with which you tasked us."

It was no small retainer that had already been electronically transferred, from funds hopefully untraceable to General Products, with the promise of another payment upon success. "Your report," Nessus prompted again.

"Can I send you a file?" Ashley Klein's most prominent feature was a Belter Mohawk dyed shocking neon blue.

Her pale blue eyes seemed almost colorless by comparison. She towered over her colleague. The question was evidently rhetorical, because data appeared in an input buffer before Nessus answered. She said, "There have been billions of births on Earth in the past century. The overwhelming majority are what you would expect: one or two children approved for obviously healthy parents, and all Fertility Board rules clearly followed."

Nessus surveyed the file as she spoke. Those billions of births had been plotted against several different parameters. Every chart showed a nice bell curve—which meant every graph had outliers. "Clearly some couples had a third, or even a fourth child. A few applications were approved far quicker than the typical review period. There have been pregnancy complications, and a scattering of congenital disorders, despite all the screening."

"It's what I'd expect," Ashley said. "There's no more variability here than you'd predict with so many cases to be evaluated. Less, to be honest."

Nessus placed little weight in the self-professed honesty of criminals. Even his own. Even when, with only the evidence of their eyes and his virtualized transmission to guide them, he must appear a human she. "And you cross-matched those exceptions with family income?"

"Of course, since you asked." Ashley shrugged and referred him to another graphic in the file. "It's the same lack of pattern."

A pattern would have been nice; a few data points would suffice. Nessus sorted a list of the outliers against family income. While proving nothing, it yielded more than a million cases of *plausible* connivance. He transmitted back his version of the data. "Here. Now look for associations with anyone working for the Fertility Board, or to their relatives and friends."

Miguel smiled humorlessly. "Then we put the squeeze on them?"

Unsavory and picaresque. The turn of phrase was new to Nessus, but its meaning was obvious. "No. For now, let the data trickle out. Reporters. Rumors. 'Net gossip. Be creative."

Ashley rubbed her chin. "Where's the profit in that? It'll only cause chaos."

"For you it will cause money." They had the good sense to be silent when Nessus paused for any further objection. "Good. Here is another credit authorization code."

"We'll head back into the solar system then," Miguel said.

Was there a nuance of complaint at Nessus' insistence on a remote rendezvous? He did not care. Closer to the sun would make detection that much more likely. Closer to the sun, he would be within the singularity, unable to flick away from danger by hyperdrive.

Thought of departure, however premature, reminded Nessus of another transaction. "There is something I would like you to acquire for me. A collection, actually." He transmitted the details.

The humans twitched in surprise. "You're serious?" Miguel asked. "That will cost you *serious* money. A few million, I'll say five, just to determine feasibility. Much more if it can be done."

"Approved." Fifty million would hardly touch the General Products accounts here in Sol system, and Nessus could hardly come all this way without bringing Nike home a souvenir.

OMAR LOPED ON the treadmill, sweat plastering his hair to his forehead. Only the wet hair suggested that he had been exercising for long. Sweat evaporating almost instantly through his nano-cloth jumpsuit kept the rest of him cool. He said, "I would defy even Nessus to find a threat down there."

Down there: the watery planet they had now orbited for twenty-two shifts. Close observation of Oceanus by remote-controlled sensors had revealed hive creatures, like especially retarded bees, and forests of sedentary sea-bottom creatures sieving the currents for the local algae-equivalent. Geometric structures in the ocean had provided the only suggestion of artificiality, an intimation that proved to be false. Except in progress reports to Hearth, the three of them never doubted these assemblages were naturally occurring reefs. Still, experience with the Gw'oth justified checking out the undersea features with methodical indirection. To stall while Eric mended.

Which, to Kirsten's relief, he had. She pinned Eric's feet as he did sit-ups. "Do you think we'll ever know where Nessus was sent?"

"Doubt it," Eric grunted. "Forty-nine. Fifty." He flopped back onto his mat, breathing heavily but with none of the wheezing that had been so scary. "I'm ready to go back."

"To Arcadia?" Omar stepped off the treadmill. Sensing the disappearance of its load, the machine came to a stop.

"To the institute."

"What?" Kirsten asked. She had championed that first excursion, arrogantly certain they would root out long-hidden secrets. That *she* would find a way into the computers, because that was what *she* did. "Why?"

Eric wiggled his feet. "Let me up." She did, and he stood. "There had to be meaning there. I keep looking."

"You keep looking," Omar said. "Present tense. How, exactly?"

"Where did I put it?" Eric looked around until he spotted his communicator, tossed into a corner when he began exercising. He tapped at its touch screen. "Here."

A holo swallowed his hand. "Enlarge."

Kirsten stepped back to take it in. "That's . . . the institute's main floor." She peered between the virtual railings at the remembered area below. In miniature, Citizens walked about, mimed conversation, guarded stepping discs, and labored at their workstations. Shadowy images floated above, phantoms of holograms past. The sequence ran less than a minute before looping back to the beginning.

"I took this video while you crept across the gallery floor to that terminal," Eric said.

"And you never said anything," she said.

"It shows us nothing." Eric shrugged. "The problem is, I can't help but believe that it should, or that it would have, if I had taken more."

"Can we enhance this?" Omar asked.

"I wish we could," Eric answered. "Now if we had a bigger computer we could safely put this on—but that's not going to happen until we're home."

"A bigger computer? We have all we could need." Kirsten leaned over, squinting. The indistinct images tantalized her. "With the superuser privileges I cloned from Nessus, I can delete all traces afterward."

Omar broke a long silence. "Let's do it."

A THOUSAND-PLUS ENVELOPES materialized at the appointed time inside as many unlisted transfer booths. The originating coordinates recorded by the receiving booths were nulled and untraceable. The compulsory authentication checks had been similarly bypassed. The identifications implicit in supposedly mandatory real-time payments were blanked out, should any of the recipients dare to inquire of the network provider. Lest the manner of message delivery be insufficiently instructive, each envelope bore in animation the snarling, ever watchful, three-headed guardian of Hades: Cerberus.

It was enough, Nessus thought, to instill dread in the recipients even before they saw what waited within.

Subverting the humans' primitive teleportation system was easy, since the underlying technology had been licensed from General Products in the first place. The device Nessus had provided his minions for the task would have self-destructed after use. The time might arise when he wanted to trust the transfer-booth system's integrity—in the sense of knowing that its vulnerability remained intact and unsuspected.

The envelope contents were as carefully selected as the recipients. Off-world bank statements with embarrassingly large balances. Dates and places of trysts. Intimations of various cooked books, stock manipulations, tax evasions, rigged bids, undisclosed product defects, and sordid collusions. Enumerations of criminal investigations stymied or inexplicably gone dormant, of pardons granted and sentences commuted. Gambling debts, drug habits, spousal abuses, embezzlements, youthful indiscretions . . .

It required an appreciation of human society far deeper than Nessus' to grasp exactly why most of the hinted-at disclosures were problematical. That lack of understanding scarcely mattered, because his minions understood. All Nessus had required of Miguel and Ashley was invisible influence.

He sought comfort from the beginnings of progress. Riots against Fertility Board corruption had begun. Those who would provide him with influence had been put on notice. Soon enough, the recipients of those Cerberus-emblazoned envelopes would be told the price of keeping their secrets. For most, the price of forbearance would be advocacy for Fertility Board "reform." For a few, the price would be much higher. Nessus would see into the ARM itself.

For all this preliminary success, Nessus trembled. The pungency of synthetic herd pheromone could not disguise the knowledge that he was alone, the only one of his kind for light-years. It could not hasten the manipulation of the wild humans. It could not purge his fear of failure. It could not heal his aberrance, or make him more attractive to the one he loved.

Not directly, anyway.

The deliberate unfolding of the plan had one advantage. The gift Nessus wished to obtain for Nike *was* obtainable.

Its acquisition would also take time.

THE VIDEO WAS low resolution, blurry, and shot from an oblique angle. Kirsten could do nothing about the angle, but everything else was amenable to computed corrections. She enhanced edges, interpolated new scan rows to sharpen the overall picture, compensated for the worst reflections, and adjusted for Eric's tremulous camera hand.

That was better.

Scattered letters that remained ambiguous to Kirsten were nonetheless identifiable by character-recognition software. Whatever had blurred and smeared the letters had likewise distorted the rest of the image. She dug into the character-recognition algorithms, and pulled apart the pattern-analysis and pattern-matching logic. One routine at a time, she experimented.

Eric, whom she had doubted, had persevered. She had despaired, and it shamed her. Not even the deflection of the Fleet's course away from the Gw'oth had cheered her.

Never again.

Step by step the image improved.

Omar ambled onto the bridge. "Welcome back."

She realized she had worked through the sleep shift. Her hands never left the keyboard. "What do you mean?"

"I mean, Kirsten, that you were whistling."

That made her stop, if only for a moment. "I guess I was. I could kill that Eric, if he hadn't almost done it to himself already. This is *good data.*"

"Only in your hands. And only when you were ready."

Omar was right, of course.

Her fingers kept working. There was always one more tweak to try. "Wish me luck." The still image hanging before her shimmered, then settled into crisper focus: the globe of NP5. This latest addition to the Fleet was always wreathed in cloud, still early in its transformation into a haven for Hearthian life. Beside the cloudy sphere hung an icon and a string of numerals.

"Luck." Omar settled on the arm of the crash couch beside her. "That looks clearer. See anything useful?"

Finally, Kirsten lifted her hands from the keyboard. She turned to look Omar squarely in the eye. "My guess is 'useful' seriously understates it.

"There's a General Products #4 hull circling NP5. For

some reason we can't yet imagine, that ship matters to the Human Studies Institute. And *this*," and she poked her hand into the cleaned-up holo, to the string of numerals, "is the key to the stepping disc network aboard that ship."

· 19 ·

With sinuous perfection, a thousand lithe figures twirled and leapt. Hooves kicked: unerringly straight and high, impossibly precise, preternaturally synchronized in each stroke against the rock-hard stage. Voices rang out, ineffably poignant in cadence and counterpoint, melody and mode. Lines formed, split, and reformed. Formations melded and reemerged.

A thousand exemplars of perfection became one. A distraction, from questing humans and political ambition alike, that Nike sorely needed. As he watched, a much-needed calm washed over him. His heads swayed sensually, drawn to the rhythms of the dance.

"Excellency," someone whispered.

Nike's heads whipped around. Who would *dare* at such a time? The troupe had dedicated this performance to *his* honor.

"Excellency," repeated the aide. His heads drooped with chagrin and embarrassment. "There is an utmost-urgency call for you."

Whispering apologies to friends and colleagues *he* had invited to the performance, Nike pressed through the throng filling the private viewing room into a corridor empty but for some of his security detachment. The closed door muted the singing, but had no effect on the pounding of three thousand hooves. The vibration of the building continued unabated as the performance continued despite his absence.

He accepted a communicator from the cringing aide. "That's all right. It was your responsibility to tell me."

"Hello?" squawked the communicator.

"With whom am I speaking?"

The name at first meant nothing to Nike. Then the cocky attitude registered, and Nike remembered. This was the General Products employee Nessus had dubbed Baedeker.

"Deputy Minister, your staff resisted putting through my call. I insisted." Baedeker's throats rasped with emotion. "The situation is unacceptable."

Why would this engineer think to contact him? "Start at the beginning."

"It's the three Colonists, aboard *Explorer*," Baedeker said. "I can't hear them."

A ship lost? The staccato rhythms of three thousand hooves waxed and waned, making the hoarse voice on the communicator even more difficult to understand. "I don't understand. How can a ship be lost? One of *your* hulls!"

"No, sir. The ship is fine. I can't hear the crew. I can't *over*hear the crew."

For this he had been called from the grand ballet? "Continue."

"We equipped *Explorer* with listening devices with which to monitor the unsupervised Colonists. Their conversation is multiplexed into the outgoing telemetry stream."

Unsupervised Colonists. Nike chose to ignore the undertune of disapproval about the mission *he* had authorized. "What could interrupt the telemetry?"

"Nothing has. All data streams continue unabated. The Colonist recordings are fiction. Fiction!" Baedeker lapsed briefly into an unhappy hum. "They evidently altered the sensor feed into the telemetry subsystem."

Nike waited out a torrent of words about sampling techniques and autocorrelation. The details hardly mattered. *Explorer*'s crew had substituted random repeats of recorded conversations and ambient noises—and Baedeker had noticed only now. First the altercation aboard the General Products factory, and now this. Twice the Colonists had bested the engineer. Nike kept his amusement to himself, giving the Colonists credit for maintaining their privacy.

Citizens rarely wanted privacy. Colonists often did. Nike wished he could see *Explorer*'s crew, observe their clothing and jewelry. That would tell him much about their mindsets, almost what he could glean by observing a Citizen's mane. Of course a Colonist was a laborer. Laborers had little time for proper grooming of their manes. They took much less time over programmable clothing and nano-spun jewelry.

Thunderous ululations from the packed theater announced the end of the second dance movement. Nike asked, "What about the reports from *Explorer*?"

"They seem credible," Baedeker said.

That was rather grudging. "Do you see any inconsistencies in the data? Odd results? Any reason at all to question their findings?"

"No. If anything they are ploddingly thorough in their studies."

"Then let us accept their desire for privacy, and let them do their work for us." Setting aside thoughts of humans and Colonists alike, Nike reimmersed himself in the beauty of the dance.

OMAR AND ERIC were rehearsing dialogue for a fresh voice recording, another faked bridge conversation. They were ad-libbing a little, trying to crack each other up, defying with their laughter the nothingness of hyperspace.

Kirsten stood unseen outside the relax-room door, listening, and asking herself one last time: Do I want to do this?

And realized that she very much did.

It scared Kirsten to remember how often she had spurned Eric's advances. Would he now spurn her?

He had matured into someone confident, supportive, and self-deprecating—into someone she very much admired. Perhaps that growth meant he would no longer have interest in her. She had to make a grand gesture.

She had to risk rejection as publicly as she had rejected him.

Kirsten stepped into view. "Eric," she called out. "May I have a word with you?"

Both men turned, and stared.

Eric followed her in silence into her cabin. The room was cramped, not much more than sleeper-field plates equipped with crash webbing. Eric managed to close the door without brushing against her. For a long time, he was at a loss for words. "About your outfit," he finally managed.

Her jumpsuit shone a fiery red, trimmed with warm yellow accents, the colors more vibrant than any she had ever seen him wear. "I hope you like it."

He looked like he wanted to ask: why? Instead he said, "You already know my medical problems. They're genetic."

Kirsten took his hands. "I have wisdom teeth." When he looked puzzled, she explained. "Extra teeth. Too many for my jaw. If I hadn't had surgery, they could have grown horizontally or pushed out other teeth. In many people, the crowding causes jaw pain and headaches." The problem was easily corrected, and in fact the extracted teeth could be saved for transplants, but she wanted to make a point. No one was perfect.

His eyes narrowed appraisingly. She imagined he was weighing the risks to their hypothetical children, as society expected. All he said was, "That's not so bad."

"Anyway, now you know. And my grandfather ruptured an artery in his brain. He was hiking alone. Help didn't come in time. He was only seventy-one. I thought I should tell you."

Eric gave her hands a squeeze. "You're beautiful and fun and *brilliant*. How could teeth possibly matter? Kirsten, could you consider me a proper mate?"

"Yes. Yes. You believed in me. You brought me back when I had given up." Releasing his hands, Kirsten put her arms around his neck. He had been sweating.

He enfolded her waist. It felt right.

Like Citizens, Colonists seldom spoke about mating

practices, but they did touch, and frequently. She could not help wondering: How much of this behavior is *human*? How much has been imprinted—inflicted—on us in hopes of more and fitter laborers?

She shook off the sudden cynicism. Now was not the time.

"Not being a total idiot," Eric said, "I want to join our lives. Shall we?"

"I bind myself. We'll still need genetic counseling," which was mandatory before a union could be made official, "but—" Kirsten trailed off, at a loss for words.

"And I bind myself." Eric broke into a grin as goofy as the one she knew she was wearing. "I have *got* to change the color of my clothes." To the pastels of a mated man, he probably meant.

"No," Kirsten answered. "You need to take them off."

· 20 ·

"You're sure about this?" Omar called from the bridge.

"Yes!" Eric and Kirsten answered in unison. "For the last time," Kirsten continued, as she sifted backpack contents. "Are *you* ready?"

"We're holding position. Thrusters are working hard to do it."

Kirsten peered out the relax-room's view port. Even at full magnification, the institute's mysterious GP #4 hull was invisible. NP5, around which it orbited, loomed largest of the six worlds of the Fleet.

Explorer, under power, raced along a distant arc concentric with that orbit. Only a chance visual sighting could reveal their presence. *Explorer*'s space-traffic-control transponder was silenced, and its stealthing mode was active.

In theory, everyone in the Fleet thought *Explorer* far away, still studying Oceanus. In practice, Omar relayed reports and fictitious telemetry through the hyperwave buoy they had left behind. The doubled distance made no difference to instantaneous communications, and Hearth received the incoming signal from the expected bearing.

Are we really clever, Kirsten wondered, or delusional?

"We *are* better prepared," Eric said.

Could he read her mind? The unstated comparison was to the expedition she had planned, to the Human Studies Institute. Or, more accurately, had scarcely planned. She answered, "If the stepping-disc network is configured as we expect."

"Even if Citizens weren't systematic by nature, why *wouldn't* there be a standard addressing scheme used aboard ships? Why waste the energy to invent one each time?"

If Eric were correct, the addressing scheme on that GP4 ship matched the stepping-disc network on *Explorer*. They would reappear unattended in a storeroom aboard the mystery ship. And if he were wrong? They could pop up anywhere. In a mess hall. Onto the bridge. She had never seen a Citizen's toilet—

"Guys," Omar prompted.

"We're ready," Eric said. Communicator in hand, he tried the first address in the presumed subnet range for storerooms. "Still here. Do you suppose there'll be gravity?" He tried another. A third.

And vanished.

Kirsten gave him ten seconds to pop back, if he had found himself somewhere unfortunate, or with a witness, or otherwise to simply vacate the destination disc. "Omar, wish us luck." She took her backpack and stepped—

INTO A CAVERNOUS storeroom, dancing briskly toward a wall.

Eric caught her, sparing her from a fall. "It happened to me, too," he said. "Not the best velocities match."

What was the magic number? Two hundred feet per second was what she recalled. They must have been just on the cusp. A bit more velocity difference and the paired discs would not have allowed the transfer. A bit less and the momentum compensation would have been perfect.

If Citizens never envisioned an intruder crossing a few miles of predator-free forest, they *surely* never imagined a hundred-thousand mile jump between ships matching courses and speeds. "Under the circumstances, the match seems plenty precise to me."

They walked quickly through aisles until they found a terminal. Eric knelt to unload his backpack. He was still wearing pastels and a topaz ring that matched her own. "Look around while I do this. Keep an ear open. If we get caught, we're courting and a little goofy."

As though that would excuse a stolen starship and sneaking aboard one of the best-kept secrets in the Concordance. Kirsten smiled but said nothing.

The plan was simple. Crew communicators were portable; hence ships had wireless networks. So: In some deep recess of the storeroom, hide a network sniffer. It would catch and store the radio packets flying by. Also hide a vidphone with good lines of sight and hearing on the terminal.

On some future visit, they would retrieve the stored data. Keyed or verbal commands the gear captured during inventory draw-downs would provide an unencoded data sample with which to crack encryption on the shipboard network. Crew login sequences, if they could catch one, would be a bonus, although tongueprint biometrics was more likely.

Kirsten explored as Eric worked, snaking through aisle after aisle of tanks and bins. Finally past the raw-material repositories, she made her way between shelves piled high with everything from complex photonic components to large structural assemblies. Those must be either too complex or too large to synthesize quickly.

"Eric," she whispered. Almost certainly their communicators would go unnoticed here, but why take even that small chance? In her mind's eye, Nessus bobbed his heads, up/down, down/up, approving her caution. "Eric. How's it going?"

"Sniffer is hidden," he whispered back. "I'm working on a power hookup. It would be a shame if we couldn't get back aboard before the batteries drained. How are we doing for time?"

Her wrist implant was in stopwatch mode. "Eight minutes left." Eight minutes until Omar attempted another precise velocity match to enable their return. Thereafter, Omar would match courses again every five minutes, pacing the unseen ship.

She walked on. More bins and parts, components and supplies. Spare synthesizers. Emergency rations (grass and grains) in case the synthesizers all failed at once. Nothing instructive. The next glance at her wrist showed six minutes. "Eric?"

"I found accessible power lines for the sniffer and vidphone. I can use inductive taps. I'm snaking our power lines behind stacks of stuff."

Clever. Kirsten wouldn't have thought of that. An inductive coupler clipped over a power line, drawing off energy without ever interrupting the electrical flow. Very stealthy.

She reached a dead end. "Four minutes. I'm coming back."

The anticlimactic smoothness made her want to scream. We haven't *learned* anything, Kirsten thought, except that we can get aboard. In minutes they would return to *Explorer*.

"Done," Eric called. "Come on back."

There *must* be something here, some further clue in the long series of signs. To wait until they next managed to return, hoping to find decipherable data—it was intolerable.

Three minutes. Kirsten reversed course past emergency rations, chemicals, parts. . . .

She sped right passed Eric, rushing through the aisles she had not yet explored, looking for something very specific and low-tech.

The storeroom held emergency rations and large structural elements. Survival gear would not be accessible only by stepping disc. Big stuff would not fit through the only stepping disc they had seen, in the storeroom's center. Logically, the storeroom had to have a physical door—and she still wasn't *sure* until she saw it.

A big square door with an inset window.

"Eric," she called. "Come here."

"Time's almost up," he answered from aisles distant.

"Now, Eric." She stared out the window, across a broad corridor, through a clear wall. A vast space, the central volume of the giant GP4 hull, gaped before her.

Suspended in its center, was, undeniably, an alien spaceship. A ramscoop.

Faded English letters on its scarred and ancient hull declared it the *Long Pass*.

REBIRTH Earth date: 2650

21

Side by side, Kirsten and Eric stared at *Long Pass*. Their wrist implants beeped almost simultaneously. Eric panned a quick view of the ramscoop with his communicator. "Omar will be matching course in a minute."

"Go ahead." Beyond the door and to Kirsten's left, a light flickered randomly. "I'll be right behind you."

Eric strode back into the maze of shelves. She took the cessation of footsteps to mean he had teleported back successfully. "In a few minutes, that is," she clarified now that he couldn't argue. *One* of them had to take back word of their find before anyone—she—took yet more risk.

She had seen old dates embedded within the serial numbers of some stockpiled parts. Dust covered the shelves themselves and most items on them. The flickering light outside the storeroom removed all doubt from her mind: This region of the ship had gone unvisited for a *long* time. Citizens would not leave a failing LED along the route to emergency supplies.

With a faint squeak, the door opened to Kirsten's touch.

She peered into the hall and saw no one. Feeling like a very small fish in a very large fishbowl, Kirsten ran, clutching her communicator, along the curved corridor to the spidery catwalk which led to *Long Pass*. With luck, software would compensate for the shaking and bouncing to render a good picture. She crawled onto the catwalk . . . but yes, there was gravity. She could safely run across.

Heart pounding, Kirsten dashed through the derelict's airlock, its hatches both open. Her wrist implant showed nearly four minutes until her next opportunity to return to *Explorer*. Thinking any ship must have something like a bridge, and that bridges belonged in the bow, she headed forward.

Crisp-edged corners, without trace of the melted look

favored by Citizens. Beds and chairs glimpsed through open doors: Colonist normal. The latches on those hatches: equally ordinary, mounted at a height natural for Colonists. The ceiling glow that brightened when she stuck her head into a cabin was pleasant to her eyes. The holo cube she found lodged behind a small fold-down shelf showed men, women, and children.

In countless small ways, the vessel was undeniably Colonist. Or was the correct term *human*?

Kirsten kept shooting video as she sped through the ship, still seeking the bridge. Scarcely a minute until the next pick-up opportunity. She *should* return to the store-room and its stepping disc.

She plunged ahead.

Another cabin, as familiar as anything on NP4. A larger room of uncertain purpose, on whose wall hung a mundane to-do list on curled, brittle paper—the tasks handwritten in English. Holos everywhere. An apparent cargo hold, its deck half empty, its shelves picked nearly clean. Tiedowns and braces on all the shelves. Gravity or free fall, the ship would accommodate both.

Beep. "I'll be back in five more minutes." Kirsten was not sure to whom she made the promise.

At last: the bridge. Crash couches. Controls meant for hands like hers. More holos.

Kirsten froze. That empty cargo hold! Without a doubt, its contents had been removed to Hearth for study. Its cargo probably resided deep in the bowels of the Human Studies Institute.

Maybe this GP4 ship had landed on Hearth, and the cargo had been extracted there. Maybe the cargo had been moved to a docking bay for offloading into a smaller Citizen ship for a flight to Hearth. It didn't matter which. The insight was that the cargo had been removed—and surely not over that narrow catwalk.

Kirsten raced back to the empty cargo hold. She found a stepping disc on the deck between two mostly empty shelves. Although she had expected to find it, the disc looked out of place. Grafted on. Her wrist showed a bit more than two minutes until Omar next matched course and speed. That gave her more than ample time in which to collect a souvenir.

She had noticed a decoration in one of the cabins, a handicraft of some unfamiliar kind. It hung on the same bulkhead as the hatch. No one could see the artwork's presence—or absence—without entering the cabin.

The artwork crudely rendered an image of flowers and shells in thousands of tiny knots and stitches. The background was tightly woven material. Texture could be a hologram, so she brushed it with her fingertips. Knots and background alike felt like natural filaments of some kind. The colors were muted—faded?—and the wooden frame battered. She took the decoration and frame, unsure why they seemed important. One corner of the wooden frame bore matching holes on its front and back edges. She guessed at a small animal's tooth marks.

Less than two minutes.

She dashed to *Long Pass*'s cargo bay. Her wrist beeped softly and she took one last video image. Then she activated her transport controller—

And stepped into *Explorer*'s relax room.

"Kirsten's back!" Eric said, presumably for Omar. "What happened?"

"I took a quick look around." She handed him the primitive picture in its wooden frame. "Impulse buy."

Omar appeared at the doorway. "Kirsten, what were you *thinking*?"

She projected the newest image in her communicator. The holo showed a small portion of the cargo hold, a stepping disc, and a nearby fifteen-digit label. "I was thinking that with this address and *Explorer* for course matching, we can board our ancestors' starship at will."

22

Thousands of humans swarmed the wide boulevard, waving placards and chanting slogans. Tens of thousands more shouted from behind barricades. Golden spheres the size of a grapefruit floated overhead: copseyes. The remotes carried sonic stunners; the beams they emitted were invisible, but not their effects.

The crowd grew frantic as more and more people fell. Then black-armored ARMs surged into the holo, shoulder to shoulder, rank after rank. The crowd stampeded, trampling anyone unfortunate enough to lose his footing. Soon the avenue was empty but for a few broken bodies and abandoned signs. A hand-lettered banner fluttered by, folds and tangles obstructing much of its message. "Bir . . . otteries Justic . . . eople." Sirens wailed, Doppler effects differentiating police vehicles in pursuit of the protestors from ambulances on approach.

"Where is this?" Nessus finally asked.

"Kansas City, Missouri." His holographic avatar must have conveyed incomprehension, because Ashley added, "That's a middling city in North America." She had come alone this trip, perhaps reassured by the knowledge that Nessus would only meet her over hyperwave relay.

"How many dead?" Nessus told himself these few had been sacrificed to spare countless more. Before spending months with only Colonists for company that rationalization might have quelled his guilt.

"Twelve in this incident." Ashley squinted at him—at his avatar, anyway. "Why exactly is birthright policy so important to you?"

"How many worldwide?"

"Hundreds." She tossed her head, and her Mohawk quivered. Today it was bright orange. "Nessus, why are we *doing* this?"

"Conscience seems inconvenient in your line of work." Or his own. Nessus blanked the holo of riot coverage. "Never mind. The important question is: Has the ARM been diverted?"

"Some. Look, Nessus, Miguel and I had no idea you meant to stir up so much trouble."

Bribery, intimidation, and rumormongering raised no objections. It was comforting somehow to see his minions exhibit traces of conscience. "The right to have children should not depend on your political connections." Stealing a glance at a holo of Nike, Nessus wondered whose political system he questioned.

"Why don't we just focus on our business," Ashley said at last. A brittle tone conveyed her disapproval.

That was fine with Nessus. He had questions about several of Miguel's recent reports. How credible was the coerced information? Had new prey been made aware of incriminating deposits made in their names? Had spying devices been planted as Nessus had requested?

It all *seemed* to be unfolding according to plan. Sipping carrot juice, Nessus asked, "What news about that item I want to purchase?"

"It took most of your five million to be sure, but we feel we can acquire it." Ashley straightened in her seat. "Forty million more. Half up front, half on delivery."

"How soon?" he asked.

"Give us a month."

"Agreed." Nessus transmitted bank codes. "You and your colleague do excellent work."

"I guess we're done. Same time, next month?"

"Yes." Even a smuggler's ship, capable of doing thirty gees, needed time to reach the fringes of the solar system. He could not expect his Earth minions to come so far any more frequently. As Ashley reached out, likely to sever their hyperwave radio link, a new thought occurred to Nessus. "Wait."

Her hand paused in mid-air. "All right."

There were more ways to stir the pot. "The problem we

have highlighted is that a few of the politically connected have bought birthrights. Perhaps we should separate the political and financial aspects. Surely the ability to make money is a proven survival characteristic. Why *not* sell birthrights legally?"

"You're kidding, right?" she said. "If that notion gets out, we'll have class riots, too."

"If you don't care for my money . . ."

Ashley swallowed but said nothing.

"See to it." Nessus had still another idea: gladiator fights. Winner gets a birthright; loser dies. Everything balances.

It turned his stomach, too. Maybe he would wait to bring that up. "I'll see you in a month."

BUT FOR HIS piercing, dark-brown eyes, the figure in the holo was unimposing: short and thickset, middle-aged, and moonfaced. His dark hair was thick and wavy, and a thin mustache was just growing in. The man paced in a small and cluttered office. He wore a jet-black business suit, doubly stark for being worn on Earth by a native, a flatlander.

His name was Sigmund Ausfaller, and he was the enemy.

Miguel's report, no matter how often Nessus reviewed it, never got better.

UN officials were no less corruptible than anyone else. If it were worth doing the calculation, Nessus thought he might find they were more corruptible. That this holo video had found its way to him proved that venality reached deep within the world government.

One problem with paranoids, of course, was that they assumed any temptation was a trap. Ausfaller had shunned all attempts to compromise him. At least, Nessus thought, the incorruptible ARM was on occasion within view of officials with fewer scruples.

Nessus returned his attention to the surreptitiously made recording. The holo had been taken by someone standing in Ausfaller's office doorway. The video caught an oblique view of the Bureau of Alien Affairs logo that shimmered on the surface of the open door.

"Sigmund is being secretive about his work, even by his standards." The comment was presumably dubbed after the video. "Maybe his computer display will tell you something."

Nessus zoomed in on the 3-D scatter plot that hung above Ausfaller's desk. Once he had reoriented himself to the human convention of showing galactic north on top, the holo looked like a star chart of Human Space and its immediate neighborhood, centered on Sol system. Almost certainly it was an information-free privacy image, popped up when Ausfaller heard footsteps approaching.

He fidgeted with his mane. Almost was not certain. "Match image with onboard navigational data," Nessus directed.

"All star positions match," the bridge computer answered.

A useless report—or was it? "Star *positions* match. Do the indicated stellar attributes differ from your records in any way?"

"Colors differ for some stars," the computer replied.

"Exaggerate color differences." Nessus craned his necks, eyeing the holo from all sides. The revised image muted most stars to a common dimness while brightening a few scattered suns. It still told Nessus nothing. "Which are the populated solar systems?"

Several stars grew pale haloes, both among the faint majority and the highlighted few that might be of interest to Ausfaller. Nessus still did not understand why. Perhaps Ausfaller's present obsession had nothing to do with the Concordance. The brighter dots clustered near the center and at the top of the map.

If the stars told Nessus nothing, perhaps starships would. The reports that had brought Nessus here said Ausfaller was investigating missing starships. "Computer, correlate this graphic with public records of interstellar travel." Such data was a very small part of what his minions had provided.

It was an expansive request. Nessus stared at the frozen image of Ausfaller as he waited for a response. "What are you looking for?" he warbled softly. The holo was as unforthcoming as the man.

"Computer, are all color discrepancies the same?"

"Yes."

This was getting him nowhere. Perhaps the star chart *was* merely a paranoid's meaningless decoy for the benefit of passersby. Am I not insane enough, Nessus thought, without inventing new reasons?

"I have a match," the computer interrupted Nessus' musing. "The falsely colored stars correlate with selective reports of human hyperdrive-ship disappearances. The selection criterion appears to be disappearances unassociated with incidents of warfare."

Nessus twitched. So much for his hope the display could be dismissed. "How many such ship disappearances have there been?"

"Twelve."

Humans had had hyperdrive for about four hundred years. Twelve ships gone astray in that time . . . excluding known Kzinti "incidents" . . . weren't many. Why was Ausfaller looking at this?

The cluster near Sol system made sense: human traffic concentrated here. Whether by equipment failure or pilot error, logically most accidents would happen nearby.

Why was there a second cluster?

"How recent are the three events near the top of the display?" Nessus asked.

"This one"—a dot momentarily flared—"two Earth years ago. The others, this year."

Suddenly Nessus realized why those dots bothered him. These recent ship losses appeared to involve exploration to the galactic north just beyond Human Space—

In the general direction of the Fleet of Worlds.

NIKE REFUSED TO identify the scout responsible. Abstractly Nessus respected that. Who hardly mattered. What did matter was the bad judgment involved.

Not very long ago Nessus had by reflex almost triggered a deep-radar scan of Sol system. Such was not only *his* engrained habit. Most pilots—of all species—did it, certainly whenever they entered a new solar system.

The intelligent species of Known Space prized similar worlds, orbiting similar suns. The biological requirements were like enough and colonizable planets rare enough to have engendered wars, most recently between humans and Kzinti. Knowing which solar systems would most quickly draw explorers, Nike's unnamed scout had set traps in the wake of the Fleet.

The bait was elegantly simple: large masses of neutronium orbiting the most appealing planet of the most suitable solar systems. Neutronium occurred naturally only in the core of a neutron star—the collapsed remains of a supernova. Neutronium was incredibly dense. At one-hundred billion metric tons per cubic centimeter, a neutronium sphere a mere few meters in diameter was an enormous mass.

Arriving pilots, conditioned to scanning each new solar system with deep radar, would see what appeared to be a stasis container abandoned since that ancient war of extermination. Pilots could hardly be expected to wonder whether a compact opacity seen in their deep radar scans might be neutronium.

The lure would be overwhelming.

When an unsuspecting ship too closely approached the tiny moon, the gravitational attraction would be likewise irresistible. No ship. No report. No likelihood of exploration yet further into the unknown, and with it the possible chance discovery of the Fleet.

They had failed to consider what a few such disappearances could reveal to a paranoid like Ausfaller.

Nessus pawed restlessly at the cabin deck with a forehoof—but where could he run? Ausfaller could not be bought. He could not be coerced. And not even Earth's worst civic unrest in centuries had distracted the man.

Perhaps it was time to eliminate Ausfaller. For enough more money, Nessus' minions might well undertake that.

Succeed or fail, how could that not raise suspicions? What sort of in-the-event-of-my-death message would someone as paranoid as Ausfaller have arranged?

Nessus pawed again, and with feeling, at the deck. He knew just where he had to run: toward danger.

The situation was not irremediable, not quite. He thought he saw one way out. It required that he have help—very specialized help—and not the sort of service Miguel and Ashley were qualified to provide at *any* price.

He would have to go deep into the solar system and enlist just the right physicist.

· 23 ·

Burning profligately through their energy reserves, Kirsten eased *Explorer* through the atmosphere of NP4. The ship's thrusters whined in protest and strain.

Explorer was matte black and radar stealthed, the better to scout in secrecy. Its traffic-control transponder, silenced since their unauthorized return to the Fleet, remained off. Their deliberate, energy-gulping descent eliminated the fiery heat and ionization trail of a normal reentry. The only way their return might be detected was visually. Over the remote expanse of ocean she had selected, and at night, that risk was vanishingly small.

The ship settled into the water with a splash. Protective force fields activated by the impact squeezed Kirsten momentarily. "Is everyone all right?" she asked.

"In a mildly bruised way," Omar answered. He occupied the other crash couch on the bridge. "You, Eric?"

"I'm fine." Eric's answer came by intercom from the engine room.

Explorer wallowed in the swells, the undulating ocean surface sparkling by NP light. Clouds rose and fell in the view ports. Kirsten tuned out her queasiness to focus on status readouts. "The main thrusters are a bit warm, but that's the only off-nominal condition I see. Is everyone ready to submerge?"

"And get off these waves?" Omar looked pale. "I'm definitely ready."

"I will be once you release the refueling probes," Eric said. The probes were emergency equipment, little more than self-propelled stepping discs fitted with filters. They would transmit deuterium and tritium from seawater directly into *Explorer*'s tanks.

Kirsten ejected the probes, and imagined she could hear the splashes. Their hydro-jets started on command. "Probes away and reporting normally." There was no alternative to a low-power radio link for monitoring and directing the probes. "Down we go."

She pressed the bow into the water with maneuvering thrusters, and then engaged more thrusters to drive *Explorer* slowly beneath the surface. Air-filled, the ship was very buoyant; it slewed disquietingly until it slipped completely underwater. She increased thrust, driving them toward their target depth of three hundred feet. They hoped to be invisible there, even under daylight conditions.

I'm in an indestructible hull, she kept reminding herself.

"This is really eerie," Eric said from the corridor just outside the bridge. He stood in a slight crouch, the better to peer through the bridge view ports.

Kirsten looked up from her instruments. Through the deepening gloom she caught glimpses of ocean life, more often due to its bioluminescence than because it approached the hull.

Hearthian ocean life, she thought, surprised at a sudden rush of bitterness. What animals teemed in the seas of her ancestral world? If *Long Pass* had carried any specimens, she knew of none that had been introduced into the oceans of this world.

A bevy of creatures fluttered past, their maneuvering more reminiscent of Hearthian birds than the— humanistic?—freshwater fish Kirsten knew from Arcadia.

She squinted, grasping for detail before they swam out of sight. She had to settle for impressions rather than a clear image. Webbed tentacles, undulating. Bioluminescent patches, in purple and gold. Ropy integument. With no way to measure the distance and nothing to use for scale, the swimmers' size was unknowable.

"Approaching three hundred feet," Omar said, watching the radar readings. "The sea bottom is down another four hundred feet."

"Thanks." Kirsten adjusted thrusters to just offset their buoyancy, and then cautiously engaged the autopilot. This was their first opportunity to test the software she had retrofitted to manage underwater hovering. *Explorer* wobbled and weaved as she lifted her hands slowly from the controls. Tilting and surging unpredictably, the ship jittered about the position where she meant it to stay. Kirsten tweaked program parameters until their orientation stabilized—which was, unfortunately, long after Omar had vomited explosively.

"I'll clean this up," Eric told Omar. "Change your clothes. Wash up. Do whatever you need to do." Omar smiled wanly, and left to comply.

After scrubbing and wiping down the area, Eric settled into the empty crash couch. He pulled up status holos. "The probes are working properly, and we're getting fuel. In a few days, we'll be adequately fueled for flying around the Fleet." His expression seemed to ask where she thought they might go next.

Omar's return spared her from speculating. He had replaced his soiled ship's suit with formal attire. "I look forward to getting onto dry land." He swallowed hard as the ship trembled in its hover. "*Solid* land."

Kirsten adjusted her own garb until she judged it suitably casual for her next stop. "Eric, will you be all right here by yourself?"

He nodded.

She checked the content of her backpack one last time.

"Then Omar and I will be on our way. Take care." She hugged Eric hard.

She walked with Omar to the relax room. He paused beside a stepping disc. "Join me when you can, Kirsten. I'll message you with the coordinates. Encrypted, of course."

Then Omar was gone.

Her communicator was preset with another address. Kirsten activated it and stepped—

To the public square nearest the Colonial Archives. She was thousands of miles from *Explorer,* and a string of suns hung near the horizon. Barring emergency, it was past working hours here.

Her "chance" meeting with Sven Hebert-Draskovics, seemingly so long ago, had not resulted in an exchange of communication codes. The publicly available code for the archivist connected her only to his voice mail. Rather than leave a message, she went inside the archive building and accessed the lobby directory.

Using a public communicator and a name randomly chosen from Custodial Services staff, Kirsten called Sven's home. The little boy who answered listened uncritically to her story of a plumbing leak in the archive building and sent a location code for his father.

Kirsten stepped from the bustling square to a grassy expanse. Shouting children of all ages greatly outnumbered the watching adults. Some children flew kites, some climbed the monkey bars, and many ran about without apparent purpose. Most engaged in team sports. Shading her eyes with a hand—the suns here were directly overhead—Kirsten scanned the park.

That was Sven, along the sidelines of a football field. Young girls ran from one end of the field to the other, pursuing the black-and-white ball with far more enthusiasm than skill, kicking shin guards far more often than the ball.

Watching the girls play made Kirsten smile. She had been terrible at football. Citizens discouraged the game, calling it antisocially competitive. Football's ubiquity across Arcadia was a rare display of independence. Perhaps meeting Sven at a football game was a favorable omen.

"Which is your daughter?" she asked Sven. The grass had made her approach silent, and he startled.

He pointed. "Vicky. The tall girl with the curly black hair." After a long silence, he added, "I don't recall that you have children." The unstated question was, "Why are you here?"

"Then you remember me," Kirsten said. "Do you recall the rest of our conversation?"

"We discussed early NP4 history. You said something rather droll about finding the abandoned ship from which the Concordance rescued our ancestors." Cheers rang out: a goal. Sven clapped enthusiastically. He turned, finally, to face Kirsten. "This meeting is no coincidence, is it?"

"May we speak in private?" She began walking toward a nearby stand of trees without waiting for an answer. He followed. They stopped beside the copse, Sven waving vigorously as Vicky looked around for her father. "Sven, I have a brief recording for you to review."

The video, its projection kept small lest the game-watching parents take notice, came from Kirsten's dash to and through *Long Pass*. Sven watched without comment. The recording ended in the cargo bay, in a close-up of the grafted-on stepping disc. He studied the close-up from all angles. When Kirsten was about to burst from frustration, he finally looked at her. "That is quite interesting."

The disc? Not the ship? Her mind roiled.

"Once more please." Sven waved again at his daughter. "Slower, if you don't mind."

At one-fourth real time, Kirsten relived her too-brief exploration. The cavernous central volume of the GP4 ship. The exposed dash over the walkway to the scarred hull of *Long Pass*. Corridors and cabins aboard the ship itself, simultaneously ordinary and exotic. The cleared-out storeroom. The few neatly patched bulkheads evoked the same doubt and anger as always. A derelict abandoned in space?

What a lie!

"Interesting," Sven said. Head canted, he again studied the stepping disc through which she had returned to *Explorer*. He finally acknowledged her confusion. "Video is data. Data can be faked. This disc, though . . . zoom in, please?"

They *needed* Sven to believe. "What is so special about this disc? What about the *ship*?"

"Zoom in, please," he repeated. "Closer still. See the controls inset along the edge? Citizens are cautious. They upgrade their technology slowly. The stepping disc in this image is a model hundreds of years out of date. I've seen few like it. It lends a scrap of credibility to this recording. May I have a copy?"

"In confidence, of course."

"Of course." Squeals of glee rose from the field. Sven waved again at the players. "I don't suppose you will tell me how you came into possession of this recording."

"I shot it. I was aboard." As Sven's eyes grew round, she slipped off her backpack and removed a parcel wrapped loosely in cloth: the threadwork she had taken from a cabin aboard *Long Pass*. "Sven, how would you like to analyze a really dusty old record?"

AMID THE HUSHED clutter of Sven's laboratory, Kirsten waited anxiously for Omar's message. The quiet would last only until the next workday and the return of staff. Before then she had to be gone, if not to the meeting Omar sought to arrange, then back aboard *Explorer*.

Sven flitted from workstation to workstation, all chewing on scene analyses of the video, and among the lab instruments with which he examined the artifact. About an hour ago, he had begun humming tunelessly. Kirsten allowed herself to hope that the droning denoted good spirits, and his good spirits the onset of belief in her report.

She had teleported ahead to the lab while Sven took his daughter home. Idly, Kirsten wondered what excuse he had given his family for returning to work. An archival emergency seemed *so* unlikely.

Then again, so did archival laboratories.

Sven shushed her when she asked about his progress, and tsked whenever she lost focus while answering one of his many questions. How long had it been since she last slept?

And *still* no word from Omar. He must be encountering the same skepticism as she.

Kirsten paced, eyeing lab equipment. Some she recognized: microscopes, both optical and electronic; spectrometers; chromatographs; crystallographic imagers. Some were mysteries.

A discreet buzz interrupted her survey. Her communicator, finally. It was Omar, and he looked exhausted. The backdrop of the holo told her nothing. "Kirsten, how is it going?"

From the minimal privacy behind a tall and unrecognized bench instrument, she brought Omar up to date.

"Is Sven convinced?"

"I think he's getting there. At least he seems excited about that framed art I brought from *Long Pass*. He refuses to say why. How are you doing?"

"I contacted some people I know in the Self-Governance Council," Omar said. "That led to a very exclusive meeting. I've been answering questions nonstop for hours."

"And now?" Kirsten asked.

"Now it's your turn." He transmitted a stepping-disc address. "Finish what you're doing and come here."

She could have asked if Sven were welcome—and didn't. Why ask, when she might not like the answer? "Sven." He looked up from a holo display in which cryptic codes slowly scrolled. *Genomic data*? "Sven, I need to go." She related what little she knew about the government meeting. "I would like you to join me."

Sven shook his head. "Not until I know more."

She could hardly drag him to the summit. He might even be correct in his priorities. "Here is the address, if you change your mind."

Kirsten stepped through into a dimly lit shed. Well-used farm equipment surrounded her, vaguely familiar from childhood tours of the factory where her parents worked. She had not known what to expect. Not this, certainly. An overhead door rattled open.

She blinked in the suddenly bright light. Omar signaled her to be silent. She followed him into a field that stretched to the horizon in every direction, the crop obviously Hearthian but otherwise unknown to her. Fibrous orange seed clusters pinched the dangling, red-and-yellow mottled tendrils that served as leaves. Combines floated in the distance, spraying orange streams into tiny floating trailers, from which the grain must teleport directly into weatherproof storage. Parallel rows of mulched stems and leaves showed the progress of the combines.

They topped a low rise. Kirsten blinked again, this time in surprise, at the people who stood below.

A slender woman with lustrous black hair and striking violet eyes stepped forward. She exhibited the indeterminate age modern medicine eventually bestowed on all Colonists, but she moved with a grace and economy of motion that hinted at advanced years. Her pink-and-red blouse was boldly checked with a matte finish. Her suede slacks had a luxurious nap. Texture and pattern alike bespoke great stature.

The hand extended to Kirsten bore a massive progeny ring, with four small rubies and at least ten emeralds: tokens of children and grandchildren. "I am Sabrina Gomez-Vanderhoff." The introduction was entirely unnecessarily. Gomez was the governor of Arcadia's Self-Governance Council, and the colony's senior elected official. "My colleague is Aaron Tremonti-Lewis." He was the minister for public safety.

Public safety involved putting out fires and dispensing aid after storms and other natural disasters. It had never occurred to Kirsten that the function might extend to protecting Colonial society from its supposed patrons. She pondered where to begin.

"May I call you Kirsten?" The governor did not wait for an answer. "Kirsten, excuse me for being brusque. We are here," and her expansive gesture encompassed the broad fields to all sides, "lest we be overheard. Needless to say, we two disappearing for any length of time would raise unfortunate questions."

Citizen questions, that was. "I'll get right to it then," Kirsten said. "It all began . . ."

Gomez cut her off. "Omar explained. As interested as we are, for now we must limit the discussion to the review of a few points."

The questions came fast and furious, with follow-ups and artfully leading paraphrases repeatedly interrupting Kirsten's answers. She was being tested. So many overlapping questions and comments kept her too busy to gauge the politicians' belief or disbelief. Was she telling the story the same way, citing the same facts, as Omar? Was she credible? This cross-examination was meant to shake her, to bare any weaknesses or inconsistencies in their story.

The governor had had her own dealings with Nike, especially since the last change in government—the Conservative Hindmost refused faces-to-face contact with Colonists. Sabrina's firsthand knowledge made her questions all the more incisive.

No wonder Omar looked drained.

Doggedly persisting through the interruptions, Kirsten conveyed the essential facts. Concern for the Gw'oth evolving into skepticism about Concordance policy to other species—including their own. The quest for hard data in computers aboard *Explorer*, then on the continent of Elysium, and even later on Hearth. The hunt for the Institute for Human Studies. The lightning visit to *Long Pass*, hidden in plain sight in orbit around NP5.

"Thank you for your patience," Gomez finally said. "Excuse us for a moment."

The hint was obvious. From a stream bed at least one hundred feet removed, Kirsten and Omar tried to read meaning into indistinct whispers and veiled expressions.

Purple pollinators, Hearthian bees, chirped nearby. "How do you think it's going?" she finally asked.

"I honestly don't know." Eyes closed, Omar rubbed his temples. "I feel like I've been through a meat grinder."

Gomez shook her head insistently. Tremonti's face flushed. They disagreed about something. What? Kirsten resisted the urge to sidle closer. They would learn soon enough what the leaders concluded. "Omar, do they even believe us?"

Omar looked away, doubt plain on his face.

The debate ended abruptly. Gomez gestured to them to return. "We find ourselves unconvinced by your report, which has more inferences than facts. Assuming that everything you have reported is correct, it would still remain unclear how best to use the information."

"Assuming? Respectfully, Governor, these *are* facts." Kirsten shrugged off the hand Omar had laid on her forearm. Obsequiousness and restraint would accomplish nothing. "The Concordance has lied to us about our past. They have kept us from the ship in which we might find answers. For all we know, they obliterated our ancestors' home world.

"Don't you want to *know*?"

"Young woman, that's enough," Gomez snapped back. "Do you imagine you are the first to worry about the inconsistencies in our history? The first to encounter an anomaly? Don't flatter yourself. There is a *reason* your captain has our ear.

"Speculation and skepticism come easily. Before anyone accuses the Concordance of lying, let alone of whatever heinous scenarios you have imagined, there must be *proof*.

"You may be ready to put at risk the unprecedented opportunity of the Colonist scouting program. I am not. What if you found a replica, a recreation, of some sort? What if your loyalty—and by extension, the colony's loyalty—was being tested? Perhaps you were *allowed* to find—"

"Hello?" The greeting floated over the hill, tentative and worried. "Kirsten?"

Kirsten needed a moment to remember having given Sven this address. Proof? Perhaps *he* had it. "Over here!"

Sven crested the hill, clutching the odd artwork from *Long Pass*. He stumbled as he recognized the high-ranking officials. "Am I interrupting?"

"I know you. You're the archivist," Gomez said. "What brings you here?"

"I invited him," Kirsten answered. "He may have the proof you're looking for."

Sven squirmed. "Kirsten asked me to assess her recordings . . . and *this*." He waggled the artwork. "It's very interesting, actually."

Tremonti coughed. "First, the data. Does that hold together?"

"It does, at least through a few hours of inspection." Handing the framed picture to Kirsten, Sven took a communicator from his pocket. "I've downloaded my main tests and correlations. We can access the raw data, if you like. But Governor . . . this artifact is the compelling evidence."

"Compelling?" Gomez frowned at the stitched flowers and shells.

"Let me explain." Sven straightened. "It's the materials that matter: the cloth backing, the fibers used in the design, and the wooden frame. Since they're organic, I carbon-dated them. These materials are thousands of years old."

"Thousands?" Omar repeated. "How can that be?"

"Exactly," Sven beamed. "Thousands of years seriously predates the official history of the rescue. It would make this artifact much older than all our records."

"How do you explain it?" Gomez asked.

Sven bounced on his toes in scarcely constrained excitement. "By recalling an underlying assumption of the method. Carbon dating is planet-specific. Carbon 14 can be more or less prevalent on other worlds. If this artwork is not an NP4 artifact, it might be any age."

Gomez considered. "Any age. Perhaps quite new, fabricated with materials found on a scouting mission."

Kirsten winced. Did her souvenir actually *hurt* their credibility?

"That would only deepen the mystery," Sven said. "I ran other tests. The materials are clearly related to materials we use."

"Clearly related." Kirsten was as lost as the rest. "Meaning?"

Sven tapped the wooden frame. "This is clearly oak—only it is of no species known to the archive. If it doesn't grow on Arcadia, where did it come from?"

Kirsten remembered Eric's disclosure about a human presence on NP3. Did the council know about that? "Could the artifact have come from another world in the Fleet?"

Sven gestured dismissively. "Calculations using the published atmospheric data for the other worlds gave me different results, but none any more credible. The organics would appear older still if they came from NP1, NP5, or Hearth. And there's too much C-14 for any of this to have originated on NP2 or NP3.

"Now consider the cloth fabric. Without a doubt it is linen, meaning its threads are made from the fibers of the flax plant. That's not merely a comment about superficial appearance, but consistent with what I saw under the microscope. Only . . ."

"Only *what*?" Gomez demanded.

Sven struck a pedantic pose. "You are aware that only a small part of a genome, any genome, serves a purpose? That most DNA consists of inactive segments, partial repetitions, and the like."

Tremonti nodded. "Junk genes."

"Exactly." Sven stroked the linen. "Most genes are junk genes, so most mutations have no meaningful effect. Not biologically meaningful, that is. Most mutations occur in the unused segments. The genetic drift rate then makes a fair molecular clock."

"A clock timing what, exactly?" Gomez asked.

"The interval since the harvesting of the flax in this linen." Sven paused dramatically. "Roughly five hundred years. I also tested several strands of the cotton floss. All imply the same approximate age."

Kirsten's thoughts raced. Five hundred years: scarcely longer than the supposed age of Arcadia colony. Those were Fleet-standard years, of course, the rotations of the NP worlds having been synched to the preferences of Hearthian biota.

A great bird soared lazily overhead, clearly Arcadian, undeterred by the extent of the alien fields. An eagle, Kirsten thought. It was majestic.

She hoped it was an omen.

Arcadian wood, either not of this planet, or thousands of years old. Flax and cotton as old as the colony. Surely now the politicians would have to accept—

"Excellent," Gomez said. "Perhaps there *is* something to this tale." She locked eyes with Sven. "You will accompany these two and their other crewman and find out for certain."

· 24 ·

The summons was not unexpected. The venue was.

Nike materialized in a vast semicircular room whose great arc of transparent wall overlooked a wooded park. Far below his hooves, the undulating, multicolored leaf canopy glowed by the light of arcology-wall sun panels.

Abandoning the spectacular view, Nike scanned the room itself. Its floor was lush with meadowplant. Overstuffed pillows and dramatic holo-sculptures had been tastefully scattered all around. The ceiling, extravagantly tall and wasteful for an arcology, soared far above his heads.

A sinuous masonry partition subtended the clear arc. Water burbled down the rough-hewn rock face into a low, stone-rimmed pool. An unseen force field bent the water around the wall's central opening, which provided access to a long corridor in which many more doorways could be seen.

"Welcome." Eos, the long-time leader of the Experimentalists, capered through the vaulted archway. He was tall for a Citizen, with striking white patches around his eyes. He wore his mane informally today, in elegant waves confined by a few orange ribbons. He brushed heads with Nike in greeting. "Welcome to my new home."

New home? When had Eos come to possess such wealth? Nike managed not to react. "Your invitation referred to the upcoming consensualization."

"We will speak inside." There were ample benches and cushions—and privacy—in *this* room. Proposing somewhere else to talk failed to disguise an unasked-for tour of the residence.

They arrived finally in a den merely twice as large as Nike's office at the Ministry of Foreign Affairs. The few wall holos somehow emphasized the burnished wood paneling. Eos indicated a tall pile of cushions. "Sit, please. Now as to invoking the voice of the people—it is a critical matter, Nike, and one to which I have given much thought. I have concluded this is an inauspicious time for political uncertainty."

"I do not understand," Nike said. The party leadership had focused on awakening proper concern within the Concordance since the first news of renewed attention by the ARM. "The Fleet flees toward the unknown, while wild humans hunt us from behind. Circumstances could not better suit the Experimentalist cause." The mission of safeguarding the herd from its own complacency . . .

"Our travels into the unknown will last a very long time. How is *this* moment different?" Eos stared two-headedly, daring Nike to argue. "Some may think the Fleet is on a journey, a transient stage fraught with danger. I have come to embrace a different view. The Fleet has transitioned to our new way of life." The subtext went unarticulated: With the transition complete, governance was appropriately entrusted to the Conservatives.

A decadently opulent new home. The abrupt renunciation of party belief. Eos' timing could not be more—

"I should share another matter with you." As he spoke, Eos traced vertical circles with his heads: a gesture of confidence and trust. "We live in challenging and perplexing times, Nike. The people call out to us, their leaders, for unity. I hear those voices, and so I am joining the present government."

The irony was unbearable; it demanded all Nike's self-discipline not to look himself in the eyes. He had dispatched Nessus to corrupt the wild humans with their own funds, money recycled through General Products Corporation. The Hindmost had co-opted and corrupted Eos with only a government penthouse.

However ironic, the situation was unambiguous. The near future would bring no appeals to or reassessment of the communal wisdom. This unnatural alliance between the leaders of the two parties doomed any possibility that a new vision might be forged.

Nike could scarcely bear to look at Eos. Looking around the room, feigning interest in this obscene ostentation was safer. This lavish home might even have been *his*. The offer had been clear enough. Now that Eos had been bought, temptation was being dangled once more.

The leaders of both factions were consumed with political and personal advantage, even as peril surrounded the Fleet on all sides. Whom the gods would destroy . . .

"Thank you for your hospitality." Unfolding his legs, Nike emerged from his nest of pillows. "If you will excuse me, however, pressing matters at Clandestine Directorate demand my attention." Surrendering to his roiling emotions, Nike left without awaiting a response from Eos, intent on locating the nearest stepping disc.

For affairs at his office *were* pressing. Having spurned the enticements of the Hindmost and Eos, Nike wondered for how much longer Clandestine Directorate would be his concern.

NIKE CHARGED FROM stepping disc to stepping disc— across vast plains, around continental coasts, from remote island to teeming megalopolitan plaza to towering mountain crest—as fast as the ever-crowded walkways allowed. In impressions almost stroboscopically fleeting, he drank it all in: the sounds and smells of the crowds, the casual intimacy of brushing flanks with countless strangers, the randomly chosen waypoints.

Whenever Nike was troubled, a frenetic gallop across Hearth like this never failed to soothe him.

Until now.

The corruption of the elite threatened to overwhelm him. How tempting it was to find a quiet nook somewhere and then curl himself away from the world.

Tempting, but ultimately futile. Withdrawal would fail to console him just as this mad dash around the globe now failed to distract him. The problem was larger than him, larger than the world. Something, whether maturity or insanity Nike could not judge, demanded that he take a larger view. To hide beneath one's belly or on a single planet—the difference was only of degree, not of kind.

Sides heaving from exertion, Nike made his way home. This evil alliance between the Hindmost and Eos put the burden of safeguarding Hearth on *him*. If he were to be removed from Clandestine Directorate, who would address the *true* risks that confronted the world?

He had to retain his post, doing whatever that took— whatever the cost to his self-respect.

The sonic shower dissolved a patina of sweat but left Nike's thoughts as dark as ever. So many had joined him at the grand ballet, those he considered his friends and colleagues—and yet there were none with whom to share these doubts and misgivings. With a start, Nike realized the only one he knew to whom this star-spanning anxiety might make sense: Nessus.

What little order remained to Nike's coiffure after his mad dash had slumped in the shower. He sat before a mirror, a comb in one mouth and a brush in the other, trying to—

Bzzt.

An alert buzzer, insistent with harsh undertones. Only his most senior staff could get past his voice mail. An iconic image floated above the buzzing communicator. The still holo showed Vesta, his most trusted aide. "Nike."

Nike waited.

"I am sorry to disturb you." Vesta's voices trembled, and his necks slumped with worry. Tufts and gaps in his coiffure bespoke recent plucking. "An urgent matter has come up."

"There is no need to apologize," Nike answered. He had just flattered himself that he was irreplaceable. How fitting that there should be an immediate crisis. "What is the news?"

"We received a report from NP4. If only we had processed it sooner." Vesta lowered his heads submissively. "An unsolicited account by an informant."

"And?" Nike prompted.

A holo inset popped up, of a dour Colonist whom Nike did not recognize. "Her name is Alice Jones-Randall. She works in an office complex used by the Self-Governance Council on Arcadia."

Evidently she also informed on her coworkers to the directorate. Vesta's hesitance began to worry Nike. "What does she have to say?"

"She claims she saw Kirsten Quinn-Kovacs yesterday."

Kirsten was light-years away, aboard *Explorer*—but Vesta knew that. "Come as quickly as you can."

His aide teleported in moments later. "Thank you, sir. If I may? This video comes from a security camera." A new holo appeared, this one an urban setting. A timestamp counted up in a corner. Offices. Arcadian vegetation. Colonists everywhere.

Vesta extended a neck into the image. "Watch here."

Here was one end of a pedestrian mall, its surface tiled with stepping discs. Nike watched streams of Colonists walking around, appearing and disappearing. Vesta froze the image as yet another Colonist materialized.

"It could be her." Even side by side with an image taken during a visit *Explorer*'s crew had made to his office, Nike was uncertain. "Or not. See the pastel clothing. Kirsten is not mated."

"Facial recognition software says it is her," Vesta said. "We used a recent holo from her personnel file in the scout program."

"Run it again, with this image from my office."

Vesta reran the comparison. Another match.

Point by point, Vesta laid out the evidence. The suspected Kirsten walking across the mall into a government building. A second video watched her enter the lobby and scan an office directory. A match between her on-file DNA and dust from the lobby. Apparently humans regularly shed hair fragments and skin cells.

"How sensitive *is* that test?" Nike asked.

Vesta checked his files. "In such a well-traveled space, cleaned daily, all detectable traces would be gone in three to five days."

The proof seemed incontrovertible. Nike reluctantly accepted the identification. "Why was Kirsten there? Whom did she see?"

"We don't know." Vesta picked fearfully at his mane before unfreezing the latest video. In it Kirsten left the lobby without speaking to anyone. Returning to the pedestrian mall, she disappeared by another stepping disc. "This is our only sighting despite extensive searching of surveillance data. We might not find her again if she avoids security cameras."

And of course the stepping-disc system kept no records of transfers between public areas.

Only by good fortune did he know of Kirsten's unexpected return to the Fleet. How long might it be before anyone spotted her again, or found her crewmates?

Or, far more critically, their ship.

Eyes fluttering with surprise, Baedeker took Nike's unexpected call. "Your Excellency."

"We have a problem." Nike summarized the proof of Kirsten's surprise presence on NP4. "How can that be?"

Baedeker dipped a head in wary thoughtfulness. "She must have teleported off *Explorer* before it left on its mission. That's why the Colonists falsified the onboard audio recordings: so we would not detect her absence."

"Must have," Vesta echoed skeptically.

"Of course. Traffic control tracked *Explorer*'s departure. They still send their reports from . . ." Baedeker trailed off as a possibility occurred to him. "Perhaps *Explorer* returned secretly to drop her off."

"Perhaps? You don't track the location of their ship?" Harsh dissonances underscored Nike's displeasure. Had the Colonists deceived this arrogant engineer *again*?

"We know it by inference, Excellency. We continue to receive reports about Oceanus, and answers to our occasional inquiries, by hyperwave radio, always from the correct direction. It just occurred to me"—Baedeker lowered his heads submissively—"that a hyperwave relay could be involved. Hyperwave radio being instantaneous—"

"The ship could be anywhere," Nike said, completing the thought. "An indestructible ship designed for stealth, controlled by a deceitful crew."

No one spoke for what seemed a very long time. No one needed to. This was a nightmare scenario—and it was of their making. Sufficiently accelerated and aimed at Hearth, *Explorer* would be an apocalyptic device.

The corrupt pact between Eos and the Hindmost that had threatened to consume Nike receded into a distant, minor hazard. "Before *Explorer*'s departure, I assume General Products outfitted it with a failsafe."

High/low, low/high, high/low: Baedeker's heads bobbed enthusiastic agreement. Did he see this as redemption for his many failures? "Of course, your Excellency. I did not use any ordinary paint—"

"I don't need to know details." It had been a mistake to meet the crew, Nike realized. He did not *want* to know details. That he had come to see Kirsten, Omar, and Eric as *people* made what must now be done that much more difficult. Possibly none of them remained aboard the doomed ship. He hoped that was the case. "Just do it."

· 25 ·

"Welcome to Earth," Traffic Control said.

"It's good to be back," Nessus lied. He hoped his avatar had an honest face. As far as anyone in this solar system knew, this was a human ship.

The Mojave Spaceport sprawled in all directions. Rugged mountains loomed in the distance. Maintenance had evidently suffered since Nessus' last visit—greenery poked upward through cracks in the tarmac, a few grown tall enough to be recognizable to the ship's computer as young yucca and Joshua trees.

Aegis would look no different from many of the vessels around it. Despite the deep recession caused by the abrupt disappearance of General Products Corporation—or perhaps because of it—the company's indestructible hulls remained prized here. A used GP hull cost more now than it once had new.

Nessus trembled with excitement on his command bench. A manic phase was upon him, and it would be foolish not to act now. "Computer, proceed as planned." Then, since the plan relied upon the unwitting cooperation of a human victim, he went to the relax room to wait.

For a while he sampled the human media. Innuendo about Fertility Board corruption. Unruly protests. Opportunistic politicians endorsing Birthright Lotteries. Vigilante attacks on "bought babies."

Necessity seemed such a facile excuse. Repelled by

what he had caused, Nessus stopped watching. The reports would be in the archives when he could bear it again.

He was concentrating on one of the human histories that Nike so prized, by a flatlander named Plutarch, when an alert tone chimed. A caption appeared over the biography Nessus was reading: Sangeeta Kudrin, UN deputy under-secretary for administrative affairs.

He looked up. Behind a one-way mirror, a woman had materialized inside a booth made of hull material. She was petite with almond-shaped eyes and many facial piercings. She wore a conservative brown-and-orange suit; what little Nessus could see of her skin-dye job favored spirals in an assortment of blue tones.

She looked panicked.

Nessus set down his reader as his guest began pounding on the booth walls. "You will not be harmed."

"Where am I?" she demanded. "And who are you?"

Not: *How did I get here?* Nessus was impressed. She had already ascribed her abduction to subversion of the transfer-booth system. "You may call me Nessus."

"Where am I, Nessus?"

"That is unimportant." He let her ponder that for a while. "You have ceased to report as ordered." Ceased to leave information in designated transfer booths at designated times, so that his minions could retrieve it.

Sangeeta swallowed. "I have provided a great deal of information."

"Nevertheless." Her body heat would quickly warm the enclosed space. The filter-equipped disc in the booth's ceiling exchanged oxygen for carbon dioxide, but she could not know that. He waited.

"What do you want?" she finally asked.

"Information about Sigmund Ausfaller."

She flinched. "That is not feasible." Nessus waited until she added, "What about Ausfaller?"

"I want regular reports on his work."

"You want me to spy on *Ausfaller*? The man is a raving

paranoid. Maybe you don't understand what that means. It means he suspects *everyone*."

Nessus waited in silence as beads of sweat appeared on Sangeeta's forehead and trickled down her face. Her eyes darted around, seeking an exit that did not exist. He said, "The ARM is part of the United Nations. There must be reports."

"I can tell you one thing." Furtive glances. "Ausfaller *knows*."

Nessus pressed on. "What does he know?"

"About the extortions! I'm trapped in here, but he's trapping *you*!"

"Explain," Nessus said softly.

"I'm guessing that you chose your victims, at least some of them, by clever data mining. I don't see how else you could have found *me*. My . . . creative use of UN funds." She slumped against a wall of the booth. "It appears Ausfaller had worried about just such an attack on the UN. He created a persona in the personnel files, gave it a suspect-looking past, just to entrap anyone doing exactly what you're doing."

Nessus quivered, his mania spent. "How do you know?"

"For the reason you wanted me here. I have limited access to his reports. At least I *had* access. He severely restricted everything soon after you tried to coerce his decoy." She laughed bitterly. "I wouldn't be here if I'd followed his example. He stopped using transfer booths right after the fake persona got an envelope with your Cerberus sigil on it."

What if Miguel and Ashley had, unknowingly, tried to blackmail the ARM? They would get disinformation from Ausfaller, surely. And Ausfaller would think to seek out other coerced parties, *real* UN personnel whom the hidden blackmailers might have threatened. If Nessus and his minions could find ways to intimidate them, Ausfaller could do the same.

Nessus quivered, wondering how much false data he might already have swallowed.

He resisted the urge to paw at the deck as the implications became clear. Assume Ausfaller knew the transfer-booth system had been compromised. Puppeteers were the obvious suspects. And the ARM already sought in the direction of the Fleet . . .

"Nessus!" His prisoner peered at the mirror, panting, hysteria in her voice. "Are you still there?"

He got his fear under control. "I have many sources at the UN. Ausfaller cannot know them all. I advise you to say nothing about our relationship or this conversation. If you inform him, I *will* find out."

Sangeeta shivered. From relief at the implication she would be released? In terror, that Ausfaller would learn of her thefts? Maybe both. "I'll say *nothing* to him."

Conscience aside, Nessus had no choice but to release her. The disappearance of a high-ranking official would only stoke Ausfaller's suspicions. If she *did* speak with Ausfaller, all she could reveal was the fact of her abduction and questioning. It would not endanger Nessus.

And Ausfaller himself? He remained untouchable. Nessus had to assume the paranoid had arranged an in-case-of-my-disability-or-disappearance message for authorities.

Nessus tongued the command that teleported Sangeeta from her cell to the transfer booth anteroom of her home. If she meant to keep her word to Nessus, she would need a moment of privacy in which to regain her composure.

As Nessus needed to regain his own composure. Without it, he could hardly expect to enlist a first-rate astrophysicist.

· 26 ·

Darkness and an eerie silence greeted Kirsten's return to *Explorer*.

An unfamiliar acrid reek filled the air. She felt her way through the relax room to a light-activating touchpad. Dimmed LEDs she could have understood, but off? Her left shin smacked something massive as she shuffled toward the control.

Blazing lights revealed unfathomable disarray. Supply cabinets gaped open, their contents spilled to the deck. The treadmill lay on its side. Wall panels hung awry, baring the painted interior surface of the hull. "Eric?" she called.

No one answered.

As Kirsten forced open the suddenly stiff hatch, a flicker of motion registered in her peripheral vision. Sven. She said, "Clear the disc for Omar, but stay here."

The corridor, too, was dark. She tapped a lighting control to reveal chaos. Torn and shattered objects lay everywhere, the scraps scarcely recognizable. Scorching covered the bowed-in walls of the corridor.

What had happened here?

"Eric," she called. Silence. "Eric," she tried again, a little louder. She crept through the clutter to the bridge, where the situational holo cast enough light to hint at more madness.

Omar joined Kirsten as she studied the status display. Despite the all-encompassing disorder, despite consoles slid away from the walls to the limit allowed by their cabling, everything registered as nominal. "What *happened* here? Where is Eric?"

"I don't know." Her answer covered both questions. Kirsten swept a pile of clothing off her crash couch and sat to scan the instruments. "*Explorer* is where we left it, deep in the ocean. The refueling probes are working. Readings for temperature, oxygen, everything we routinely monitor, they're all fine."

Omar activated the intercom. "Eric." Silence. "Kirsten and I are on the bridge. Report."

Sven appeared in the doorway, looking anxious. "Is everything all right?"

She threw up her hands. "Honestly, we don't know. The readouts are fine, but *something* happened here. And Eric . . ."

"I'll search the bow," Omar said. "Kirsten, take the stern. Sven, stay here. We'll keep in touch by intercom."

Kirsten struggled aft through cluttered corridors. These halls had been empty, their walls straight and clean, just a day earlier. She activated lights as she went, checking inside each cabin, hold, and closet, finding only disarray until—

Eric sat on the engine-room deck, arms wrapped tightly around his knees, rocking, amid a jumble of tools and spare parts. Main thrusters and the hyperdrive were unbolted from their deck mounts and rudely shoved aside. A flicker of recognition appeared on Eric's face but he said nothing.

"Eric is in the engine room," Kirsten called into the intercom before settling beside him. "Eric. Eric!" No response. She shook his arm. "Eric, what's the matter?"

"I've been a fool," Eric said softly. "A fool," he repeated as Omar ran in.

"Are you all right?" Omar asked.

"Yes." With a shiver, Eric came out of his funk. He looked around as though noticing the disarray for the first time. "Welcome back."

"What happened?" Omar asked. "Why is everything torn apart?"

Leaning against an overturned cabinet, Eric got to his feet. He handed each of them a slender copper tube from a heap on a workbench. Wires protruded from one end. "While you two were away, I decided to look for any more hidden sensors."

"For *that* you tore apart the ship?" Omar snapped. "With the telemetry bypassed, the sensors were harmless. We never revealed that we knew about hidden sensors. How do you propose to disguise this destruction when *Explorer* gets its next overhaul?"

Eric's eyes demanded Kirsten's attention. He seemed so *sad*. There was more to this mess than sensors. "Eric, these aren't listening devices, are they?"

"They're electric detonators." Eric laughed humorlessly at their evident shock. "After I found one, I got a little crazy. I found them all through the ship."

"Detonators," Kirsten repeated. "To detonate . . . what?"

"A good question." Reaching behind an upended supply cabinet, Eric scraped off a fleck of the paint-and-insulation layer that lined the hull. He sealed the paint chip, a detonator, and a sledgehammer inside a little GP #1 hull, one of many *Explorer* carried for use as free-flying probes. He strapped everything down on a workbench. "And presto."

Kirsten barely heard a loud *crack* before the engine room's noise cancellers kicked in. Vibrating madly, the GP #1 hull seemed unharmed—only its transparent shell had suddenly turned black. When Eric opened the probe's hatch, heat puffed out, and a stench of metal. She realized what now coated the orb's inner surface: the vaporized metallic head of the sledgehammer.

"The Citizens never trusted us. We were expendable." Eric's voice trembled with grief. "They were prepared to blow us up."

"They wouldn't . . . they planned for some remote contingency. . . . I don't see how . . ." Kirsten grasped for an explanation for the inexplicable.

"You think? Come with me." Eric led them toward the bow. "This could almost be funny. A lifetime's deference to the Citizens almost killed me."

As they approached the burst hatch of Nessus' former cabin, Kirsten's jaw dropped. An explosion had destroyed everything inside.

DRIFTING OFF TO sleep after hours of backbreaking labor restoring order to the ship, Kirsten realized why Eric looked so different. It was more than the pain in his eyes.

The elaborate braids and colorful dyes—every trace of the Citizen-mimicking coiffure Eric had so long affected—had vanished.

From adulation to doubt to anger and shock. Kirsten could not imagine how upset Eric must be.

Nor could she help thinking the Citizens would someday come to rue it.

Julian Forward was a fireplug of a human, short and squat. He had arms as massive as most men's legs, and legs like columns. Forward was a Jinxian, and Jinxians bred for strength. That made sense on a world with nearly twice the gravity of Earth.

Nessus was happy to be thousands of miles distant.

Forward peered curiously and unknowingly into the hidden camera. His eyes, as though with minds of their own, kept sliding off axis. "Interesting," he finally said. He left briefly. Reappearing with a broom, he poked it into the transfer booth. Then, with a wry smile, Forward dropped the broom. He stepped inside the booth and picked up the package Nessus had sent.

This one was smart, Nessus thought, as quick as Kirsten. Forward's mind had leapt from the extra-dimensionality of the package to distrust of transfer booths to the realization that, had abduction by teleportation been intended, it would have happened without warning.

Optics far beyond human capabilities reconstituted the scene from rays scattered by their contorted path into the package's interior. Nessus watched Forward carry the object to another room. The nearest window offered a spectacular view of the Coliseum. Other windows gave equally striking views of the Grand Canyon, the Great Wall, and the pyramids at Giza. Boxes were piled all around, some still open, spoiling the simulated views.

All did not run smoothly in the life of Julian Forward.

"Whenever you're ready." Forward sat on his sofa, legs apart, facing Nessus' parcel. His eyes continued to slide off. "You have my attention."

"You are very perceptive, Dr. Forward," Nessus began.

Forward smiled. "You have a beautiful voice. Transfer in and give me a look at you."

"You are very calm for a man in your circumstances."

Forward brought his hands together, making a tent of his fingers. "A tesseract is a singular gift with which to get my attention."

"Your fame in astrophysical circles brought you to mine. But tesseract? I am unfamiliar with the term," Nessus dissembled. It was a small test.

"A four-dimensional 'cube.' Modern cosmological theories invoke additional dimensions beyond those we experience." Forward patted the tesseract; his fingertips bent oddly as they entered the volume of manipulated space. "To manifest one of those dimensions at macro scale—that *is* exceptional. And of course transfer booths somehow access those hidden dimensions to accomplish teleportation."

He was right, of course, on all counts—including, from the human perspective, that "somehow." General Products did not share the underlying science when it licensed transfer-booth technology. "Do you like Earth, Doctor?"

"Call me Julian. And you are?"

"Very cautious," Nessus answered. Over Forward's hearty laugh, Nessus added, "I wonder if you might consider a new professional opportunity."

"As to Earth—no, I don't much care for it. It's much too crowded for my taste."

"And yet here you are, Julian," Nessus said. "You have spent years on Earth. Attempting to prove a theory about the Tunguska Event, I believe."

"You have the advantage of me again . . . whoever you are. Yes, something fascinating happened in Siberia in 1908, something still unexplained. For all the devastation, that 'something' left no crater. And yet, trees remained standing near the epicenter. The accepted explanation, that a meteorite struck, simply fails to fit the facts." Forward frowned. "You need not have gone to such extremes merely to discuss my investigation."

Nessus knew all about Forward's research. After a hasty study, Nessus knew about most leading cosmologists in Sol system. Unfortunately, excitement and enthusiasm drove genius. It could not be coerced.

Few at the apex of human physics had seemed approachable. If the Jinxian would not serve Nessus' purpose, no one would.

And then Ausfaller would continue to stalk the Fleet.

"You are only the most recent to advocate that a quantum black hole, not a meteorite, struck Siberia that night. What you cannot answer, Julian, is when and where your hypothetical black hole, having passed through the Earth, then exited. If you determined *that*, perhaps you could deduce the black hole's orbit. And the historical records, such as they are, are all on Earth."

Forward stiffened. "This grows tiresome. Get to your point."

"The Institute of Knowledge funds your research, does it not?"

"It did." A scowl. "Apparently I failed to show sufficient progress."

And so we arrive at the hearts of the matter. Of course Nessus had the advantage. He knew why the Institute had *truly* canceled Forward's funding: they were bribed. Hence Forward was busy packing. "Then perhaps you would consider an alternative employment."

"Your convoluted methods do not evince confidence," Forward answered.

But they would evince curiosity. "All I ask for now is your confidentiality and consideration," Nessus said. "You will receive a handsome remuneration for this consultation." With the flick of a tongue, he severed the connection.

"HELLO, JULIAN," NESSUS began.

Forward had taken the call in his living room. Towers of boxes climbed higher than ever; today, only one box remained open. A sealed box hid the tesseract and blinded its camera. He removed a large box from the sofa and sat.

"An unforgettable voice. And now an unforgettable face to put to it. When do I get a name?"

Forward had lifted the box effortlessly. The stack he had brushed past had tottered. These boxes were empty: props. The scientist was tempted—by the large honorarium, if nothing else.

Aboard *Aegis,* Nessus winked; his image in the call smiled. The avatar wore Kirsten's face. "You may call me Nessus."

"An unusual name for an unusual circumstance. What can I do for you, Nessus?"

"As I suggested in our last conversation, I have a complicated task that you might help me with."

Julian leaned forward. "Related to black holes?"

"Something less weighty." Nessus had his avatar smile again. "But only a little."

"And the work would be performed on Earth?"

"That is one of the complications," Nessus replied. "It's best to perform this project at a distance. You see, we're going to produce neutronium."

"At a distance." Forward's eyes narrowed. "Yes, some separation *would* be desirable, given that it takes a supernova to make neutronium."

"Is that a given, Julian?"

"Perhaps not." Forward stood. "Perhaps not for your kind."

Nessus somehow resisted the urge to snatch at his mane. He had no idea how the avatar program would represent that mannerism. "My kind?"

"Puppeteers." The silence stretched uncomfortably. "Now I have *your* attention."

"Do I *look* like a Puppeteer?

"You look like an angel, which is hardly conclusive since this is a vid call. You *sound* like a Puppeteer. General Products pulled up stakes just five years ago. It takes much longer than that to forget just how sexy a Puppeteer sounds.

"More to the point, Nessus, is the tesseract you sent to

get my attention. It embodies technology for which humans have no scientific foundation—much like making neutronium.

"While you consider that, Nessus, allow me to share an observation. In past dealings with humanity, General Products considered blackmail a perfectly acceptable business practice. The tesseract, and everything about it—and about you—that I know and could surmise, have been entrusted to a friend."

Nessus relaxed. *Blackmail* was a human term. Among Citizens, this was merely a stage of negotiation.

He had his native expert.

CRASH!

Furniture suffered when Forward grew frustrated. His newest table toppled, its top dented and a leg shattered by this latest blow. Tables, fortunately, were simple to synthesize.

"What now, Julian?" Only the relative safety of *Aegis* enabled Nessus' philosophical detachment. His native expert fulminated from inside the research center to which *Aegis* had berthed, the mined-out and repurposed Oort Cloud object immodestly renamed Forward Station. The Institute of Knowledge nominally owned the base; Nessus had anonymously arranged its lease.

"This derivation makes no sense. The third postulate here, to start . . ."

Forward ranted, not expecting a reply. The process had become all too routine. Experts in the Fleet would send isolated bits of theory, entirely out of context lest too much be disclosed. Then their responses to Forward's inevitable questions would be as unforthcoming as the incomplete information that had raised questions in the first place. As often as not they failed to grasp the limitations of human technology, blithely assuming Forward had access to instruments and means of fabrication available only in the Fleet.

An intellect any less brilliant than Julian's would have made no progress at all.

Despite the considerable pay Forward was accruing, he took no step until he entirely understood every nuance and implication. But for the passage of time the Fleet could ill afford, Nessus would have approved. The vast energies that they employed deserved the utmost caution.

So time passed—too much time—as Forward made the tools to make the tools to make the tools. It brought to mind Kirsten's musings, so seemingly long ago, about Gw'oth progress. How were his Colonist scouts faring? Nessus wondered. Nike declined to "distract" him with their progress reports.

How much quicker things would proceed if Nessus could only return to the Fleet for a neutronium generator! Alas, hyperdrive notwithstanding, he could not make the trip. Too much here in Sol system relied upon his constant attentions: Guiding his minions. Fomenting the Birth Lottery unrest. Anxious and indirect monitoring of Ausfaller.

And no one, regardless of Nessus' importuning, was available to deliver a neutronium generator to Sol system.

It all too often seemed that the fate of the Fleet rested on far too few freaks like himself. The pressure made Nessus yearn all the more for oblivion in a tightly rolled ball. For Nike, he reminded himself, countless times each day . . .

"I said I'm going to drop offline for a bit."

Nessus had once again let his attention wander. "Sorry. Doing what, Julian?"

"Uploading new calibrations for the implosion effect to the stasis-field generators. Baedeker sent new specs." Forward nodded at the holo of a nearby icy mass, its surface dotted with test gear. "While I do, perhaps you can recheck the instrument constellation." He referred to the halo of microsats, each a GP1 hull, which would monitor the coming experiment.

"Of course. And this"—the nearby mass of ice and rock, miles across—"will make how much?"

Forward grimaced. "About a cubic centimeter, Nessus. I hope this process scales up well."

To reproduce a neutronium trap here, to mimic what the ARM might find at any time in the Fleet's wake, Nessus needed a twelve-foot sphere.

They had their work cut out for them.

· 28 ·

The acrid stench of explosives tainted everything. By the time *Explorer*'s scrubbers eliminated the last of the fumes, all traces of herd pheromone were also gone.

Somehow, Kirsten thought, that seemed fitting.

Sven was dazed, indifferent to symbolism, overwhelmed by his plunge without warning into intrigue and peril. The Concordance had tried to kill Eric, Omar, and Kirsten; *he* was endangered by staying anywhere near them. But if the authorities already suspected his involvement with the three, going home could be just as dangerous.

Perhaps, for as long as the Concordance believed *Explorer* destroyed, the safest spot for them all was onboard.

Kirsten shrugged. They would accomplish nothing by playing safe.

She found Sven in his cabin. The room had been hers until she had doubled up with Eric. Despite the bulging satchel at Sven's feet, he seemed reticent to leave. She said, "We're about to learn secrets every archivist before you would have given his right arm to know."

Sven smiled wanly. "I find I'm very like a Citizen. This seems foolhardy."

"Course match in ten minutes," Omar announced over the intercom. "Eric is waiting in the relax room."

She touched Sven's arm. "No one can make you come— but if you miss this opportunity, you'll regret it for the rest of your life."

Nodding, Sven picked up his bag. "You're right. Let's go."

KIRSTEN MATERIALIZED IN the ancient storeroom, its crisp right angles and emptied shelves just as she remembered. Sven stood nearby, his fears forgotten, enthralled by the handwritten list on a yellowed scrap of paper pinned by magnet to a bulkhead. Eric, who had previously only glimpsed the ship's exterior, looked about in awe.

At Kirsten's approach, Eric shook off his distraction. He burrowed into his backpack for a motion detector. It was just one of the devices he had prepared for this expedition. "Nothing detectable," he whispered.

For all Kirsten's certainty that this ship was abandoned, its contents long offloaded to Hearth for study, she sighed in relief. "Then why whisper? Let's look around."

"First things first." Tellingly, Eric did not attribute the expression to Nessus. "We've got sensors to distribute." One by one he dispatched tiny flying sensors to stepping discs throughout the huge GP4 hull. The robots, if anyone was aboard to notice them, resembled flutterwings midway through their nymph stage. For secrecy and power conservation, the robots would report only sporadically, in highly compressed low-power bursts. "All right. *Now*, let's look around."

Kirsten led them through the ship. Sven alternately muttered and rubbed his hands, declining attempts to draw him out. Eric clutched the motion detector, checking it ever more frequently as they neared the airlock. "Still nothing," he said. "Of course, *Long Pass* could be filled with or surrounded by sensors like those we distributed. A motion detector wouldn't see mobile devices that small."

Kirsten thrust her hands into her trouser pockets. "Clearly nothing was watching me during my last visit. If I had been spotted then, someone would have changed the storeroom's stepping-disc address. We wouldn't have gotten aboard at all, or we would have materialized inside a locked room with a receive-only disc, or been greeted by guards, or . . ." Her voice faltered. This expedition could have gone badly in so many ways.

And still might.

Eric laid the motion detector on the deck, facing the open airlock and catwalk. "If anyone approaches, we'll know. If the remote sensors spot anyone aboard the main ship, we'll know. After I reprogram the storeroom stepping disc to require authentication, we'll be safe from surprise callers."

They followed that quick walkthrough with a systematic survey along each corridor and stairwell, and into every room. *Long Pass* was mostly machinery; there wasn't that much in habitable volume. Kirsten videotaped everything, narrating as she went. Data crunching would turn those recordings into a detailed 3-D map, complete down to the last closet, cabinet, drawer and cubbyhole. It would be too easy to overlook something vital without such an aid.

All the while, their teleported sensors found nothing to report. The big ship that enclosed *Long Pass* was unoccupied. They decided it was safe to explore separately. Eric began in the engine room. Sven began a more detailed examination of cabins and the mostly empty holds. Kirsten headed forward.

A savory aroma followed her onto the bridge. She tried to ignore the smell. Sven had mentioned planning to reconstitute one of the ancient packaged meals found in what she considered the relax room, but whose door was labeled "Dayroom." She would bring the sample to *Explorer* for testing when she traded places with Omar. However inviting the food here smelled, it might have turned poisonous. And its edibility would further prove whose ship this surely had once been.

Stomach growling, Kirsten inspected the instruments and controls. Their operation should be obvious, she thought. The keyboards had the familiar, inexplicable QWERTY layout. Cryptic icons shimmered in the holo display once she flipped a console's plainly labeled POWER toggle.

That was as far as she had gotten.

One does not randomly push buttons on a starship bridge. The almost familiarity of the controls stymied and frustrated her. Somewhere here were controls for navigation, shipboard status, external sensors—functions *Explorer* provided, functions any starship must implement. Functions she *should* recognize.

Drawers beneath the console ledges offered only dried-out pens, brittle papers covered in doodles and handwritten poetry, and the powdery remains of (she guessed) ancient snacks. What if the whole ship were like this? What if everything useful had been removed for study elsewhere?

"Eric," she called. The intercom controls, at least, like those of the synthesizer, were obvious and intuitive. "Have you figured anything out?"

"Mostly that this won't be easy," Eric answered. "We're hundreds of years distant from the people who built this ship. We're generations removed, Kirsten."

"Have you found any manuals?" she persisted.

"Sorry. No."

"Thanks anyway." She released the intercom button. "I need help," she admitted to herself.

One of the many enigmatic icons, a cartoon-ish head with somber expression and handlebar mustache, flashed twice. In a comically unctuous voice, the animation said, "You may call me Jeeves. How may I be of service?"

SVEN AND ERIC had come running. When they talked over each other, Jeeves got confused or didn't respond. They learned patience. They laughed a lot. Hours passed while they played with the Jeeves program. At some point Eric stepped aside to cook several meals from their packs. They took turns napping, and had to be briefed when they woke.

After so long a search, so much had finally been

revealed—everything, it seemed, except the one important thing: the location of Earth. Numbly, Kirsten tried to absorb it all.

From the captain's log: *Long Pass*'s discovery of and message to the Ice World, proven unambiguously by its ice-covered continental outlines to be NP5 en route to the Fleet.

From the video archives of shipboard safety systems: the takeover of *Long Pass* by robots clearly of Citizen design. Robots like those in the hold of the very ship that currently enclosed *Long Pass*. They had all seen such robots before, toiling alongside Colonists in fields and forests.

From an entertainment collection, musical recordings both familiar and wondrously fresh. How it must have amused Nessus to claim credit for *Ride of the Valkyries*!

From the ship's manifest: a listing of what, and who, had once been aboard, most notably the embryo banks and hibernation tanks that had given rise to a colony of laborers.

And the crew whose misfortune it had been to signal icebound NP5? Of their fate, Jeeves could offer no clue.

Gradually their questions ran slower. When Kirsten checked her watch, twenty-seven standard hours had passed. That long? *Only* that long?

Kirsten chewed without tasting something Sven had put in her hand. Part of her was overwhelmed. Part of her marveled at having come so far. Nodding belated thanks for the sandwich, she found herself remembering the football match from which she had so abruptly taken Sven. Girls running and screaming, embracing a game universally discouraged by Citizens.

Even Citizens didn't always get their way.

Kirsten went aft to the engine room, where Eric knelt staring in concentration into an open wiring closet. His new look, a long ponytail with no trace of Citizen-style coiffure, still made her pause, but she liked it. She gave him a long, hard kiss.

"I'm not complaining," Eric said, "but what was *that* about?"

She smiled. "It's about taking joy in making progress."

* * *

OMAR SNIFFED APPRECIATIVELY as the dayroom synthe-sizer filled a foamed plastic bulb for him. Coffee. She doubted he had tasted a normal beverage since the synthed food here on *Long Pass* checked out.

Normal? That was, despite her efforts to retrain herself, backward thinking. What this ship dispensed *defined* the standard. Black bitter stimulant. Bulbs for use in free fall, with a flat bottom because sometimes you had gravity.

"I've asked Eric this already." Omar paused to squeeze a sip from his coffee bulb. The nonchalance seemed feigned. "When do you feel we'll be ready to report back to Sabrina?" It went unstated that reporting back meant traveling back.

Omar had not mentioned Sven. There was no need. A few shifts earlier, every garment, doodle, or dust bunny aboard had fascinated the archivist. Now, with Jeeves' assis-tance, Sven had several hundred terabytes of databases to explore. He could not wait to analyze it on familiar comput-ers running familiar applications.

First the casual pose. Then the ever so carefully worded neutrality of the question. *Omar* wanted to return.

Regardless, Omar raised a fair question. What *did* she think? Were they ready? "We don't know yet where we, where *humans* come from. We only have names: Earth, Sol system, human space."

"We may never know," Omar said. "If the coordinates aren't lost, I would think Sven and the archivist's lab pres-ent our best chance at recovery. He's copied everything accessible.

"Soon enough, *Explorer* will be declared missing—maybe by whoever tried to destroy it, maybe because we're no longer communicating—but by someone." Sad eyes added, "My wife and children will think me dead." He shrugged off the hand she had sympathetically laid over his. "I know. I can't contact my loved ones even after we're back in Arcadia. But the sooner we report in . . ."

And her family, and Eric's.

It would be *so* easy to answer: I can mine the data anywhere. Easy, but was it true? Her gut spasmed. "I don't think we're ready, Omar. I'm working as fast as I can."

Her own hot bulb of coffee in hand, Kirsten headed for the bridge and more conversation with Jeeves.

"THAT DATA HAS been corrupted," Jeeves said. He always sounded apologetic, although he had spoken the same sentence scores of times. Any of a Citizen's devices, or any Colonist, would have become exasperated.

Kirsten rubbed her eyes. She was exhausted. How else could she approach this problem? She had asked in countless paraphrases about the location of Earth, Earth's sun, human settlements, human-settled solar systems, and any near-neighbors of Earth's sun. "I'd like to see this ship's course data."

"That data has been corrupted."

"Show me the stars used for navigational reference."

"That data has been corrupted."

Sven occupied the other crash couch on the bridge. An intricate, many-colored graphic, relating various recovered data files, she thought, floated over his console. He glowered—at her, Kirsten suspected—but said nothing.

"Show me the external sensor data for the five years before robots boarded this ship."

"That data has—"

"Kirsten!" Sven snapped. "All location data is gone. You have to accept it."

"Why is this one category of data gone?" she asked. "Did Citizens destroy it?"

"That data has been corrupted," Jeeves intoned.

"I don't begin to have your skills with computers," Sven said. "Maybe, given enough time, you can recover something. But think: Citizens have held this ship for generations. If the data were here, wouldn't they have gotten it somehow?" His expression softened. "Don't you *hope* the data is inaccessible?"

She shivered. If primitive chemical rockets made the Gw'oth a potential threat, how would the Concordance have reacted to her starfaring ancestors? How react, that was, beyond their unprovoked seizure of *Long Pass*? All too easily she imagined the preemptive destruction of human civilization. Trillions of people, in Kirsten's imagination, on human worlds spread across the sky, until the Citizens came. And after?

More than ever, she wanted to find Earth. She wanted to *know* the fate of her people.

"Jeeves," she tried again. "I would like to see data about astronomical observations made during the flight."

"That data has been corrupted."

Sven stood, shaking his head. "I'm getting coffee. What can I get you?"

"Coffee," she repeated mechanically. As Sven was leaving, she managed not to ask Jeeves about astronomical objects not examined during the flight. How tired *was* she? Even if that data weren't corrupted, the set of unexamined objects must encompass most of the universe.

And yet . . .

There was something else to try. She was sure of it. Something she *knew*. Something she had done before. Something about comparing two mutually exclusive sets.

By the time Sven returned with her coffee, Kirsten was pondering the fact that Jeeves deemed several terabytes of memory neither inaccessible nor accessible.

· **29** ·

The nondescript stony lump that Julian had dubbed Forward Station waxed slowly in the radar display. In the forward view port, with photomultipliers set to maximum, evidence of habitation emerged: airlock hatches, strings of emergency lights, antenna dishes, the faint impressions of past ship landings. Nessus cautiously lowered *Aegis*, pressing another dent into the primordial surface.

Julian Forward netted in from an underground laboratory. "Welcome back, Nessus."

"Thank you, Julian. Are we alone?"

Forward's nostrils flared. "Nessus, I *told* you we would be alone, just as I've promised not to tell anyone about you."

Dismounting his padded bench, Nessus stretched necks and legs. "This must be a short visit, Julian. I would like to get directly to your progress report."

"Come in, and we'll get started," Forward said.

"This will go faster if I stay aboard." Had Nessus not worked closely with Colonists, he might not have recognized that rigid pose. Forward was offended—and strong enough to snap Nessus like a twig. Nessus hoped the Jinxian never learned how his research grant got canceled.

Colonists. Nessus did not want to think of them now. "Julian, your status?"

Forward never needed much encouragement to discuss his work. As always, the nuances surpassed Nessus' understanding, so he made noncommittal answers whenever a response seemed expected. He recorded everything for the experts on Hearth.

Still, the broad outlines were plain enough. More experiments: some successful, as many not. Imploding a stasis field was hard. So was maintaining symmetry as the field collapsed. Even harder was ascertaining what occurred, or failed to occur, within. Time stood still inside, within nanoseconds of the stasis field's activation. Thereafter, nothing but the mass within could be measured from outside.

"I'd make faster progress with proper equipment." Forward crossed his arms across his chest.

Ah. Nessus finally understood Julian's attitude. Freighters seldom called at Forward Station, deep within the Oort Cloud. A supply ship had recently come and gone—without the bulky, custom-built gravity meters Julian had ordered.

They, together with more mundane cargo items, had been displaced, at Nessus' intervention, to make room for the merchandise from Miguel. "I apologize, Julian, but I need those packages. Are they ready for loading?"

Station cameras followed Forward down a dimly lit corridor into a cavernous storage space. He gestured at stacks of crates. Shimmering holograms showed the seals remained intact. "What's in these? Rocks?"

"They don't concern the project, Julian."

"They do when they delay critical instrumentation that I—"

"Julian, please." Unseen behind his avatar, Nessus plucked at his mane, resisting the urge to remind Julian who worked for whom. He dare not demotivate his native expert, especially just as it became necessary to leave the human unsupervised. "A time-sensitive matter has arisen. I leave immediately, and those crates must go with me."

Julian leaned against a crate, eyes narrowed in calculation. "When will you be back?"

A few months, at least, considering merely the round-trip transit time—assuming he came back. Nessus was not about to provide even that slight hint to the location of the Fleet. "To be determined, but we can keep in touch by hyperwave radio." And via repeater buoys ejected along the way to disguise *Aegis*'s path.

Nessus also answered as best he could the unasked question: Would the project continue? "Funds already provided should last for a while. Your priority remains the prototyping of a neutronium generator."

"And do you expect to return before the money runs out?"

"To be determined," Nessus repeated. "I'll release other funds, if necessary. Can we load while we talk?"

"Do you expect to return?" As he spoke, Forward casually set the first crate into a transfer booth. Nessus got the impression Julian would be happiest if the funds and knowledge transfer continued without the oversight.

The box was practically weightless here, but microgravity

had no effect on inertial mass. What Forward shifted effortlessly, Nessus struggled to lift off a stepping disc. Box by box, deflecting queries as he labored, Nessus moved the cargo by floater into *Aegis'* main hold. The overflow filled the relax room and several corridors.

Would he return? Nessus honestly did not know. If he did, he would bring a proper neutronium generator. There would be no further need for Forward's services.

Clandestine Directorate's latest message raised more questions than it answered. *Explorer* was missing, its crew unaccounted for. Nessus was recalled immediately, by implication to scout ahead of the Fleet.

Nessus launched as soon as he had secured the shipment. The sooner *Aegis* reached the Fleet, the sooner Nike would tell him the nature of the emergency.

And the sooner he might know what had happened to three friends.

· 30 ·

Explorer's relax room, its exercise equipment and furniture temporarily crammed into cabins, barely and uncomfortably accommodated the gathering. Considerations more basic than comfort had determined the meeting location. They dared not be overheard. If heard, they must be behind an impregnable hull.

Sweat trickled down Kirsten's forehead as the ventilators ran full out trying to cool the overcrowded room. Elsewhere heaters ran, as the frigid ocean depths sucked the warmth from a starship submerged beneath NP4's cold sea.

Sabrina Gomez-Vanderhoff stood in the doorway. "Let's begin," the governor said. "I don't see it getting any comfier in here."

No one had met everyone, so they circled the room doing quick introductions. Sabrina. The three crew. Sven.

Aaron Tremonti-Lewis: minister of public safety. Lacey Chung-Philips, short and brunette, in the drab garb of widowhood: the economics minister. Lacey peered about the relax room, craning to see into the corridor, as though aboard a spaceship for the first time.

With a nod, Sabrina signaled Sven to begin. He projected a hologram. A spherical spaceship, backed by a storm-wracked rim of NP5, now glowed in the center of the room. "Eric, Kirsten, Omar, and I recently spent several days aboard this vessel. You probably associate ships like this with grain transport. Not in this instance." The picture changed into a panoramic view of *Long Pass*. "This is inside."

"Our ancestors' supposed starship," Aaron said. Lacey just stared.

"That's what we're here to discuss," Sabrina said. "That and what it would mean. Please let the man continue."

Sven laid out his findings, voice firming as he proceeded. Hull repairs consistent with the attack that began the colony's official history. The many artifacts aboard for people shaped like themselves. A primitive synthesizer that offered safe and nutritious food. Needlework art whose floss and linen predated the founding of Arcadia colony. The almost-as-old stepping disc retrofit to the ship.

"Suppose you *are* right." Lacey's tone dripped skepticism. "Why would the Concordance withhold this information? Why not admit that they had located our ancestors' ship?"

Kirsten took the projector controls. "*Here's* why."

Lacey gasped as Citizen robots overran *Long Pass*. She finally asked, "Can you authenticate this?"

Sven squared his shoulders. "It appears real, with no evidence of tampering."

"Sven is our expert," Sabrina said. "So: Presume *Long Pass* is our ancestors' ship. How do we handle the situation?"

"Situation?" Lacey asked. "While this information remains secret, there is no situation. Not until we confront the Concordance—if that's what you decide to do."

"Suppress what we have uncovered? Ignore it?" Kirsten quivered with anger. "You can't mean that."

"I may not *like* it," Lacey said, "but I mean it. Silence is our wisest course. Picture thousands of Colonists becoming as enraged as you. Imagine the chaos."

"Colonists reacting with hostility, you mean. Rebelling." Kirsten struggled to express herself with terms that described teenaged misbehavior. How did one articulate anger and purposeful enmity between neighboring cultures? There ought to be a word.

Jeeves spoke English. Clearly, so had the crew of *Long Pass*. Did English—true English—have vocabulary appropriate to their circumstances? What else had Citizens expunged, besides all clues to the location of their ancestral home, of Earth?

Maybe it didn't matter. Maybe hostility and rebellion would suffice. Perhaps the time had come for Colonists to grow up and take charge of their fate.

"Yes, rebellion," Lacey said. "That's exactly the problem. Suppose that we lash out like an immature teen. We could damage some Hearthian crops, certainly, or disrupt food shipments. We might even imprison or threaten the few Citizens on NP4. How do you suppose the Concordance would react? Before you answer, remember that they grew food on the nature preserves long before they found *Long Pass*.

"The truth is, the Concordance does not need us."

"Kinetic weapons," Eric said to himself. "Like the rigged comet in the Gw'oth system."

"What?" Sabrina asked.

Eric grimaced, struggling for a brief explanation. "The details don't matter. Smack a planet with something moving fast enough, and it wipes out everyone and everything."

"That's why we were attacked! *Explorer,* I mean." Kirsten was sure of it. "Someone realized we weren't following orders, and worried that we might use the ship to strike Hearth. But they already had the exploding paint in place! They were *prepared* to betray us."

Pensively, Aaron rubbed his chin. "So possession of a starship gives us leverage. What if we also seized the ships at Arcadia spaceport?"

"Stop it!" Sabrina shouted. She glared about her. "How quickly your minds turn to mass murder. We don't even know that the Concordance ordered the attack on *Long Pass*. Yes, an attack followed a message to the world which would become NP5. I assume a Citizen vessel was there to coordinate the planet's migration, probably the same ship that now encloses our old ship.

"Everyone here knows Citizens personally. Is it so difficult to believe that the crew on that ship panicked, that they lashed out on their own? Perhaps the Concordance has since done its best to make amends."

Lacey nodded. "Whatever happened happened long ago. Long-dead Citizens attacked our long-dead ancestors. If rebellion ever made sense, that time has passed."

Kirsten stared, her fists clenched. "I don't believe this. At the least, the Concordance hid that past—*our* past—from us. The lies continue to this day. How can we keep serving them? How can we live with them?"

She shrugged Eric's hand off her arm. She didn't want to be calmed. "Sabrina, there are things I must know. That every Colonist deserves to know. Where do we come from? Did the Concordance treat that civilization any more gently than it did *Long Pass*? Is there some way our people can go home?"

"*Yes*, Kirsten. We really *must* decide what we want. Not just information, not just apologies, but a way to confirm these things. And is it only information we want? And what do we have to . . . negotiate . . . persuade them with?" Sabrina too was having trouble with an English stripped of too many concepts. "One tiny spacecraft. I suppose exploding paint cannot be exploded twice, and we have you for a pilot and codes to fly it. But compare *Explorer* to—" She waved at the nearly featureless holographic sphere: a General Products #4 hull. "They have thousands of those."

Eric said, "As for what we want . . . ? I suppose we want to leave."

Lacey: "Leave our *homes*? For what? This lost Earth?"

Aaron: "Maybe. If we knew enough."

The debate raged, every option unpalatable. Exile for a few, fleeing—to where, no one could say—aboard stolen starships. Futile acts of revenge. Provoking their own destruction. Shame and dishonor if they did nothing.

Kirsten finally stopped listening. Symbolic resistance or horrific destruction. Surely there was another way! Stomach churning, she mentally retraced the circuitous path that had brought them so close to the truth about their past.

The Ice Moon of the Gw'oth. The woods of Elysium. The General Products factory. The arcologies of Hearth. The Human Studies Inst—

The General Products factory and *Explorer*'s very thorough overhaul. Kirsten mused aloud. "While Nessus still commanded, this ship carried a fusion drive." The others stopped talking. They were actually listening to her. "General Products replaced the fusion drive with thrusters before we three were given control. Nessus had a fusion drive aboard for a purpose. Just as surely, the fusion drive was removed on purpose. I think I just realized that reason.

"A fusion drive directed toward a planet's surface would also be a weapon—precise, controllable, and horrible. Easier to point—more effective, maybe more credible—than a kinetic weapon."

Pointing at the hologram of an old ramscoop that still floated in the center of the room, Eric articulated the thought Kirsten guessed had leapt into everyone's mind. "*Long Pass* carries a fusion drive, if only we can use it."

Aaron shook his head. Lacey snapped, "Use it? It's—"

"It's locked in a box," Sabrina said. "An impenetrable shell. Whatever horror you're thinking of perpetrating, that old ship is of no use to us."

"Actually," said Eric, "It just might be the easiest part."

Their edges sharp, their corners treacherously pointed, Nike thought the crates stacked before him looked out of place even here in the bowels of the alien-artifact-filled depot of the Foreign Affairs Ministry. They'd bite you as you passed. Warning signs encircled the boxes, and a wide aisle encircled the signs. Cargo floaters, material-handling robots, and burly workers streamed all around, giving a wide berth to the mysterious delivery.

A worker shuffled forward, heads bowed. "I apologize, Your Excellency. Containers kept appearing, offloaded from the spaceport, marked to your attention."

The ministry depot, like almost anyplace on Hearth, was a mere step from his office. "You were right to contact me," Nike said. Besides his name, every container bore a prominent label: *Aegis*. Nessus' ship. Nike could imagine no peril here. He thought: I'm the *last* person Nessus would endanger.

He also thought, with less surprise each time it occurred to him, how much he had missed the scruffy scout. He would debrief Nessus soon enough, once Nessus rested from the tiring, long-distance, solo journey.

"What can you tell me about the contents?" Nike asked.

The worker straightened. He was short and broad, with dark brown eyes. Only the cloth gloves which covered his heads were transparent—and, of course, gas-permeable. The rest of the protective garment that covered his legs, torso, and necks had been turned blue to show his foreman status. Clothing on a Citizen, however appropriate the context, was jarring. The covered mane, scarcely discernable through the sturdy fabric, seemed especially disfiguring.

"Excellency, whatever you've been sent is very heavy. Scanners show only slabs of rock in foam padding. Nothing obviously dangerous."

Why would Nessus send a shipload of rocks? "Show me one." As the foreman stepped toward a wheeled scanner, Nike clarified, "Open one."

"Your Excellency?"

"It will be fine," Nike said. He sufficiently understood Colonists to recognize curiosity when, unaccountably, he experienced it himself. Or was this Nessus' influence again?

With impatience surely akin to the unaccustomed curiosity, Nike watched from behind a safety barrier as a robot carefully lowered the top crate from a stack. It pried off the top and sides of the container. Workers in protective garb converged to peel back the packing material. Finished, they stepped back in confusion, revealing figures carved with wondrous detail from the marble slab.

Nike wriggled his lips in unrestrained delight.

NIKE ROSE AS an aide ushered Nessus into his office. Nike was, as always, poised and immaculately coiffed. His mane gleamed today with gold and orange gems. "Thank you, Vesta," Nike said.

Vesta backed out, closing the door behind him.

"I see my gift arrived," Nessus said, admiring the marble sculptures that hung from one long arced wall. Heroic figures, on whom the draped cloth was elegant. Wondrous beasts. Flawless craftsmanship. Despite the spaciousness of the office, only a small portion of the art could be displayed. "They are finer than I dared to imagine."

"They are magnificent, Nessus. Are they what I think? The Frieze of the Parthenon?"

"Most of it," Nessus replied. "Acquired from the British Museum." Acquired was a neutral-enough term, and the humans themselves had quarreled for centuries as to the rightful owner. "Given your interest in human mythology, I hoped you would like them."

"Very much so." After a glance at the closed door, Nike crossed his necks flirtatiously.

How long I have waited for this moment, Nessus thought.

And how circumstances have changed. He walked around Nike's desk, the better to study two groups of seated figures facing each other. "Even human scholars cannot agree on its meaning."

Nike moved closer.

"The frieze is said to celebrate the creation of the human kind," Nessus continued. "Some say these scenes represent a Council of the Gods, debating the wisdom of that creation. We see that the two groups, representing both points of view, are closely matched."

And humanity's fate again rests in the balance.

"It's time, Nike, to tell me exactly what happened with *Explorer.*"

KIRSTEN FOUND LIGHT-YEARS distant from where she belonged. The entire crew conspiring. *Explorer*, intrinsically a deadly weapon, missing under the control of the duplicitous Colonists. The destruction of the ship made perfect sense.

Logic did not lessen the pain.

Nessus slumped on a bench in Nike's office, the triumph of his gift washed away by grief. Months without sightings of or communications from the three. They were surely dead.

He wondered who would tell little Rebecca.

For all his anger at the Colonists' deceit, Nessus accepted his responsibility in the tragedy. He had selected them. Taught them. Championed them.

Evidently, he had failed them.

Nike stood before Nessus, stroking his mane, massaging his tense shoulders, intoning a wordless dirge. "It had to be done, Nessus," Nike said. "Truly, I'm sorry."

"I know." Nessus shivered. "I'll heal."

"I liked them, too," Nike said. "But they chose their path."

Nessus could not bear to dwell on his loss. "I assume this ends the Colonist scouting program. Once *Aegis* completes overhaul, I'll go out again."

"In time." Nike began combing Nessus' mane. "For now, I'm glad you are here."

NIKE AND NESSUS circulated slowly through the crowd. Nessus sneaked another peek at their complementary braids. The hair artist so hastily summoned to prepare them could have been no more surprised than he.

The harmonized manes; the side-by-side walk, with flanks pressed together; their necks entwined in public, the introduction to each other's friends—all were affirmations. All were traditions that invited the scrutiny and approval of the community.

They were hardly mated, but a process had begun.

"Clio." Nessus repeated the name in greeting. "I am honored to meet you." His trilling sounded flat and discordant, but no one commented. How could he remember so many names? This social meadow in Nike's arcology teemed with Nike's friends, neighbors, and acquaintances. On the periphery, blending seamlessly, a virtual herd spread far into the distance.

They wandered among holo sculptures, dance performances, scent fountains, and mellifluous choruses, admiring the many forms of art with which most people filled their time. Sneaking another look at their coordinated manes, Nessus truly appreciated how much Nike and he had in common. They both worked.

Somewhere in their meandering, he and Nike joined a group of dancers. Legs flashing, hooves kicking high, voices raised in joyful accompaniment, Nessus realized: I'm *happy*.

This was not the mating dance, of course. Mating, should it happen, was far into the future. Still, amid the rich stew of crowd pheromones, sides heaving in exertion, throats thrumming accompaniment of a familiar ballet, Nessus allowed himself to envision the day he and Nike would walk together into the lush pastures of the Harem House.

In his imagination, Nessus saw a cluster of Companions. They grazed on a nearby hill, each lovely, each shy.

A Companion of surpassing delicacy and beauty glanced up from her nibbling. Twirling and leaping, he and Nike lured the fragile Bride with the perfection of their movements. She slipped between them and joined the dance, more graceful than anything he had ever seen. Their motions grew ever more intricate and sensual.

She broke free, and Nessus held his breath. This was the moment of decision.

The little one gazed up the hill to her friends. She could rejoin them, and resume the idyllic life that was all she had ever known. Or—

She looked back at her suitors. Slowly, she walked into the nearby circle of scarlet hedge. She settled onto a bed of lush meadowplant—

Their Bride.

A roaring crescendo celebrated the end of the dance. Nessus awoke from his reverie, sweat trickling down his flanks. Nike stood nearby, breathing deeply. Friends watched them both, blinking approval.

Never had the Bride-to-be been more real in his mind's eye.

Nessus permitted himself a moment of sadness for the Bride he had yet to meet. For after that glorious dance, after the tender moment of conception, after a year of doting by himself and Nike, would come childbirth.

And in giving birth to a Citizen, the Companion invariably died.

EXHILARATED AND EXHAUSTED, Nessus settled onto a pile of cushions. He owned only one small room deep inside an arcology, but Nike had a suite with an exterior wall. Craning his neck slightly, Nessus glimpsed woods below. The wall lighting panels were in their night setting, but the forest canopy shimmered in the light of the worlds.

Nike synthed a glass of carrot juice and another beverage for himself, then settled onto more heaped pillows. He seemed oddly withdrawn.

"What's wrong?" Nessus asked.

Silence greeted the question. Finally, Nike stood. He stared out the window, appearing not to focus on anything. "I would value your opinion on something."

"Anything," Nessus said.

"Do you know where we're going?" Nike began. As though with a will of its own, a forehoof scraped at the floor.

"We?"

"The Fleet, Nessus."

Had he ever seen Nike not in total control of himself? Nessus' mind whirled. "To the galactic north, I think. That is our shortest path from the galaxy, to open spaces where we can set a straight course without stars to be dodged. Then outward, far from the core explosion."

"And then?" Nike prompted.

What odd manner of conversation was this? "To another galaxy, of course."

Nike exhaled a minor chord of great sadness before raising his heads high with resolve. In dire and portentous chords, he spoke—

Of the races the Concordance had wronged. Of Sisyphus seeking endless, eventless stability in the darkness between galaxies. Of Eos' corrupt bargain. Of Nike's own worst fear: That the Concordance, devoid of stimuli, was doomed by its timidity to self-absorption, decadence, and eventual decay.

Nessus' mind had never ranged through fields this wide. Nike's ambitions were frightening. He would shape the race itself.

"What would you have us do?" Nessus asked.

"We should go inward, *closer* to the galactic core. To a place rich with stars and resources, yet past the risk of a supernova chain reaction. To a place vacated by potential competitors, where, in temporary isolation, we can con-

sider how better to coexist with other races. En route we
will find species who could not flee, who will welcome our
help."

Compared to the fate of the Concordance, Nessus
thought, how trivial his worries seemed, even the deaths of
three Colonist friends. As he searched for words of solace
and hope, an alert buzzed stridently. An icon materialized,
and Nessus recognized one of Nike's aides.

"Connect," Nike said. "What is it, Vesta?"

"Excellency, my apologies. You will want to see this
immediately." Vesta looked surprised to find Nessus in
Nike's home, but also relieved. "You, too, Scout."

"Speak."

"This must speak for itself," Vesta said. His off-screen
head tripped something, and a hologram replaced him:
humans, life-sized, too many.

· 32 ·

As the old Colonist woman walked into the close foreground, Nessus screamed in chorus. He settled into the
meadowplant rug, heads snaking under his belly . . . then
pulled one out, and the other. Weirdly, terribly, he saw Nike
doing the same.

The woman glared. "I am Sabrina Gomez-Vanderhoff,
Governor of the Arcadia Self-Governance Council. I speak
for the humans who have been repressed and exploited on
Arcadia for half a thousand local years—"

Humans! How did she know that word?

But it wasn't just her. It was everything. Nessus forced
himself to watch, made himself believe. *Preserver,* the
ancient grain ship converted for exploration, and *Long Pass,*
the old human-built interstellar ramscoop, and tiny *Explorer,*
somehow unharmed. The three ships were in computer composite, surely not part of a physical scene, but their mere

juxtaposition spoke of terrible secrets now revealed. In the foreground stood a crowd of Colonists as close-packed as Citizens. Despite his shock Nessus was relieved to see his three friends, still alive, among them.

Sabrina talked. Nike and Nessus listened.

"We have had enough of secrets and lies," Sabrina finished. "You will accept our demands, or pay a very high price. To begin, we are prepared to broadcast your secrets across the Fleet unless you contact us very quickly."

TURF FLEW AS Nike pawed the floor in anger and fear.

Long Pass, long hidden, now revealed. Colonists further provoked by Baedeker's botched attack on *Explorer.* The Colonial government threatening to reveal everything. Predictions—thinly veiled threats—of civil unrest and food-export disruptions. Insistence upon free access to everything pertaining to their past, on every world of the Fleet.

And they demanded what no Citizen would dare admit to knowing: the location of Earth.

He and Nessus had stepped through to his office at the ministry, where the marble tableau now mocked him. The Council of the Gods, debating the wisdom of creating humans, arrived just as the wisdom of creating the colony arose anew.

Nessus sidled up, pulling at a mane again unkempt. "They know too many Fleet secrets to ever have contact with wild humans. But to tolerate a hostile world within the Fleet—or to undertake to destroy a world here within the Fleet—both choices are mad."

Nike quivered agreement. He had seen simulations. A kinetic-weapon strike that eradicated the Colonists would blast loose mountains of debris. Most would fall back.

Some wouldn't.

How much of the ejecta would fly free? How much be captured by the complex gravitational dance of six co-orbiting worlds? How much would bombard Hearth itself? These were questions beyond the capacity of any computer to determine. Flaming mountains falling among the arcologies—

And no what-if scenario had ever considered that a Colonist-controlled, stealthed starship might retaliate in kind against Hearth.

And yet . . .

Nike willed his posture to straighten, his hooves to cease their restless pawing. Slowly he paced, pausing only once to seek inspiration in the eyes of Zeus.

"Nike," Nessus said. "Are you recovered?"

The demands of the Colonists. The needs of the Concordance. The futility—for all sides—of open hostilities. Secrets now beyond keeping and secrets yet secure. Possibilities and perils coursed through Nike's thoughts. "I'm fine, Nessus. Give me a moment."

Flight from the galaxy had somehow become familiar to the masses. But aggrieved neighbors living on a world so near as to raise tides on Hearth? *That* danger had no precedent, and Experimentalists always took their opportunities when the danger was most extreme.

It seemed the Colonists meant to restore *Long Pass*. They might intend only an act of respect for or identification with their ancestors. They might have come to the wily realization that a fusion drive loose in the Fleet would affect the strategic balance. It mattered not. Locked safely inside a General Products hull, even a restored ramscoop represented no threat— except to the complacency of the Conservatives.

A well-managed crisis here within the Fleet would bring Experimentalists—dare he hope? Would bring *him*—to power.

Only more deception would do, perpetrated by one with great skill at controlling humans. "Nessus, do you love our people? Do you love *me*?"

"Yes and yes!" Nessus sang. "What do you need?"

As Nike summarized the plan—as much, anyway, as anyone but himself needed to know, he felt the eyes of gods boring into him.

He tried not to worry about the warning from Euripides.

Omar loped on the dayroom treadmill, confident and secure, and not at all the obsequious shipmate Nessus had once known.

"Tell me about Oceanus," Nessus said. He had seen enough reports to know that nothing there represented a danger to the Fleet. The distant ocean world was merely a neutral topic of conversation.

"Wet. Primitive. Probably a good . . . refueling station." Omar blotted his forehead with a towel as he ran.

"Refueling?" That was perceptive. The Fleet would not pass Oceanus for years, during which time much deuterium and tritium could be extracted from its seas. Hearth's own fusion resources needed periodic replenishment, while the less depleted oceans of the Nature Preserves served as emergency reserves. "Good idea."

The treadmill slowed. Omar adjusted his pace. "How much about this did you know?"

"This?" Nessus asked.

"*Long Pass*," Kirsten said. Nessus' right head whipped around. He had not seen her enter the dayroom. "NP5. The way to Earth. Who did this to us."

"Hello. I wish I could answer your questions"—which was true, however misleading—"but you ask about things no one can know. Still, I know more than some."

He knew more than the technicians did. These were a dozen Citizens whom Nike had provided to work with the Colonists on *Long Pass*. They served as proof of Nike's good intentions. They brought technical skills or an interface to factories that could fabricate unique parts. They did not carry dangerous historical knowledge. And they were instructed not to share what little they might know about the Colonists' past.

"Separately, I want to congratulate you on your new relationship with Eric."

"Which you have, several times now. You can't change the subject forever, Nessus."

"My apologies. I mean no offense."

Coffee smell permeated the dayroom as she synthed a serving. "So how much about this did you know?"

"Which *I* have explained repeatedly." Nessus chose his words carefully. Since leading the small Citizen team to *Long Pass,* he doled out a bit more information with each repetition.

"Most Citizens don't know these things. You can believe that much! I could not have known you would buy histories while on Hearth. We're dealing with information held by a few officials. These are long-suppressed secrets the current government would still resist revealing."

Secrets that made it plausible this alliance of convenience must remain clandestine and restricted. Nike had convinced the Colonist leaders, at least for now, that this coerced cooperation must remain confined aboard this ship. That Experimentalist agents and Colonist rebels alike must avoid the suspicions and scrutiny of Concordance security authorities. Doubtless Sabrina and Nike both thought to exploit what they learned, to improve their negotiating positions later on.

Just as the technicians aboard conveniently knew only approved history, Nessus guessed he knew only a fraction of Nike's plans. That was for the best. Nessus could not let slip in error what he did not know.

He would rather that Nike trust him completely.

Omar and Kirsten exchanged skeptical looks. Nessus took it as a sign he was being too coy. "I've told you what I know about *Preserver.*" The ship that encased the little ramscoop. "*Preserver*'s crew deployed the planetary drive on the Ice World. As they escorted that world toward the Fleet, a comm laser contacted them. They panicked.

"Extrapolating the migratory planet's course, your

ancestors would have been looking at the comet band around Red Star. They'd have seen five worlds in clearly artificial orbits. A gravitational rosette is stable, but it doesn't happen naturally.

"Then as now, the Concordance considered the secrecy of Hearth's position essential to our safety. *Long Pass* was attacked lest it signal the Fleet's position. By hyperdrive, the trip was a matter of days."

The treadmill stopped. Omar hopped off. "Nessus, that doesn't make sense. We're discussing two ships nearly a light-year separated, communicating by laser. *Preserver* responded to a year-old message. *Long Pass* had that same year to signal home."

"*Preserver*'s crew lost all reason to their fear. In a way, it appears they guessed right. Your ancestors evidently had not yet signaled home." Nessus could hardly admit *knowing* that human records made no mention of a wandering Ice World. *Long Pass* itself appeared in UN records, the official cause of its disappearance "unknown."

Unofficially, everyone blamed technical failure.

A ramscoop swept up interstellar hydrogen for fuel, using intense magnetic fields hundreds of miles wide. Fields that intense were deadly to advanced life, so ramscoop technology was reserved for robotic craft. Crewed vessels, carrying their own fusion fuel, followed robotic scouts to the stars at much slower speeds: slowboats.

Long Pass's designers had built a bubble in the magnetic field, a safe zone to contain the life-support compartments. The briefest interruption would have killed everyone onboard. Ramscoops were proven technology. At the time, safety bubbles were not. Everyone assumed bubble failure had doomed *Long Pass*. What else could happen in the emptiness between stars?

More than two centuries had passed before humans crew-rated another ramscoop.

Eric said, "Guessed right. They *guessed*?"

"Please understand, I do not condone the attack." Nessus didn't back away from Eric's rage, but it was hard. "I meant only, strictly for keeping secret the Fleet's location, that they met their goal."

"You so carefully always say *they*," Kirsten observed. "Were you involved?"

The long-awaited question. "Absolutely not. This all happened before I was born."

Being entirely honest about something felt good. The opportunity so seldom presented itself.

PRESERVER, MORE THAN a thousand feet in diameter, enclosed twelve cargo holds, three parks, hundreds of cabins, a network of interlocking hyperdrive motors, miles of corridors—and, in the central cavity which once transported a reactionless drive of planetary scale, *Long Pass*.

A visitor setting hoof anywhere in *Preserver* inevitably spiked the temperature reading of some room sensor, the effect slightly more pronounced for Colonists than Citizens. By calibrating reporting thresholds with room sizes, Nessus turned the environmental-control subsystem into a serviceable tracking system.

Within the privacy of his cabin, Nessus watched the Colonists wander about *Preserver*. Some things about humans never changed, with curiosity high on the list. Eric soon limited his forays to the engine room and its technical files. Kirsten mostly visited the bridge. Omar and Sven entirely lost interest in the great ship. Despite crowding, they spent most of their waking hours aboard the ramscoop.

Then came the flash of empathy. *Long Pass* was built wholly by and for humans. It incorporated no Concordance technology. It made no compromise for the caution or convenience of visiting Citizens. In every detail, from ambient lighting to color combinations to door-latch and table heights to the taste of the air, the ramscoop proclaimed its independent origins.

No Colonist had experienced such an environment.

That the long-emptied ramscoop ship called to the Colonists made it simpler to keep them from coming upon anything unfortunate on *Preserver*. For that, at least, Nessus was grateful.

He burrowed deeper into a mound of cushions. Much had changed between him and his erstwhile crew, some subtly, more often not. Eric's close-cropped scalp was only the most glaring instance. Kirsten and Omar remained, warily, his friends. The newcomer, Sven, might become one.

Gone was the deference inculcated by generations of indoctrination. It was as though Nessus shared *Preserver*—and its many secrets—with wild humans.

Disaster loomed, and Nessus trembled.

A dot blinked red on the wire-frame holo of *Preserver*, which floated before Nessus. A warm body had appeared on the bridge. With a two-throated lament, Nessus stood. *Preserver*'s bridge was but a step by disc from his cabin. He guessed he would find Kirsten there.

It would not do for the Colonists to know he tracked them. Rather than onto *Preserver*'s bridge, Nessus stepped to the disc closest to the gangway onto *Long Pass*.

He found Sven in the dayroom, deep in conversation with Jeeves. Eric and Omar stood in the ramscoop's engine room, discussing technical esoterica with a General Products specialist.

Something suggested Colonist progress, something that Nessus could not at first put a tongue on. Then he had it: the absence of the fat power cable that had snaked from an auxiliary fusion generator in *Preserver*, through the open airlock, along corridors and down stairways, to the main power-distribution panel in this room.

Long Pass was now sufficiently repaired or refueled to generate its own power.

Nike needed time for a purpose not yet shared with Nessus. Let the Colonists waste that time restoring this ship—it would never fly again. Nanotech had sealed the great doors that once opened to swallow *Long Pass*. Like entropy itself, the extension of the super-molecule was irreversible. *Preserver*'s hull, except for small hatches, was now seamless.

It must be Kirsten's body heat that had set off the temperature sensors. She was unattended on *Preserver*'s bridge, where, doubtless, she poked about in the main computer. Data archeology was an activity for which, Nessus had belatedly recognized, she had few equals. "Where's Kirsten?" Nessus asked to cover for what he already knew. "I wanted to talk with her."

"The big ship's bridge," Eric interjected into the ongoing technical conversation. The rudeness miffed Nessus, although it spared him having to elaborate his story.

A stepping disc later, Nessus found Kirsten leaning against a padded bench on the bridge of *Preserver,* head tipped backward, eyes closed in thought. Holos surrounded her: navigational, graphical, and textual. "Hello, Kirsten."

She started. "You surprised me."

"I wondered how you were doing," Nessus said. "Eric said I'd find you here."

"You wondered *what* I was doing."

"There's no need to think that, Kirsten."

"Yes, there is. Too many secrets have been kept from us Colonists. We've been told too many lies. *I've* been told lies."

She didn't say by whom. She didn't need to. "Yet here you are, aboard this ship. Tell me truthfully, Kirsten. Did your path to *Long Pass* ever stray from total candor?"

She reddened. "We were inventive, of necessity."

Nessus said, "Then perhaps you can understand I also operated under constraints."

"You can see I'm fine." She turned away from him.

One of the floating holos caught Nessus' eyes: more material Kirsten might find troubling. "The planet en route, I see."

She enlarged that video.

At many times real time, the world that would become NP5 spun, swirled in clouds. The star that was no longer its sun shrank to a spark. Something in the display logic— Kirsten's contribution?—maintained apparent brightness as the star receded.

Storms raged as land and oceans surrendered their heat. The cyclones grew and merged, and the ocean spawned yet more storms, until thick cloud completely hid the surface.

"A world in its death throes," Kirsten said, her tone flat with disapproval. She set the playback rate yet faster. Cloud churned and whirled, its texture subtly changing. The clouds thinned. "Lakes and streams have frozen. Finally ice coats the oceans themselves, starving the storms." She fixed him now with a hard stare. "Now the atmosphere itself freezes, one gas at a time, covering land and ocean ice alike with new layers.

"Fast-forward, to arrival at the Fleet." Necklaces of little fusion suns streamed across space to ring the ice-sheathed planet. Storms formed anew as the atmosphere started to thaw. "An almost instant, oxygen-rich atmosphere, ready for eco-forming. Nothing above single-celled life could have survived the deep freeze to compete with Hearthian life forms."

Nessus straddled one of the bridge benches. "It was a primitive world. It would not otherwise have been taken."

"Primitive. Like Earth?"

Nessus jerked, realizing: *She thinks us monsters.* "Not even like Oceanus."

She did not respond. The silence grew oppressive. "You *know* the Concordance eco-forms worlds," Nessus said. "First, NP1 and NP2. They were arid worlds relocated within our original solar system, but further out. Before moving them, we bombarded them with comets. The collisions melted the ice. We massively seeded the new oceans with tailored single-celled organisms. Transformation of the primordial atmosphere took thousands of years."

Nessus pointed at her holo. "A world with ocean and oxygen-rich atmosphere is quickly productive, ready for soil treatment as soon as the thawing storms dissipate."

"Like NP3 and NP4, I suppose," Kirsten said. "And NP5, soon enough."

He had to appear to cooperate with the rebellious Colonists. That precluded blocking her access to *Preserver*'s computers. What he couldn't block, though, he might monitor—and so he had hurried here. Better still would be to divert her interest.

Computers aboard the old ramscoop had been exhaustively studied. Earth's location was *gone*. Nessus was supremely confident that not even Kirsten could recover the coordinates of any human world from those computers. He was far less confident that no proscribed data lurked in *Preserver*'s systems, if not residual from the ill-fated mission, then carelessly uploaded after its return to the Fleet.

He needed to distract her.

"The strange thing, Kirsten, is that the Fleet flees an abundance of worlds just like that." He extended a neck at NP5, huge beneath the bridge view port. "Every once-habitable world in the galactic core has been wiped clean. More and more will be sterilized as the radiation front passes. Millions of worlds, Kirsten, ripe for eco-forming."

Swiveling his heads, Nessus looked himself in the eyes. "If only those worlds were safe to approach before all that wonderful but reactive oxygen recombines."

With a shiver for effect, he dropped the ironic pose. "Enough gloom. Let us return to *Long Pass* for coffee and carrot juice."

As she vanished, stepping ahead of him, he permitted himself a much needed stirring of his mane before following.

NIBBLING DELICATELY, NIKE sampled the grass-and-fruit medley offered to him. The simplicity of the snack emphasized the naturalness and freshness—the expense—of its ingredients: another transparent offer. "Excellent," Nike said. With delicacy was exactly how he had to manage this meeting. "Thank you for agreeing to see me, Eos."

Eos gestured expansively. At the luxurious dwelling his venality had gotten him? At politics and life? At the presumed deal about to be made? "Of course. Always glad to see you. Have you considered what we discussed on your previous visit?"

"I have." Nike bowed a neck with feigned unease. "Will the Hindmost definitely propose a unity government?"

"Very soon," Eos said. "The time is right. The migration proceeds smoothly."

Smoothly? Wild humans still sought them. By disregarding that truth, Eos had betrayed his position. Had forfeited the right to continue as leader of the Experimentalists.

Nike decided: My conscience is clean. "A point worth making when you and the Hindmost announce your association."

"Indeed." Eos paused from refilling his trencher with more grain-and-fruit medley. "Is that important to you, Nike?"

"As leader of Clandestine Directorate, I am expected to watch objectively for problems. . . ." Another contrived bending of the neck.

"I see," Eos said. In the head not encumbered with a snack, lips wriggled with amusement. "It is more appropriate for you to agree that our circumstances are safe, especially to a suggestion *I* offer, than to volunteer that same assessment."

Nike lowered his heads submissively.

"I see your point." Setting down his trencher, Eos whistled a wry, double-throated arpeggio. "Then we have an understanding."

"We do." Nike straightened. He felt no shame for his lie.

Once Eos made his ill-advised declaration, and the Colonist crisis followed almost immediately, the whole Concordance would reach an understanding:

The current leader of the Experimentalists was unfit.

· 34 ·

Snoring softly, Eric turned lazily on his long axis, releasing Kirsten. Finally. She collapsed the sleeper field, easing them to the deck. She stood aside and reactivated the field before he stirred. He snorted in his sleep and she smiled.

Resenting her insomnia—or his easy sleep—accomplished nothing. Kirsten headed to the relax room for a sleeping pill from the autodoc. En route, she changed her' mind. She stepped directly from *Explorer* to *Long Pass,* the former docked alongside *Preserver*'s outer hull, the latter locked within.

After a detour for coffee, Kirsten went to the ramscoop's bridge. She found Sven already there.

"Oh, hello," he said. He continued shuffling papers.

"I'm sorry to see you can't sleep either."

"Coffee. We're all addicted."

She took the other seat on the bridge. "I hoped to chat for a bit with Jeeves. Will that bother you?"

"Nah." Sven spread the papers across a console ledge. "If it does, I'll move. I'm only here for a change of scenery. I can as usefully be stumped in my cabin or the dayroom."

"Thanks. I'll talk quietly." She swiveled toward the console, giving Sven the semblance of privacy. "Jeeves, this is Kirsten."

A cartoon of a round head with a moustache, smiled widely. "Good morning." It was, just barely, by ship's time.

"What can you tell me about Earth?" she asked.

"Very little. It's where humans come from. *Long Pass* was built in and launched from high Earth orbit."

"And you don't know where Earth is." Kirsten sighed. She already knew his answer.

"That data has been corrupted," Jeeves said regretfully.

She slouched in her chair, still not tired, but weary. Discovery of the ancestral ship was supposed to provide answers. Kept busy restoring the ship, Eric and Omar did not share her frustration. She did not share their intuition that mastering their forebears' technology would prove useful. Somehow.

Concentrate, she chided herself. "Could we, Colonists, live on Earth?" She had transferred basic knowledge to him, files about Hearth and the Fleet, about NP4 and Arcadia, hoping something would correlate with an otherwise useless scrap of his memory.

"Presumably," the AI said. "You can live in this ship."

"We may never know," Sven said, rearranging and crinkling papers. "The Concordance wants no one to know its location. Earth's authorities might have felt the same. Perhaps the data was only in the navigator's head. Perhaps they had a plan to erase it if they encountered others."

However logical the speculation, Kirsten could not bear to accept it. So *much* had gone into getting here. In the end, would they be left with only Citizen fables of their past? The possibility broke her heart.

She leaned back and stretched, stiff joints cracking. Sven had again rearranged his stack of papers. Task lists. Sketches. Snippets of inventory, some items checked or lined through. "Jeeves has terabytes of data. Why spend so much time dealing with these few bits?"

Sven shrugged. "The crew also had those terabytes. They found this worth recording by hand. It's worth a fraction of my time to wonder why."

"But doodles? At that, mostly doodles of flowers." Kirsten was reminded vaguely of the needlework she had taken her first time aboard. "Sure, we found them all over. After years in this cramped, sterile environment, I'd yearn for a bit of nature too."

"Even the flower drawings are interesting," Sven said. "You recognize them, of course."

Kirsten sipped the dregs of her coffee, now scarcely tepid. "A few. Buttercups and daisies. Irises, I think. That means the ship carried the seeds."

"Tyra, my wife, is quite the gardener. I recognize all these flowers, except maybe one." Sven tapped several sheets. "It looks like a fuchsia, except that every fuchsia I've ever seen has four petals. These all have five petals."

"Odd," she mused. "Maybe they brought seeds for those, too, but the breed didn't take."

Sven stifled a yawn. "Jeeves?"

"My inventory never included such a seed." The AI paused. "At least I do not think so."

In the corner of Kirsten's eye, Sven yawned again. She said, "Don't let me keep you up."

"Fair enough." He gathered up his papers. "So you see why I look to these few papers. The fuchsia discrepancy may mean nothing. Or it may show us that not only navigational data has problems." Big yawn. "But more likely nothing." He shambled off the bridge, presumably bound for his cabin.

Not even Sven's yawning had any effect on her. "Jeeves, remember the block of corrupted memory we last talked about?" The region somehow neither accessible nor inaccessible, of whose content and purpose Jeeves denied all knowledge. "Show details."

A graphic materialized: a fast-scrolling hexadecimal dump. The data sped past, telling her nothing. At so low a level of detail, how could it? "Pause. Is this program code or data?"

"A little of each," Jeeves said. "It's mostly meaningless."

Neither program nor data? "Is this unassigned storage? Something released by a program and not put back into use?"

"Unlikely," Jeeves said. "It's not queued for reassignment. Nor has it been initialized for reallocation."

Kirsten drained the last of her coffee. She had studied Citizen computers, not human computers, but surely they shared some common underlying principles. No one worked with such minutiae as memory allocation—such bit shuffling had long ago been optimized and standardized—but obviously data structures underpinned everything. "Jeeves, does this mysterious block belong to *any* data structure?"

"Yes," he answered. "Not a useful one. It's tagged not to be reused, as though it had a physical fault. If so, the fault is transient, because it passes all my diagnostics."

Back and forth the conversation went, without progress. Her mood darkened under the futility of it all. Jeeves did not know what he did not know.

What *she* did not know was simple: how to give up. "You said there is some data in this region. Does it use any data structure with which you are familiar?"

Jeeves shook its animated head: no.

Hmm. "You also said there is program code. That *must* correspond to a meaningful structure, or else you could not distinguish it from data. Correct?"

It nodded, the tips of its mustache bobbing slightly.

Kirsten jumped as the ventilation fan kicked on. She had ground to a halt. Maybe she might yet get some sleep this shift.

But first—"Jeeves, I'm thinking we should try to execute the suspected code segments. Can you recognize and intercept anything unsafe they might do, before they do it?"

"Clarify unsafe."

She thought. "Changes to program or data. Operation of shipboard systems." Attempting to fire the fusion drive while inside the enclosed space of *Preserver* would kill them quick.

"Then, yes, I can."

Kirsten rubbed her eyes. After disallowing all that, how would she know if those mysterious programs did anything at all? "Corrections. One, permit memory modification within only the anomalous region we're discussing. Two, on this console," and she pointed, "allow display and speech."

"Done," Jeeves said. "Shall I begin running the suspected code segments?"

"Go ahead."

The corrupted memory region held eight possibly executable code segments. Four, given the opportunity to run, did nothing. Three tried to transmit garbled commands over the main shipboard network; Jeeves blocked their attempts and terminated them.

The final segment opened up a primitive hologram at Kirsten's console: a narrow rectangle with a blinking square at one end. It might be nothing.

Or, she thought, it might be a login dialogue.

* * *

NOT LONG AGO, to bond with Nike had seemed the unlikeliest of occurrences. Somehow, though, that had happened. So perhaps the news broadcast from Hearth should not have surprised Nessus.

Instead, Nessus found himself struck tuneless.

The Hindmost himself had invited Eos to join the government. Eos himself had agreed, citing the new era of security well established by years of uneventful Fleet voyaging. The sanguine announcement mentioned neither questing ARMs nor rebellious Colonists.

Nike refused Nessus' calls, pleading pressing duties.

Behind his locked cabin door, heads below the delusional safety of his belly, Nessus marveled. There were forms of insanity far worse than scouting interstellar space.

PRESERVER STORED HUGE volumes of deuterium and tritium. Like *Explorer,* but on a much grander scale, its tanks were refilled through stepping discs and molecular filters. Operated in transmit mode, those same discs refilled the fuel tanks of fusion reactors across the ship. Thus were all of *Preserver*'s auxiliary vessels refueled, and its robots, and even its trash disposals.

Once Eric completed retrofitting a few stepping discs, *Preserver* would also replenish *Long Pass*'s tanks.

While Eric attended to refueling, Omar and Sven consulted with Jeeves about old inventory records, Nessus sulked in his cabin, and the Citizen technicians ignored them all to debate the latest political news from Hearth . . . Kirsten fretted.

After finding that single semi-functional code fragment, she had been too excited to sleep. No, be honest: too depressed. Say that she had found a hidden application. How could she possibly log in? Her exhaustion went beyond coffee's powers; she switched to stim pills.

Arms folded on the dayroom table, head down on her

arms, Kirsten visualized the display invoked by that mysterious code. The blinking square was likely a cursor. Presumably the long rectangle was a data-entry field. If so, the field accommodated six characters. Random typing had proven the field did not expand to permit more.

So, twenty-six letters and ten digits. She would be an optimist, and assume the password contained no punctuation marks. Six character positions. That made thirty-six to the sixth possibilities. Two billion, more or less.

Guessing would not solve this problem and whoever had set *this* puzzle was doubtless wily enough to have defended against a brute-force attack.

Guessing would not solve this problem.

When the stim pills finally kicked in, Kirsten noticed she was hungry. She tried another experiment from *Long Pass*'s synthesizer: pepperoni pizza.

Sven had covered one dayroom wall with old flower doodles. She couldn't tell most flowers apart, except for their differing numbers of petals. Why had someone spent so much time drawing these things?

The synthesizer disgorged her pizza. It smelled wonderful. The first bite seared the roof of her mouth.

Flowers everywhere. Flowers on that handicraft from her first time aboard. If those flowers meant something, why were the fuchsias drawn wrong?

More cautiously, she took a second bite. Pizza tasted wonderful. An Earth recipe, she decided.

And Earth flowers? Was a message hidden in the flowers?

Kirsten stared at the wall of drawings, desperate to see a pattern. Messy sketches. Many varieties. Petals and leaves. Something about the petals. The number of petals?

On one sheet, flowers with three, five, and twenty-one leaves. On another sheet: three, eight, and five. The next: eight, three, and five. Something teased her memory.

Across all the drawings, the flowers exhibited only a few distinct numbers of petals. She sorted the list: three, five, eight, thirteen, and twenty-one.

She saw a pattern, but no meaning. Three and five are

eight. Five and eight are thirteen. Eight and thirteen are twenty one.

She finished the pizza and went to the bridge. A Jeeves animation was deep in discussion with Sven and Omar. There was no room for her inside. "Jeeves," she called from the corridor. The AI could multitask. "Three, five, eight, thirteen . . . what comes next?"

"Twenty-one, thirty-four, fifty-five. They're all in the Fibonacci series, Kirsten. Starting with zero-one-one-two, every number in the series is the sum of the two that precede it."

Omar looked up, impatient at the interruption. "Kirsten, can you play number games later?"

So the series had a name. Did it have a purpose? "Jeeves, what is the meaning of that series?"

"The Fibonacci series occurs frequently in nature. In botany, for example, Fibonacci patterns appear in the spiraling of petals, leaves, and pine cones, the clustering of seeds, and the growth points at which plants branch and rebranch. In zoology, the Fibonacci numbers appear in the dimensions of successive compartments in the shell of the nautilus. The so-called golden rectangle . . ."

"Kirsten," Sven grumbled. "I've found my way to a listing of species once carried on this ship, including marine species new to me. Can your fun with numbers wait?"

She ignored Sven, too. "Jeeves, you said the pattern occurs in nature. Did you mean all nature, or earthly nature?"

"Earthly nature," Jeeves said.

So: She had found a code fragment, with what might be a dialogue box. A secret program hidden in the earthly computer, possibly accessed by a secret password. A secret *earthly* password?

Might the flowers everywhere carry a message? Something that only humans might notice? Fibonacci numbers. Flowers with three, five, eight, thirteen, and twenty-one petals.

She was stumped.

Kirsten sat on the corridor deck, back against a wall,

staring into the bridge. 3-5-8-13-21. Seven digits. The suspected password field allowed six.

"Sven!" He looked up at her yell. "You said fuchsias have four petals, not five?"

He nodded and went back to his work.

Discard the five as disinformation. 3-8-13-21. Six digits meant 720 permutations. She could *do* that. She climbed back to her feet.

Light-years and generations and centuries . . .

Would the Colonists' secret past finally be revealed through a brute-force search? For all Kirsten's excitement, the aesthetics of that possibility offended her. *Logic* had brought them here. *Logic* should complete their quest.

What else did they know?

Flowers and Fibonacci numbers. Badly rendered flowers. She recognized only some of the flowers, but even she knew real irises grew much taller than real daisies.

Kirsten searched her pocket computer for an image of the ancient needlework. Of the many flower representations, only that one was in color, obviously labored over the longest. Short irises and tall daisies. Might tallest representation denote the most significant digit? "Jeeves, run the last program fragment we found, with the same isolation measures. Into that text box, enter 8 3 21 13."

A trumpet fanfare rang out. A human hologram appeared, seemingly in a cabin of this ship. No, Kirsten thought, it *is* this ship. The needlework she had taken still hung on the wall behind the apparition. Sven's mouth fell open. Omar froze.

The man in the holo had dark eyes, hair, and complexion, and a face of indeterminate age creased with worry lines. His jumpsuit, of a curious plaid pattern, did not disguise a pudgy body build. His eyes were worldly wise and weary, and yet they conveyed a hint of humor. Kirsten could not help but think: I would like to have known this man.

He spoke. "I am the navigator of starship *Long Pass*. I have a story to tell.

"My name is Diego MacMillan."

Nike plunged into the murmuring throng that filled a randomly selected outdoor mall. Vesta struggled to keep pace. Sunlight panels shone from arcologies all around. Jets of water shot high into the air from a fountain not otherwise visible through the crowd, the spray cool on Nike's hide. Herd scent embraced him.

"Excellency," Vesta wheezed. "Please wait."

Poor Vesta could not understand the fleeting nature of this moment. Soon, there would be no more opportunity to mingle with the crowd, at least not for Nike.

Voices warbled and chanted, crooned and trilled. The main topic of conversation, today as ever since the recent announcement, was the prospective unity government. The harmonies: acceptance, trust, concurrence. The every-day-fewer discordances: doubt, anxiety, resignation.

Experimentalism obsolescent. Exhilaration and fatalism. Consensus emergent.

"Excellency," Vesta huffed. "This new government will happen. These harmonies cannot be denied. Accord is crystallizing." His voice quavered with the undertunes that, with no answer expected, asked, "Why?"

"Do not worry." Nike's undertunes rang with confidence. "This partnership cannot last. We do not live at the end to history."

For I am making history.

The Colonist rebels must have grown complacent sharing *Preserver* with Citizens. Trusted guards from Clandestine Directorate were in place aboard *Preserver,* in the guise of technicians. All the robots were refueled, fittingly the same robots that first took over the ramscoop built by Sol's wild humans.

Vesta finally caught up. He lowered his voices questioningly. "I do not understand."

"Patience, my friend." Nike swerved to brush flanks. "All will be well."

The picture grew ever sharper in Nike's mind's eye. All four Colonists would be taken prisoner aboard *Preserver*. *Explorer*, docked alongside *Preserver*, was harmless even if the prisoners never revealed the stepping-disc codes needed to reclaim it. Noisy but ultimately impotent furor among the Colonist rulers on Arcadia. Let the Colonists protest about the secret of *Long Pass* so long denied them—the deeper truths that might bring that unrest to a boil remained hidden.

Soon Eos would be proven wrong. Soon Eos would be proven unfit and unworthy to lead the Experimentalists. And soon a new party Consensus must turn to the one who had stopped a crisis here in the heart of the Fleet.

And, if public disappointment raged loud enough? Might the time be ripe even for a new Hindmost?

Very soon now . . .

· 36 ·

"I am the navigator of the starship *Long Pass*. I have a story to tell. My name is Diego MacMillan."

Omar, Sven, Eric, and Kirsten hugged the walls of *Explorer*'s relax room. The holo recording shimmered at the center of the room, projected from a copy downloaded into Kirsten's pocket computer. The message Diego had so elaborately safeguarded could be meant only for Colonist eyes and ears.

"I speak human to human, ancestor to descendant. Despite everything that has gone wrong, I retain hope humans will find this message. I had to hide the key in plain sight, trusting my ability to make the clues meaningful only to humans.

"And yet . . ." Diego scowled. "I cannot depend on that.

If our descendants are viewing this, I know how you must yearn for the location of your home, the planet Earth. To leave you *that* information would risk revealing it to the Citizens and leading these murderers to Earth itself. That I will not do."

Eric pounded the wall. Sven and Omar exchanged looks of frustration. Kirsten cursed. No matter that she respected Diego's reasoning: The road could not end here. It must not. She couldn't bear that.

Diego's scowl quickly passed. "On our way to settle a new home—New Terra, we agreed to name it—we encountered something amazing. Something awe-inspiring. We found a world traveling between stars. My observations suggested a steady acceleration for years. Reasoning that intelligence must be moving the Ice World, we signaled it by comm laser.

"Earth is a peaceful place, at least in my day. We believed that peace and prosperity arise naturally with advanced technology. We never considered that the knowledge to move worlds might come without wisdom. None of us, that is, except Jaime."

A lovely blonde woman appeared, a holo within a holo. "This is Jaime, my wife," Diego continued, his voice become ineffably sad. "You'll hear more about Jaime, and why she does not take part in this journal. She is the ship's doctor. Barbara is our captain, Sayeed our engineer.

"When we found the Ice World, Jaime dared to wonder: 'What if the aliens *aren't* friendly?' And because she worried, and because I love her, I took the one precaution I could. I prepared a computer virus that would obliterate all astronomical and astrogational data."

Kirsten slumped further. The way Diego had hidden this journal was brilliant—in ways, a kindred spirit. She could not imagine recovering a secret he had intentionally expunged from the ramscoop's records.

"We knew how long our signal would take to reach the Ice World. We even threw a party when the planet continued on its extrapolated course long enough to receive our message. Our physics makes no allowance for faster-than-light communication or travel. We expected a long wait for a response.

"How naïve we were!

"Within hours of our celebration, a ship arrived, a whale of a ship, large enough to swallow us. Faster-than-light drive, obviously. Much faster. And so began our slavery to the Concordance." Diego smiled wickedly. "But *not* before I released the virus."

Whale was clear enough from context: something big.

"Slavery?" Omar asked. "Anyone know that word?"

"Human beings defined and used as property," Jeeves said. The notion didn't bother him.

The definition and its accompanying shock of recognition further blackened Kirsten's mood. She and all of her kind—too manipulated even to realize the depths to which they had sunk.

Wistfully, Diego admired the image of his wife. "We had shown we could track the Ice World, whose course pointed toward their home. Toward Hearth. We were attacked lest we reveal Hearth's location distantly orbiting a red-giant star. And so we were taken to the Fleet of Worlds, the secret place, the place from which, they tell me, we may never leave.

"There our nightmare became far worse.

"*Long Pass* carried more than ten thousand passengers, mostly frozen embryos. Our masters say their Concordance took pity, that they could not let so many perish. A few Citizens admit—but only to us, the few forever trapped on board—that they intend to turn our helpless passengers into a slave race. I believe they're at least being honest." Tears glimmered in his eyes (and Kirsten felt stinging in her own). "Two of those little ones are Jaime's and mine.

"The Citizens removed our onboard hibernation tanks to the world they call Nature Preserve Three. They lied to those they awakened about a derelict found adrift. Even so, most people had their doubts. When Citizens encouraged them to start their planned colony, the women resisted immediate implantation with embryos.

"*Long Pass* also carried embryos of mammals, cows and sheep and such, we meant to introduce on New Terra. Of course we had artificial placentas for those animal embryos. The Citizens were determined to have their colony. They experimented with implanting human embryos into artificial animal placentas. They 'refused to accept our voluntary extinction.'"

Kirsten squeezed Eric's hand. He had trembled since the reference to NP3.

"There were spontaneous abortions, horrific birth defects, and developmental problems." Remembered tragedies brought Diego to an eye-blinking halt. "To our masters, those were 'experiments.' To us . . . each was someone's child. Several women agreed to be surrogate mothers to stop the 'experiments.'

"Following a few successful pregnancies, our masters demanded that all women be surrogates. None would. The Citizens brainwiped a few. The rest submitted. Citizens saw nothing wrong with men alone rearing the babies, if it came to that. My guess is that Citizen females aren't sentient. The few men who rebelled—ran amok—were reunited with the four crew still imprisoned on this ship. Us. It's from them that I know the NP3 part of this sad history.

"Then one day, Jaime and Barbara were taken." Diego trembled with loss and rage. "Someone decided their uteruses offered more value than their minds. I know they couldn't be allowed to talk about the attack on *Long Pass* to the uninformed adults on NP3. They must have been brainwiped before joining the colony."

Diego got his voice under control. "And the men still aboard this ship? We counsel our masters how to structure a human society. We try through our advice to alleviate a bit of the suffering. We're trying to reduce forced pregnancies, especially by brain wiping. All the men insist that the mother's active role in child rearing is critical. Two centuries of gender equality is a small sacrifice to save women's minds.

"We do what else we can. Sometimes that's in the vocabulary and concepts we try to retain in the sanitized English taught to the children. Sometimes it's undoing the effects of Citizen mistakes." He smiled, almost despite himself. "Citizens are hardly beyond error. They wear no clothing, so they considered Colonist clothing a waste of resources. They learned quickly enough that nudity does not go with their disapproval of birth control *and* their hopes of controlling the bloodlines."

The smile faded. "I fear they suspect our indirect interference. We've been told of a new colony, this one on NP4, started with only children under Citizens' supervision.

"All that remains for me is hope for the children. If you viewing this recording are like me, are human, know this: You descend from an accomplished people. We settled our whole solar system. We planted colonies, *peacefully,* on the worlds of other suns." Diego swallowed hard. "I wish I could give you the way home. Earth is a beautiful world."

"And if you viewing this recording are Citizens, I wish you go straight to hell."

· 37 ·

Beneath the watchful eyes of Zeus, Nike decided: It is time.

He reached Nessus in his cabin aboard *Preserver,* the moment too auspicious to mind the nearly ten-second round-trip delay. "Nessus, the Directorate will soon release an urgent communiqué. I wanted you to hear about it first from me.

"It announces the seizure by renegade Colonists of a Fleet facility in orbit around NP5. Our self-sacrificing crew, aboard to monitor eco-forming progress, were taken hostage, but a few"—he kept speaking over Nessus' protest, finally arriving after a few seconds at light speed— "a few hostages escaped. They radioed a report to authorities and will attempt to reassert control. Clandestine Directorate has surrounded the facility with ships, so that those responsible cannot escape."

"Nike." Nessus waited to be sure it was his turn to talk. "Nike, we *agreed* to the small Colonist presence aboard. The technicians are not hostages—although I suppose neither are they merely technicians. How can you call the Colonist presence a seizure?"

"How can you *not* understand?" Nike demanded. "Promises we made to the Colonists we made under duress. We owe them nothing. Our paramount duty is recovery of *Explorer,* or at least its removal from Colonist control."

The comm channel fell silent for much longer than light-speed delay could explain. Pawing the deck, Nessus finally asked, "And when the Colonial government protests?"

"Who will believe them when *Long Pass* no longer exists?" With a graceful wave of the neck, Nike dismissed the certain response before it could arrive. "We have learned by now everything that that primitive spacecraft has to tell. It is only a memento, and we have surely seen that keeping it is an unnecessary risk."

Nessus shuffled in his cabin, too confined to pace. "And the four Colonists? I consider them friends."

"I am not cruel," Nike said. The questions began to irritate him. A budding relationship did not excuse the implied criticism. "They will be taken to the NP3 compound." *If* they survive the takeover, Nike admitted to himself.

With a shiver, Nessus got his feelings under control. "I understand, Nike. I would not want to get in the way inadvertently. Can you tell me exactly what will happen when?"

Relieved by the change in attitude, Nike did.

NESSUS STEPPED TO one of *Preserver*'s empty cargo holds. There he circled and circled, amid the clop-clop-clopping echoes of his hooves. Music skirled and resonated as Nessus muttered to himself. It sounded like a small herd in here.

Were the Colonists a threat to the Fleet or merely an embarrassment to the government? Or were they—and he—puppets in some play he did not understand?

He could say nothing—but silence would betray his friends. He could warn them—but of what, exactly, and how much? Would he be betraying Nike?

Nessus set aside the troubling question he had no time now to confront: Could he love one so deceitful and manipulative?

Nessus tugged at his mane. So many questions! All he knew for certain was that Nike had lied to him. As *he* had lied, on many an occasion, to his crew.

The assault was imminent. This impotent agonizing would soon become a decision. A decision with likely outcomes Nessus did not believe he could live with.

He stepped back to his cabin. The surveillance system showed no Colonists aboard *Preserver*. On *Explorer*, then. He called Kirsten's communicator. Nothing.

Finally, she answered, looking wary. "Yes, Nessus?"

Why wary, he wondered. Could she possibly know? "I need to speak with you four. Where are you?"

"We're busy right now," Kirsten said. "Can this wait?"

Nessus straightened, wondering if the body language would make any difference to Colonists, especially skeptical ones. His conscience demanded he try. He had to convince them. "Go to a secure channel." Her image dissolved to kaleidoscopic writhing, then reformed. "Kirsten, we've been betrayed. If you return to *Preserver*, you will be arrested soon. *Explorer* is completely boxed in by other ships, so you cannot escape that way.

"If we act immediately, I think I can sneak you back to NP4 aboard *Aegis*."

"ERIC, COME ON," Kirsten shouted. "What are you doing, anyway?"

"Almost done," Eric said, his face scrunched in concentration, his fingers flying over a bridge console. "I don't have time to explain." Eric rapped the console. "Done."

They ran to *Explorer*'s relax room and stepped through to the dayroom aboard *Long Pass*.

Sven and Omar had stepped ahead to *Long Pass* to admit Nessus through its airlock. The stepping disc aboard the ramscoop remained secured with codes they were loath to share with any Citizen. Nessus, looking more unkempt than usual, opened his communicator. "Colonist translation mode, on. You know Nike. Now watch and listen."

Kirsten steadied herself against a wall. "Nessus, how can we trust you? You've lied to us before. You've withheld information from us. Maybe the trap is aboard *Aegis*."

Nessus plucked at his mane. "You are wise to doubt me. You are wise to doubt *any* of us. If this is a ruse, I am as much a dupe as you. You have been restoring this ship. Can it receive vid broadcasts?"

"I'll go to the bridge," Eric said. "What should I look for?"

"News from Hearth. I would hope an interstellar receiver can receive leakage from local transmissions."

Eric left. Minutes later, full-textured warbling burst from the intercom. Nessus' communicator translated.

Hostage crisis. Government crisis. Disgrace of the not-quite-formed unity government. The nearly converged Consensus, dissolved and condemned. Swelling clamor for Nike and his Permanent Emergency faction.

Did she trust Nessus' translator?

Eric shared her doubts. "I'm switching to an independent translation."

"Resources under the authority of Clandestine Directorate expect to recapture the facility soon," boomed Jeeves. And in lower tones, "I was taught to translate over the years."

"We must hurry," Nessus insisted. "This broadcast is real. The assault will be real. You will be attacked by robots such as attacked *Long Pass* long ago."

The translated broadcast cut off. "Nessus is right, at least about that," Eric said. "Hull cameras show a dozen Citizens and many more robots converging on the gangway. I've put an override on the exterior airlock controls. That won't keep them out for long."

"Hurry, please," Nessus pleaded. "Step through to *Aegis,* if it is not already too late. When the security forces realize I am with you, they will take over *Aegis* or block it in as well."

Sven's eyes darted like a trapped animal's. Remembering the old video of robots cutting their way in? "Nike's message to Nessus spoke of *removing* this ship. Is *Long Pass* repaired enough to fly out?"

Omar grunted. "*Preserver*'s hull is sealed. I can't find any trace of cargo doors. Nike must mean to remove *Long Pass* in tiny pieces. Or maybe they'll drop *Preserver* into a star with this ship still inside."

Kirsten's mind raced, desperately seeking an escape. But even if they were doomed, their report must get out. "Eric! Can we transmit, too? If so, send the Diego MacMillan recording to Hearth and NP4."

"Diego MacMillan?" Nessus' heads pivoted in confusion. "Who is that?"

"Will do, Kirsten," Eric replied. "But I need you on the bridge."

She uploaded a copy of Diego's message to Nessus' pocket computer—he should know they would no longer be taken for fools—and ran for the bridge.

Holos floated all around Eric, some status, some system specs, and a few apparently real-time video. In the largest holo, robots approached the gangway. "What can I do?" she asked.

He asked without looking up, "Do you trust me?"

"You and not much else." They were running out of time. "If you have an idea, try it."

Ruby-red, a laser beam blazed out from near *Long Pass*'s bow. Decking bubbled and steamed at the robots' feet. "Comm laser," Eric explained. "Teach them some caution." The smaller holos flickered and danced all around him. "Jeeves, status check on the ramscoop?"

"Ready on your command," Jeeves said.

Eric opened another holo, real-time video of the day-room. "Nessus." The scout was rapt in Diego's recording. "Nessus! Listen to me." Eric raised the intercom volume and whistled sharply. "Nessus!"

Heads snapped up, startled. "Yes, Eric."

"In two minutes, I'm activating the ramscoop field. Do you know what that will do?"

Kirsten had no idea, but Nessus shook like a leaf. "It will kill everyone within hundreds of miles, except here in the life-support area."

Eric fired the comm laser again, scything a robot in half. "No, Nessus. Just everyone else within *Preserver*. The GP hull will contain the field. Everyone now has a minute, forty seconds to teleport off this ship. You need to tell them because they won't believe a Colonist. Then get out yourself—unless you trust us and truly want to help. A minute and thirty seconds."

Nessus screamed, like the pulling of a hundred rusty nails. His torso heaved. In seconds he mastered his fear, or anger, or whatever emotion had immobilized him. He war-bled rapidly and emphatically into his communicator.

Nike's security team must be somewhat mad, to plot violence against the Colonists aboard *Long Pass,* but they weren't much madder than most Citizens. They pivoted and ran for stepping discs. The robots paused in their tracks—but only briefly. Nike's agents resumed their remote-controlled attack from the safety of their docked ships.

Nessus had not moved.

"Nessus . . ." Kirsten trailed off, at a loss for words.

"Because you do not deserve what has been planned for you," Nessus said. "If nothing else, I offer myself as a witness."

In the composite panorama from the hull cameras, three broad I-beams, one supporting the gangway, converged to support *Long Pass*. All three supports terminated in the massive band that suspended the ramscoop ship in *Preserver*'s vast central cavity, against *Preserver*'s gravity generator. Writhing shadows on the cavity wall hinted at robots scuttling along the hidden undersides of all three approaches. The comm laser could not reach them without severing the support beams and sending *Long Pass* crashing.

Eric called, "Omar, Sven, Nessus. Get aboard *Explorer*. I think you'll get a chance to get away."

Omar's voice snapped, "Then both of you come too!"

"I must be here to give you that chance," Eric said. "Kirsten, you'll be safer with them."

She massaged his shoulders, taut with tension. "I'm staying with you."

"Where will I be most helpful?" Nessus asked.

"Here on *Long Pass*." Eric opened another display. A wire-frame map of *Preserver*, Kirsten thought. A red dot pulsed on the hull, its significance lost on her.

"Sven, Omar, go!" Eric shouted. "In about a minute, all hell will break loose. Your autopilot will kick on. That's your chance."

Kirsten watched them vanish from the dayroom. Nessus remained, pawing at the deck.

"We're hemmed in, all right," Omar reported a moment later. "Right up against *Preserver*'s hull. I don't see how the autopilot can help that."

On the distant, curved wall of the central cavity, the scuttling shadows seemed closer. They would begin carving their way into the hull at any moment.

Eric never looked away from his keyboard. *Long Pass* appeared now inside the wire-frame drawing, with a faint line connecting the ramscoop with the mysterious red dot. "What happens now?" Kirsten asked.

"Now we see if I'm worthy of you." As Eric spoke, the communications laser blazed out from *Long Pass*'s bow, far brighter than before. Bright enough, Kirsten marveled, to reach between the stars. The beam punched through *Preserver*'s cavity wall like tissue paper. Molten metal dripped from the hole. As the beam traced a spiral, the hole grew. Chunks of wall and decking fell inward.

Eric finally looked at Kirsten. "Remember the General Products factory? Remember how unhappy Baedeker was at my questions?"

Through metal vapor and a maelstrom of in-falling debris, she glimpsed a tunnel that gaped to *Preserver*'s hull. There the ruby-red light vanished, the absence of scattering in a vacuum rendering the beam invisible. "Baedeker?" she repeated. "He didn't say anything about light. Anyway, we know the hull is transparent to visible light. How does the laser help us?"

The shadows had almost reached *Long Pass*'s hull.

"Remember what Baedeker refused to explain. Nessus said there's a power plant embedded in the hull. The power plant reinforces the interatomic bonds of the hull supermolecule. I found it. The hull—the supermolecule—is transparent to visible light.

"Kirsten, we know we can't find Earth. We need to concentrate on what we want from the Concordance when we win."

"We're *winning*?"

TERAWATTS OF COHERENT light poured from *Preserver*'s General Products #4 hull—all but the tiny fraction of the questing beam intersected by a sealed, lifetime-fueled, embedded power plant. A tiny fraction, but still gigawatts of focused power.

The fusion reactor overheated and shut itself down.

Artificially constructed interatomic bonds were suddenly without reinforcement. The super-molecule that was *Preserver*'s hull regressed into ordinary matter. To Kirsten's view, a wave of opaque gray spread across the big ship's hull.

The dust shell around *Long Pass* held, bulged, then blew away like a dandelion puff in a tornado.

Air pressure exploded the flimsy decks and partitions, spewing shrapnel large and small. Lights, gravity, communications—every system died. Kirsten gasped as the floor fell out from under her. Eric didn't twitch.

Explorer, whose autopilot Eric had set to dart *inward* on full thrusters, bulldozed through the debris, away from the ships that had confined it.

Now *Long Pass*'s laser flicked downward, severing the massive support beams. Attitude jets set *Long Pass* spinning, faster and faster, hurling away any robots that still clung to the stubs.

"Jeeves," said Eric steadily, "We're getting too much radiation. Way too much. How are you doing with the ramscoop?"

Kirsten needed a moment to decode that. Orbiting NP5 with neither *Preserver*'s hull nor the planetary force field for protection, radiation induced by the Fleet's own velocity was blasting the old starship. Was blasting *them.* They needed the ramscoop's magnetic field to divert the oncoming muck.

"Working," Jeeves answered. "Working. Hydrogen density is adequate, velocity is adequate. Ramscoop fields in place. Accelerating at point zero zero three gee and rising. Eric, *Long Pass* is surrounded by rubble."

"Use the comm laser on anything that's in our way. Kirsten." Eric's voice shook with tension and exhaustion. "I could really use a good pilot just now."

"You got it," Kirsten said.

Atop a miles-long column of blue-white fusion flame, *Long Pass* set its course for nearby Hearth.

38

Shouting.

Nessus squeezed himself yet more tightly, and the muffled noise faded. Then a rough kneading began, the heads—no, hands—unfamiliar to him. Colonists!

He remembered the gravity dying, then spinning, faster and faster. He'd been flung off his hooves. He had tucked himself into a tight ball just as he hit the dayroom wall.

Nessus cautiously unclenched a bit. A man's voice called his name. Eric's voice. Nessus unclenched a little more. "Where are we? Are we safe?"

"We're on *Long Pass,* on our way to Hearth. As to our safety, the circumstances don't permit an easy answer. Come out so we can talk."

"*Preserver* is going to Hearth? Why?" Nessus asked.

"*Preserver* has been destroyed. It's just *Long Pass.*"

With a wail, he compressed as tightly as he could. Eric's voice became unintelligible until suffocation forced him to loosen a bit. Then Nessus heard: "Less than an hour to Hearth."

Shuddering convulsively, Nessus unrolled and stood. He was still in the dayroom. The room's main holo showed a telescopic image: a cloud of debris glittering by sunlight against the stormy backdrop of NP5. Gases faintly aglow, streaming past in primary colors, converged aft: the ancient ship's ramscoop come to life.

"*Preserver* destroyed? That's impossible! It would take large amounts of antimatter." Nessus waited out an involuntary tremor. "Are you bringing antimatter to Hearth? You play with star-fire energies as casually as you put edges on furniture!"

"You've kept many secrets, Nessus." Eric grinned unpleasantly. "I have mine. I suggest you consider more pressing matters. Kirsten"—he raised his voice—"What's our status?"

"I'm here." Her voice over the intercom sounded frighteningly tense. "I've been beaming Diego's final message to Hearth for the past twenty minutes. We arrive in another forty."

Nessus sensed an unarticulated question in her tension: What then?

He nipped and tore at his mane, thoughts churning. Freed of *Preserver*, the Colonists hardly needed antimatter to threaten Hearth. A low orbit while operating the ramscoop field would quickly kill billions on the ground. A drifting hover over almost any populated area would kill mere millions. Lacking hyperwave radio, *Long Pass* carried a comm laser powerful enough to beam across light-years. At short distances, it, too, would be fearsome.

Eric watched silently, appraisingly. Nessus thought: I'm meant to work through the horrors of this situation. He knows they have a position of strength.

Forty minutes. What could possibly stop this ship? Very few Citizen pilots were insane enough to fly anything other than routine food transfers. That was why the Colonist scouting program began in the first place. Who would be *so* insane as to board a ship now, knowing that it could be dissolved around him?

Hearth was *hidden,* not *protected.* How could a planetary defense be organized in mere minutes?

Shaking violently, Nessus battled his useless instinct to flight. Where could he go? Where could anyone go? "You said I would be most helpful here. What would you have me do?"

"Kirsten?" Eric prompted.

She answered in a firm voice. "Radio the Concordance. Persuade the authorities that the price of Hearth's safety is immediate freedom for all Colonists, publicly promised."

"We arrive in minutes!" Nessus said. "The government is in chaos. You cannot expect—"

"We do expect," Eric interrupted. "Time changes nothing except their ability to conspire against us."

"Call Nike," Kirsten said. "Do it now. Convince him we're serious, so that we do not have to show *how* serious. However chaotic the government, Nike will know whom to contact."

"Freedom from what? What do you want?"

Kirsten said, "I think we want NP4."

Nessus whistled a wordless query.

"I can't think of a safe way to claim just the continent of Arcadia," Kirsten said. "We'll have to take the whole planet. Does NP4 still have its motor? Of course it does, we've been accelerating for years. Nessus, you wouldn't still want us as neighbors, would you? After this is over, we'll have to be gone, one way or another. We're too dangerous."

Nessus' thoughts raced. Less than forty minutes until the end of the world. "I'm coming to the bridge, if that's satisfactory."

Eric shook his head. "You can talk from here."

Did they think him insane enough to attempt to retake the ship from them? Perhaps so: Eric now held a flashlight laser. Nessus shook with fear and rage. "I'll stay." He plunged a head into a belt pocket to tongue communications codes. "This will get us through to Nike."

THE HOLO BROADCAST was ubiquitous: in millions of stores and dining halls, in billions of homes, and, magnified to many times life-size, in public spaces around the globe.

Even here in the remote island retreat of the Hindmost.

Everywhere, Diego MacMillan glared at his oppressors. Nothing short of a Fleet-wide network shutdown might interrupt the damning recitation. Nothing short of a

Fleet-wide network restart might purge all the copies. Even then, countless billions would remember it.

I do not believe in ghosts, thought Nike, and yet here one is.

Nike did his best to ignore the dissonant clamoring that filled the room. The Hindmost let his ministers, Eos newly among them, prattle on, obsessing illogically on how best to explain or excuse or resuppress centuries-old tragedies. Did no one wonder why the Colonists had released this history?

Maybe a few did. The more practical among the ministers had succumbed already to the dubious safety of their underbellies.

Unexpected trilling released Nike from his futile musings. Only Vesta held the access code that could reach him now. Nessus had known it too, Nike thought sadly. There had been no word from Nessus since the destruction of *Preserver*.

Nike took the call, wondering: What new catastrophe has occurred?

Nessus appeared in a small holo, and Nike felt a glow of relief. "You're alive!"

"For now," Nessus said. He stepped backward to reveal a hard-faced Colonist with flashlight laser in hand. "You remember Eric. He and Kirsten now control *Long Pass*."

The Hindmost extended a neck at the unexpected holo. "You dare to take calls at this time?" he roared.

Nike did not flinch. "The Colonists now command a weapon of frightening potency. Clandestine Directorate has an agent aboard, and he is our best source of information. Report, Nessus."

Voices quavering, Nessus spoke: Of the dissolution of *Preserver*. Of Citizen ships fleeing from NP5. Of *Long Pass,* a fearful engine of death now rushing to Hearth. Of Colonist demands and dire threats.

Incomprehensible but nonetheless familiar English translation droned in the background.

"And they have antimatter," the Hindmost asked, focused finally on a real problem.

Nessus plucked at his mane. "How else can one dissolve a General Products hull?"

Antimatter or fusion flame? Did the precise mechanism of megadeath truly matter? Nike whistled over the swelling fear of the ministers. "Describe their demands."

Nessus moaned. "Ceding all of NP4 to the Colonists. The right to withdraw NP4 from the Fleet, if and when they choose, and our cooperation in doing so."

"We're humans, not your colonists. Not any longer." Eric bared his teeth in a feral snarl. "We also require the repatriation of all humans to NP4—regardless of the world on which you now hold them."

"These are extraordinary demands," the Hindmost said with undertunes of fear and dread. "It is impossible to meet them before your arrival. Impossible."

"In a few minutes," Kirsten said flatly, "you will receive a demonstration. It may make you reconsider what is achievable." Her disembodied voice made the warning all the more chilling. "An arcology or two seared in the fire of suns."

With a howl of despair, the Hindmost collapsed. He rolled into a tight ball.

A few ministers remained on their hooves. They turned as one to Nike, and an eerie calm came over him. This was *his* moment. "Kirsten and Eric, I have a proposal. Reverse course immediately and return control of your ship to authorities. In exchange, the government will publicly pledge to honor your demands."

"Trust you?" Eric laughed humorlessly. "We tried that before, Nike."

"Then what would you suggest?" Nike asked.

"You publicly commit the Concordance to our freedom," Kirsten said. "We keep *Long Pass,* but promise not to use it against the Fleet." Unless you renege, she did not bother to add.

"Five minutes," Eric reminded.

The attempt on the Colonists' lives had failed. So had his more recent and elaborate betrayal. Perhaps, Nike mused, it was time to consider a new approach toward the Colonists.

Respect.

Assuming a confident, wide-legged stance, necks extended high, Nike said, "The Concordance accepts."

ODYSSEY   Earth date: 2652

39

Transfer-booth abduction still worked.

"Welcome back," Nessus said to the woman trembling before him. Unobservable behind a one-way mirror, he yanked at his mane. Hull material enclosed his guest—which was not the comfort it once had been.

He scarcely recognized Sangeeta Kudrin. Only in part was that due to the skimpy black evening dress in which he had found her. Her facial piercings were gone; the bold blue dye job he remembered had been exchanged for muted greens; and new muscle hung on her petite frame.

"Two years," she finally said. "I had dared to hope you were gone for good. It's Nessus, isn't it?"

"Correct." On his exterior views, Mojave Spaceport was emptier and seedier than on his last visit. "I hope to make this brief."

Sangeeta said nothing.

"You prospered during my absence," Nessus continued. Public databases now listed her as a UN undersecretary, no longer a mere deputy.

She sighed. "You kidnapped me before for information. Is that why you've taken me now?"

"It is." Nessus shifted in his nest of cushions. "Information about Sigmund Ausfaller."

Sangeeta stiffened. "Him again. He's still away chasing pirates."

That was too cryptic for Nessus. He queried through the spaceport network for a definition. Armed thieves operating on a water surface? "Go on."

"Back when you first contacted me, Ausfaller was obsessed with distant ship disappearances. Then starships much nearer began disappearing."

"Where?" Nessus asked.

The question surprised her. "On the fringes of Sol

system. Around the third disappearance, other systems started shunning us. Ship captains here began refusing to leave. Ausfaller declared the situation a threat to the state, and launched an investigation."

Her hands wandered, vainly seeking pockets in which to hide. "In a few months, eight ships vanished. The last communication with any of them was from the Oort Cloud, which the newsies took to calling 'The Borderland of Sol.' Then Ausfaller himself went after suspected pirates, using his own ship as bait."

Ausfaller diverted from the scent of the Fleet by pirates. It seemed much too convenient. Nessus disbelieved in coincidences, especially those that worked to his advantage. "Continue."

"How can you not know about this?" Sangeeta asked incredulously.

"I was busy. Tell me more."

"Ausfaller's reports are highly classified. No administrator, even a full undersecretary, has access."

"So he reported pirates." A suspicion came over Nessus. Yes, the Oort Cloud was an immense region. It was still odd that he could not contact Julian Forward. It was odder still that public databases made no mention of Forward Station since shortly after Nessus' hasty return to the Fleet. Nessus ventured a guess. "Pirates operating out of Forward Station?"

Her eyes widened. "How did you know?"

"Then you *do* know something more," Nessus said.

"Nothing certain. You have to understand." She swallowed hard. "There were rumors everywhere about conspiracies and cover-ups. One of the most prominent scientists in Human Space, gone without a trace. Ausfaller was suddenly questioning gravity theorists, cosmologists, every manner of esoteric physicist. Interstellar commerce shut down for months. People feared to leave the inner system. Surely you remember how confusing everything was."

Behind the mirror, Nessus twitched. He knew all about conspiracy and confusion.

Sangeeta babbled on about witch hunts. "And the Jinx

government is still demanding answers about Julian Forward, information Ausfaller refuses to give." She leaned forward to whisper, "I believe Forward is dead, that Ausfaller killed him."

Nessus did not believe in coincidences. Sangeeta's account suggested he did not need to. "So Ausfaller is obsessed now, wondering how Forward made neutronium," he summarized.

"Yes, damn you! Haven't you been listening? No one knows much more. Ausfaller simply won't talk. After he ended the pirate attacks, no one, not even the ARM director, would dare challenge Ausfaller to reveal more than he chooses."

Nessus shut his eyes in thought. It was suddenly clear. After he lost his grant from the Institute of Knowledge, Julian had fixated about money for his research. Forward must have managed to produce enough neutronium to make a tiny hyperspace singularity, a mini black hole. Any ship passing close enough to it would be dropped precipitously from hyperspace, to be looted by Julian's lurking henchmen. Probably the looted ships and their crews were now but a bit more mass added to the singularity.

"Very good. You may go." Nessus transferred Sangeeta to a remote booth before she could comment.

Ausfaller chasing shadows. Julian Forward, and the advanced Concordance technology reluctantly disclosed to him, both gone. The Fleet, once again, safe from prying eyes.

On the other head . . .

Eight starship crews vanished, dead. Earth still in convulsion—in the final analysis, unnecessarily—over Fertility Board corruption scandals and birthright lotteries. Rather than research and tally those casualties, Nessus turned his attention to ending the mayhem.

Perhaps minions could be put to *good* use.

GLOWING STREAKS OF pink cloud alternated with impossibly azure bands of sky. Pink deepened to red, and azure to ever darker shades of blue, as the great crimson ball of Sol sank slowly behind the mountains.

Nessus watched in awe until the sky over the spaceport faded to black. Once, on sunless Hearth, he had described the beauty of a sunrise to Nike. How long ago that seemed!

How distant seemed the time until they might reunite.

An upper atmosphere wind drove the clouds steadily eastward. Stars took their place, glittering like diamonds. Nessus watched until the sun rose.

In his hearts, Nessus knew: If he and Nike were to have a future, first they needed time apart. Time to come to terms with each other's actions. Time to accept actions that could never be admitted.

When Hearth itself faced imminent catastrophe, what did a *promise* matter? Nessus had had no choice but to urge it. Nike had had no choice but to give it.

Had Nike guessed how overwhelmingly the terrified populace would support that coerced promise? That Kirsten's War, no less than the false emergency Nike had sought to contrive, would crystallize into a new Consensus? Probably, yes. Who but Experimentalists could even *look* at the *Long Pass* crisis, let alone deal with it?

But Nike must wonder whether Nessus had acted under duress. Far better *that* ambiguity than that Nike ever know Nessus' true beliefs:

The Colonists deserved their freedom.

He had never believed Kirsten capable of fulfilling her threat.

Nessus rose stiffly from his nest of pillows, grateful that his responsibilities would keep him in Sol system for a while. He still looked forward, in the fullness of time, to returning to Hearth. To never again leaving Hearth.

And just possibly, to life there as the mate of the new Hindmost.

40

Boldly striped in yellows and browns, its unbroken clouds aswirl with storms, the mighty world, ninety thousand miles wide, dominated the sky. From the Ice Moon's orbit the gas giant spanned six degrees—a dozen times the apparent size of nearest neighbors within the Fleet.

The Ice Moon itself glowed, on one side from the light of the distant sun, and on the other side, far more brightly, from the sunlight reflected by its primary. Large structures snaked across the ice, many erected since *Explorer*'s previous visit.

From the comparative comfort of her crash couch, Kirsten pointed into the holo. The incomplete ice-and-metal space station glittered like jewels. "They did it, Omar. Crewed spaceflight."

"I can almost understand a Citizen's instinctive reaction," Omar said. "The Gw'oth rate of development is astonishing." He waved off her objection faster than she could get it out. "I said *almost,* Kirsten. The galaxy would be a poorer place without the little guys. I'm happy to find them faring so well."

She was gladdest to have found and disarmed the comet bomb Nessus had insisted they rig. The recovered and reprogrammed GP #1 probe would forever orbit this solar system, reporting by hyperwave radio any abrupt change in radio chatter—such as would occur if the Concordance should ever drop a comet on them.

"They must be protected." Omar grunted agreement, but Kirsten knew she spoke mostly to herself. "We owe the Gw'oth a *lot*. Appreciating their accomplishments taught us to appreciate our own. Questioning Citizen intentions toward the Gw'oth taught us to question Concordance policy toward Colonists."

Habits died hard. She corrected herself: "I mean toward humans."

Omar stood and yawned. "I'm going for coffee. Can I bring you anything?"

"Ice cream. Strawberry," she said. One of the first changes made to *Explorer* after the crisis was new choices in the synthesizer's repertoire.

"Kirsten."

She looked up, and Omar handed her a bowl. How long had she been contemplating the holo? Omar said, "We're done here, Kirsten. The Gw'oth are as safe as we can make them. Our place now is at home."

Omar was right, of course, and yet . . . "There is one thing more we can do. A message for them. A way to thank them properly."

He shook his head. "Everyone agreed, Kirsten, before we set out. Science and technology are very new to the Gw'oth. We can't know how they would respond to alien contact."

"That isn't what I meant." She explained, and he went off to translate her words.

AND SO THEY departed—but first they left a message.

The Ice Moon's closest neighbor was a rocky, cloud-shrouded moon. It was tidally locked to its more distant primary, keeping one face forever hidden from the Ice Moon.

But not, if they continued to advance, from the Gw'oth.

A miles-long X, etched by laser, now marked the far side of that moon. A cubic structure of laser-carved stone slabs stood at the X's center. Inside that cube, sealed within a clear plasteel container, in an inert atmosphere of pure nitrogen, the Gw'oth would someday find the powerful radio buoy for which the guardian hyperwave buoy would forever listen. In every common pictographic script of the Gw'oth, ahead of instructions on operating the radio, the accompanying note began:

"Call if you ever find yourselves in need. The Gw'oth are not without friends in the galaxy."

KIRSTEN SHIFTED POSITIONS yet again, wondering how she had ever considered crash couches comfortable. More likely, the General Products couches were yet another evil device designed by Baedeker. She stood, circled the tiny bridge several times, then settled back down with a groan. The mass pointer remained empty.

Omar walked onto the bridge and handed her a bowl. Vanilla. "I'm ready for home, too. New Terra."

Kirsten patted her swelling belly. "We both are."

· 41 ·

Jeeves had described the long delay as necessary to get their ducks in a row. Eric had neither the patience nor the passivity of an AI. For him, this was personal. For that matter, Eric didn't know what a duck was.

Metaphor aside, Jeeves's meaning was clear. Many milestones necessarily preceded this mission. Repatriation of Colonists from the secret facility on NP3. The vote whether to withdraw NP4 from the Fleet. Instruction on operating and maintaining the world-moving drive. Accumulating new deuterium and tritium reserves. Acceleration of NP4—New Terra—away from the Fleet of Worlds. Learning to stealth the few starships retained by the former colony.

The painful recovery of long repressed memories.

Sharing the tiny bridge of *Long Pass Two,* Sven fidgeted with his gear and pretended to ignore the blind spot that lurked just beyond the covered view port. "How much longer?" he asked yet again.

Minutes matter when using hyperdrive. Exit a minute

earlier than necessary and you had an extra billion miles of normal space to cross. Of course waiting a minute too long could drop you into a singularity, beyond the knowledge of even Citizen science. "It's all right, Sven. No one likes being in hyperspace." Eric canted his head and assessed the mass pointer one more time. Five scarcely distinguishable lines pointed toward them. "A few more minutes."

Shadowy figures darkened Eric's own thoughts. NP3 repatriates shared too many irrational dreads to doubt a common cause. It had taken extensive painful therapy to reconstruct their—and his—repressed memories of another human facility somewhere on NP3. Neither psychotherapy nor data mining had located that other place, the compound whose existence the Concordance indignantly denied.

Traumatic amnesia, Jeeves had called the condition, and recovering the lost childhood memories was painful. As an adult, Eric understood: The coerced cooperation of *Long Pass*'s women had not ended Citizens' experimentation with human breeding.

The successes, their memories suppressed, were relocated to the main NP3 colony, or even, as in Eric's case, to NP4. The failures, those beyond the ability of autodocs to help, remained behind: crippled and scarred in ways not even therapy could force Eric to face.

What he no longer forgot, he would never forgive.

They would find out soon enough whether the pain of recovering those memories had been worth it.

Sven squirmed in his crash couch. In the mass pointer, singularities reached out to devour them. It's time, Eric thought. "Ten seconds. Five. Now." He uncovered the view port.

Five dull lights in a pentagon lay directly ahead.

MOMENTS LATER, ERIC received a radio burst: *Courageous*. After final confirmation of details, Eric took *Long Pass Two* ahead on an arcing course.

They approached the Fleet from within the plane of the

pentagon, waiting until NP3 hid the other worlds before reversing thrusters to hover. Chance observation by a Citizen ship could be disastrous. In free flight, the embedded power plant of another ship would be an impossible target. The credible threat of antimatter encouraged the Concordance to honor its commitments to Arcadia—and, of course, Arcadia had only the illusion of antimatter.

Ice caps glittered in the suns. Extensive snow cover appeared on northern and southern continents. One more duck they had waited for, Eric thought. Winter, and with it the evacuation of most Citizens from the compound. Hearth with its unavoidable waste heat, like NP4 with its polar-orbiting suns, had a temperate climate worldwide. Citizens hated the cold.

Despite himself, Eric smiled. Romping in the snow was a *good* recovered memory; he savored it while waiting for the suns to set.

Preserving samples of all Hearthian life required reproducing all Hearthian climates and seasons. NP3's equatorial suns heated higher latitudes less. In full "winter," a few suns at the end of the orbiting string went dark, for the shorter and cooler days some life forms required.

The last sun finally disappeared around the horizon. "Ready?" Eric asked.

"Ready," Sven agreed.

Viewed in infrared, the night side cooled rapidly. Scattered areas continued to glow hot. A few glowed *too* hot: hot springs and volcanoes. Other anomalies took study to identify: factories and power plants.

By process of elimination, Eric narrowed the possibilities to five heat sources. Two were at latitudes too low to fit the consensus recovered memory of long winters at the compound. High-resolution thermal sensing eliminated two more locations—

And revealed unmistakably human shapes at the last site. Sven said, "That must be it."

At some level, Eric had dared to hope the traumatic

memories false. He breathed slowly and deeply until he trusted himself to speak. "Agreed. We're going in."

Hearthian forest surrounded the compound. He set *Long Pass Two* down in the closest clearing, ten miles away, trying not to remember the hike through woods to the Human Studies Institute—or Kirsten. Better to remain focused. "Let's unload the floaters."

Stepping discs had eliminated most ground transportation. The floaters they rode from the cargo bay were essentially miniaturized but full-powered tractors. Snow swirled all around. Despite heating elements woven into his nanofabric garment, Eric shivered.

They slipped into the woods, guided by inertial navigation units in the floaters. Infrared goggles made the view bright as day. Only wind whistling through the branches and the soft hum of the floater motors broke the silence.

These woods were far denser than on Elysium or the Hearthian park. Thickets and hedges far outnumbered single-trunk trees. Their route grew circuitous as the dense growth stymied their passage. Glancing at his wrist Sven said, "This is taking too long."

"Agreed." Eric dialed a flashlight-laser down to a narrow beam that scythed through the undergrowth. Snow on the forest floor flashed to steam, enveloping them. Sap sizzled and popped, and scattered plants burst into flame. Things screamed in dismay from the winter-bare limbs of the forest canopy. "Let's go."

Seventy minutes later, with several smoldering thickets in their wake, they reached a sprawl of buildings within a tall fence. The sky remained dark. They circled the facility on foot, scanning with infrared as they went. The only Citizen IR signatures came from a single building. Unmoving: asleep. The human signatures were concentrated in a second building. A dormitory and hospital, Eric guessed. Dispersed quarters would have made their task that much harder.

Their breath hung before them in the cold. "Let's do

this," Sven finally said. Without waiting for an answer, he sent his floater soaring over the fence. Eric followed.

A few faces peered out of dormitory windows. Within moments, the windows filled. Eric bypassed the alarm on the dormitory door, then stepped back. "Your turn, Sven."

Eric followed Sven inside and jammed the door latch behind them. Sven spoke soothingly, about nothing specific at first, as Eric reset stepping discs to send-only mode. He tried to ignore the people he glimpsed as he worked. Shriveled adults, unlike anyone he had ever encountered. Short people who must be children, whose eyes revealed sad truths no child should ever have to bear. Crippled and wasted bodies. Terrified faces.

And a few faces that awakened memories in a terrifying rush.

"We have come to take you home," Sven was saying. "To where *our* kind, not Citizens, make the laws. I promise you will be cared for if you come. It is your choice, but I urge you, I implore you, to join us. You must decide now, and quickly.

"I bring you something of our past to help you decide." Sven activated his pocket computer.

The image of Diego MacMillan appeared. "I am the navigator of starship *Long Pass*. I have a story to tell."

As people wept and moaned, and the younger children stared with incomprehension, Eric radioed *Courageous*. "Loading to commence within minutes," he said.

"Copy that," replied Terrence, the pilot. "We're standing by, burning fuel like mad to hover ten thousand miles over your heads."

In other words: hurry.

"There were spontaneous abortions, horrific birth defects, and developmental problems," Diego said. Tears streamed down the faces of the inmates. They understood all too well.

When the recording ended Sven added, quite simply, "These reprogrammed stepping discs will bring you to our ship, for a short flight to a better world. A *human* world."

A bent and wizened woman stepped forward and disappeared. An emaciated man with horribly gnarled limbs followed. Parents gathered their weeping children. With a shuffling gait, people formed lines. The lines shortened. Shortened. Disappeared.

"Time to go," Eric said. He had never felt so drained. He retrieved the stepping-disc address that would return them to *Long Pass Two*.

Sven was gone.

"Over here!" Sven's voice echoed down a long corridor. Eric followed. He found Sven gazing through a massive plasteel window into a lab. Shiny metal cabinets covered in gauges and buttons lined the walls.

"Look at those corners and edges!" Sven gestured at the cabinets. "Humans built those. And from old records I've seen, I'm sure I know what they are! Embryo banks. Egg banks. Incubators and placentas. They must be from *Long Pass*." Sven pounded on the window in frustration. "Is there a way to deduce the stepping-disc address for inside?"

Embryo banks! Eric shook with rage, unable to speak. He sliced a door-sized opening with his laser. The slab teetered, then toppled inward with a crash.

Sven rushed to the cabinets. "This one has sea life: sea turtles, squid, all kinds of fish. Some names I've encountered, more I haven't." He looked at the next case. "Big mammals: lions, polar bears, elephants." And the next case. "Dozens of bird species, including ducks."

"*Courageous*," Eric called. "We've sent all the people. Now we have cargo for you." He ignored Sven's oblivious excitement at some seed findings.

"Copy that, Eric. Standing by."

Sven's computer clattered to the floor. His face was ashen. "More human embryos. Almost a thousand."

He'd found what Eric feared—and somehow knew—they would.

They did not step back onto *Long Pass Two* until they had teleported every earthly seed, egg, and embryo to the cargo ship hovering overhead.

* * *

ONCE MORE THE nothingness lay in wait, inches away.

Eric scarcely noticed. Maybe, he thought, he was getting used to hyperspace. Or maybe he had not realized just how many emotional scabs the mission to NP3 would rip open.

He only knew that he could not wait to get home to New Terra.

Sven also ignored what lay outside, lost in data he had recovered from the lab. Every few minutes he would murmur or nod or exclaim cryptically.

"Take over for a while. I'm going for some soup. Anything for you?" Eric took the shrug he got to mean, who has time for food?

He returned to the bridge to find Sven smiling strangely. "What now?" Eric asked.

"One of my uploads is a genealogical database. Breeding records—for NP3 and also from Arcadian hospitals."

Eric couldn't understand why that made Sven smile. Then Sven showed Eric an excerpt from the database, and Eric grinned, too.

He and Kirsten had decided to name their baby Diego or Jaime. They meant it as a token of respect.

It was a far more fitting choice than they had known. Diego and Jaime, Eric now read, were Kirsten's great-to-the-sixteenth grandparents.

· 42 ·

Sudden murmuring among his aides, the words indistinct but the significance unmistakably familiar. Nike sighed. Another problematical state of affairs, about which those in the next room debated whether to disturb him.

They already had.

The universe was strange, Nike thought. The most

significant changes could manifest themselves in the subtlest ways. Only two NP worlds presently hung overhead, and yet their slightly increased spacing shouted that another world was set free to wander.

He would be happier when it had wandered farther. A fraction of a light-year still made the rebels close neighbors.

He stood alone on the grand balcony of his favorite mountainside estate. The view down to the sea was as spectacular as ever. The wind, blowing now from just the wrong direction, carried a hint of something rank—another of those small but essential reminders. Removing a world from the Fleet had complications. Ocean surges had washed ashore great piles of still-rotting sea life.

So many changes, Nike mused. Nessus would adjust quickly—when he returned to the Fleet, that was. It was best for them both that Nessus stay away for a while.

When would his doubts, anger, and loss finally sort themselves out? Nike stared upward, determined to consider anything other than his feelings toward Nessus.

Five worlds, not six—surely a small thing. Within his grandfathers' lifetimes, the Fleet had comprised but five worlds. Within his grandfathers' lifetimes, those worlds had coped without human servants.

The exquisite irony delighted Nike. Everything returning to so recent a norm had swept *out* the Conservatives and brought *in* the Experimentalists. Of course it was a Conservative government that had allowed the Colonists to get antimatter. His security forces had yet to determine how, but Nessus had had it right: How else could *Preserver*'s GP hull have been destroyed?

No wonder the people had rebelled.

Still the aides murmured inside. Nike pressed through the weather-resistant force field into their room. "What now?" he warbled impatiently.

"Apologies, Hindmost," one of them offered. "Vesta insists on speaking with you now."

"Then bring him!" Nike blasted enough harmonics to

make a point. To *this* Hindmost, foreign affairs mattered. Vesta was now the Deputy Minister directing Clandestine Affairs.

Permitted access, Vesta arrived immediately. They brushed heads, and Nike led Vesta back to the balcony. "What has happened?"

"We have a problem on NP3," Vesta said. He bowed heads submissively. "A Colonist raid. The breeding compound was evidently not so secret. They removed everyone and everything."

Overhead on NP5, cyclones raged worse than ever. Energy from the recent ocean surges must have strengthened the storms. Nike listened to the report. "Are our people safe?"

"Yes, Hindmost."

At the base of the mountain, great combers washed in. The tide: now one of eight daily, not ten. Another reminder to embrace change. "Perhaps it is for the best," Nike decided. "If we still had the ability, we would surely be tempted to create new servants. Recent events suggest we are better off without them."

Vesta pawed at the marble tiled floor. "We should punish the Colonists."

"No," Nike said adamantly. "And it would be best, my friend, if you stopped thinking of them as Colonists. The humans reclaimed their own. I think I respect them for that."

"Understood, Hindmost."

"And of your human agents on New Terra?" Nike asked.

Vesta straightened. "They radio according to schedule, Hindmost. Our hyperwave buoy just beyond their planetary singularity continues to relay. I expect regular updates to continue."

"Excellent." Citizens could also play tricks with hyperwave radio buoys. Would Baedeker appreciate that? Probably not, Nike decided. Hard labor in the fields of NP1 left little time or energy for such abstract musings.

In a few hundred years, the Fleet would rise above the

crowded galactic disk. A consensus no longer existed as to which way to turn next.

Of course, that was a decision the "liberated" humans would now have to make first.

Perhaps, according to planted hints, they would turn toward the galactic center. Inward, to where they could at least hope to encounter their ancestors. Inward, to where myriads of newly sterilized worlds lay fallow. Inward, and away from the now-hated Fleet.

But *inward* was exactly where Nike meant for the Fleet to go. How much better, then, if an unwitting world of scouts could first draw the attention of any intelligent races that still survived in the core.

These Colonists were quite mistaken to believe their fate and the Concordance's fate could be so easily disentwined.

• Turn the page for a preview of •

JUGGLER *of*
WORLDS

Larry Niven

AND

Edward M. Lerner

Available now from Tor Books

TOR® A TOR HARDCOVER

ISBN-13: 978-0-7653-1826-8   ISBN-10: 0-7653-1826-1

. 1 .

Sigmund Ausfaller woke up shivering, prone on a cold floor. His head pounded. Tape bound his wrists and ankles to plasteel chains.

He had always known it would end horribly. Only the when, where, how, why, and by whom of it all had eluded him.

That fog was beginning to lift.

How had he gotten here, wherever *here* was? As though from a great distance, Sigmund watched himself quest for recent memories. Why was it such a struggle?

He remembered the pedestrian concourse of an open-air mall, shoppers streaming. They wore every color of the rainbow, clothing and hair and skin, in every conceivable combination and pattern. Overhead, fluffy clouds scudded across a clear blue sky. The sun was warm on his face. Work, for once, had been laid aside. He'd been content.

Happiness is the sworn enemy of vigilance. How could he have been so careless?

Sigmund forced open his eyes. He was in a nearly featureless room. Its walls, floor, and ceiling were resilient plastic. Light came from one wall. I could be anywhere, Sigmund thought—and then two details grabbed his attention.

The room wasn't quite a box. The glowing wall had a bit of a curve to it.

There were recessed handholds in walls, floor, and ceiling.

Panic struck. He was on a *spaceship*! Was gravity a hair higher than usual? Lower? He couldn't tell.

Plasteel chains clattered dully as Sigmund sat up. He had watched enough old movies to expect chains to clink. Even as the room spun around him and everything faded to black, he found the energy to feel cheated.

* * *

COLD PLASTIC PRESSED against Sigmund's cheek. He opened his eyes a crack to see the same spartan room. Cell.

This time he noticed that one link of his chains had been fused to a handhold in the deck.

Had he passed out from a panic attack? *Where was he?*

Sigmund forced himself to breathe slowly and deeply until the new episode receded. Fear could only muddy his thoughts. More deep breaths.

He had never before blacked out from panic. He could not believe that *this* blackout stemmed from panic. Yes, his faint had closely followed the thought he might be aboard a spaceship. It *also* had occurred just after he had sat up. Sigmund remembered his thoughts having been fuzzy. They seemed sharper now.

He'd been drugged! Doped up and barely awake, he'd sat up too fast. *That* was why he had passed out.

More cautiously this time, Sigmund got into a sitting position. His head throbbed. He considered the pain dispassionately. Less disabling than the last time, he decided. Perhaps the drugs were wearing off.

Some odd corner of his mind felt shamed by his panic attacks. Most Earthborn had flatland phobia worse than he, and so what? True, he'd been born on Earth, but his parents had been all over Known Space. Somehow they took pleasure in strange scents, unfamiliar night skies, and wrong gravity.

On principle, Sigmund had been to the moon twice. He had had to know: Could he leave Earth should the need ever arise? The second time, it was to make sure the success of that first trip wasn't a fluke.

He listened carefully. The soft whir of a ventilation fan. Hints of conversation, unintelligible. His own heartbeat. None of the background power-plant hum that permeated the spaceships he'd been on. Gravity felt as normal as his senses could judge.

Recognizing facts, spotting patterns, drawing inferences . . .

he managed, but slowly, as though his thoughts swam through syrup. Traces of drugs remained in his system. He forced himself to concentrate.

If this was a ship, it was still on Earth. Someone *meant* to panic him, Sigmund decided. Someone wanted something from him. Until they got it, he'd probably remain alive.

They.

For as long as Sigmund could remember, there had always been some *they* to worry about.

But even as Sigmund formed that thought, he knew "always" wasn't quite correct. . . .

IN THE BEGINNING, *they* were unambiguous enough: the Kzinti.

The Third Man-Kzin War broke out in 2490, the year Sigmund was born. He was five before he knew what a Kzin was—something like an upright orange cat, taller and much bulkier than a man, with a naked, rat-like tail. By then, the aliens had been defeated. The Kzinti Patriarchy ceded two colony worlds to the humans as reparations. In Sigmund's lifetime, they had attacked human worlds three more times. They'd lost those wars, too.

Fafnir was one of the worlds that changed hands after the third war. His parents had wanderlust and not a trace of flatland phobia. They left him in the care of an aunt, and went to Fafnir in 2500 for an adventure.

And found one.

Conflict erupted that year between humans on Fafnir and the Kzinti settlers who had remained behind. His parents vanished, in hostilities that failed to rise to the level of a numeral in the official reckoning of Man-Kzin Wars. It was a mere "border incident."

Everyone knew the Kzinti ate their prey.

So *they,* for a long time, were Kzinti. Sigmund hated the ratcats, and everyone understood. And he hated his parents for abandoning him. The grief counselors told his aunt that that was normal. And he hated his aunt, as much as she reminded him of Mom—or perhaps because she did—for allowing Mom and Dad to leave him with her.

The same year his parents disappeared, the Puppeteers emerged from beyond the rim of Human Space. A species more unlike the Kzinti could not be imagined. Puppeteers looked like two-headed, three-legged, wingless ostriches. The heads on their sinuous necks reminded him of sock puppets. The brain, Aunt Susan told him, hid under the thick mop of mane between the massive shoulders.

So *they* came to include these other aliens, these harmless-seeming newcomers, because Sigmund didn't believe in coincidence. And then *they* came to include *all* aliens—because, really, how could anyone truly know otherwise?

That was when Aunt Susan took him to a psychotherapist. Sigmund remembered the stunned look on her face after his first session. After she spoke alone with the therapist. Sigmund remembered her sobbing all that night in her bedroom.

He had a sickness, or sicknesses, he couldn't spell, much less understand: a paranoid personality disorder. Monothematic delusion with delusional misidentification syndrome. He didn't know if he believed the supposed silver lining: that it was treatable.

What Sigmund did believe was the other consolation Dr. Swenson offered Aunt Susan—that paranoia is an affliction of the brightest.

In time, Sigmund understood. Trauma can cause stress can cause biochemical imbalances can cause mental illness. A day and a night asleep in an autodoc corrected the biochemical imbalance in his brain. But a single chemical tweak wasn't enough: Knowing the world is out to get you is its own stress. Three months of therapy with Dr. Swenson addressed the paranoid behaviors Sigmund had already learned.

Dr. Swenson was right: Sigmund *was* very smart. Smart enough to figure out what the therapist wanted to hear. Smart enough to learn what thoughts to keep to himself.

* * *

TREMBLING, SIGMUND TRIED again to shake off the drugs. Reliving old horrors served no useful purpose—especially now. He needed to focus.

Start with *them*. They weren't Kzinti: The room was too small. Kzinti would have gone crazy.

They wanted something from him; how he responded might be the only control he had in this situation. Who might *they* be?

Others might see in him only a middle-aged, midlevel financial analyst. A United Nations bureaucrat. A misanthrope dressed always in black, in a world where everyone else wore vibrant colors.

Sigmund saw more. All those years ago, Dr. Swenson had been far more correct than he knew. Sigmund was more than bright. He was brilliant—in the mind, where it counted, not in gaudy display.

Who were *they*? Probably somebody Sigmund was investigating. That narrowed it down. The bribe-taking customs officials at Quito Spaceport? The sysadmin at the UN ID data center who moonlighted in identity laundering?

Sigmund's gut said otherwise. It was his other ongoing investigation: the Trojan Mafia. The gang, known by its reputed base in the Trojan Asteroids, engaged in every kind of smuggling, from artworks to weapons to experimental medicines. They killed for hire—and, more often, just to keep the authorities at bay. They were into extortion, money laundering . . . everything. Every other analyst in Investigations refused to touch them.

Surely that was *who*.

How was more speculative. A "chance" encounter in the pedestrian mall near his home, he guessed, by someone with a fast-acting hypo-sedative. He stumbles; his assailant, to all appearances a Good Samaritan, helps him to the nearest transfer booth.

Where? Other than somewhere on Earth, Sigmund wasn't

prepared to guess. On a world bristling with transfer booths, he could have been teleported instantaneously almost anywhere.

And when? Blinking to de-blur his vision, Sigmund raised his hands. His left wrist hurt—not much, but it hurt. The time display had frozen. Ironic that, since the subcutaneous control pips felt melted: tiny beads beneath his thumb. Clock, weather, compass, calculator, maps, all the utility functions he normally summoned by fingernail pressure . . . all gone. He guessed his implant had been fried with a magnetic pulse. It fit the program of disorientation.

They weren't as smart as they thought. The room had no sanitary facilities, not so much as a chamber pot, and so far he felt no need to pee. His black suit was clean, if rumpled. It wasn't an ironclad case, but Sigmund guessed he had been snatched from that pedestrian mall no more than a few hours ago.

Footsteps! They approached along the unseen corridor beyond the out-of-reach door. The door flew open.

A tall figure, easily two meters tall, stood in the doorway. A tall fringe of hair bobbed on an otherwise bald head: a Belter crest. And did not Hector, mightiest of the Trojans, famously wear a helmet with a plume of horsehair?

It all fit with the Trojan Mafia.

Sigmund blinked in the suddenly bright light, unable to make out details.

"Good," the Belter said. "I see you're awake. There's someone who wants to speak with you."

"YOU SEEM UNSURPRISED, Mr. Ausfaller."

An eerie calm came over Sigmund. "Someone had to put through all the requests for reassignment. Someone had to tolerate one unproductive investigation after another."

"Your boss," his captor said.

"Someone had to authorize those transfers. Someone had to accept the department's persistent failures." Sigmund mustered all the irony he could. "Sir."

"Meaning me." Ben Grimaldi, Undersecretary-General for Inspections, leaned casually against the wall. Body language somehow added, *Your suspicions make this easier.*

That was self-justifying nonsense, of course. Grimaldi would not have shown himself had there been any chance Sigmund would be let free.

Grimaldi broke a lengthening silence. "I need to learn what you know. More importantly, I need to know how."

Once I reveal that, Sigmund thought, *I'm dead.* He shifted position, his chains clicking dully. *Change the subject.* "Why the Trojans?"

Grimaldi smiled humorlessly. "We prefer Achilles. The Trojans were losers."

The Trojan Asteroids fell into two groups, those orbiting the L4 Lagrange point, 60 degrees ahead of Jupiter in its orbit, and those orbiting the L5 point, 60 degrees behind. The Greek Camp and the Trojan Camp, as they were sometimes called. Achilles was among the largest asteroids in the Greek Camp. Of course Hector *also* orbited there, so named before the labeling convention began. . . .

Sigmund pinched his leg, desperate to unmuddle his thoughts. "How much dope did you give me?" he demanded.

"Enough." Grimaldi looked pointedly at his wrist implant. "I must be going soon. Your stay here will be much more pleasant if you answer our questions voluntarily."

More pleasant, perhaps. Also shorter? Did buying time matter? "Why the Trojans?"

"Why would you think, Ausfaller? They made a generous offer for my assistance. Official scrutiny is bad for their business.

"You're an odd one, Sigmund, but I admit you're capable. Persistent. I truly wish I thought we could buy you. Sadly, you inherited piles of money. You still chose to work for a pittance at the UN." Grimaldi shook his head. "You live like a monk. You dress like a monk. Why offer you money when you ignore the wealth you already have? It seems too likely you have principles."

And there it was, the memory Sigmund had struggled

for. Money. He tried and failed to blink away the fuzziness. "Perhaps *I* can pay *you*."

A reflexive flash of contempt—and then, more slowly, an expression of low cunning. Grimaldi said, "You'd still have to tell everything you've learned about me and my associates. And every detail about *how* you learned. It won't do for someone else to discover what you did."

"Understood."

"You wouldn't try to trick me, now would you?" Grimaldi asked.

"Of course not," Sigmund answered.

Grimaldi smacked his hands together; strangely, that assurance had sufficed. "Stet. There will be no negotiation. One million stars, transferred into the numbered Belter account I will give you. Don't bother to protest. I know you're good for it. When your weekly reports began to show progress, I made it a point to learn about you. Here's the deal, Mr. Ausfaller. You pay. You tell all. Then we let you go."

He'd never be let go, but Sigmund acted as though he believed. Anyway, the million-and-change he thought Grimaldi could trace was merely the fraction of Sigmund's wealth he intended to be visible—and it wasn't as though there were anyone to leave his money to. At worst, the charade might make his final hours less unpleasant.

Sigmund raised his arms, clanking on purpose. "For a million stars, I want these off. I want a nicer room. A suite with plumbing would be good."

"We'll see about that after the funds clear. Until then, maybe a pot." Grimaldi took a sonic stunner and a handheld computer from pockets of his bodysuit. He whispered inaudibly into the handheld, set it on the deck, and then slid it with his shoe tip toward Sigmund. Handheld and foot never came within Sigmund's reach. The sonic stunner was fixed on him.

"I'm logged into an anonymous account. All other comm functions are locked out. Moments after my funds are received, they'll be shifted elsewhere." Grimaldi laughed.

"My colleagues, as I'm sure you know, are skilled in anonymous transfers."

My funds. Sigmund held in his anger. "Funds transfer from Bank of North America." He paused for the voiceprint check. "Account: five . . . four . . . one. . . ." He articulated slowly and distinctly, leaving no chance for misinterpretation. Account number. Subaccount. Access codes.

The good news was the response time. He was still on Earth.

The stunner never wavered. He'd be lucky to utter a suspicious syllable without being zapped. "Four . . . two . . . niner. . . ."

The bank AI spoke a challenge code. Grimaldi snorted in disgust. He wiggled the stunner, just a bit, in warning.

Sigmund shrugged. Clank. With the challenge-response feature set, a bank would accept transfer authorizations only in real time. Challenge-response defeated coerced recordings. What rational person *didn't* configure his account this way?

Sigmund could authorize the transfer with a duress code. That would alert his bank, but so what? Money laundering was big business for the Trojans. Within minutes of the money's release, it would be laundered through a dozen shell companies, off-world tax havens, and other anonymous venues. The duress code would accomplish nothing.

If he purposefully aborted the transfer, Grimaldi would know instantly—and the coming questioning could become a *lot* less pleasant. Or—

Dr. Swenson had been right: Sigmund *was* paranoid. And now, he thought, we'll see if I've been paranoid *enough*.

SIGMUND REMAINED IN CHAINS, but he'd been offered a chair, an improvised chamber pot, and a greasy drinking bulb with tepid water. For a million stars, there should have been at least a leaded-glass tumbler and ice.

Grimaldi was long gone. He had delegated the detailed questioning to the lanky Belter Sigmund had met earlier.

His interrogator disdained to offer a name. Sigmund chose to think of him as Astyanax: Hector's little boy, hurled from the ramparts of Troy. Like Achilles' son, Sigmund wanted no more kings of Troy.

Slow, pensive sips didn't buy much time.

All crimes lead to tax evasion. Sigmund had concentrated his quest for the Trojans there. He discoursed methodically on forensic techniques in spotting hidden income, waxing ever more pedantic. Whenever Astyanax began looking impatient, Sigmund offered a tidbit about which banking investigations had suggested what line of further investigation. A few such admissions evoked surprisingly astute questions. The Belter was something of an expert himself on income-tax evasion.

A handheld in Astyanax's pocket squawked in alarm. There was sudden pandemonium in the corridor. Thudding footsteps. Thudding bodies? The unmistakable zap of sonic stunners.

Astyanax dropped his own stunner, and took a utility knife from his belt. Low-tech but lethal.

"Don't," Sigmund said. "You'll only make it wor—"

He gasped in shock at the sudden agony in his stomach. His shirt and Astyanax's hand were bright red. Lifeblood red.

"Nothing personal," Astyanax said.

As Sigmund slumped, a squad of battle-armored ARMs burst through the door. To the frying-bacon sound of stunners, as everything went dark, Sigmund thought: Too late. . . .

· 2 ·

Sigmund awoke. The incredible pain in his gut was gone. His wrists and ankles no longer throbbed from tight restraints. He was clearheaded and full of energy. Rested. Content.

It scared the hell out of him.

He opened his eyes. A transparent dome hung centimeters from his face. Reflected LEDs shone steadily, all in green.

He was in an autodoc.

Readouts told Sigmund that the 'doc had replaced his heart and part of his liver! And two liters of blood, and— he stopped reading. He raised the massive lid and sat up, to echoes of pain in his chest and belly. Logically, those pangs were in his head, since the 'doc had declared him healed. They hurt regardless.

The room seemed chilly, but that might only be because he wasn't wearing anything. You never did in an autodoc.

"Welcome back."

His head swiveled. A stranger in a drab bodysuit occupied the room's only chair. She was lean, almost gaunt, but also massively muscled. He guessed she worked out obsessively. She would have been striking, if not exactly pretty, if she didn't scare the bejesus out of him.

The stranger stood and handed Sigmund the robe that hung from a hook on the door. She did not turn her back. "You'll want this, I expect. Then we should talk."

"Where are we?" Sigmund asked.

Instead of answering, she waved a blue disc at him. A holo shimmered, Earth, and a bit of text: Special Agent Fiona Filip.

It appeared to be an ARM ident. Perhaps she had answered him.

The Amalgamated Regional Militia was the unassuming name for the UN military forces. Understatement sufficed when merely to see an ARM made most people quail. Everyone knew the militia was how the United Nations maintained control, not just civil order.

Sigmund slipped on his robe and climbed out of the autodoc. Everyone knew what someone meant everyone to know. Grimaldi? The people for whom Grimaldi worked? Maybe the rescue had been staged, Sigmund's stabbing a bit of theater for credibility, to hear what he'd tell those he thought were the authorities. To see whom he'd contact next.

"Sigmund, this will be hard for you. I understand better than you can know." The stranger sighed. "Let's start over. I'm Fiona Filip. My friends call me Feather. I'm an ARM—but not the kind that extracted you. I prefer to avoid guns and knives. People can get hurt with those things. As you recently learned."

When had they become friends? "Where am I, Agent Filip?"

Her smile looked wrong, somehow. Unpracticed rather than insincere. "A SWAT team extracted you from an interplanetary freighter on the tarmac at Mojave Spaceport. You were dying of a stab wound. You were also, by the way, pumped full of truth serum.

"They always bring autodocs on raids. The squad leader popped you into a field 'doc and delivered you to the nearest ARM District Office. That's Los Angeles. Hollywood, more precisely, if you know the area."

Sigmund remembered saying he wasn't trying to trick Grimaldi, and the bastard had taken his word for it. Truth serum explained it. He had told the literal truth. He hadn't been *trying* to trick Grimaldi—he *was* tricking him.

If any of this was real, of course.

"I want you to trust me, and that doesn't come easily to you, does it?" Filip turned the chair and sat, legs straddling the back. "I don't expect an answer, by the way. As I said, I understand you. I'll answer the questions you don't dare to ask. For starters, you're not a suspect. Not for anything."

Sigmund's mind raced. Except for the usual fresh-from-the-autodoc burst of energy, he felt normal. Normal for *him,* that was. How could that be? "Then I'm free to go."

She flashed an I-know-something-you-don't-know grin. *This* smile looked natural. "Yes, but you won't, because you need to know more."

If Filip was who she said she was, she must know how he had signaled for help. If she wasn't . . . to even reveal that he *had* signaled could bring on retribution. It would, at a minimum, make the Trojan Mafia hide him better.

"You're dying to know how you were rescued. No, let's be

honest. Sigmund, you're wondering *if* you were rescued." She laughed at his twitch of surprise, but it wasn't a cruel laugh. "You're kind of cute in an intense way. Just hear me out.

"You came into a fair amount of money when your parents died, part inheritance, part insurance. You took control of that money once you reached twenty-one. The interesting thing, Sigmund, is what you've done with that money."

"Nothing." Sigmund willed his voice to stay level. In fact, he'd divvied the money into several accounts, two directly in his name, the rest far more subtly registered. He hadn't broken any laws in doing it—*they* certainly watched for that—but he had, arguably, bent a few. "It's my rainy-day fund."

Filip shook her head. "Hardly. You sloshed your wealth around in very unusual ways. You triggered trip wires in more money-laundering audits than I care to admit." She cut off his objection before he could do more than open his mouth. "Relax. You did nothing illegal. Not quite. You kept the individual funds transfers *just* below the banks' required filing threshold. And once my colleagues determined the ownership of all the blind trusts, they saw none of the money had even changed hands.

"Given what you do—you're very good at it, by the way—you knew exactly what would happen. You knew the pattern of activities would flag those accounts. Sigmund, you went to a lot of trouble to create bank accounts the authorities would forever watch."

Sigmund shrugged. He could feign nonchalance all he wanted, but were sensors even now picking up the pounding of his brand-new heart?

"Rainy-day fund? It apparently poured yesterday in the Mojave," Filip said. "From an account long idle, suddenly there's a million-star transfer into a numbered account in a Belter bank haven. It set off all kinds of alarms. I wondered: If you *wanted* attention, why not just make the transfer using a duress code?"

Because a duress alarm wouldn't say enough! If a duress

code caught your eye, you might not look any further. Wasn't that obvious?

"I dug a bit deeper," Filip said. "You could have used any of those red-flag accounts. Did your choice matter? Banks assign account numbers, but account owners choose their own access codes. So: I ran your access codes through crypto software. Each of your funny accounts had its PIN derived from the name of a high official in the UN Inspections Directorate. The PINs changed, but not the pattern." She patted Sigmund's arm and he flinched. "The PIN that released those funds decrypted as 'Grimaldi.' He was at Mojave Spaceport when you authorized the payoff."

Sigmund couldn't help shivering. He pulled his thin robe more tightly closed, but he doubted it fooled her. Then it *was* true: ARMs traced people through the transfer-booth system. He'd always worried about that. Transfers had to tie back somehow to people, for billing purposes.

Or the Trojans were even cleverer than he'd feared. Grimaldi might have recorded his PIN as he authorized the transfer. If Trojans had decrypted his code, they might be testing him now. . . .

"Sigmund! Come back." She laughed, somehow kindly this time. "Who but a paranoid sets traps with the ARMs to implicate their co-workers? You came out of the autodoc as paranoid as you went in. I see it in your eyes. Surely *you* noticed. Have you asked yourself: Why?"

He sat still, afraid to speak. Why *hadn't* the autodoc reset his brain chemistry?

Filip said, "Here's where we become friends, Sigmund. You've heard the rumors. Senior ARM agents are paranoids. It helps us with the job. We get that way chemically. We're pumped up for the workweek, and pumped out when we go off-duty. Most ARMs, that is. Like you, I'm a natural schiz. I'm drugged before they send me home for the weekend.

"The thing is, today is Wednesday. A workday. After your little mishap, you went into an autodoc. Ours see nothing unusual with a bit of schizo brain chemistry. It's no accident you're as messed up as ever.

"Sigmund, that's the reason I understand you. We're the *same*."

He wanted to believe. Of course, he'd heard the stories. Who hadn't? The thing was—

"Sigmund," she snapped. "Stay with me. You're thinking: ARMs put out the rumor that they're paranoid to trick you into revealing that you're paranoid. I did, too."

For the first time since Sigmund had climbed out of the autodoc, she peered directly into his eyes. "Bright and paranoid is a license to be miserable and alone. Miserable maybe I can't help. But alone—that's something else."

He accepted the new ident chip she offered him. When he held it just right, a blue globe and his name shimmered above it. It was supposedly keyed to his DNA and would get him into the ARM academy in London. He struggled into the plain, black suit she whisked from a cabinet. It didn't surprise him that it had been synthed to his size and preferred style.

He admitted nothing, promised nothing. He was, finally, apparently free.

Free to go? Free to be followed? Festooned with tiny cameras?

Beyond the clinic door, an office buzzed with activity. No one paid Sigmund any attention. Ignoring the transfer booths, he found his way outside. Large five-pointed stars shone in the pedestrian walkway. Grauman's Chinese Theatre stood across and just down the street.

He turned. Above the double doors through which he had just exited, stone-carved letters read: Amalgamated Regional Militia, Los Angeles District. A faux ARM office could hardly be fabricated in such a public place.

Sigmund fingered the ident chip Agent Filip—Feather— had given him. It suddenly seemed possible, after more than a century alone, that he had finally discovered a place where he could fit in.